To Jacki, Happy Birthday!

12 - 10 - 2016

Five Years Under The Swastika

Through A Child's Eye

Five Years Under The Swastika

Through A Child's Eye

Frits Forrer

Holland's Glory   P.O. Box 488, Gulf Breeze, Florida, 32562

Contact the author at:
fritsforrer@cox.net
www.fritsforrer.net
850-607-7147
850-384-5363

This book was prepared for publication by
Ghost River Images
5350 East Fourth Street
Tucson, Arizona 85711
www.ghostriverimages.com

ISBN 978-0-9714490-0-8

Library Of Congress Control Number: 2002401772

Printed in the United States of America
December, 2009
10 9 8 7 6 5

Dedicated
to the memory
of
Joop and Clasien

Other books by Frits Forrer

The Fun Of Flying
ISBN 0-9714490-3-1

Tampa Justice
No Money, No Justice.
ISBN 0-9714490-5-8

Smack Between The Eyes
ISBN 0-9714490-6-6

To Judge Or Not To Judge
ISBN 0-9714490-7-4

The Golden Pig
(El Cochino de Oro)
ISBN 0-9714490-8-2

Brothers, FOREVER!
ISBN 0-9714490-9-0

The Curse Of The Black Mamba
ISBN 978-0-9822207-0-2

Golden Nuggets
ISBN 978-0-9822207-1-9

Contents

Hof van Holland

CHAPTER I
May 10, 1940

"BOOOM...BOOOM..BOOM..BOOM.."
"HERMAN EN IDA.....DE MOFFEN ZIJN HIER..."
"HERMAN AND IDA....THE KRAUTS ARE HERE...THE KRAUTS ARE HERE.."
"WAKE UP!"BOOM...BOOM..BOOM..Uncle Otto is banging on the back door...
"WAKE UP...WAKE UP..!"
It's barely four in the morning and still dark in the little town of WINTERSWIJK, near the German border.
"THE KRAUTS ARE HERE!, WE'VE BEEN INVADED!"
Two heads appear out of an upstairs window.
"WHAT HAPPENED?" hollers Herman with an accent that immediately tells you he is not from that region.
"THE KRAUTS HAVE CROSSED THE BORDER JUST TEN MINUTES AGO AT DEURNE, THEY WILL BE HERE IN A FEW MINUTES!" cries OTTO hysterically.
"WHAT DO YOU WANT ME TO DO?" asks Herman unperturbed, *"STOP 'EM?"*
"I don't know." Otto's calming down, "What are you going to do?"
"Stay inside for the moment, wake the kids up and get 'em dressed and wait. There won't be any fighting here anyway."
"See you later!" "TJU"
Heads disappear and Otto retreats to his back door, just a few steps from Herman and Ida's door.
Ida is Otto's older sister. Three years ago, she moved back to the little eastern town where her German mother and Dutch father raised her.
When "OMA" died in 1937 at age 59, Ida and her family returned from Belgium to take over her parents' "Hotel-Café-Restaurant "GERMANIA," so her father, "OPA KWAK" could retire to a little house down the street.

Presently, they are following their own advice and are getting themselves and the kids dressed in a hurry as Herman runs downstairs to get the radio going.

Radio broadcasts are normally never available at this early hour, but a German station is broadcasting the BLITZKRIEG invasion into Holland, Belgium, Luxembourg, Denmark and France. It sounds like a long string of victories even though the war is only 30 minutes old.

The kids come running into the bar, the "CAFÉ," where the big floor-model Phillips radio is blasting away.

"PAPPA,PAPPA, GAAN WE NOU VECHTEN?"

"Pappa,Pappa,are we going to fight now?"

"Be quiet!"

Pappa Herman's German is very limited and he is frantically trying BRUSSELS and HILVERSUM I and II, the Dutch stations, for reports.

Finally, a Dutch voice comes through on HILVERSUM I announcing the invasion along the Dutch border and the fighting that is already taking place. The DUTCH are victorious all over too.

"What fighting, what victories?" asks Pappa. "We live ten minutes from the border and we haven't heard a shot!"

"Mama, I'm hungry," says FRITS, who is eight years old and blue eyed like his brothers and sisters.

"You are always hungry!" is Mama's reply.

Mama is a solidly built Germanic looking woman of 35 with a quick smile and sparkling blue eyes. Her broad face, fairly broad shoulders and big hands seem to say; "I don't mind hard work and I'm tough!" but her eyes belie that toughness.

"I'm hungry too!"

This time it's PAULTJE.

Paultje means: little Paul, though Paultje is a chubby squirt with straight white PIGS hair.

"Fix 'em something, damn-it, I want to listen to this!" shouts Herman, who's getting colder and irritated. "I told 'em, I told 'em, I told 'em a thousand times that the KRAUTS were going to invade this time. They're not going to respect our neutrality like they did in the WAR!"

It had not gotten to the point in history, where this war would be known as WORLD WAR II, so the war Herman is referring to is actually WORLD WAR I.

Screaming at the radio rather than anybody in particular, Herman rants on; "The KRAUTS will eat us alive! We have no defense, no tanks, no airplanes! What are a bunch of boys going to do? Put on boxing gloves?"

Clasien, seven and pretty, with every curl in place and carefully dressed takes it all in with a serious look on her face as if she understands. She sits on the carpeted floor holding her little sister HEDWIG, who's not quite three.

These children have already learned that when Pappa hollers, screams and curses, it's best to be quiet or to stay away altogether!

"JOOP, wake up ANTOON!"

Joop straightens up from his slouched position, draped over a barstool and runs out the door. Nobody disobeys Pappa.

Joop runs up the stairs two treads at a time and stops at the first door on the left, KAMER I.

"Antoon," KNOCK, KNOCK, KNOCK! "ANTOON!" Shouts Joop. He hears a grunt from inside. *"OPSTAAN! D'R IS OORLOG!"*

"Get up, there's war!" Joop yells and off he is, down the stairs, three treads at a time, so he won't miss but a second of the broadcasts.

Joop at ten is the oldest, the tallest and possibly the most intelligent of the five children. His hair is darker than that of the other four kids. He was quite blonde until he was about six, when his blonde curls gave way to straight darker hair. He's quite a handsome boy, tall, gangly and a bit clumsy, which has earned him the name of "SHLEMIEL" from his father.

Meanwhile, a sandwich in hand, Frits is upstairs at the window facing the street between room number one and room number two, KAMERS I and II, where the big MANGEL stands against the wall, patiently waiting to be turned again next Tuesday to press the linens.

The front windows face south. Across the street he can look into the blacksmith's shop, but by leaning out of the window, he can see at least four blocks to the EAST. One block east, a V in the road is where the main roads from GERMANY meet from the directions of BORKUM and BOCHOLT. Either way, the border is only eight kilometers from his house and as far as Frits is concerned, the GERMANS should be here any minute.

Unbeknownst to them, the German troops have already passed them by.

As they found out later, at precisely 4:00 AM, a German soldier appeared at each border crossing, surprised the Dutch soldier standing guard, took his rifle and took him prisoner. Other commandos meanwhile stormed into the guardhouse and had the Dutchmen surrender without a single shot being fired.

A "PANZERZUG," armored train, rolled across the border at 4.01 AM and stopped one Kilometer into Holland just before a derailing lock. A soldier got off the train, fired into the lock, kicked it off the tracks and the "PANZERZUG" rolled on. That was the only shot fired in that whole sector.

"DAAR KOMEN ZE"

"THERE THEY ARE!" Frits hollers at the top of his lungs as he runs to the stairs.

"MAMA,PAPPA,THE KRAUTS ARE HERE,THERE THEY ARE........."

He looks back through the window and continues; "What is this? NO tanks? Motorcycles?..Personel carriers?.... Little jeeplike vehicles? Trucks with soldiers, holding their rifles between their legs. More motorcycles with sidecars, but no tanks, no shooting. "What kinda war is this?"

"GET AWAY FROM THAT WINDOW! Shut that window, close the curtains."

Pappa is in rare form. Pappa and Antoon are standing at the side of the window, peering behind the lace curtains.

Antoon van Brummelstroete is their only lodger in the Hotel. He's a distant cousin of Mama's, twenty years old and very quiet. He is disqualified from the army for health reasons and is actually a boarder, rather than a hotel guest. In other words, he eats in the kitchen with the family, instead of in the dining room like a hotel guest.

Meanwhile, sandwiches in hand, Frits and Paul are in room IV, furthest away from Papa, next door to the sole bathroom on the floor, hanging out of the window. The convoy is really moving now, truck after truck, directed by a motorcycle soldier, who has parked his machine across the side street right next to the house and he's waving on the traffic.

With his huge green rubber coat, boots and helmet, a submachinegun slung across his back, he is an imposing figure to the boys. Each time he turns towards the house, the big oval shield hanging across his chest glistens in the reflection of the corner streetlight.

Frits is trying to figure out the writing on the shield as the sun is starting to cast a glow against the sky behind the advancing Germans. He manages to spell it out: "F-E-L-D-G-E-N-D-A-R-M-E-R-I-E."

"FELDGENDARMERIE, Paultje, that's the police, like in Belgium, remember?"

Paul was two and a half years old when the family moved back to Holland in '37, but caught up in the excitement of the moment, he whispers; "YA, YA." He doesn't remember a thing, but his brother's excitement is contagious and even though he's scared, he stares at all that military power rolling out of the sunrise past his house disappearing toward the west.

They keep coming from the direction of the town's swimming-pool on the outskirts of town and hustle along at an even paced fashion as if they're going on an exercise instead of off to war.

Nobody in the convoy is laughing, really, but they also don't seem concerned and certainly not poised for action.

"Tanks, Paultje! Look! Tanks!... No, no. Over there, way out, way over there!"

Indeed, in the distance the guns and turrets are silhouetted against the now orange ball on the horizon.

The engine noise is getting louder and louder and diesel fumes hang in the street and creep into the open window. Not a sole civilian is in sight. Only curtains moving here and there give the only hint that the homes are not deserted.

Most of the homes are ordinary two story buildings interspersed with stores. Across the street is the blacksmith, JONKERS, with his store full of coalstoves, hearths and gas stoves.

Then swinging east is old man BAUMAN, the butcher. Then the baker, KAANDORP, and at the very end of the block, some ten homes down, THE SPAR, the big store. Beyond the V-junction, the only building in view that is taller than two stories is the Theater/Concerthall with it's rounded roof.

Coming back on this side of the street are all private homes until close by where WIGGERS has his vegetable and fruit store.

Then the corner store of PECHT, the butcher across the side street from Otto's bicycle shop, which is adjacent to Hotel-Café-Restaurant HOF VAN HOLLAND.

HOF VAN HOLLAND is the name now, because Herman did not like the name GERMANIA, so he changed it. OPA hated that, but OPA hated almost anything anyway.

There, right over the "HOF" of HOF VAN HOLLAND are two young faces, crowned with white and blonde hair staring at the parade of tanks..... on FLATBEDS. They must have been rolling into the lowlands at 40 to 50 kilometers per hour, not expecting any opposition and not getting any. Now dozens of cannons, pulled by trucks, rumble by. WHAT A WAR ALREADY!

When Frits starts waving, an occasional soldier in an open truck waves back. Pappa, peering behind the lace of the hall curtain realizes what is happening in one of the other rooms. Storming down the hall, opening the doors of room II, III, and IV, he yells; "I told you to stay away from those windows!"

Ducking and covering their ears with their hands, the two boys run past Pappa into the hall and are relieved that they did not receive a slap about the face or a swift kick in the pants.

Pap must be mellowing; This is the first time in their young lives, that the kids have eaten a sandwich at an irregular hour without sitting at the kitchen table precisely on time and after having said grace.

First a sandwich at 4.30 AM, then no punishment.....Pappa must be excited about the invasion too.

Normally a jovial, outgoing and loving man of 45, Pappa's feet were frozen while sitting at attention on a supply wagon waiting for inspection by QUEEN WILHELMINA. Even though HOLLAND was not involved in WORLD WAR I, HOLLAND'S army was mobilized and Herman served five years, from '14 to '19. "Supply" was his command and he ran a two-horse wagon. He lovingly referred to his horses as the *"STAANDE VRETERS EN LIGGENDE SCHIJTERS," THE STANDING EATERS AND LYING SHITTERS."*

The incident of the partially frozen feet had made him hate the Army, Wilhelmina and the whole Royal Family. Besides that, somehow, frozen feet had caused ulcers and when his feet got cold or his temper flared, his ulcers would flare up and he'd be in real pain. He'd crouch in a corner on his haunches and swear like a dockworker if anyone disturbed him.

Right now, though, he's busy. He runs down the stairs to catch the latest news and back up to catch a glimpse of the Germans. The convoy is slowing down to a trickle and only an occasional staff car or a motorcycle streaks by their door. Now and then a vehicle races by in the opposite direction, back to the FATHERLAND.

HILVERSUM continues to blare out heavy resistance at the Rhine near ARNHEM, at the IJSEL near ZUTPHEN and heavy fighting against the German paratroopers near ROTTERDAM. It sounds like HOLLAND is beating the daylights out of the German monster.

Otto, meanwhile has joined Herman and Antoon at the radio and he gets Herman to switch to a German station.

Well....They're winning too. All over the western front, the Germans are pouring into the low countries at a rapid pace. Within the first hour, they've rolled 60 kilometers into Holland it seems and they are now trying to cross the rivers.

Every few minutes, the radio blares out the first few lines of the "HORST WESSEL SONG...... "DIE FAHNE HOGH, DIE REIEN FEST GESCHLOSSEN... S.A.MARCHIERT....." and then "SONDER-MELDUNG... SONDERMELDUNG. We have just conquered this town or that town. We clobbered X amount of tanks, crossed X rivers, captured tens of thousands of prisoners" and on and on... then..."DEUTSCHLAND, DEUTCHLAND ÜBER ALLES"... their national anthem.

Herman switches the radio back to Holland's HILVERSUM I while screaming at Otto; "I told you stupid asses that Germany would not respect our neutrality, but you..."

"Oh, shut up. What the hell makes you such an expert? Because your Mother-in-law was German, you're an expert on German mentality and strategy?"

"What's the matter with you Otto? Are you stupid and blind? For years we've seen the Jews stream across the borders. We've seen the military build-up. We've seen what they did in SPAIN and then how they waltzed all over SUDETENLAND and CZECHOSLOVAKIA, grabbed AUSTRIA and just ran over POLAND. What do you think? That we are different, special or something? Like hell! Well, let me tell you something, maybe it's a Godsend.

We're starving to death here and have been for ten years or more and the Queen gets wealthier as her people rot. Well hell, this may be a blessing and....."

"Herman, I swear, you're crazy!"

"Otto, Herman,..hold it..hold it" pleads Ida as she joins the group in front of the radio.

Clasien is still on the floor holding Hedwig with very serious looks on their angelic faces. They don't like it when Pappa is mad. They have seen him fight with customers that got drunk and they have seen him beat up the boys and they don't like it. He's never hurt his little girls, but he has hollered at them and it frightens them.

Ida pops in; "What are we going to do? I've got the table set, the Krauts stopped coming, just about and I need to know what to do about church and school."

"Ida, I swear you're getting to be as loony as that northern husband of yours. What school? What church? There is a war going on. The town is crawling with Krauts and you're considering sending your kids into the street?" Otto is nearly screaming.

"Otto, shut up. Are you going to eat with us or what? You're right Mam," says Herman, looking through the front windows, "It slowed down, let's eat."

All this time, Antoon has not said one word, looking from one to the other, his face a blank, no emotion whatsoever.

Jopie meanwhile, still draped over a barstool, is drinking this all in. His eyes are wild with excitement, feeling he is part of the "men" during these historic events and even though he has not learned German at school, he can pick up the drift of the broadcasts because the dialects on both sides of the border are very similar.

In WINTERSWIJK, in the GRAAFSCHAP (EARLDOM) of the ACHTERHOOK, province of GELDERLAND, the dialect is HOLLANDS-PLAT. On the other side of the border, in WESTPHALEN, the dialect is PLATT-DEUTSCH, and there are enough common words used in either dialect and enough common expression that the locals can easily communicate with one another at either side of the border, the "GRENS."

As a matter of fact, GERARD KWAK SR., "OPA" to the kids, born in WINTERSWIJK, had married HEDWIG MÖLLER in BOCHOLT, 25 Kilometers into Germany and IDA was born there and lived there until age three and the "KWAKS" moved back to WINTERSWIJK.

As the procession reluctantly leaves the radio in the bar and meanders to the kitchen, Mama looks over their heads and asks; "Where are Frits and Paultje?"

"Jopie, look upstairs and get them down here!"

Herman loves to order people around. He should have stayed in the service as a drill sergeant.

With the sun well above the horizon now, the big live-in kitchen with its high ceiling is well lit, the tea is steaming from the cups on the large table and sandwiches are piled high on a plate.

As Otto is saying; "I'll be back!" Jopie comes in panting..

"They're not upstairs!"

Herman, instantly annoyed, lifts the bottom half of the large kitchen window. "Frits....,Paul...Come in!" Nothing happens..."Hotdamn it!" Herman is ticked off and he literally runs to the front door across the mosaic floor of the long hallway. He yanks open the door that is supposed to be locked, gingerly steps outside, still framed by the walls, and peeks around the corner. Left first, but that's enough. Paultje is standing on the edge of the sidewalk in front of Otto's shop and Frits is standing in the middle of the street, talking to the Feldgendarm, while playing with the knobs on the motorcycle.

"What's that on your chest?" Frits wants to know. The German may not have understood him 100%, but nonetheless, he knows what the boy means.

The boy could have been his own. The big blue eyes, blonde hair and fair complexion. The kid could have been German, Dutch or Polish. He has seen kids like this in AUSTRIA, SUDETENLAND and DANZIG. The kid is cute and inquisitive.

"This means; "field police" says the soldier in German. "I direct the traffic. In five more minutes, I leave for my next post."

"Where are you going, are you going to shoot somebody?"

The blue eyes of the soldier smile back at him, "Probably not..Hey buddy, your father doesn't look too happy. You better run."

"Er kommt schon!" addressing Herman now.

Herman, visibly relaxed, starts to walk towards the man with the sidecar cycle. Apparently, the sidecar is not built for passengers to ride in, but holds a radio with a long antenna protruding from it.

Herman's German is atrocious. After living in the ACHTERHOEK for three years and eight in Belgium, he still sounds like a northerner from HAARLEM, up north in HOLLAND.

The soldier makes the most of it and carries on as if he understands every word Herman is saying and Herman thinks he's doing great.

"Look at that idiot!" exclaims Otto. He and Tante Cato are overlooking the scene in the street below their bedroom window. "Now he's fraternizing with the enemy!"

The soldier seems animated. Every so often he steps forward and waves on a passing vehicle and presently he says:

"Verzeihen sie mir!" takes off his helmet and shield, slips his big rubber coat over his head, folds it meticulously on the creases and tucks it next to the radio in the sidecar. He keeps right on conversing as he replaces his helmet and shield.

The sun is now well above the horizon and the temperature is well over 50 degrees already. It's going to be a nice day in Holland.

Paultje has now joined the little group in the middle of the street and fiddles with every switch and knob that Frits has already played with and yells: "OUCH!" as Joop slaps his little hand.

"Don't touch that, BOER."

Paultje has been nicknamed "Boer" by Pappa. It means FARMER because of his ruddy, chubby looks with the straight, white, piglike hair standing straight up on his head.

Paul kicks in the direction of Joop's shins; "Why don't you go back inside? You're not the boss!"

Everybody is outside now. Ida is standing in the doorway, holding Hedwig, while Clasien is standing next to her. Antoon is passively leaning against the wall, taking in the scene, some 50 feet away.

Pecht, the butcher, strolls out of his front door into the street and breaks out in perfect German,

"Guten Morgen, wie gehtst?" Translated, he says; "Good morning, how are you?"

"Good, thank you....and you?" replies the soldier.

"Good, thanks, where are you from?"

"I'm a SCHWABERLANDER, near the Black Forest."

"You're far from home, "says Pecht, as he waves his son BERNIE, eight years old, back to the sidewalk. But Bernie joins Frits and the group at the fascinating machine, where he's now exploring the radio.

Otto can't stand it anymore; "Got to see what's happening!"

With that, he moves down the stairs, but as he opens his front door, the German kicks his engine into life, saddles in and with a *"GRÜSZ GOTT,"* he noisily takes off.

As the men are joined by WIGGERS, the fruitman, the kids group together as Frits is heatedly telling them:

"I know how he started it. He turned the gas on, then the key and he folded out the kicker and he stomped on it."

Feldgendarmerie

"Yes, I can do that too!" says Bennie coming in.

"But you're not strong enough to kick-push that thing down," observes Frits.

"Oh yeah? Wait till another one comes along. I'll show you!"

"Oh man, you can't even reach the pedals. How are you gonna give it any gas?" teases Frits.

German paratroopers in Rotterdam, May 10, 1940

Nobody in the young group realizes that the gas is not controlled by foot, but by hand. With their youthful imaginations, it doesn't really matter what's right in their young minds.

"Laten we nou eten!" says Ida, getting impatient. "Let's go eat!"

The strict disciplined routine of eating, sleeping and working is seldom deviated by as much as a minute, but right now her schedule has been rudely interrupted.

"Boys, go eat!" says Herman, but he's too busy running the world's affairs on that street corner to be bothered with food. Jopie lingers on the edge of the group, intent on being part of the "men," but Pappa says: "Go eat!" and slaps in the general direction of Joop's left ear, but Joop expertly ducks it and reluctantly retreats into the house.

As other neighbors join the group, they move to the sidewalk in front of Otto's store and ponder the future. The war is barely two hours old and the battle lines are already drawn.

Herman and Pecht are on one side and Otto, Wiggers and Jonkers on the other.

Team ONE: "Holland will be on its knees in 30 days and things will get better. The Germans will turn over Holland to a new government and then things will improve around here."

Team TWO: "You talk like a damn Nazi. The Germans will never cross the Rhine and the British will land and join our forces at the GREBBEBERG and then push the Germans all the way back past Berlin into Poland. The Krauts made a big mistake by invading Holland. They just blew it. We'll whip their ass!"

It could have gone on a lot longer, were it not for another convoy rolling in from the direction of BORKEN, led by some racing motorcycles. One of them, a Gendarm with an attaché case slung over his shoulder on a brown leather strap, slows down calling at the debaters:

"DRIN, DRIN!" "Go inside. Get off the street!"

The kids are just finishing their sandwiches as Herman enters the kitchen. He is fussing. The kids are quiet. Kids do not speak at the table.

"That idiot brother of yours thinks he knows everything. Well, he is wrong. He has no idea how well-organized and how well-armed these Germans troops are!"

All eyes are on Pappa, which gives Frits a chance to sneak a slice of GELDERSE WORST, a spicy sausage.

"Mama, Frits is snitching worst!" tattles Clasien, who always seems holier than thou. But Mama is absorbed by Pap's conversation.

Herman continues: "Did you see how they don't even bother to run their tanks in on their own? They were on flatbeds, so they can move much faster and save a lot of gas, right? Do you know why? Do you know? Because of their intelligence, that's why. They know exactly where they're going to run into resistance and at that point, they will unload the tanks, put the infantry on top of them and move out. Why do you think they call it a "BLITZKRIEG? They move like LIGHTNING, that's why. They will be all over Holland in thirty days, I'm telling you, right then and there...."

An earsplitting roar makes everyone jump. A flight of planes roars over at treetop level causing the windows to rattle and the girls to scream.

"UNDER THE STAIRS!" Pappa commands. Antoon drops the sandwich he just made, but otherwise remains motionless.

Frits is under the table with Paultje and scoops up the sandwich. Paultje's face looks like he's going to cry any minute but Frits isn't crying so Paul won't either. Mama and the girls run out of the kitchen door into the closet under the stairs. Joop has just decided that he will stay with Pappa, who has flung himself to the floor, as another flight comes over with enough noise and vibration to convince him to join the girls under the stairs.

Frits is letting Paultje bite off the sandwich too. It has chocolate "MUISJES" sprinkles, their favorite.

Low flying German twin bombers

After another flight roars by, a little further away, Herman realizes that they are merely flying over on the way to a distant target. They are not attacking WINTERSWIJK. He gets up and says: "That's nothing, they're just flying over, get used to it. Get the kids ready for school."

He returns to the bar to resume his vigilance of the radio.

"To school? Is he crazy?" says Mama as she emerges from the closet wiping Hedwig's eyes. "It's okay now baby, don't be scared."

Clasien seems recovered and starts cleaning off the table, just before Frits gets hold of another slice of salami.

"No school...no school. There's a war on. We can never go back to school anymore!" sings Frits.

Paultje joins in the celebration: "No school!..No School!" He's been going to kindergarten now for two years already.

For once, Joop agrees with Frits.

"Mama, we can't go to school. It's dangerous out there, we could get run over, we could get shot. We've gotta stay home."

Joop still has a trace of a Flemish accent even though he sounds mostly High Hollands, like his dad.

"I'll go talk with Pappa."

He thinks, that being the oldest gives him seniority and authority, a bone of contention between him and Frits at times. He's back in a minute. "Pappa says it's a school day and that's that."

Frits is having a change of heart. Going to school means being away from this house and away from Pappa. That means freedom.

"Come Paultje, wash your face and hands and we'll be gone."

This is the first time in his 8½ years that Frits has volunteered to wash his face. He's standing on a chair in the "BIJKEUKEN," the pantry, combing his hair while looking in the mirror over the sink.

Bending over, after wetting the comb again, he tries to do something with Paultje's hair. The "BOER" is standing in front of him, head bowed, subjecting himself to the beauty process. It's hopeless. Paul's hair looks the same as before the treatment, except wetter. His hair is sticking up in all directions.

"Did you wash behind the ears?" asks Mama as she grabs a washcloth and washes a protesting Frits behind and over the ears and over his neck and chin.

"Paultje, you're not going." Mama is rubbing Frits dry. "Go kiss your father in the Café, bye!"

She gets a fleeting kiss from the skinny kid with the boundless energy who's just glad to get away from those big hands.

In the bar, Pappa's already lecturing Clasien and Joop.

"You hold hands at all times. Stay on the sidewalk. Straight to church and straight to school. You hear? No stopping. No detours and straight back after school, understand? Make sure you are absolutely clear when you cross the street, okay? Got it? No screw-ups Frits. You listen to Joop, you hear?"

Pappa gets fleeting kisses, except from Clasien, who hugs her Daddy. Frits watches with disgust. She always has to act so mushy and she's giving Pappa the works.

Finally, there they go. Two brothers identically dressed in their white shirts, blue and white knit ties, black shorts, gray knee-length stockings and black shoes.

Clasien in a white dress with pink frills all over. They are clean-scrubbed Dutch looking kids. They are poor but clean, walking along, holding hands.

It's going on eight o'clock and the May weather is really here. It must be 60 degrees by now and the smell of blossoms is heavy in the air. Holland is at its prettiest this time of year. In the west, the tulips should be in full bloom and all of the country is dark green with millions of blossoms and flowers decorating the countryside. It's a pretty country and the Germans picked a good time to invade.

Traffic is fairly sporadic by now and the kids are making normal progress. They pass the Carpenter's place, the coal distributor, Old Bram's leather shop, Bastiani's bicycle shop.... "Bastiani?"...

What's this Italian name doing in this remote part of Holland? The kids don't know. The kids don't care.

May 10, 1940. German bombers on the way to the target

"Why are there no planes now?" Frits is dying for some more excitement.

The street is deserted, with no civilian movement whatsoever. Not even the horsedrawn milk carts are around. Normally, they would be streaming into town in one long procession from all directions, converging on the milk processing plant.

The soil in this area is very rich, making for rich grass, in turn providing big healthy cows with lots of healthy, creamy milk.

Fluttering curtains are the only indications of life behind the two-story façades.

In the next block, the houses are a little taller, three stories mostly. As the threesome passes quickly by the druggist, "DE GAPER," (the yawner), past the "SPOORSTRAAT," (railway street) leading to the railroad station, Frits breaks loose, crosses the street in a dead run, while both Joop and Clasien are loudly urging him to come back. He stops in front of the corner building on the southwest corner of the WOOLDSTRAAT/SPOORSTRAAT intersection.

Oproep

aan de bevolking van Nederland

Het door de Duitsche troepen bezette Nederlandsche gebied wordt onder het Duitsche Militair-Bestuur geplaatst.

De Legerbevelhebbers zullen de maatregelen, noodig voor de veiligheid der troepen en voor de bestendiging van rust en orde uitvaardigen.

De troepen zijn gehouden, de bevolking, voorzooverre zij zich vreedzaam betoont, onder alle opzichten te ontzien en haar eigendom te eerbiedigen

In geval van loyale samenwerking met de Duitsche overheden zullen de Openbare Besturen op hun post gelaten worden.

Van het gezond verstand en het inzicht der bevolking verwacht ik, dat zij alle onbezonnen handelingen, elken aard van sabotage, van lijdzamen of daadwerkelijken weerstand aan de Duitsche Weermacht zal nalaten

Alle verordeningen van het Duitsche Militair-Bestuur zijn stipt en on- voorwaardelijk te volgen. Het zou de Duitsche Weermacht spijten, moest zij zich, gedwongen door vijandelijke handelingen van onverantwoordelijke elementen der burgerbevolking, tot scherpe maatregelen tegen de gansche burgerbevolking genoodzaakt zien.

Dat ieder aan zijne arbeid en op zijn post blijve, zoo dient hij niet alleen zijn eigenbelang maar de belangen van zijn Volk en van zijn Vaderland.

De Opperbevelhebber van het Duitsche Leger

May 10, 1940

24

"Come here!" Frits commands as he waves his hands at his frightened siblings across the street. "Come here! Look up here!"

On the wall is a poster in bold black and white with a German eagle across the top. "OPROEP." It seems to scream at him. That's how big it is. Then it continues in Dutch and repeats itself in German on the bottom half. It states that the occupation forces of the "Duitsche Weermacht" are in full command, that all activities should continue as normal and that the citizenry of Holland is guaranteed civil rights and protection by the occupation forces as long as there is only collaboration and no resistance.

The whole thing is signed by "DE OPPERBEVELHERBBER VAN HET DUITSCHE LEGER"

Though he's only a third grader, Frits is a good reader and except for a few words, like "collaboration" and "resistance," the whole thing makes good sense to him.

Joop and Clasien have reluctantly joined him. They had to cross the street somewhere anyway and now Joop is getting into the excitement of it all. This is a real war. This is going to be interesting and Joop, nearly quoting Oom Otto verbatim, is vehemently denouncing the Krauts and adds that the Dutch will beat the tar out of them.

In all the excitement, Frits starts to tear at the bottom of the proclamation, but Clasien interferes by grabbing his hand;

"They'll shoot us dead!" she cries, "Let's get away!"

The reality of dying is too much and as by command, Joop and Frits grab Clasien by the hand, one on each side and go flying down the street. Past the Big Hotel, left into the alley behind the toy store, around the corner into the WINKELSTRAAT, (the store street), across the street again into the churchyard and into the church.

They are five minutes late!

After three years of making Holy Mass at eight o'clock six days a week, seven o'clock Mass and ten o'clock High Mass on Sunday, Vespers at 5 PM and 7 PM in May and October and 'tLof at 7PM on Sundays and Holidays, this is the FIRST time they have ever been late.

In the Forrer family, NO-ONE is ever late. Never, never! Everything is on a schedule. There are no exceptions. The wrath of Herman's temper wouldn't tolerate anything else. This time, May 10, 1940, they are FIVE minutes late. Blame the proclamation!

But....no harm done.

Mass has not yet started. The KAPELAAN, (assistant Pastor), is at the altar conferring with Mr. COMMANDEUR, the Headmaster of the school. One, just one old lady sits in a pew on the right side of the church. That's it! Not another soul is in the whole church. JESUS on the cross over the altar looks to be in more pain than usual in his deserted church.

The Priest and Headmaster look up as the beam of sunlight pouring in the door announces the entrance of something or somebody.

As the children shyly shuffle forward to their customary seats, (they normally sit with their respective classes.), the Kapelaan and Headmaster wave them on and start approaching them.

"Frits," ask the Priest, "you served Mass, didn't you?"

Out of all things, Frits blushes. He remembers having been dismissed as an altar boy when he and his friend Eric, were found nipping from the Holy wine.

"Yes, Mijnheer Kapelaan."

"And you, Joop?"

"NEE Mijnheer Kapelaan"

"Okay Frits, get in there and get dressed. Joop, sit with your sister and you Mr. Commandeur can assist on the left side, Okay? Okay!"

"Let's go!"

As the Kapelaan gets things ready and Frits reappears from the SACRISTY in a black frock with a long white overshirt bordered with lace, Joop and Clasien climb into the first pew.

Normally, Joop would have sat back at least twenty rows with his classmates, (the further back, the more important you are, you see.) but today, he does not mind sitting with his little sister in the front. There is nobody here to see him in this belittling, embarrassing position anyway.

The Priest is now going through his routine;

"DOMINUS VOBISCUM" recites the Priest.

"ET CUM SPIRITU TUO," Frits duly answers.

Joop marvels at the fact that: WAR, PLANES, TANKS, SOLDIERS and OCCUPATION don't seem to be of any importance to the Priest at all.

The Kapelaan continues his well known ritual, "GLORIA TIBI DOMINUM" while Frits hustles back and forth ringing his little bell and carrying napkins and decanters on schedule.

He seems to know what he's doing and the Headmaster, looking out of place in his street clothes, follows right in time with the proceedings.

Joop and Clasien stand, kneel and cross themselves right on cue and before they know it, it's "SANCTUS, SANCTUS, SANCTUS," and Holy Communion is being offered. Nobody comes up to receive communion. Nobody! Joop, Frits and Clasien have eaten already so they cannot receive communion. Mr. Commandeur must have eaten too. The little old lady? Joop glances over his shoulders at her, but she's not budging.

"Strange," he thinks, "Do you suppose she ate or maybe she committed a sin and needs to go to confession first."

Joop is wondering what kind of sins an old lady would commit. He knows what type of sins Frits would commit, but an old lady? Maybe she cursed the Germans. Yeah, that's it! She may have cursed. Joop doesn't even have the nerve to think about what kind of curse words she might have used, but his reverie is interrupted anyway as Mass is over and it is time to kneel one more time and leave.

In the vestibule of the church a conference between the Kapelaan and the Headmaster is taking place with the kids eagerly listening in. Frits is still out there cleaning up and Joop is wondering if he'll have the nerve to nip of the wine again. "It's real sweet," Frits had told Joop. "Just like that RED CROSS wine that Mama has. The stuff that's supposed to be good for your blood." Joop knows about that one. That's good stuff.

It's decided that Mr. Commandeur and the children will go to school and see if any other teacher or students will show up. The little group meanders off to cover the two short blocks from the church to the KATHOLIEKE school.

In this part of Holland, only twenty percent of the population is Catholic. Some ten percent are DUTCH REFORMED and they have their own school too. The rest are mostly PROTESTANTS, most of them just in name only. The JEWISH population is maybe less than one half of one percent, that's all.

As they pass the BEWAARSCHOOL, Paultjes school, Frits wonders where the NUNS are this morning and why they weren't in church. Maybe they already went to 7 o'clock Mass or maybe not at all.

Just then, planes roar over, not directly overhead, but close. Mr. Commandeur explains that they are "STUKAS." "STURZ-KAMPF-FLUGZEU-GEN." His German sounds real German, Frits is thinking. The planes pass over in waves of 5 in V formations. There must have been 30 of them. The Headmaster explains that they are "DIVE-BOMBERS."

"See the bombs? Hanging under their bellies? Those are bombs. They knocked the dickens out of the POLACKS last year." The Headmaster continues. "They even hit targets as small as tanks. Right now, they're probably on the way to the GREBBEBERG, but our boys will be ready for them. We have some awesome FLAK, you know!"

"What's FLAK?" the boys ask, as they resume their stroll to the next building; the KATHOLIEKE SCHOOL.

The Headmaster is enjoying this. "FLAK means FLIEGER-ABWEHR-KANON, or anti-aircraft-gun. The British call it ACK-ACK, but we prefer FLAK, don't ask me why."

At the school, meanwhile, there sits just one boy, looking forlorn. It's Gerrit Beukeboom, Frits' classmate. Everything else is deserted. No bikes, no teachers, no students and no noises are to be found around the usually bustling school. Just 9 year old GERRIT, that's it.

"My Dad made me come!" says Gerrit, sounding like he's apologizing.

"That's Okay, come on in guys." Mr. Commandeur leads the way as he unlocks the door. He tells them to go to the eighth grade classroom while he makes some phone calls.

"WOW!" The benches and desks are really big. Much bigger than those in third grade, where Frits would normally be at this hour. They are also much bigger than the ones in second grade, where Clasien belongs. This is fun. They are climbing over the benches, checking out the chemistry set in the back corner by the sink and studying the world map on the inside wall. Joop is explaining how long the frontline is from Denmark all the way down to Switzerland. The "MAGINOT-LINE" in France, the "ARDENNES" in Luxembourg and Belgium, the hills of Limburg in Holland, the Rhine and IJsel rivers and the former Zuiderzee are all the areas where Germany will be beaten badly today. The kids are impressed. Joop suddenly seems much older. Frits even gains some respect for his older brother.

WINTERSWIJK and even the ACHTERHOEK are barely specks on the global chart. Holland is sooo little, compared with Germany, especially as Joop points out that Austria, Czechoslovakia and Poland are all part of the THIRD REICH. Frits' enthusiasm subsides considerably and he asks, "Why do they want to attack us then? We didn't do nothing to them."

Joop starts his explanation of National-Socialists, the N.S.D.A.P. and their greed for LEBENSRAUM as Mr. Commandeur enters the classroom. He looks somber. The few long hairs on either side of his bald head are hanging down kinda straggly as if he's been sitting with his head in his hands. The kids square themselves away in the front row benches without being told.

As Mr. Commandeur is running his hands through his hair, front to back, trying to plaster his hairs back to the sides of his head, he says to no one in particular;

"Nobody is coming to school today. The royal family has fled to England by boat. Her Majesty has urged our soldiers to fight bravely and she's confident we'll win."

He seems devastated by the news. The kids sit quietly as if they feel the seriousness of the occasion.

"Paratroopers have landed near Rotterdam, but they are meeting heavy resistance. In Limburg, they've crossed the Maas at one point and..and...and..."

He looks at his rapt but youthful audience, stops abruptly and says; "We're going home. Stay together. Gerrit, you stay with the Forrers until you get to the WILLINKSTRAAT, then you race home. Okay? Stay on the sidewalks, don't stop and be careful. We will probably start school again tomorrow."

Stukas over Holland, May 10, 1940

Stuka—Bombs away

Impressed and suppressed, the children file out the door. Even Frits is subdued as he says, "Dag Mijnheer Commandeur!" on his way out. Dutifully, the four hold hands as they make their way past the Bewaarschool, past the church, then left into the WINKELSTRAAT. Just as they are about to turn right into the alley, they see a FELDGENDARM bring his tricycle to a stop in the middle of the intersection of the WINKELSTRAAT, WOOLD-STRAAT and MEDDOSESTRAAT, just about half a block up ahead. He positions himself in the intersection like a traffic cop.

He waves the traffic to his left as they come out of the WOOLDSTRAAT and turn right into the MEDDOSESTRAAT past the old St. JACOB'S church.

Originally, the St.Jacob's church was the only church in Winterswijk, but that was before reform days when everyone was still Catholic. Now it is the major Protestant church in town and the Catholics built a new smaller St.Jacob's church, where the kids attended Mass this morning.

Spellbound, the children watch as they edge closer even though Clasien is saying that they really oughta turn here.

"Goody goody gumshoes!" Frits is thinking. "This kid is sick. No normal kid would be good all the time."

Joop, for once, seems to feel the same way as Frits. "It doesn't matter whether we turn here or at the next corner!" Slowly, they progress to the next corner where the convoy is turning.

An open car with a leathercoated officer in the backseat stops at the tricycle. A soldier gets out, does something to the radio in the sidecar and hands a telephone to the man in leather. He has to shout into the instrument because the traffic noise is overwhelming. He checks a map in his lap, shouts some more, hands back the phone and takes off as soon as the soldier is back in the front seat.

The depression that hung over the kids is gone. This is the most fantastic day of their lives. Truckload after truckload of soldiers rolls by. Covered trucks that must be carrying ammunition, according to Joop, or other supplies, just keep coming and coming. Cannons with their barrels pointed backward make for an endless parade as motorcycle riders with briefcases slung over shoulders, race by in either direction. The convoy slows down as if there's a traffic jam up ahead, which would not be surprising in these narrow, age-old streets.

More people are now hanging out of their windows on the second floors and even though, from this vantage point, one can see three or four more "Proclamations" plastered on different walls, nobody seems to be conducting "business as usual." The large ALBERT HEIN supermarket on the corner is locked solid, but has people hanging out of the second story windows.

Up ahead, nearly across from the old St.Jacob, soldiers are moving in and out of the HOTEL STAD MUNSTER.

Just as Clasien is saying, "We should be going home. Pappa will be mad." The column starts up again slowly.

The delays seem to be just beyond the OUWE JACOB at the market place. Joop agrees with Clasien, "Let's go!" he says.

Frits turns loose of Clasien's hand that he's been holding since they left school half an hour ago. "You go! I'm staying."

"No, you can't! You're coming with us. Pappa will beat me up because I'm the oldest and he'll hold me responsible!" pleads Joop, as he lets go of Clasien's hand in an attempt to grab Frits'.

Joop is not quick enough. Frits darts behind the Gendarm directing traffic and then crosses the intersection toward the church. On the opposite side of the street he stops and hollers;

"Gerrit, come on, let's go!"

Joop is close to tears, more from sheer helpless frustration than from fear of his daddy's beating. He tries once more. "Come on now, you brat!" He turns, knowing the hopelessness of the situation, grabs Clasien and starts back down the WOOLDSTRAAT towards home. Even though he is twenty-one months older than his brother is and nearly twice as tall, he has never been able to control the stubborn brat. He's beaten him, yes, many a time, but Frits has never given up. "One of the these days. Just wait."

Meanwhile, Gerrit has joined Frits across the street and the two of them leisurely move toward the church, taking in everything that attracts them and that's just about anything that passes by. Gerrit looks like the squat little farmboy that he is, with his ruddy face, wooden shoes and heavy clothes that have seen better days.

Passing the restaurant windows of the HOTEL STAD MUNSTER, they stop and stare at the officers sitting at the tables, eating heartily and drinking beer. The clock on the Jacob church strikes eleven. As they pass the front of the old church, they dart across the street between a cannon and a supply truck and stop in sheer amazement of the scene that unfolds in front of them. The ancient market place just crawls with soldiers.

The center of activity revolves around two great big stainless steel kettles on wheels. Trucks are parked in neat rows that change constantly as some trucks leave and arriving ones line up in their places. Soldiers get off, stand their rifles in perfect little circles and line up at the kettles for chow. With their food, they sit down somewhere, anywhere. Against the church-arches, the trucks, the old houses that line the square and even against the

Rifle pyramids, relaxed German soldiers, May 10, 1940

cannons. Most of them have taken off their steel helmets and seem to be happy and relaxed.

They certainly do not appear afraid or anxious. They act as if there is no war anywhere in the world. Frits and Gerrit start moving among them and nobody seems to care. As a matter of fact, some of the soldiers start talking to them and Frits sits down with them and chats right back. The fact that the soldiers don't speak Dutch and Frits doesn't speak German doesn't bother anyone as they rattle right on.

The marketplace, Winterswijk, May 10, 1940

Gerrit, who had drifted away, returns with a brown, grayish slice of bread in his hand. He's happily knawing on it as he approaches. Frits is on his feet instantly.

"Where'd you get that?" the always hungry Frits wants to know.

"Over there!" Gerrit points toward the kettles where on a table loads of loaves are lined up.

Frits is up there in a second. "Mag ik er ook een?" he asks.

"Natürlich" is the answer.

There is no language barrier here. Besides that, the soldier giving the okay, is not the cook anyway, so he doesn't care.

"Boy, this bread is tough and a little sour, but otherwise Okay." Frits thinks to himself.

There are a couple of other boys in the marketsquare. They're older, maybe twelve or thirteen. Frits does not know them. They must be protestant, because they're not from his school. They are just hanging out, talking with the soldiers, carrying things and helping out around the kettles. That's cool, man. This is a signal for the third graders to loosen up a little too. The beautifully stacked rifles certainly capture their attention. As they're sitting on their haunches admiring the weapons, Frits shows off to Gerrit;

"This is what you pull to shoot! Bang, bang, bang!"

He has read many books by CARL MAY about cowboys and Indians, so he knows all that stuff. In his enthusiasm to educate Gerrit in this new-found warfare, he pulls a trigger a little harder than he intended and thank God, the safety is on, so the weapon doesn't fire but it collapses the perfect little pyramid. With an awful lot of clanging and banging the whole stack of rifles smashes to the ground. Soldiers startle and jump and Frits and Gerrit are gone like a shot.

They race off, in between and around the trucks, into a little sidestreet, into an alley behind the houses and out again into another quiet street with not a soul in sight, not even Gerrit.

Catching his breath, Frits starts for home. Nobody has followed him apparently and his heart gets back from his throat into his chest. He ducks back into an alley until he gets to the WILLINKSTRAAT, behind the Dentist's house with the tennis court. He stops, looks up and down the street and as he turns north, it dawns on him that the factory, the WILLINK's factory, named after the owner, WILLINK, is not making any noise. It's closed. His curiosity gets the better of him and he decides to check it out. As he approaches the main gates to the plant he sees several cars, one Dutch and several Mercedes' or Opels.

The factory is dead quiet. No machines are grinding noisily, no turning out of rolls and rolls of fabrics.

He inspects the cars. Nice cars. One open car has a leather coat draped over the passenger seat. A brown leather belt lies on top of it with a cute little gunholster attached to it. Standing on the runningboard he can reach the pistol. The lock on the holster gives him a hard time, but finally he figures it out and soon he stands in awe of the shiny black weapon in his hand. A sudden noise makes him stick it back fast and he nearly breaks his neck as he jumps away from the car. Apparently, someone started up the machines inside the plant, that's all. He screws up his courage again, steps back onto the runningboard, takes the belt and pistol, wraps the belt around his middle twice, buckles it after some trouble and takes off out of the yard into the alley.

He races the length of the alley behind all the houses till he gets to the WILLEGENBOS, the willow woods. He stops, gently taking out his new-found treasure and admires it with a loving look in his eye. It's so small, a grown man could hide it in his palm, but for him, it feels just right.

After putting it back into the holster, he jumps the creek and out of the woods, crosses the pasture behind his house and climbs the fence into his yard.

Willink Factory

He crosses the backyard, moves through the long hall to the Café door and stops in front of the gathered war analysts in front of the radio. Out of breath, but beaming with pride, he says,

"Hey, look what I got! This war is fun!"

CHAPTER II
May 10, 1940   12 Noon

Every noon, as the factory whistle blows the dinner hour, BRAM, the old saddlemaker, walks half a block to the Hof Van Holland, sits at the bar and sips two glasses of BRANDEWIJN and shuffles on back home.

"It's good for the digestion," says Bram, "and you'll live longer."

He ought to know; heaven knows how old he is. Today, however, he has considered not coming at all with all that commotion out front, but after putting his wife of 55 years at ease, he decides that his digestion should not suffer because of war.

Inasmuch as he has not done a lick of work today, he walks out even earlier than usual and that's a good thing, because the factory whistle isn't going to blow today.

Now he's on his THIRD BRANDEWIJNTJE and is up to his eyeballs in politics. OOM GERRIT, Ida and Otto's brother, who lives caddy corner to the west in KWAK'S SLAGERIJ, another butchershop, has joined Herman, Otto, Pecht, Jonkers and Antoon.

Gerrit is even more vocal than Otto about Holland's ability to whip the Germans and even though the Royal Family's fleeing to LONDON was a terrible letdown, he still has all the faith in the world in the Dutch soldier.

In between "SONDERMELDUNGS" on the German station, the amateur analysts argue the pros and cons of the German broadcast. Bram is about to make a point as he's rudely interrupted by Frits' appearance with a belt circled around his waist twice, with a holster smack on his belly. He's about to pull out the pistol to show it off, when Pappa calls out,

"Don't pull that out. Where'd you get that thing?"

"From the Germans, of course!" Otto cuts in.

"Oh, shut up Otto! How'd you get that? No, don't take it off. I want it out of here, we could get shot having that thing around the house. How and where did you get it?"

He might have slapped Frits about the ears, but somehow Frits being armed made a difference.

Frits starts to talk but Bram interrupts, "That's good quality leather. Expensive, must have..."

"I don't give a damn about the leather, take the damn thing back where you found it. WHERE did you find it?"

"Pappa, I'm sure he stole it!" Joop has to put in his five cents.

"Oh, shut up everybody. Where did you get it?" His ulcer flares up and his temper is about to explode.

"Well, at the WILLINK factory..."Frits begins...

"The factory didn't even open today!" Otto interrupts.

"Otto, for the last time, stay out of this! What about the factory?"

"Well, there were a bunch of cars and this was just laying there...." He starts to take the pistol out again.

"Leave that alone!" Pappa is beside himself now.

"So I put it on and came home!" Frits continues.

"Take that belt off and let me see it!" This time it's Oom Gerrit.

"Like hell you will, Frits. take it right back where you found it and come straight home thereafter and you won't leave this home no more for the rest of the war!"

"Hold it, hold it!" Otto again. "Give it to me. I'll return it so we won't get this boy in trouble!"

"Just get it the hell out of there, that's all I want..."

"But Pappa, can't I keep it, then you can keep the belt...and..."

"No way, Otto go admire the damn thing someplace else and you Frits and you too Jopie, get out of your school clothes, but if you stick as much as your nose out of this house, you'll get the beating of your life. You'll spend the rest of your life as a cripple!"

"Excellent quality though," Bram drains his third BRANDEWIJNTJE.

Herman walks behind the bar for another refill just as the radio starts another, *"DIE FAHNE HOCH,"* another SONDERMELDUNG coming up.

"Can I have another beer, please?" Antoon must be speaking his first words of the day.

"Food is on the table!" Ida sticks her head around the door and withdraws immediately.

"Be right there!" Herman is listening intently to the German newscaster who, in glowing terms, announces further advances. Bram downs his fourth drink and says; "Tot Kiek!" and shuffles out the front door. The sun is now shining into the bar and into Bram's eyes. He adjusts his cap and shuffles on home.

Herman is handing Antoon his beer and asks, "They broke through where?" "In Belgium, in CHARLEROY, I believe they got the MEUSE bridge intact."

"How did they get to the MEUSE so fast? Paratroopers?"

After checking everybody's drinks, Herman and Antoon walk to the kitchen, Antoon beer in hand, leaving the rest by the radio.

The kitchen is the main living area for the family. It is large with a high ceiling and dominated by the table.

It easily seats all eight of them and is surrounded by high-backed chairs and Hedwig's highchair, her KINDERSTOEL.

Pappa occupies the chair at the head of the table and Antoon sits at the far end. Mama sits with her back to the stove for easy access. The room has three stoves, one coalstove, where most of the cooking and baking is done, one modern miracle, an electric stove and burners. That thing was installed three years ago, anticipating lots of restaurant business that never came. (Mama still says, "I should have gotten a gas stove!") The third one is a potstove that's meant for heating the large kitchen, but will be removed now that the evenings are not that cold and humid anymore.

Frits is neatly telling Paultje about all the activity at the market square and even though Joop would like to kick him in the shins from across the table, he's hanging onto every word, kinda annoyed that he's missed out on all that fun, just by being good.

Pappa and Antoon enter right at the part about Officers eating at HOTEL STAD MUNSTER and wants more details as to;

"How many? What time? Could you see what they were eating? "BIEFSTUKJES?" "Damnit, they get all the breaks. Here we are, Hotel-Café-Restaurant, and they drive right by us by the thousands, while we're starving for business. Well, damnit, let's pray!" "Jopie!!!!"

Dutifully, Joop leads in the Sign-of-the-Cross, the Lords-Prayer, Ave-Maria, another Sign-of-the-Cross and then SMAKELIJK ETEN!" Mama starts serving potatoes, carrots and fish. The weekly supply of meat was already gone by Monday, the soup by Tuesday but today being Friday there's plenty of fish. Vanilla pudding concludes it all. In typical old-country-style, the main meal of the day is the NOON DINNER. School's closed from 12 till 1:30. The stores close during that same time and the factory closes from 12 to 1 PM. So everyone sits down to dinner as the ANGELUS sounds from the church tower.

On normal days, nobody speaks unless spoken to, but today is not a normal day, obviously, and Frits gets both bellylaughs and worried looks as he tells his story about the noisy collapse of the rifle pyramid. When the question comes up again about the pistol, Mama nearly freaks. "You've got that thing here? I don't want that thing in the house. I don't want anybody…"

"Ida, Ida, calm down. It's gone already. Otto took it."

"Otto? What's Otto going to do with it? He'll get in trouble. Now, Frits, you stay away from that stuff, you hear? We don't want problems. Who knows what's going to happen now, maybe we will get bombed too and we'll have war here too and fighting and everything and...and.." Her nerves are getting frazzled, the tension starts to show.

"Come on, slow down, the war just passed us by, we'll be alright, as a matter of fact, this may very well be the end of the depression for us!" Herman sounds really soothing.

For the first time Antoon speaks up, "So you really think Holland will fall, Herman?"

"I give it thirty days, that's it!"

"I don't know. If England lands its troops tomorrow like they said, they may throw the Germans right back and we may be in the middle of it!"

"Let's finish and we'll go back to the Café, Antoon. Frits, you stay in and peel potatoes. Joop, let's pray!"

"In the name of the Father....," all heads bowed, grateful for the meal, it may not have been the greatest, but today? Who cares?

At least Frits is allowed to peel potatoes in the backyard where the German Shepherd HILDA can keep him company.

OPA KWAK, who now lives in a neat little house at the end of a row of neat little houses, has gotten up the courage to walk over to his old GER-MANIA, now, Hof Van Holland. He still actually owns the building, with Otto and Cato occupying about one third of the building on the eastside and Hof Van Holland in the other two-thirds. Otto has been paying on his mortgage for twelve years already and is well on his way toward paying it off.

Herman and Ida are slow and behind all the time, partially because they bought the place in '37 when the depression was at it's worst in Holland and it hasn't improved much since.

OPA blames Herman. "He is a good talker, but not a good business-man, as a matter of fact, he talks too much. In the bar-business, people don't want to listen to anyone, they want to be listened to. Now Ida, she has a way with people and a way with a penny. She makes everyone feel at home, while turning every penny over ten times before spending it. If it wasn't for her, I might have foreclosed on the place a long time ago and sent them back to Belgium!"

Now, as he saunters into the backyard with his walking cane and cigar, the dog comes running up to him, wagging her tail in friendly recognition.

"How are you, old girl? Is the world treating you all right? Good girl, Good Girl!" He's patting the dog on the neck as he's talking and moves up the path toward the back of the house.

One thing he has to give Herman credit for is his yard. The man has a way with flowers. He has changed the straight dirt path into a half circular-path ending in a circle around the old ACACIA tree. A one-foot strip of grass on one side and a beautifully manicured lawn on the other borders the path. Flowers line the left side that borders the stalls and Otto's property and the lawn on the right is dotted with flowerbeds of all colors and varieties. The tulips and narcissus dominate the scene this time of year, while lilac trees are laden with white and purple flowers. It is hard to imagine that this garden spot, so peaceful and so pretty is only fifty yards from a street where thousands of tons of death and destruction have rolled by all day.

Frits sits on an old kitchen chair under the acacia, hacking the hell out of a basket of potatoes. As OPA walks up he greets him with a "Hi Opa!"

"This kid is alright!" says Opa to himself, "even though he takes after his father, I think." "A quick wit, an easy smile, intelligent blue eyes. Maybe there is some KWAK in him anyway!"

"You're hacking away the best part of the potato, boy. Here, hand me one."

As Frits hands him a potato, Opa retrieves from his vest pocket a little knife, unfolds the blade and commences to peel the potato from the top in nice even circles, turning the potato constantly till he's down to the very bottom. He dangles the peel, in one piece, in front of Frits, who observes that the peel is so thin he can nearly see through it, and it's nearly blue in color.

"Don't you know that the best part of the potato is under the skin, boy?"

"Ha, ha, ha," Frits cracks up. "Opa, the whole potato is under the skin!" Ha, ha, ha.

"Ya, but at least you shouldn't be throwing away half of your potato, like you're doing! Now do it like I did!"

He walks to the backdoor muttering to himself, "That kid is too smart for his britches."

Frits meanwhile mutters too. "You're not my father, I don't have to listen to you!"

But as he sticks his tongue out at the disappearing old man, he concentrates on getting a thin blue peel started from the top, round and round. His effort is not really rewarded. The peel either breaks off or is cut off and halfway 'round the 'tato he gives up and resumes his hacking.

Opa, as always, dressed to a Tee in his darkgray three-piece suit with goldchain watch and shined shoes, walks into the barroom to join the rest of the war analysts now seated in front of the radio.

The blacksmith, who normally only has a beer on Sunday, is already on his forth beer and if Ida had not come behind the bar to note it down, nobody might have known how many he owed for. Bram's tab hasn't been marked either, but Herman seems to remember that he had four instead of his customary two at dinner, for which he pays each Saturday. Ida dutifully marks that down too and even Antoon is onto another beer. Opa orders an OUDJE (an old GENEVER, Dutch gin), hoping his daughter won't charge him for it.

The Dutch troops seem to beat the Germans at the rivers and very heavy fighting is reported near Rotterdam. British planes have joined the air battle, but the Dutch Air Force is just about to fall apart. There was no Air force to speak of to begin with. British troops have landed along Holland's southern border and in ANTWERP, Belgium, as well as in northern France. Holland is holding it's own, it sounds like, but the Germans are pushing far into France and Belgium. Denmark sounds like a pushover according to the German broadcasts, one SONDERMELDUNG after another.

The mood in the Café varies up and down with the newscasts. Shouts of encouragement at one point and grunts when they hear some bad news.

"Why can't those lousy Frenchmen hold these Krauts at their MAGI-NOT line? It's supposed to be stronger even than Germany's SIEGFRIED line. This MAGINOT line is supposed to be impenetrable and yet the Krauts broke through it on the first day and are pouring into France."

Herman, having lived in Belgium for eight years, exalts the courage of the Belgians and their readiness. He's told to, "Shut up!" as a new sight attracts their attention. A convoy of four trucks with red crosses painted on white squares are coming from the west and slowing down right in front of Hof Van Holland and start turning left between Otto's bicycle shop and Pechts Horsemeat market.

At the end of the EELINKSTRAAT is the ALGEMENE ZIEKENHUIS, the General Hospital, and that's where they must be headed. Everybody heads out the backdoor, drinks in hand.

From under the acacia tree they can see the trucks racing to the Hospital and they're wondering if those are German or Dutch wounded? How many? How badly? And how many are dead or dying? All of a sudden the seriousness of the war hits 'em like a ton of bricks. All of a sudden all the excitement is reduced to death and human suffering. Everyone becomes quiet and subdued.

As they turn slowly to saunter back indoors, Herman notices the chair, the basket with potatoes and peels and a stainless bucket with "peeled" potatoes. "Frits!" he says…"FRITS" he shouts…"Frits," he hollers in the direction of the street, expecting Frits to have run after the ambulance trucks.

"He's up there!" Pautlje volunteers that information as he points to the top of the three tall willow trees that line the property.

"Ya PAP," he greets cheerfully as he waves down at the gathering under the acacia tree. The whole flock moves from under the acacia toward the street, so they can see him on his perch up there.

There he is, way up in the center tree, swaying back and forth as if the tree is a swinging cradle.

"Oh my God!" Mama, who has joined the crowd out back, puts both hands on her bosom as she takes in gulps of breath. Opa adds, "That boy is gonna kill himself!"

Pappa doesn't seem as worried but he shouts just the same, "Come on down, you dumb idiot!" but he knows his monkey will be alright.

Frits gives no indication that he's planning to come down, but instead hollers at them, "They're putting a big red cross on the hospital roof and there's a banner over the entrance, a big white banner with big black letters!"

"What's it say?" All of sudden the fear for the young lookout disappears.

"I can't read it, they're moving it too much. Oh ya, wait a minute, it says KRANKEN something…"

"KRANKENHAUS" Otto volunteers,

"That's KRANKENLAGER," now I can see it, KRANKENLAGER."

"That damn boy must have eyes like an eagle." Gerrit mutters more to himself than to anyone in particular.

"Or it's a very big sign." Opa cuts in.

"No, no, no, that boy has great eyes!"

Herman is too proud of that monkey to stay mad, so with more tenderness than he realizes he shouts upwards, "Okay you monkey, come on down and peel those potatoes."

Frits starts working his way down slowly, purposely making the time drag as best as he can. This is more fun than peeling potatoes anytime. He sways the tree back and forth between the other towering willows. One of these days, he's going to jump from one tree to the other like TARZAN in the comics.

TARZAN and PRINCE VALIANT are his heroes and he can't wait for the SATURDAY EVENING POST or the PANORAMA to arrive, so he can read about his heroes and what they're up to in the next episode. The willow tree sways less as he gets lower and lower. He'd bet that he could sway this middle tree so far one way or the other that it would touch the other trees and then he could grab a branch and latch on. These willows can handle it. Willows are what wooden shoes are made of, the wood will give but not break or splinter, that's why he makes his bows from willow branches. They're tough and yet elastic.

By now he's on the ground and sighs when he thinks about his peeling job, but Mama is waiting there, bucket in one hand, chair in the other.

"Pick up that basket, you're coming inside. No wait, where are your

KLOMPEN? Wooden shoes? "In the BIJKEUKEN Mama." "Wait, put that basket down, go get your KLOMPEN, wash your feet out here and come in through the BIJKEUKEN. You're staying in, young man. No more nonsense today."

Frits kinda washes his feet and his knees and dries them with the blue and white checkered kitchen towel. Most of the dirt is now on the towel. This is the way it goes as long as he can remember. "Wash your hands and knees before coming in!" The only differences being, in Belgium, they had a pump outside, here they have a regular faucet. He's dried off and now he dries the BOER, who has joined him at the faucet. Paul tags along most of the time. Wherever Frits goes, Paultje goes. Paultje doesn't relate to Jopie at all, he's too bossy. Frits is neat, they do things. The grown-ups may not always appreciate what they're doing, but at least they do stuff.

Now they enter the kitchen through the bijkeuken. Mama turns away from making sandwiches to greet them with;

"Where are the potatoes?"

"Oh, the potatoes? I'll get 'em." He returns with the basket and Mama takes him through the far door into the hall next to the stairway.

"Here you sit and here you stay. Don't budge until you're done with these PIEPERS and don't peel so thick, leave some potato. Paultje, you come with me!"

Left alone, Frits can ponder his sins, but he has better things to do. He cuts a face on a large potato, complete with holes for the ears and eyes. The stupid AARDAPPEL, the potato, smiles at him in a crooked way and Frits makes a face back at the potato face. The AARDAPPEL face reminds him of a Jewish man who sat just on the other side of the wall across from him. He had come with his family, about eight of them, and they had eaten in the VOORKAMER, the good room, where the kids were only allowed at Christmas time.

Frits had looked in on them in wonder as they prayed with their hats on. That was just the opposite from the Catholic Church, where the women went to church with a hat on and the men took them off when they prayed.

What was even crazier, when the man who looked like the potato was through praying, he took off his hat and then he still had a little round knit cap underneath.

While he sits there, dreamily remembering the scene, he cuts off the rear top of the potato and now it looks even more like the Jewish prayer man with his funny little cap.

There were a lot of Jews coming through at one time. Walking, on bikes, pushing handcarts or pulling baby carriages full of stuff. Some came in cars, but most of the ones that stopped at Hof Van Holland were the walking crowd. Hof Van Holland was nearly the first restaurant that they encountered after crossing the border from Germany. At one point there was a steady stream coming across and most of them were tired and hungry. They must have come a long way. What puzzled Frits was that most of these people did not eat in the EETZAAL, the dining room, but ate in the VOORKAMER.

"How come they're allowed in there and we can only get in there for Christmas?"

The answer about religion and KOSHER food from Bauman was well over his head and why meat from Oom Gerrit and Pecht was not good enough and it had to come from Bauman Senior or Bauman Junior was absolutely beyond him.

As he studies his Jewish AARDAPPEL he wonders why they stopped coming about a year ago. Something about HITLER closing the borders. Anyway, all Jewish traffic stopped and the electric stove hasn't been used since.

He's interrupted in his reveries by the noise of more trucks and motor-cycles coming through and he sneaks to the corner of the hallway to see what's happening.

Just then, Pappa storms out of the Café, followed by Oom Gerrit and Antoon, "Get back to those potatoes!"

"Damn!"

He peeks after them and then lights up the stairs, two treads at a time. Just as he is in good position at the hall window near the MANGEL, Joop appears with the same seat in mind and his immediate reaction is typical, "You're supposed to be downstairs working on your PIEPERS and I'm going to tell Pappa that you're up here!"

"CREEP, LOUSY BASTARD!" Frits retreats but instead of turning downstairs, he heads upstairs to the attic, the ZOLDER. The attic is pretty barren and the wooden floor is dusty from all the leftover dirt from the flowerbulbs.

Just about ten square feet of newspaper is still down with some dahlia bulbs and they'll go in the ground, probably this week.

Every fall, all the bulbs are dug up, cleaned, spread on newspapers in the attic, not touching. When they touch one another, they rot, they can't have that. All the little bulbs that were born during the year go in separate beds, not to bring forth flowers, but to grow and get ready for next year. Frits is learning all that stuff from his dad and he loves it.

Meanwhile, Frits is trying to get a good look through one of the few little lift-up windows that light the attic, but the view is very limited. He can't even see the street in front of the house.

"DARN."

Only one thing to do. He gingerly lifts one of the red barrel tiles and slides the lower one underneath. "NEAT." Now one more and one more."Okay," Now a few down and he has a foot square opening. The roof is neat. The rafters going up to the crown of the roof, are covered with 1 X 2's running lengthwise like a giant ladder. He gets an old chair, stands on it and now his whole upper body sticks through the roof.

"That's better!"

Now he has the best seat in the house.

"Yeah, man!" He can see nearly as far as the swimming pool, well, at least to the railroad crossing.

Just then, a PANZER train comes into view. The road traffic has been stopped and the train rolls by in the distance. "Oh Boy," more tanks, some bigger, some smaller. Behind the two locomotives is a flatbed with a 4-barrel cannon on it. FIERLING FLAK, he'll learn later.

"WOW!" He can see it from up here, but the people below can't, because the houses are in the way. Even Jopie on the second floor can't see this, the dumb ass. He always thinks he's so smart, and he is, schoolwise, but when it comes to real smart, like Frits thinks of himself, he's just dumb and clumsy.

Directly below another Red Cross truck returns against the traffic. It turns left, just under Frits' nose. He cranes his neck, but the roof is in the way and blocks his view and that can't be helped unless he creates another look out on the other slope of the roof. He's just considering that, although the PANZERZUG seen from this side still holds his imagination when the sound of aircraft comes again, but from the other side of the house, direction KRANKENLAGER. His mind is made up in an instant. He works his skinny body through the lathe work that forms the roof and in ten seconds flat he's crawling up the roof on hands and feet. With his bare feet he has great traction and the roof is not all that steep. Before you know it, he straddles the crown of the roof and takes in the scenery. The airplanes are not the same Stukas as this morning and not as many, maybe ten. They're fading fast into the setting sun. It must be going on six o'clock, Frits figures. The hospital with it's huge white flag and the Red Cross on it is in full view from here and he can even see the garbage dump beyond the last house of the EELINKSTRAAT. That flag has to be 20 X 20 meters he figures.

He's wondering if they brought that thing with 'em or if they made it here. He decides they must have brought it.

The fighting must be really close if they're bringing their wounded all the way back here. He doesn't really know how far Arnhem or the rivers are from here, but he does know that when he's gone to see his Tante Paula and Ome Henk in Arnhem during summer vacation it took about an hour by train with some six stops.

Military supply trains. Reason for bombing

The radio and the men have been talking about that area, that must be where the action is. The Panzertrain has passed the crossing and must by now be in the yard being switched to the north for ZUTPHEN or to the northwest for ARNHEM.

Now that the guard has been raised, (the operator must have come to work.), the column starts approaching again and for a better view, Frits gets up and walks toward the nook on Oom Otto's house. With both arms stuck out at his sides, he gingerly balances his way, tile by tile, to the corner, where he's spotted by Mrs. Kaandorp. The Baker's wife is hanging out of the upstairs window, caddy corner across and her attention was drawn from the scene of activity below, to the skies because of some new aircraft rumblings.

"HERMAN!" she can see him on the sidewalk in front of his door. "HERMAN!" he's looking up at her. "FRITS IS ON TOP OF THE ROOF!" All eyes turn upward. Pappa, Pecht and Otto race across the street toward Pecht's doorsteps, so they can see him and there he is.

"Pap, you should come up here, you can see the whole works!"

Even the soldiers on the trucks, some riding on running boards, see him now. Frits waves at nobody in particular, but some wave back. Young Bernie Pecht catches the spirit of it all.

"I'm coming up too! Wait for me."

"Like hell you will!" booms Pa Pecht. "You stay right here, young man!"

Pappa Forrer starts boiling fast, "You come right down!" He sounds serious. Frits balances his way back to where he came up, goes down on his hands and knees and starts slowly down the slope towards the hole he's created in the roof. For the first time, panic sets in. He really doesn't have any foothold or anything to hold onto. Suppose he'd start sliding and he can't stop. His hands get clammy, but he has some hold on the rounded edges where the roof tiles overlap. His feet seem to have enough friction so he carefully inches his way down. Pappa meanwhile appears in the original lookout hole and grabs his feet the moment he can reach them. He gingerly lowers Frits through the opening, all the time holding onto his feet and easing Frits inside the attic.

Before Herman even attempts to replace the roof tiles, he sets himself on the old chair, folds Frits over his lap and proceeds to whack the blisters out of him.

Frits starts screaming immediately with the first blow and keeps screaming, though his eyes are dry. With Pappa, if you don't scream he'll keep beating till you do, so it's better to scream immediately. Pappa puts him down, breathing hard, grabs Frits' ear and screaming louder than Frits can scream, "NOW IN BED, NO SUPPER AND DON'T YOU MOVE!"

Down the stairs, nearly flying, past a grinning Jopie, "BASTARD!" and into room VI. Out of his shorts and shirt, under the blankets, puffing. "Well," he says to himself, "it beats peeling potatoes!"

CHAPTER III
May 11, 12, 13, 14, 1940

The morning is nearly normal as if yesterday never happened. The milk wagons are rattling down the street as usual. Jopie is sent across the street for a loaf of bread. Other than Pappa sitting by his radio, instead of at the breakfast table, things appear like any day of the week in the beautiful month of May.

May always seems to be beautiful. Mama Ida Forrer-Kwak was born in May. "5-5-5." May fifth, 1905 and she would tell anyone who wanted to hear it, that in all her life, it only rained once on her birthday and then only a little.

This morning is no exception. The air is heavy with blossoms and yesterday's diesel fumes have mostly evaporated.

Pappa has talked to Mr. Commandeur and the three oldest ones are going back to school again. Some of the neighbors are still going to keep their children off the road, but generally, the little town is returning to normal. The regular trains aren't running yet. Nobody wants to go anywhere anyway and fruit and produce don't come in by rail.

Every now and then a small truck roars by or an ambulance returns, but that's about it.

The motorcyclists with their green rubber coats and briefcases slung over their backs are the most regular sight.

The planes are also pretty steady customers and some formations can be spotted at higher altitudes, bombers presumably.

News about intense fighting keeps pouring in and at one point a truck with Dutch Prisoners of War comes cruising through from west to east. Here's where the first outpouring of patriotism becomes evident. People stop to cheer and applaud our boys, although they are a sorry lot. Mostly bareheaded, some bandaged, all filthy and raggedy, they look somber and rejected. The German soldiers, guarding the Dutch boys at riflepoint don't seem to care one way or the other. They must be a battle hardened bunch already.

The kids leave the house at 7:45 as always, neat and clean, shoes shined and hair combed. Hand in hand, they make good progress, but they're not joining many other kids on their way to school.

When it's time to cross the street near RUPERT, the toy store, they have to wait several minutes before being able to dart into traffic between trucks and cars. The milk wagons, with all their milk cans tied behind a chain are lined up here, stranded behind a traffic jam. The kids hurry on, Frits is holding onto Clasien's hand like a good boy, while Joop holds onto the other.

Pappa gave Frits a stern talking-to this morning. That, with the hunger pains from not eating last night, has made him see the light as to the fact, that being good always pays off.

Besides that, Pappa said things like, "In the difficult times ahead, I have to be able to count on you, not worry about you and I need you to carry your share of the responsibility for our family. Can I count on you?"

Handshake, hug, slap on the shoulder and Frits felt ten years older. So far, so good. Church is normal, but only one third full. The walk from church to school becomes more interesting, because now Frits has an audience and he has the tallest tales to tell. Most of the dull boys have done nothing yesterday and don't believe much until Gerrit joins the group and they relive yesterday's experiences up to the point where they somehow got separated after the rifle incident.

Only one other boy has an exciting tale about Germans stopping by their farm, searching the grounds and spearing the haystack with bayonets. He doesn't know what that was all about except, that the family was scared to death. He felt that his mother, speaking German, had saved their lives by talking the Germans out of killing them. "Boy, that's some story!"

The school bell rings and as the students line up in their customary spaces, it becomes obvious that only half the kids and less than half of the teachers are present.

Frits' teacher, Mrs. Bijlsma, the oldest teacher in the school, is not there and the third graders join the fourth graders in the class of Mr. Raes.

This should be fun. Mr. Raes is a young teacher with funny little glasses from the islands of ZEELAND along the Belgian border. He talks funny, as far as the locals are concerned, but what's more important to Frits, he has a reputation for not having a knack for discipline. He was Joop's teacher last year and Joop had not developed a great reputation for the FORRER name. Neither has Mr. Raes gained much respect in the FORRER family.

Frits whispers to Gerrit, "This is going to be fun!"

Much to their surprise, Mr. Raes uses the events of the day to teach geography, starting with his own province of ZEELAND.

"LUCTOR ET EMERGO" is the slogan of his province and its crest is a LION on his hind legs rising from the sea. "I WRESTLE AND COME UP" is what "Luctor et Emergo" stands for and in the picture, the lion is certainly coming up.

Mr. Raes takes their young minds from Antwerp, in Belgium, where the British have landed with large troopships that are now being bombarded by German planes. They cross the broad waters of the OOSTERSCHELDE through Zeeland, across all the other waterways that Frits can't remember, to the MAAS river at Rotterdam. He outlines the events of the war as he knows them. He must also have been listening to the accounts of both the Dutch and the German broadcasts and when he's asked, he replies, "Very true! Plus we monitored the BBC and Brussels and between all their accounts we're getting a pretty good picture!"

When asked, rather bluntly, by some chubby girl, "Why has the Queen deserted us and is she really a traitor?"

Mr. Raes stammers a bit, realizing that this girl is verbalizing the attitude in her own home.

"Staying in The Hague, taking a chance at being bombed, would not really help. She is safer in LONDON and from there she can oversee the defense of our country just as well as from The Hague!"

He doesn't sound too convincing, but the topic of discussion remains interesting.

He now produces a big map of GELDERLAND and on this map, compared with the world map in the eighth grade yesterday, this map shows everything really big.

Now Frits understands why rivers are so important and why the GREBBEBERG and all the other hills, north and west of the rivers, are so important.

Now he understands why the Germans poured out of Winterswijk in two directions. We're at a strategic junction and according to Mr. Raes, it's our good fortune that Holland's Army did not defend us any better than they did, because the Germans would have obliterated us in order to grab this town.

Wow, the children are fascinated and as the breaktime bell rings, they mill around Mr. Raes and the maps and tell the stories of their own experiences. Playing soccer on the playground is forgotten and most students don't even file outside. Occasionally the drone of aircraft disrupts the class, but trucks and trains cannot be heard from this point.

It's still hard to realize and understand that not too far from school people are dying in bitter fights.

Just before the noon bell rings, Mr. Commandeur walks into the room with an announcement for the parents,

"Please tell your folks, that this afternoons classes will be suspended, "HURRAH," "but Monday all schools will resume their regular schedules, "BOOOO." "In a conference with "MIJNHEER DE BURGEMEESTER," German authorities and the public school principals, it has been decided that normal life will resume in Winterswijk!" "BOOOO!"

Without further ado, without prayers, before the noon bell even rings, Frits, Gerrit and three other boys are on their way to the railroad station. It's kinda on the way home, anyway. "KINDA!" Maybe a little out of the way, but KINDA.

They reach the tracks to the west of the station, where the big silos are being built. That's where the warehouses are and the ABATTOIR, the slaughterhouse. The abattoir seems to have normal activity with one exception. The white-coated butchers, sliding carcasses on the overhead rails, are wearing BOOTS instead of KLOMPEN. They are German soldiers doing the butchering and big boxes of cut meats are being loaded on military trucks, probably heading for the front.

Fascinated, Frits has forgotten all about his promises to Pappa. He doesn't even think about Joop and Clasien. This is too intriguing.

Also, there's one more of those big kettles on wheels and a jovial cook in a white frock, having served every soldier in sight, asks the boys, "Wollsts auch was SUPPE?"

"SUPPE?" That sounds like soup to them and it being dinnertime it sounds like a good idea.

The cook digs up some metal dishes and spoons, but as three of the boys step up to get some soup, two take off for home. They must have been taught things about FRATERNIZING with the enemy. The soup is pretty good as a matter of fact. The boys are sitting on the edge of the loading platform, their legs dangling over the edge, heartily engaged in eating soup and making conversation.

One of the cooks is telling them about; *"Wenn ich noch ein lauschbub war!"* When he was a little brat, he did this and made that..., but the boys can't follow all of that and the cook kinda gives up just as a large group of planes comes over.

"Heinkel Bomber!" explains one of the Germans.

Boy, they're noisy, it feels as if the ground even vibrates. The butcher reappears carrying something disgusting in his hand. He walks over to a wall faucet, rinses and washes whatever he has and comes and stands in front of the boys as they're eating away at their soup. There are lots of chunks of meat in it, green peas, potatoes and slices of spicy sausages.

Frits grins to himself as he thinks about potatoes.

"Wonder who ended up peeling them last night?"

The butcher is blowing his lungs out on the thing he's holding and he blows it up as if it's a balloon. Wow! It gets big, twice as big as a soccer ball. He ties a knot in the end, whips out a sharp knife and starts scraping stuff off the taught skin of the balloon.

"Oh, neat, what's that?"

"A pigs bladder!"

Gerrit chokes on something, just thinking about that this man just had that thing in his mouth, blowing in it.

The butcher keeps clearing fat, string and other gook off the bladder,while telling them, "When it's dry, it makes for a great drumskin and if you don't have an innerball for your soccer ball, you stick it inside your soccer ball, blow it as hard as you can, wait for a few days for it to dry and you'll have a great ball. Who wants it?"

Frits has already snatched it, but regrets it instantly because the stupid thing is slimy and where it hits his shirt and tie it leaves gook, like snot, all over it.

"Now, let it dry for a few days, Okay?"

That sounds good. Frits asks for some "TOUW." But the Germans can't figure that one out and he can't seem to get across that he wants some rope to tie onto it, so he can carry it without having to hold on to that gooey thing. Well, we'll think of something.

He hands his metal dish back to the cook, who points to the faucet on the wall, where the soldiers have been rinsing their utensils.

"Eat with them, then act like them!" he seems to say.

The bladder balloon is clumsy, because he has to hold it as far from his body as possible so Gerrit rescues him by washing his dish for him.

The soldiers seem to have enjoyed their company and get back to work, cutting, loading, driving meat.

"*Grüss Gott!*" someone says and that's easy for the boys to pick up, so with a lot of "Grüss Gotts" they leave a lot of smiling Germans behind.

At the silo not much is happening, but at the warehouses, trainloads of boxes are unloaded and then loaded onto trucks.

Underneath the loading lid of the truck lies a box that must have been dropped, because it looks crushed and busted.

"Let's check it out!"

With that, they duck underneath the truck, while the bladder keeps banging into them, into the sides of the truck, the wheels of the train, leaving it's slimy marks wherever it touches.

The box proves to contain cans of sardines in olive oil. The boys are not sure what that is, but the picture of fish surely indicates that there is seafood in the cans.

"Let's take some home!"

"No, no, no, that's stealing!" This kid Robbie gets panicky.

"No, we found it, right Gerrit?"

Gerrit agrees, "We found it!" as he's trying to work a can into his pants pocket. The can's too big, so he unbuttons his shirt and sticks the can in his blouse.

Robbie takes off!

Gerrit and Frits look at one another and Gerrit points to his temple with his index finger, meaning; "He's nuts!"

The boys put about 4 or 5 cans behind their blouses and even though they "found" their bounty, they're whispering to each other as the Germans continue their loading right over their heads.

As they crawl away, Frits whispers, "Come play at my house!" and Gerrit nods as they straighten up and walk away from the warehouse.

As they pass the front of the truck, Frits spots a soldier's cap on the fender and swipes it with his left hand without missing stride.

After they round the corner and out of sight, he puts on the cap and nearly drowns in it. It hangs all the way down to his collar.

Gerrit howls with laughter at first, but then asks, "Can I try it on?"

Now it's Frits' turn to howl.

This time they walk into the front door of the Café rather than the back door like he did yesterday with the gun on his belly.

Besides, they came from a different direction.

Approximately the same men are in the Café as they walk in, but now they're sitting around the "reading-table" as the newspapers are running again and several have been delivered.

There stands Frits, soldier's cap on his head, sardine cans in one hand blown-up bladder in the other.

"Hey, Pappa, look what I got!"

"BACK TO THOSE DAMN POTATOES!"

At least, this time he has company. Gerrit stays with him under the acacia tree and even helps a little.

"No, Mrs. Forrer, my parents aren't worried, they think I'm at school. No that's okay, we don't have a phone, I'll go home at four, okay?"

"Okay!" Ida shakes her wise head saying to herself, "How can parents let a kid like that just roam the streets? I don't understand this modern upbringing. In my day that type of thing would not happen." She mutters to herself on the way back to the kitchen.

Paultje needs to hear all about the bladder and the sardines and how he got that cap. Again the cap is under Oom Otto's control, but everyone enjoyed the sardines. Ida put them on sandwiches and Frits couldn't remember ever having had sardines before, though his Mama,said in the better days in Belgium he had eaten them.

Anyway, they were good and the men in the café said, "They went great with beer and Jenever," so that worked out beautifully.

First, it was insisted that Gerrit keep his cans, but after a while the men accepted one of his anyway. In the kitchen the boys learned from Mrs. Forrer, standing on chairs along the counter, how to open them with the little keys and now Gerrit is down to three cans to take home.

Knowing how good they taste, he knows his parents will enjoy them.

The bladder is gently blowing in the breeze overhead where Pecht has hung it up, explaining, "As it dries, it shouldn't touch anything!" (sounds like tulip bulbs) and you wanna be sure that dogs and cats can't get it."

So string was provided, tied on and with the help of a stepladder it was strung from one of the acacia branches.

The dog might not be able to jump that high and the cat couldn't get to it, even if it climbed on the branch, but the flies are certainly on it. At least two dozens of them.

Mama's protests about that "SMERIGE DING" and, "it should go in the garbage!" hasn't fazed the men at all because they were young too and they would have loved to have had a drum.

Frits doesn't really know how he's going to make that drum, but he's convinced that he'll manage.

"Gerrit, let me tell you one thing, from here on in, I'm going to hide the things that I find. I've got secret places. Every time I get something neat, Oom Otto ends up with it. Yesterday, that neat pistol, you should have seen it, small and black and shiny and today it was my cap. MY CAP, I found it. If he wants a cap so badly, why doesn't he go and find his own? I don't like this, I'm gonna keep all my stuff! That's it!"

"Where are your secret places, Frits?" Paultje wants to know.

"I'll show you someday, but you can't tell nobody, you'll have to swear!" "What's swear?" He's barely five years old, but he's intrigued by everything that Frits says or does...

"That means, promise on your soul, may you die if you tell!"

"Boy that sounds serious."

At that point an open MERCEDES or BMW or something drives up the drive and Frits chokes. That's the car he "found" the gun in yesterday and now they caught him. He considers running, although he knows Oom Otto is really the one who should worry. "He's got it, not me!"

But the Germans smile as they get out and even wave at the boys.

Three of them, with leather overcoats, walk toward the backdoor as Ida comes out to greet them. "Can I help you" She asks in German.

"We would like to eat something, is that possible?"

"Of course, of course, Natürlich!"

A load off her mind. She thought they came to arrest the conspirators around, the "leestafel" in the Café.

"Follow me, please!" She leads 'em into the Café, nearly creating an exodus. Nearly all of the men jump up, but one of the Germans waves them back down.

"Setzen Sie Sich!" Sit down please!"

Well, they do sit down, but not a word is spoken.

Ida shows the Officers to a table near the window, while Herman is already tapping beer, following a command, "DREI BIER BITTE."

Pecht meanders over to the threesome and in perfect German asks general questions as to how things are going, where they're from and were they on other fronts and have they seen action?

The reading table listens intently.

Ida gets an order from the Germans and instructions to also feed the soldier in the car and disappears into the kitchen. Otto slithers out with her. For a guy, who's half-German he seems strongly Anti-Deutsch.

Frits has conveniently deserted his potato peeling and is getting an education in German Military Insignias.

The cap the driver is wearing is identical to the one Frits owned just a little while ago and it's an army cap. The button up front denotes infantry. The driver is a Corporal and when he makes GEFREITER, sergeant, he'll be an Unter Offizier. He'll then get a yellow thin band around his cap and a stripe on each sleeve.

The other markings on his arms mean two campaigns. He was in Spain and in Sudetenland and NO, Frits can NOT have his belt buckle.

"In Spain? Germany fought in Spain? I never heard of that?"

Before the soldier can answer, Ida brings out a "SINAS," a cold bottle of soda, and takes his order. He's going to eat out here.

The lesson continues.

Inside are a Major and two Hauptmannen,(Captains) They're Officers and they handle intelligence.

That's the reason for the long antenna attached to the back bumper. They carry a powerful radio, and "NO," they can't see it.

"Can we sit in the car?" "NO?" "Can I steer?" "NO!"

Gerrit announces, he'd better go. The clock in the car indicates 4:45. Gerrit doesn't know that the Germans are working in a different time zone;

it's only 3:45. Anyway, he's off!

"TJU!"

"TJU," answers the rest and they, Joop has joined them, continue their inspection and interrogation of the soldier and his vehicle.

Mama brings him a plate with sandwiches and homefries and tells Frits; "I may need those potatoes tonight already, instead of tomorrow!"

Then to the soldier, "Kaffee?" A nod sends her scurrying back to the kitchen.

The chair, basket and bucket are moved closer to the car, so they can have uninterrupted conversation flowing.

In between swallows, the soldier answers, "Yes, I've been shot at, no he's never killed anyone yet, no, he's not married and no, he has no children and this is the second time he's in the army. He had left to work in his Dad's business, but he'd been called back and "NO" all he wants to be is a chauffeur and on and on and on.

The kids are picking up the language fast. It doesn't seem all that foreign anymore.

Joop is draped over the front fender, raptured and involved, smirking at Frits because of his crummy chore with the potatoes.

Mama reappears with the coffee. The soldier refuses the saucer, just like he earlier refused the glass, but drank from the bottle instead.

"Just some sugar, thank you! You speak good Deutsch, Dame!"

"Yes, I was born in Bocholt to a German mother and lived here most of my life and at age 11, I went to German classes and I've never forgotten it!"

The girls, Hedwig and Clasien, had come out with their mother and stare at her in wonder. Mama's talking in a foreign tongue. That sounds so funny.

They're a pretty sight in light dresses with little aprons, very blonde and glowing.

"Jopie, get out of those school clothes and come down and help Frits with those potatoes, I'm going to need a lot of them."

Now it's Frits' turn to smirk, "Goody, goody."

In the restaurant, the officers are enjoying their "biefstuk" with "bratkartoffeln" and stringbeans.

Because of it's rich soil, Holland produces healthy, big tender cows that produce lots of rich creamy milk, that makes for excellent butter and steaks, properly browned in butter, are just delicious.

Some Dutch cheeses, LEIDEN, GOUDA and EDAM, complete the meal and beer is being replaced with coffee and cognac.

"These clowns know how to live!" Herman is thinking, but it's business after all.

Pecht has meandered over with a drink in his hand and now that they're finishing up, he strikes up a conversation again.

They don't seem to mind, they are relaxed, their tunics unbuttoned, their gunbelts are slung over the backs of the chairs, while their hats dangle from the chair posts.

While Pecht is debating strategy, Herman is admiring the quality of their uniforms and boots. He's envious when he mentally compares them with Dutch uniforms, even the most modern ones.

"Boy, these guys dress first class, and those boots, they must have cost a fortune."

Antoon has joined up with the little cluster around the officers and Bram, the saddle maker just enters through the front door.

He's back again and joins the little group, while Herman goes to get his "usual" drink.

Ida is removing dishes, gently shoving Pecht aside and asks, *"SCH-MECKTS, noch mehr kaffee?"* Two "NO"s and one "yes."

She retreats just as 'Herr Majoor,' the major, says: "Holland won't last 10 days and France, maybe thirty, but that's only because of its size.

Those French aren't fighters, they think they're lovers, well, I think they stink. The Dutch are good fighters, but you guys are unprepared. Antiquated material, not one modern tank, not one modern plane. You guys don't have a chance, I'm sorry to say. See, I like the Dutch, most Germans do, but still, you are unprepared. If it weren't for your *"Verflugte"* rivers, we'd have been at your coast in twenty-four hours. Now,..your fleet is very modern, that's the crazy thing, your fleet is good, excellent even, but what are you going to do with a fleet when you have no country? The logic escapes me!

Now the Belgians are different, they're tenacious and they have equipment, but we're going to cut them off and they really won't have a chance. I give them two weeks, maybe three!"

He's very poised, soft spoken and he demands respect with his slightly balding high forehead and wire rimmed glasses.

He's nearly unemotional, yet he keeps his audience spellbound. "Oh yeah? I still think we'll whip your ass when the British get into it!"

Antoon, of all people. He must have drunk beer all day. This is not like him at all, but the alcohol may be making him courageous.

The Major is unperturbed, although one of his HAUPTMAN nearly jumped up. "The British are very selfish people, my friend, they're going to sell you out and leave you to the vultures. Just remember the war of '14-"18 and you Dutchman better remember the BOERENOORLOG, the BOERWAR. Churchill and his animals only beat you guys and KRUGER, by putting your women and children in concentration camps and that made your BOERS surrender. No, my friend, the Brits will desert you when you need them and you better start looking to the Germans as your partners, cause we will bring you prosperity and peace!"

A hush falls over the little crowd, the authority that radiates from this man quiets everybody down.

Getting up, he addresses Herman, "Check, bitte! Excellent, Herr Eigner."

Herman rushes back to the bar to figure the tab as the officers retrieve their coats from the deer rack coat hangers.

They buckle up their belts, adjust their holsters to the back of their hips and after one of the HAUPTMAN pays for everyone, including a huge tip, the trio departs out of the back door amidst "Grüsz Gott, Gutten tag and Gutte Fahrt!"

All of a sudden, everyone talks at the same time.

Herman leaves them alone as he rushes into the kitchen, showing Ida the money he's taken in. More than what they took in all last week.

This war is just a day and a half old, but all of the sudden it doesn't look so bleak anymore.

Clasien comes into the kitchen with cup and dishes, retrieved from the chauffeur and while Herman holds the door for her, he sees Joop and Frits fighting in the backyard. They're rolling in the dirt and Joop seems to be having the upper hand. In two seconds, Herman has the both of them by the scruff of the neck and separates them.

"If any beating takes place in this house, I'm doing it, you hear!"

"Ya, but Pap, he.."

"I don't care, get back to those potatoes!"

PATS, he slaps Frits smack on the ear as Frits tries to kick Joop behind his back.

"Sit down, before I beat you to a pulp!"

"Ya, but Pappa!"

"Shut up and peel!"

He picks up little Hedwig who's crying. She doesn't like it when the boys fight and she doesn't like Pappa to hit Frits.

Pappa wipes her tears and kisses her on both cheeks. She snuggles her little arms around his neck and even though he's melting, he gets off a last stern. "Now, you watch it guys, no more fighting!"

He takes Hedwig into the kitchen, where he deposits her with Clasien.

In the Café, the conversation has heated up again, mostly fired up by the statements of the Major, plus some additional SONDERMELDUNGS from the radio.

Herman had the radio tuned to Frankfurt all the time while the Germans were in the café. At the end of the newscast, the officers surprised the whole group around the READING TABLE by snapping to attention when *"DEUTSCHLAND, DEUTSCHLAND ÜBER ALLES"* blasted out of the radio at the end of the newscast. One of the HAUPTMEN knocked his chair over when he jumped up, probably because of the weight of the pistol hanging from the back of his chair, but he didn't flinch or move a muscle until his National Anthem had finished.

One thing is becoming obvious, the opinions are deeply divided. Frans Vervoert, who has joined the group for the first time, is siding with Herman, they are or becoming PRO-DEUTSCH, while the rest are distinctly ANTI.

In the last two days the only people in the Café have been the occupants and the neighbors. Nobody but the kids, has ventured further than one block from home, so far.

With nothing at home but women folk and the radio, Frans just had to get out and into some serious politicking.

The beer is flowing, the voices get louder and louder and Herman, who doesn't drink, says to himself, "I hope they pay their tabs this week, it's going to be an interesting night!"

Potatoes put away, knees, feet, face and hands washed, the clan sits at the table, headed up by Herman.

Ida's behind the bar and Antoon is not interested in food.

"In the Name of the Father..!" Joop leads in again.

It's a peaceful scene.

Except for planes overhead, trucks in the street and loud radios without any music, the little town is nearly back to normal on the 12th and 13th of May 1940.

All the teachers are present and most of the students.

The factories smoke again and the noon-whistle precedes the "Angelus" chimed by the "New St. Jacobus." Antoon has gone back to work again and Gerrit and Otto have opened their shops. The chief of Police rides by again on his bike with his black "Bouvier" on the leash trotting slightly out and to the rear.

"Wonder where he's been" Herman muses as he's planting DAHLIA bulbs along the drive. They're going to be big and beautiful, he knows. Tall, very tall, three to four feet high with deep, deep purple flowers. Sometimes they're so dark, they're nearly black. One day, he'll have cultivated a black one, just like a distant relative developed a black tulip many years ago. Herman prides himself in having cultivated and developed a "Parrot tulip," much like the "Darwin tulip." Instead of smooth petals, the Parrot tulip has kind of wrinkled petals and multicolored creases and ridges. He's never been able to market his creation, or even get recognition for it, but… one of these days.

Nobody is in the bar right now. Only Bram came in at noon, that was it, so after putting Paultje and Hedwig down for their nap, Ida strolls into the yard, glancing around at the beautiful surroundings (other than that stinking bladder up in the acacia tree) and takes a deep breath.

Everything is in bloom and gives off its heavy fragrance and she can't get enough of it.

As she slowly comes upon Herman, he gets up and stretches. Ida puts her arms around his waist and pulls him toward her.

"What's going to happen, Pappie? What's going to happen to us?"

"Everything will be better than it ever was, Germany will give us independence and increase our production and prosperity and we'll do better because of it.

Hitler believes in educating the masses and our children will get a chance at a higher education, just like rich kids! It will be good for us, you'll see!"

Ida looks up at him and moves a curl back from his eyes.

"But what about that Hitler, you know what he's been doing to the Jews!"

"The Jews, they bring it upon themselves mostly, that has been projected and predicted all throughout the Bible. Besides, we're not Jewish and we have nothing to worry about!"

She wants to believe him. He's pretty worldly and he knows the Bible inside out, backwards and forward.

He's really a warm and loving person, but he can be so darn opinionated and he can flare up over nothing, especially if his ulcers flare up first.

She releases him slowly and waves at CATO, who's shaking out a dustmop through her 2nd floor window.

"She's a strange one," Ida thinks, "she never even walks next door for a cup of coffee or tea. All she does is stay home and play house, well, that's her problem."

Two Army ambulances, racing past, remind her rudely, that in spite of this local tranquility, a lot of fighting is still going on not far from here.

The kids are home by 4:20, right on time.

Even Frits is with them. This afternoon he came straight home too, but that was because Pappa made him promise. Paultje, who attended school today at the "bewaarschool" for half a day was waiting.

Frits is busy with his new project. That's what brings him home so soon. He has obtained a round metal cookie box and Oom Otto has assured him that it needs reinforcement and Pecht has told him he should have his bladder tightened over his drum-to-be and let it dry like that, so it would make a perfect fit.

"Wow, the first drum in his life and he's going to build it himself."

Hanging from the acacia branch upside down, he realizes he should have planned better. He has climbed the acacia, undid the string that holds his balloon and now the string proves to be too short to lower it far enough so Paultje can grab the string. He won't grab the "thing" itself because it is sticky, smelly and full of flies. He needs help.

"Mama, Mama!"

Through the kitchen window, Mama sees him hanging upside down with that "thing" on a string.

"Come out of that tree and get out of those school clothes!"

How did he slip by her so fast?

"Help Mama, help me!"

Inspite of herself Mama runs outside, gets talked into holding the string with the "thing" on it as far away from her body as possible, while Frits dismounts and races upstairs to change clothes.

Indeed, he's back within a minute, bare feet, old shirt, unbuttoned, fly not buttoned, but he's back.

"Why couldn't you just drop it?"

"Oh, no, Mama, you can't get dirt on it. Mam, you can't get it off, Thanks Mam!"

Off he is, Paultje on his heels, to Uncle Otto's workshop, where a wooden crossbrace is fabricated, (Man, this Oom Otto is good) and is installed across the upper inside of the round can. The can is about nine inches in diameter and is going to make a neat drum.

Stretching the messy skin over it is a different story. First, part of it is cut away with a pair of old scissors, then put over the drum. What a mess. They're doing it outside on the concrete when Otto has a great idea.

"Hetty, get me the talcum powder!"

Hetty, his daughter, six and cute, returns with the powder and soon it's less sticky and the flies stay off it.

Before continuing, they wash their hands to get rid of the slime and continue on. Otto makes "round" cuts, that way it won't tear, leaving six tails hanging down the sides of the drum. Now, upside down on a newspaper, there she goes, the tails are tied and tightened across the bottom. Again, "wash hands." Now, a thin metal wire is tied around the whole drum about an inch from the top, to secures it just below the little ridge on the can, where normally the lid would have rested.

Oom Otto makes two little loops, one on each end. "To attach your harness to, when it's dry!"

"Oh boy, I would never have thought of that!"

Some more cutting and trimming of tails and it's ready for drying from one of Otto's overhead bicycle racks.

Only one big disappointment, it has to dry two or three days before he can play it. But...he needs to make drumsticks anyway.

"Bye, thank you. Oom Otto!"

Off they are, Frits in the lead. Paultje following as fast as his little legs can carry him.

Tough break, time to eat. "Wash up, come in and sit down!"

The war is in its fourth day.

May 13 is so much near normal that it's just about monotonous.

A few customers have come in to read the papers over coffee or to discuss the war progress, but that's it.

The activity by railroad is still constant, but truck convoys consist mostly of tank trucks carrying gasoline or diesel.

A few more soldiers are seen patrolling and some of the "Feldgendarmerie" seem to be "cruising" with an armed soldier on the rear seat.

Rumor has it that the "Krankenlager" is full and that the Catholic hospital is being used too, mainly for surgery.

A local surgeon has been pressed into service and his wife is being pumped by anxious neighbors; "How many of them are our boys?" "Is there any news from the front?"... She doesn't know much either, her husband hasn't been home much, sleeping in the hospital, where and when he can.

School is nearly normal, darn it and Frits can't keep his mind on his classroom work because of the need to get home to his drum.

He's cut fourteen drumsticks so far, but only three of them are satisfactory. He's been told, "You need a "hardwood" like walnut or hazelnut for drumsticks."

He knows where there's a hazel tree and can't wait to get at it.

The hazel tree proves to be a disappointment. The owner of the tree is sitting right in her living room, looking right at it.

Her baywindow gives her a nice view of the street and her little yard dominated by the hazeltree. The leaves are auburn this time of year and they'll turn nearly black by summer before turning brown by fall.

She waves back smilingly at Frits and Paultje as they're standing on the little brick wall surrounding her property.

A foreign language pours out of her open windows and Frits summarizes, she's listening to the BBC. He only knows one English song, "It's a long way to Tipperary," but it's enough English to know that what's coming out of her loud speaker is not German.

Oh well, what to do? He's got one of Mama's butcher knives under his shirt, rolled in a washcloth, but he can't get to the branches he needs.

From their vantagepoint they can see the sign "KRANKENLAGER," although the hospital itself is obscured from this low angle by the trees surrounding it.

"Come on, Boer," They go trotting off in the direction of the Hospital. A lone sentry, his rifle slung over his right shoulder, starts at one of the brick pillars that line the entrance, walks across to the other, stops, makes an about face, walks back to the first one and then does it all over again.

He doesn't really move his head, but his eyes scan the area and as he spots the children, he smiles, but continues his march. Somehow he creates the feeling, "DON'T MESS WITH ME!" and Frits is indecisive for a moment. Fortunately for them, a pleasant interruption comes into view. Three ambulances. The sentry stops his march, positions himself near the left pillar, swing his rifle from the shoulder to the ready position and as the first Red Cross truck slows down, he seems satisfied that all's in order and waves the trucks on without them coming to a complete stop. By the time the third trucks eases its way through, Frits and the Boer have slipped into the Hospital yard, keeping the trucks between them and the guard.

Once out of his line of sight, they approach a line of parked trucks while the newcomers back up to the emergency entrance for unloading.

"Look!" points Paultje, "LOOK OVER THERE!" He's nearly whispering. "A KERKHOF." A cemetery, brand new with a dozen white little crosses in neat little rows.

"OH BOER, THEY MUST HAVE DIED RIGHT HERE! WANNA GO AND LOOK?"

"NO, NO, NO!" panic is written all over his little face. "I WANNA GO HOME!"

"Okay, okay! GIVE ME YOUR HAND!"

They're crossing behind the trucks with the red crosses on them. Frits turns loose of Paultje's hand.

"WAIT RIGHT HERE!"

"NO, NO, I'M COMING WITH YOU! THOSE ARE DEAD PEOPLE OVER THERE! I'M COMING WITH YOU!"

"Okay!" All he wants to do is check out some of the trucks, so he climbs on the running board of one of them, and peers inside. The windows are down, so that's convenient. Nothing looks interesting. Just maps and papers and a brown paper bag.

By hanging over the door he can reach the bag, pulls it toward him and says, "CATCH!" He pitches the bag to Paultje who says in pure amazement, "CHOCOLATE COOKIES!" "De Gruijters" CHOCOLATE COOKIES!, HOW ABOUT THAT?"

They each stick one in their mouth and Frits mounts another running board. Again, maps and papers.

"I WANNA GO HOME!" Paultje starts to moan now and Frits is just about to say okay! as he spots a pocketknife and some cigars up against the windshield. By hoisting himself a little higher, he can reach them and ten seconds later they're on the way home.

One thing they can't do is exit the way they came and pass by the guard, so they cross the lawn away from the white crosses and work their way through nicely sculptured hedges into the rough of the adjacent woods.

Most of the trees have been cut down and the area is now the city dump, a very interesting place to explore.

Today, though, they turn toward home and end up on the sidewalk across from the hazel tree lady.

The cookies are all gone by the time they reach the backyard and now they have time to examine the pocketknife.

It's fairly simple with a four-inch blade on one side and a little bitty blade on the other. No frills, no decorating, but it's HIS!!! His first pocket knife. "MIGHT AS WELL RETURN MAMA'S KNIFE NOW. WE WON'T NEED THAT ANYMORE."

After leaving their wooden shoes, the knife and the washcloth in the "bijkeuken," they tromp through the kitchen where the table is already set, through the hall into the Café, where the discussion group is even larger than the day before.

Frits taps his Father on the back as he's tapping beer; "PAPPA" as he holds up two cigars, "SEE WHAT WE BROUGHT YOU?"

May 14 proves to be a disaster.

The day starts alright, routine planes, some convoys, some Red Cross trucks and a new PROCLAMATION on various walls.

Other than that, a normal day. The horsedrawn milk carts are back on schedule. By eight o'clock, they're already on the way back home.

Mass, school. Everything is routine, till about 11:30.

The bell rings, everyone in the schoolyard, line up by grades, like before school.

Nobody has to be told, "BEHAVE!" or "HUSH!"

A funeral-like atmosphere hangs in the air.

Master Commandeur appears in the doorway and it gets deadly quiet.

"Our Majesty the Queen has just announced the surrender of Holland!"

Cries erupt all over. The female teachers are weeping and some of the children cry right along with them.

"QUIET!" booms the Headmaster. "Go directly home, hold hands. Tomorrow school will resume as usual, pending other news. NOW GO HOME!"

Rotterdam, demolished, May 14, 1940

For once, Frits searches out Joop and Clasien and hand in hand they walk to the "BEWAARSCHOOL," where the children are already on the front stoop, surrounded by the Nuns.

They retrieve the Boer and walk on home.

Joop starts in, "I don't understand it, we were winning, we were beating the Krauts and now we've given up. Maybe Pappa's right, we shouldn't have a Queen, a woman. Women are always chicken. At least in Belgium we had a King. I bet you, he's not surrendering, I don't understand it!"

Joop, all of a sudden, seems soo much older and wiser, that Frits or the others have nothing to add. Now that the full impact hits him, he's very subdued.

Somehow, he knew we'd win. "We can't lose! If only Holland had Prince Valiant we wouldn't have lost."

The streets are again totally void of civilians, other than children walking home. It's just like the first day except there might as well have been a dark thunder cloud overhead.

At home, the Café is crowded with a dozen men, sitting or standing near the radio in the corner. The announcer repeats his story of surrender, how a tearful Queen has read the surrender in Dutch and in English over the BBC. Frits wonders if she doesn't speak German, and for the first time the kids hear the reason behind it all.

The Germans have bombed the center of ROTTERDAM. The whole inner city is flattened. Hundreds of women and children are dead, maybe thousands.

The Queen has said things like, "No more unnecessary bloodshed." "Hopelessness of the situation!" "Cooperate with the occupation forces!" "We're with you, we won't desert you and we'll be back!"

"BOMBED ROTTERDAM, WOMEN AND CHILDREN....THOSE BASTARDS, THOSE LOUSY BASTARDS..

THOSE DAMN KRAUTS...
VERDOMDE MOFFEN...

CHAPTER IV
June 1941

It's a beautiful warm Sunday in Winterswijk.

The sky is a solid blue cover and birds are singing in every tree.

Church lets out. High Mass is over. The little square in front of the "NEW SAINT JACOBUS" church fills with people in their Sunday best who slowly filter into the WINKELSTRAAT, some turning left toward home, some turning right.

Frits races down the circular stairs coming from the balcony where he sings with the choir nowadays. He loves to sing, so does his Dad and he has a good voice like his Dad.

His Mam also sings and hums all day, but she can't carry a tune in a basket.

Singing is more fun than praying or trying to follow Mass in his Missal.

Thank God, they got rid of the few girls in the choir because girls are such a pain.

He hustles his way through the dispersing crowd and just turns into the WINKELSTRAAT as a voice reaches him, "Fritsje!" It's OPA, that old grouch.

"Come, walk home with your OPA, I don't see you that much anymore!"

"Ya, but OPA, I've gotta get home, 'cause...."

"Five minutes won't matter!"

He could hate that old man. Pappa always says that he killed OMA, by working her to death. She bore twelve children, ten living, ran the household and the restaurant and died at age 59 of old age.

Frits can't remember much about OMA HEDWIG, but everybody loved her and everybody has nothing but good things to say about her.

OPA meanwhile, fairly short, maybe 5'8, but very erect with gray hair combed straight back and a closely clipped gray German style mustache, asks, "How are you doing in school?"

"Okay!...GREAT..., maybe good!" He wishes he could run off.

"How are your grades?"

"About an 8+ on a scale from one to ten!"

"Jopie does better than that, right?"

Frits starts boiling, "I hate that, I hate that, they're always comparing me with Joop and I don't care what Joop does!"

Biting his tongue, he answers, "I guess so."

"Why don't you do better?"

"EIGHT PLUS! OPA, I'M FOURTH IN MY CLASS!"

"But you could be number ONE, couldn't you?"

"Can I go now?" He could be number two, he knows, but this one guy, who's father is the sixth grade teacher, man, he's hard to beat. He's smart and he studies all the time. Another one of these "Goody-goody-gumshoes!"

"No, walk with me. It's Sunday, you have all day. How's your Mama?"

Frits feels like saying, "Why don't you ask her yourself!" but instead he answers, "All right, I think!"

"That old bastard!" Herman and OPA KWAK had finally had it out over politics and money. Even though business was much better than before the war, Herman and Ida couldn't possibly catch up the deficit in mortgage payments left over from the depression.

They were holding their own now, but catching up was impossible,, so OPA KWAK pulled the rug from under his own daughter and family by foreclosing on the business.

His quote, "I told her not to marry that loser!"

So in the late fall of 1940, a public auction was held.

The building, the Forrer's half, was sold to a wealthy furniture manufacturer, who worked out very favorable leasing terms with them.

The "GROLSCHE" Brewery bought most of the restaurant equipment and furniture. They also worked an arrangement, based on beer consumption, that everyone could live with.

Friends, with pre-arranged conditions to buy them back as money would allow, bought some other items.

OPA KWAK showed up during the proceedings and if people hadn't restrained Herman, he would have choked him to death right then and there.

He did get across to him that he would kill him if he ever set foot on the property again and the kids were forbidden to associate ever with OPA, Oom Otto, Oom Gerrit or any of their families. (They must have sided with the old man.)

Now as they're getting closer to home, Frits is even worried about walking with OPA and he sees his chance when he notices a classmate across the street and with a "TJU OPA," he's gone in a flash.

Sunday dinner is usually at ONE sharp, instead of twelve-thirty like during the week, and Sunday dinner is usually good, because on Sunday they get meat.

Things are busy in the Café today. The warm weather makes more people stop in for a cold beer or soda and the billiard table has been busy for hours.

Business as a whole has gotten better all over, everybody's working, factories are steaming day and night and people are spending.

The restaurant and the bar business is booming, nothing extravagant, but if this had happened a year earlier, the Forrers would still own the place.

Herman has hired a girl to work the bar and the dining room and "ELLIE" adds a spark to the bar trade.

Right now, it is evident that neither ELLIE nor Herman can be spared, so Mama, the boarders and the children will start without them.

Every window and door in the house is open and a soft summer breeze makes it a day in paradise.

The distant drone of airplane engines starts to filter in with the voices coming from the Café.

"TOMMIES OF COURSE!" On clear days they come over regularly on their way to the "RUHR" area, where Germany's main weapons industry is located.

The kids are hungry and Ida decides to go ahead. Two of the three boarders are at the table, brothers Antoon and Willem, Brother Gerrit is still playing billiards.

The aircraft noise is now getting overbearing. The kids are dying to run out and watch the "LANCASTERS" crossing overhead in tight formations, but Mama says, "Jopie, bidden!"

Joop leads off as per usual and after the final AMEN the spoons dig into the tomato soup in their plates.

But...before they can even get the first spoonful in their mouths, a loud screeching sound gets louder and louder and ends with a bomb blast that shakes the house like an earthquake and makes the soup fly right out of the plates.

PANIC, SCREAMING... MORE BOMBS... VOOM... VOOM... VOOOM... VOOOM... TEN... TWENTY ... MAYBE FORTY...

The house rocks... glass shatters... people scream and run everywhere.

Ida and the kids are under the stairs, the brothers Brummelstroete are under the kitchen table and Herman is in the cellar, steadying wineracks with the help of some customers.

Ellie is flat on her face behind the bar, screaming like a pig, while glasses shatter all around her.

Customers are flat against the walls and under the billiard table.

In the street people are running in all directions and Frits is halfway up the willow tree for a better look.

It's over in less than 40 seconds.

The planes disappear toward the south, turning westward on the horizon.

People, still in hysterics, are assessing themselves and others for injuries and find that all their limbs are still attached.

Frits is out of the tree, out of breath, "Pappa, Pappa..it's near the station, the blocks before the gas holder near "OLLE WILLEM'S HUUS, OL' Willem's house."

Out the door he is, the front door this time. The brothers Brummelstroete are in hot pursuit.

Just a few blocks and the devastation is before them. An entire block of small, attached homes is gone. Another block behind it is half in ruins and OL' Willem's barn is burning.

That fire is about the only fire, the houses are just demolished but only minor fires are to be seen.

The early arrivals are helping dazed and wounded people, laying them on the sidewalk. Others are digging in the ruins, following screams and groans.

Frits is working on freeing VROUW KAMPEN, she's half buried under brick and wood. She's lucky though, the roof has collapsed on top of her. She's kinda stuck in the cavity between trusses and that's protecting her more than hurting her.

Just last week, she and MIJNHEER KAMPEN have retired from their hardware store and moved out into the little house on the side street, so they could live out their Golden Years in peace and quiet.

Just as she's freed and lifted carefully out of her trap, her son arrives on the scene. The son now runs the hardware and lives over the store. He's getting married on July 1 and his bride will move in with him.

Mama KAMPEN is being moved carefully, she has a broken leg, but only asks for her husband. "He's under there somewhere!"

Many hands pitch in as she's eased to the sidewalk. Now police, ambulances and fire trucks are on the scene.

Not many. The Germans have long deserted their KRANKENLARGER and all the Red Cross trucks have gone with them.

Now some grown-ups are telling Frits to get out of the way, but they're being told, "I WAS HERE FIRST!" in no uncertain terms. He resumes his digging, working side by side with the KAMPEN son, who keeps hollering, "Pappa, Pappa!!!" to no avail.

No groans, no screams, no nothing.

Tears rolling down his face, he keeps picking up bricks and timber, moving it aside, digging for his Dad.

Frits is being told again, "This is man's work, get out of here!" as more and more grown-ups start arriving and start pitching in.

He retreats back to the street, where a lady from across the bomb blasts offers him a drink and a towel.

All the houses on that side are intact except no one has any windows left.

Frits is a sight. He's covered with cement dust and wiping his sweaty face with the towel just streaks the dirt like warpaint on an Indian.

He sees Joop and then Pappa.

Mama has taken over the bar and Ellie, still hysterical is eating with the little ones, so Pappa can join the throng of onlookers.

By now, there's enough help, so he takes Frits by the hand and says, "We're going to eat."

"But Pappa, there are still people under there and OL'Willems barn is burning and eh and eh…"

"We're going to eat! Joop, Joop, Come on!"

Joop feels like Frits, "Here's where the excitement is!" but he doesn't have the nerve to argue with Pappa.

They meet up with other people and stop to explain what's happening out there, but eventually they walk into the Café, where things are fairly orderly and Mama looks in shock at her son and his Sunday clothes.

"Mama, Mama, I rescued Mrs. Kampen, she has a broken leg. Mr. Kampen is still under there, but they threw me out. Can I have some lemonade, Mama, can I?"

"Yes, you can have some lemonade, you too, Joop?"

She can't help but smile inspite of the ruined clothes. And those shoes! Look at them! And shoes are so hard to get nowadays.

"Now go out back, get out of those clothes, wash up and go eat! I'm sure it's cold by now! Herman, Joop, go eat too! And Herman, then relieve me here unless Ellie gets herself under control!"

While at the dinner table, just the three of them, with Ellie waiting on them, Herman talks to his boys as if they're grown-ups.

"I told those idiots at that last meeting again, that we should follow German orders and form a civilian warning system, but their attitude is, "The TOMMIES will never bomb us, so let's sabotage the German effort as best we can.

Now, look at today, no sirens, no air raid alarm, no early warning system, and no organized rescue system.

You should have seen those idiots, running around like chickens with their heads cut off while people are dying in those ruins!

Did you see any Germans dying in this raid?

Did you see any Germans coming to the rescue?

They don't give a damn, it's our job to protect our own!

Now, we'll get organized, you'll see! Now we'll get sirens! Now that some people were killed first, now things will happen!

Those damn idiots! You should hear them, "THE BRITISH WON'T BOMB US!!! WHAT WERE THESE?? KRAUTS?? And what were they trying to hit that's of military importance in this area? There wasn't even a German Motorcycle parked in that whole District and they fly all the way from ENGLAND on Sunday to do this to us?

And the BBC. Wait a minute, I should turn on the BBC and see what RADIO ORANGE has to say about this success mission. Piss on the Germans, I'm going to listen to the BBC. Maybe somebody in the bar can understand English in case RADIO ORANGE doesn't broadcast."

"WOW! He's on a roll now, isn't he?" Frits grins at Joop.

"Yep, the old man is certainly on a roll!"

This is his chance though. Frits is sitting at the dinner table in his underwear, but with Mama and Pappa both in the bar, it takes just a second to run upstairs, get into his old clothes, back down into the kitchen, then into the BIJ-KEUKEN for his wooden shoes and through the backyard, so they won't see him, and back to the excitement.

This is something…people all over the place, digging and loading, but mostly discussing the events of the afternoon.

Opinions vary widely. Some people saw 12 planes coming over, some saw as many as 200. It all seems to add up to about 20 planes.

The same about the altitude.

Some claim they were at only 100 meters and others believe they were at 5,000 meters, that seems to add up to about 1,000 meters.

One thing is for sure, about 100 bombs were dropped in just under a minute.

Frits is listening in on a conversation by officials standing in a circle, with the Mayor, the BURGEMEESTER, leading the dialogue.

They've concluded that most of the bombs were 500 pounders, with maybe some 1,000 pounders amongst them.

The flight of the squadron is the one thing that everyone agrees upon. They were flying on a SouthEasterly heading and the extensive railroad-switching yard must have been their target.

Yet not one bomb hit the tracks, but the cluster and pattern definitely indicate that the bombs would have been smack on top of the railroad yard, had they released the bombs one minute, maybe 30 seconds later.

The Mayor is saying, "The Nazi's are going to have fun with this one, they'll exploit it to the hills. I can see the headlines now."

"BRITISH BUTCHERS BOMB WORKERS QUARTERS. OLD PEOPLE, WOMEN AND CHILDREN DIE BY THE DOZENS!" O, God, why must there be this war?"

The consensus of opinion is the same all over.

Right now, dozens of horsedrawn wagons are hauling debris to a temporary dump created at the "HOGE LAND."

It's a large undeveloped field just south of the hardest hit housing area. The field is a favorite playground, especially for kite flying because there are no trees or wires, and it is now dotted with bomb craters that are being filled up with bricks and lumber.

Frits wonders why water stands at the bottom of the pits even though it hasn't rained a drop.

He wanders from one marvel to another. Every ruin is different, every ambulance offers different excitement, every wagon different treasures.

Nothing for him though. All belongings are stashed on the sidewalk and literally hundreds of people are helping or milling about.

A number of Frits' buddies are around too and the exciting tales that everyone has to tell makes it sound like it was a daylong bombardment with millions of planes.

He heard from one of the neighbors that MIJNHEER KAMPEN has been found alive.

He was sitting on the toilet under the stairs and he was knocked unconscious by the mirror that came flying off the wall. All he has is a gash on his forehead and a possible concussion, cause he seemed dazed. He's in the Catholic hospital, St. Josef's, but he should be fine.

Frits wonders if somebody had to wipe his butt and pull up his pants.

So far, only one death has been reported, a nine year old girl, Protestant probably, because Frits doesn't know her.

There must be other casualties under all this mess and hundreds of eager hands are digging all over to uncover anybody or anything trapped under there.

Someone has been smart enough to turn off the gas main, cause everyone here cooks with gas and gas was just pouring into the atmosphere from dozens of busted gaslines.

Frits and FRANS VENERIUS are exploring the extent of the bombed area and indeed the bomb craters closest to the railroad are just about 100 feet short, just on the other side of the STATIONS STRAAT, the street that parallels the tracks.

A lot of windows are shattered and that has it's advantages, because when they're finished admiring the blasted windows at the railroad station they notice an interesting scene.

To the north, in the "SPOORSTRAAT," people are boarding up the store window of the Icecream parlor/Lunchroom.

"No, we don't need help, thank you very much!" but they get an ice-cream cone just the same.

It's a good thing that it's such a warm day and that most people had their windows wide open, because the damage to the windows is really minimal, once they get away three or four blocks from the bomb zone.

The ice cream is great and the boys saunter down the street on their inspection tour.

FRANS VENERIUS is a rather dark skinned kid with coal black eyes. He's a gypsy with black wavy hair and lives in the only mobile home camp in the area and somehow they've settled down here permanently, at least for now. They work at a travelling carnival in their cute little mobile homes, drawn by two horses and decorated with thousands of bangles and beads.

Frans is a classmate of Frits' or rather, has been off and on, whenever they're in town, and he's rather quiet.

His Mama comes to church in real Gypsy clothes, but his dad dresses like the next farmer up the road.

Frans and the Gypsy camp are off-limits to Frits but that doesn't seem to matter today as they circle block after block, ending up back at the area of the worst devastation.

The atmosphere is one of a subdued carnival and not until hunger pangs and a setting sun tell him to go home, do they leave the area and with a "TJU," they part and go their own way.

Nobody jumps all over him for being late and sandwiches are still stacked on the kitchen table.

There's hardly a drop left in the milk bottle, there's no milk in the bij-keuken, so the cellar is the only source left.

Dirty as he is, he proceeds to the Café, 'round the billiard table to the SLIJTERIJ, the little liquor store where you can buy an ounce or a liter, and then down into the cellar.

There is no noticeable damage and if there was any it has already been cleaned up.

He grabs a bottle of milk and makes his way back upstairs.

Boy, the place is alive with activity. There are people here that he's never seen before. The work at the bomb ruins must have made a lot of people thirsty.

Sightseeing apparently causes thirst too, because a lot of people in their Sunday best are also sitting or milling around, drink in hand.

Although the urge to socialize is nearly killing him, he retreats to the kitchen with his milk, because he knows if he's spotted, they'll make him wash himself and then put him to work.

Before the war, he had to work every Sunday night, because they had a dance on Sundays. Joop's and his job were to keep the bar supplied with bottles of beer, sinas, cola and chocomel.

A lot of people preferred their GROLSCH in bottles instead of draughts and it was their job to cart the "empties" to their cases in the "SLIJTERIJ" and replenish the stock from the cooler cases in the cellar. Refrigeration consisted of the cold damp floor and blocks of ice, placed on top of the beer barrels.

Ladies and girls only drank soft drinks in those days and that only came in bottles, so from six to eleven, they worked their little fannies off, hauling bottles back and forth.

The good thing was all the music and frivolity.

The band struck up at seven sharp, but usually there weren't many dancers on the floor yet at seven and that gave Mama the opportunity to dance with her children.

Mama loved to WALTZ and Frits could waltz with the best of them, though turning to the left somehow came more naturally to him than turning to the right.

He also learned loads of songs as the band played all the popular songs of that era of course and he could switch from, *"It's a long way to Tipperary!"* to *"Parlez-moi d'Amour"* to *"Der Donau so Blau, so Blau,"* without ever knowing a word he sang.

The war had abruptly stopped the "BALLS" and they hadn't had a dance since.

There were no young guys anymore.

War-deaths, prisoner-of-war camps, Labor-camps, underground, even voluntary service in the German Armed Forces had all but depleted the supply of dance-aged young men.

"SHAME!" he thinks, in spite of the work involved it was a lot of fun and better than going to bed at 6:30 every night.

He can't wait till next September. He'll be a fifth grader and he'll be allowed to stay up till 8! Oh, Boy, he can't wait.

Something unusual is taking place. On his own accord Frits washes his hands and knees outside. He can't see his face, so that does not need washing, slips out of his clothes upstairs in room SIX and crawls in bed with Paultje, who's sleeping like an angel.

"IT'S BEEN SOME DAY!"

Things are changing. "Slowly!" but changing just the same.

A new MAYOR is installed. A NAZI BURGEMEESTER, Dr. BOS. He's a VET by trade. The old BURGEMEESTER was too anti German, so he's replaced.

The Dutch have a NAZI party too. It has been here since 1935, but no one seemed to notice until now. It's named after it's big brother, the N.S.D.A.P.(National Socialist Deutsche Arbeider Partei.)

The Dutch call theirs the N.S.N.A.P. (Nationaal Socialistiese Nederlandse Arbeiders Partij.)

People in black uniforms with armbands start to appear.

A lot more curtains are closed even before the sun goes down.

A lot more whispering goes on and conversations stop abruptly when children or strangers approach.

The radio broadcasts are Anti-British and even the comedy shows on Saturday and Sunday nights are slanted Pro-German.

Songs that gain popularity are, *"WAAROM HANGT DE WAS NIET AAN DE SIEGFRIED LIJN?"*(Why isn't the laundry hanging from the SIEGFRIED LINE?) That's the German defense works opposite the MAGINOT line in France. That MAGINOT line became the laughing stock of the war.

It was designed to hold off a German invasion forever, but the "BOCHE"(French for Krauts) ran over it in one day.

Other songs like *"GLORIA, VICTORIA, OUD ENGLAND WORDT AMERIKA!"* (Old England will become American) become popular.

The Germans have a new tune that's played at the beginning of every *"SONDERMELDUNG"* that involves sea battles.

"WENN WIR FAHREN, WENN WIR FAHREN, WENN WIR FAHREN GEGEN ENGELAND, ENGELAND, AHOY!"

"SONDERMELDUNGS" that have to do with the *"AFRIKA KORPS"* and *"FELD MARSHALL ROMMEL"* are proceeded by *"PANZER ROLLEN IN AFRIKA VORT!"* or something like that.

The Germans seem to be unbeatable and unstoppable and their victories lead to a sizable following in the low countries.

It's feels like everyone now knows where the battle lines are drawn and which one is definitely PRO or who is ANTI.

HOLLAND is becoming a country divided.

JEWS walk around with a yellow STAR OF DAVID embroidered on their chest with the word "JOOD"(Jew) in Hebrew letters in the center.

Jewish men, women or children cannot be seen in public without their STAR. Jewish children are taken out of public schools and now attend the "YESHIVA."

Parks and park benches have signs, "VOOR JODEN VERBODEN."

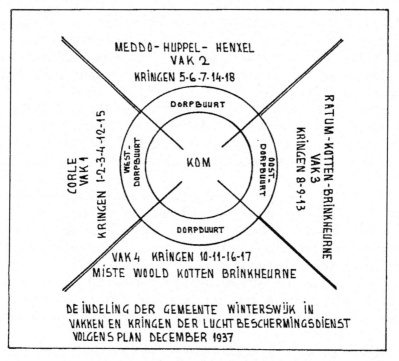

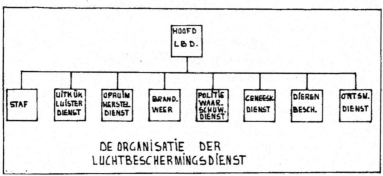

Civil air defense plan, dated 1937

(Jews not allowed). Libraries and other public places are off limits for them and even HOF VAN HOLLAND has a white sign with black block letters, "VOOR JODEN VERBODEN." Mama doesn't dare shop at Baumans anymore, neither Senior nor Junior and both their butcher shops have huge Stars of David painted on their windows with the word "KOSHER" in it.

The kids have no idea what "KOSHER" means, but they stop to admire the new sign at Bauman Jr.'s store on their way from school.

He's on the corner of the "WOOLSTRAAT" and "WILLINKSTRAAT" and next door to him is the "DROGISTERIJ de GAPER."

A big head is mounted over the entrance to the Pharmacy with its mouth wide open and its tongue sticking out as it has for the past hundred years.

At school things have changed too and as a fourth grader, Frits now has Mr. RAES as a steady diet and he has taken up, where Joop left off two years ago. He pesters the hell out of the teacher, wherever and whenever he can. His grades have plummeted and on his last report card at Easter time he only received a 5- for conduct.

As far as Frits is concerned, it's all the teacher's fault. He's such a weak disciplinarian, who screams a lot, hits the kids across the knuckles with a ruler and sends 'em to the principal's office when he can't control them anymore.

Also, a new face has appeared in class, JAN KAMPHUIS.

JAN is a very neat, clean-cut fellow from AMSTERDAM, who talks funny and acts superior.

At first, the locals with their "PLAT" dialect snub him, tease him and even challenge to fight him, but he proves to be alright.

His character is much better than his fancy clothes and his phony dialect would indicate. Besides that, he lives right around the corner in the "EELINKSTRAAT," beyond the former KRANKENLAGER and the hazel tree.

Jan's younger brother, "HENKIE KAMPHUIS" is in first grade with Paultje, so the foursome can be seen together regularly, as they make their way back and forth to school. They make quite a team; Jan and Henkie, Frits and de Boer.

Mr. Kamphuis works for the customs office and now, since passenger flights into and out of "SCHIPHOL" (Amsterdam airport) have ceased, he's been transferred to WINTERSWIJK and border patrol.

He's tall and muscular, like a cowboy hero in ZANE GREY's books.

His booming voice and the pistol he carries on his hip make that picture nearly complete. He rides a neat horse and has two German Shepherd patrol dogs that go with him on his patrols at night.

Mrs. Kamphuis is a roly-poly woman of maybe 5-feet tall with the friendliest round face and sparkling blue eyes. The woman made them feel at home from the moment they met her and the first words out of her mouth are always, "Would you like to eat or drink something?"

Henkie must take after both of them. He has his height from his dad, he's a head taller than the BOER and twice as heavy. He has the same round face as his Mama, although the sparkling round eyes in his face are the same brown as his Dad's.

The "Kamphuis Baby" is a 6 month-old baby-doll with the darkest hair, brown round eyes and a perpetual smile on her round doll-face. You'd want to hug her, the moment you'd see her.

Mr. Kamphuis is a very strict person, like Papa, and just as punctual, but because of his work shifts, he's hardly ever in sight. He's either working or sleeping. Just as good, because that gives the boys a lot of leeway, just like the ones in the Forrer home when the folks are busy with their business.

Right now, life has become rather routine. Back and forth to school, up to bed on time and not enough time to get in trouble.

Mr. Raes is in rare form today as the kids line up for class at 1:25. Some of the boys are more rambunctious than they're supposed to be and Mr. Raes' voice seems higher pitched than usual. He pulls one boy by the ear to turn him around and make him face forward like the rest of them.

The boy in question is GERRIT, the old farmboy, and Gerrit may be a quiet boy, but when you get his ire up, watch out!

Not even looking who's pulling his ear, he kicks backward with his wooden shoes and catches Mr. Raes right in the shin. At the same time he lands a punch on the nose of the boy he was scuffling with, and now that boy, DIRK, grabs him and before Mr. Raes can interfere, they're rolling across the schoolyard bricks. Blood from Dirk's nose is getting all over them.

Mr. Commandeur, at the top of the steps at the entrance, signals the 8th grade to start inside, while he rushes over to help untangle the pair. That's not easy. They're clawing, biting and tearing at one another. Gerrit is screaming bloody murder, because a thumb is lodged in his eye socket and Dirk is hollering, "Auw Auw Auw," because Gerrit has a handful of his hair and is pulling with all his might.

The fourth graders have fallen out of line to form a circle around them and they're cheering on the young gladiators.

Dirk is a much bigger boy, because he's been left behind twice in order to repeat a grade, but Gerrit is tough as nails. Farm work will do that for you.

The teachers are making some progress as they're getting the boys pulled apart and Mr. Raes finally has Gerrit subdued with his knee on his chest and his arms pinned down. Mr. Commandeur has Dirk's arms pinned behind him as Dirk is bristling and fighting to get loose, so he can get back at Gerrit.

Blood keeps running from his nose down his chin and he's swiping at it with tongue, making an even bigger mess.

"FOURTH GRADE!" booms the headmaster, "GO TO YOUR CLASS AND SIT DOWN!" Pointing at Gerrit, "BRING HIM TO MY OFFICE!" Mr. Raes has a struggle on his hands, controlling Gerrit. He breaks loose, picks up his wooden shoe that has come off in the struggle and confronts Raes with it. As Mr. Raes tries to grab him, he hits him over the knuckles with his "KLOMP" and as Mr. Raes let's out a yell, Gerrit turns and races out of the schoolyard, while the class cheers and applauds.

"What a ball!"

Gerrit slows for a second to take off his other "Klomp" and now he races even faster out of sight around the corner.

Out of breath, holding his sore hand, Mr. Raes orders, "Inside!" and the rest of the class gets swallowed by the big double doors of the school entrance.

The kids leave their wooden shoes under their assigned numbered coat racks in the hall and those who have caps hang them on the hooks above them. They pile into their respective rooms.

A lot of kids are wearing "klompen" now. Leather shoes are getting harder to come by, because production of almost anything goes to the "War Effort" and little is left for the civilians.

Besides, a pair of shoes for these boys is nearly 40 guilders, while a pair of wooden shoes is only "f2: 50."

They last about 6 months and they're better in bad weather anyway. So now the boys wear wooden shoes during the week and leather shoes to church on Sundays.

Clasien is allowed to wear her regular shoes to school. She's a girl and she's always such a good girl. She wouldn't scuff her shoes or get her clothes dirty. Yech, she makes Frits sick.

Inside their wooden shoes, they wear little black leather slip-ons or sometimes they wear an extra pair of heavy socks, but for walking around in school, the leather slip-ons are most practical.

Right now, Frits is sitting on top of his desk in the front row. Good kids sit in the back, not Frits obviously.

He's holding court. "Did you see that? POW, right across his knuckles with the Klomp. I hope he broke his bones. That oughta teach the bastard about hitting us with his ruler, the bum."

Let's chant, "MEESTER RAES, KOMMETJE KAAS, KOMMETJE INKT. RAES DIE STINKT!"

The rhyme doesn't make a whole lot of sense, but it rhymes and it belittles Mr. Raes and that's what counts.

They're just starting to chant in earnest, when the cheering stops abruptly. The door opens and here they come. Dirk first, followed by Mr. Commandeur and Raes.

"SIT DOWN!" Mr. Commandeur commands respect.

"I have had it with this class and if there's any repeat of this type of commotion, the whole class will be severely punished! Carry on!"

Dirk slides in his seat, the headmaster disappears and Mr. Raes assumes his post in front of the blackboard.

He's as white as a ghost and he breathes rapidly as if he just ran a 5-mile race. He looks as if he's going to be sick any minute. He picks up his favorite ruler. It's 75 cm long (2 ft), 1 centimeter thick and wide with reinforced copper edges. He taps the table in front of him and announces, "NEDERLANDSE TAAL, page 46, conjugations in the past tense!" "DULL STUFF! Frits cringes.

Until the 10 minute break, the class works without interruption, although the tension in the room is so thick, you could cut it with a knife.

During the break, instead of playing soccer with a tennis ball, a circle forms around Dirk and whether they like the guy or not, he's today's hero in Gerrit's absence.

Dirk says he may be suspended and his parents will be called in for a conference, but he also says that he heard the headmaster blast Raes for immaturity, lack of leadership and more. He could hear all that through a closed door. It must have been some outburst. The boys cheer, "Good for him, sock it to him. Mr. Raes, kommetje kaas!"

The spirit's back in the gang.

"Dividing" in Math is next and as Frits is good in math and some other kids need help and explanations, so he gets bored as Mr. Raes is working with some guys behind him.

He's working on a new poem, but the words aren't flowing today. His other project, the continuing saga of Prince Frederic is not inspiring him either. The character, "PRINCE FREDERIC" is remarkably familiar as if he were a first cousin to PRINCE VALIANT.

Today, nothing adventurous or courageous seems to flow from his brain, so he crumbles the paper into a ball, changes his mind and smoothes it out again. He carefully folds it and tears it into neat little strips, just right for spitballs. He folds them into little neat projectiles, the type that one of his other favorite cartoon characters would use.

This cartoon is about a dog detective "FOKKIE FLINK"(brave) and he's the crime stopper and solver of the comic pages. Jan and Henk have gotten in the habit of calling Frits, "Fokkie Flink" after their Dad called him that once.

Now the brave detective-dog prepares his "PROPJES"(spitballs), folding them scientifically till they are 1-inch long projectiles. He feels in his desk for a rubber band, locates it and spans it around his thumb and index finger. He glances over his shoulder in the direction of Raes, who's occupied with a kid in the far aisle.

JAN is bent over his desk, intrigued in something, not math, Frits is sure of that. Jan is good at Math too and he must be long finished.

Frits puts a "PROPJE" over the front string of the rubber band, pulls it towards him, crossing the rear part, aims carefully...and pffft...Missed. Too high! It lands harmlessly in back of the room. Nobody notices. "When at first you don't succeed.." Another glance at Mr. Raes..no danger there. Not a sound in the room, but Mr. Raes' whispered instructions. The only other sound is the droning of the multiplication table of SEVEN, sounded out in unison in the third grade next door and floating in through the open windows.

He'll make it a bit more interesting. He slips open the lid of his inkwell and dips the next projectile into the ink. Just a little. Now he aims again, and "pffffy"...hits Jan right on the crown of his bent-over head, creating the cutest little blue blotch.

"YIKES!" goes Jan, shattering the silence. Mr. Raes snaps to attention, grasps the situation immediately.

(After 10 months with these clowns, he knows what's happening,) He runs to the front of the class, ready to strike with his ever-present ruler. Frits isn't waiting. He's out of his seat, down the aisle to the back of the room, keeping the rows of desks between him and the aggressor.

"STAND STILL..SIT DOWN!" shouts an infuriated Raes as he inches up the aisle, but Frits moves away from him, keeping the class between them.

"STAND STILL!" he orders again. Boys are starting to cheer, girls begin to scream and the havoc raises Mr. Raes' temper and his voice even more. As he edges to the rear, Frits edges to the front and too late does Raes realize his mistake.

Frits has the advantage; he dashes to the door, through the door with Raes on his heels.

A cheering class files into the hallway as Frits rounds the corner toward the front door. No time to grab his KLOMPEN, so out the door he flies on his slippertjes.

Raes can't catch him, so he returns to his class and orders them to "Sit down and shut up!" returns to the hall, picks up Frits' wooden shoes, grabs his bike from the rack outside and takes off after Frits.

Out of breath, wooden shoes in hand, he appears in the bar at about

3:30, a half-hour before school lets out.

There's just Herman and two customers drinking beer at the round table.

"Mr. Forrer," he starts breathlessly, "where is your son?"

"Where is MY son?," with the emphasis on "MY." "He's in your class, I hope, cause that's why I send him to school, so you can watch and educate him."

"He's run away and here are his "KLOMPEN." He puts them on top of the nearest table.

"HE'S RUN AWAY??" Herman raises his voice, "WELL, YOU BET-TER FIND HIM AND FAST, BEFORE..."

"But Mr. Forrer, I need to talk to you about what that boy does to me!"

"You better talk about what I'm going to do to you if you don't get out of here and find that boy. I don't know, where you got your education, but you're no teacher, that's for damn sure. If you can't handle a bunch of ten year olds, you...you...you...OUT...OUT!"

Raes is out fast.

Herman and his customers double up with laughter as they watch Raes hop back on his bike in front of the Café windows.

"What a guy!"

"I must talk to Frits though, because his grades are slipping and he has only one month left to bring them up for the year!"

Frits, meanwhile, has no idea that Raes would go to his house. He himself would certainly not go home at this hour. Oh, no! He would appear right on schedule with the rest of the kids, hoping that Joop and Clasien wouldn't have heard of the incident, because they're bound to tell Mama and Pappa and Pappa is sure to punish him.

Besides, there's no way in hell that he's going home without his wooden shoes. He figures, as the kids pour out of the school, he'll sneak in unnoticed, so he can retrieve his KLOMPEN. Or else he can get a hold of Jan and have him go back in and get them.

Way up in the tree, on the grounds of the "BEWAARSCHOOL," he has a commanding view of his own school yard, just blocked a little bit by the trees in front of the school.

As he surveys his domain, he reflects back on the days, when he attended this very "Kindergarten" and played in the sandbox below, with IRMA, a blue eyed blonde that he was very infatuated with. She moved away since, but she would probably have become a pain in the butt by now, just like all other girls. He knows, he'll never associate with girls, they're all sick, sick, sick.

Hedwig is alright though, but she's still little, not even four yet. She's kinda alright. Yeah, he likes his little sister Hedwig.

The school bell rings, interrupting his thoughts and he works his way down quickly and makes his way over to the school, yet staying out of sight.

When he locates Jan, who's waiting for Henkie, he dashes over and gets Jan to go for his KLOMPEN. "Of course!" is Jan's reaction. Now there's a true pal!

"They aren't there. Do you suppose they took them to the principles office?"

"Oh boy, there's no way I'm going to the principal's office. Oh boy!

Now I'm gonna get it, unless I sneak around to 'tSCHUURTJE (the old shed, where old wooden shoes await their fate as kindling wood.)and match up a pair of old ones!" "Oh boy!, OH BOY!"

That takes all the fun out of the afternoon and they walk home the long way so they'll approach the house from the rear and won't be seen through the Café windows.

Pap's not crazy though. He "happens" to walk into them, just as they're approaching the acacia tree.

"Hi boys!"

"Hi, Mr. Forrer!" "Hi, Pappa!"

There they are, four little angels, two on shoes, one on wooden shoes and one on his leather slippers.

"Where are your KLOMPEN?"

"Well, Pappa, it's like this.."

"Hold it, if it's a long story, come inside and tell me. You boys go home! BOER, you change clothes."

"TJU," "Good bye!" and in they go.

Frits is still not aware of what game his Dad is playing, but the fact that his Dad is not blowing his cork, puts him at ease, rather foolishly.

"Come here, sit with us. Want some milk or limonade?"

"Limonade, graag!"

He sits down and should have been suspicious of the overly friendly attitude of the customers at the round table.

Herman pours about two fingers of orange syrup in a glass, tops it off with water and hands it to Frits with a coaster underneath.

"Where did you say your KLOMPEN are, Frits?"

At first, still unsuspecting, Frits considers concocting a story, but something tells him, that they're on to him. Damn!

So reluctantly, he starts to tell the true story and when he gets to the point where he dipped his "PROPPIE" in the inkwell, the whole table bursts out laughing. Well, that's an unexpected reaction, so now he really gets into it. As he describes the bullseye on Jan's head, one of the men nearly falls of his chair from laughing so loud and by the time he's demonstrating his

Weurden

stand-off with Raes by running halfway around the table and back, the whole group gets hysterical and it doesn't get much better as he demonstrates his escape through the side door.

Finally, the laughter subsides and Frits sits back, beaming. This is certainly much better than the beating he expected. He smiles broadly as his audience until Pappa asks, "Now where are your klompen?"

"Oh, boy!" His face drops as he gives them his opinion about the principal holding them. Herman wants to know, "How are you going to school tomorrow?" He's intent on teasing him a while, but his customers, maybe with the help of a few beers, can't keep their faces straight, so Herman gets behind the bar and produces his klompen.

"How'd you get'em?? Did Jopie bring 'em?" (That creep, he's thinking, "I'll get even with him!")

"NO!" Pappa answers, "Mr. Raes brought them over!"

"Mr. Raes?" The stunned look on his face makes them roar all over again.

"What did he say?"

"You don't want to hear!" one of the customers roars, doubling up again.

"What did you say to him, Pappa?"

"You don't wanna hear that either!" They can't stop laughing.

"What's so funny?"
"Go change, I'll talk to you later!"
"Oh, boy, oh boy! It's not over yet, is it?"
Oh well, it could have been worse.

CHAPTER V
July 1941

Lots of things are happening in WINTERSWIJK.

A "Burger Veiligheidsdienst," Civilian Safety Service," has been created. By some strange co-incidence, the basic plans were already available since 1938.

More people with armbands. Lots of tall buildings now have sirens on top of them. Air raid practices are being held in schools.

At home, the area under the stairs is being cleared of vacuum cleaners and brooms, low benches are installed and spare blankets and pillows are stored.

Last month's bombing attack has proven, that under the stairs is the safest part of the house.

The very way a staircase is constructed keeps it standing when the whole rest of the building collapses on top of it, or around it.

It needs very little re-enforcement and it's all ready and waiting.

It's July and so far it has been a good summer, not all that rain, that they're used to.

There's been one more bombing raid, but that was at night and the bombs were on their way down, before the alarm sounded.

On two different occasions, there were night alarms, but nothing happened and within 20 minutes the "ALL CLEAR" sounded.

It was exciting, though, up in the middle of the night and into your clothes, Mama and the little ones under the stairs, Pap, Joop and Frits into the backyard, checking things out.

On Wednesday afternoon, (No school on Wednesday and Saturday afternoons) the happy foursome is out and about scouting the latest bombing results. At least this time, the Tommies hit the railroad tracks. Not much damage is visible, because the Germans repaired them in one day. Some homes are damaged and a lot of windows were blown out.

Now, on Wednesday afternoon, Mr. Kamphuis with his sonorous voice is explaining with the help of a map, why this railroad junction is of such strategic value.

"FOKKIE FLINK, look here, "ESSEN," "the RUHRTAL." Here's where the bulk of Germany's coal and iron-ore mines are.

This is the center of Germany's war-machine. Here is where most of the Dutch boys are that are working in German Labor Camps. The volunteers make good money, but the ones that they pick up in their "RAZZIA'S," their raids, well, I just don't know about them.

Now here's where we come in. Along the whole North Sea coast defense works are being built and all the steel for the construction and re-enforcements comes from our own "HOOGOVENS" (steelmills) in IJMUIDEN in North Holland near Haarlem, where your father is from.

The cannons and their tracks are built in or around "ESSEN" and then shipped by rail to the coast.

That's where WINTERSWIJK comes into the picture.

See those tracks? Coming into town and going out? Well, here's where the switching takes place and here's where the trains slow down to be diverted Northward to the Waddenzee or this way, toward Arnhem and from there to the southern coastline of Holland and Northern Belgium.

Now you can bet your last pair of klompen, Fokkie Flink, that the times we were bombed, a loaded train was right here in town, full of very modern and expensive weaponry and that's what they were after!"

"How did they know the trains were here, Mr. Kamphuis?"

"Oh, the Underground keeps them informed, I'm sure."

"The Underground, like those guys that stole the projection equipment from the movies and then set the place on fire to cover that up?"

Mr. Kamphuis has to chuckle at that one. "I guess you're right, that was probably the underground, although I can't figure for the life of me, what they want with some old projectors."

"But how does the Underground tell 'em and besides, the trains are in town probably less than half an hour and it must take longer than that to fly all the way from England?"

Frits looks at Jan with admiration. This big city kid is certainly smart..

"You bet, these Brits know the moment these trains leave ESSEN."

"But how? Is there an Underground in Germany too? I thought Underground was Dutch an..."

"Yes, there are probably spies working in Germany too, they may not call them Underground, but they're there and they transmit their messages to England in CODE and.."

"What's CODE?" Henkie's turn.

Frits answers that one, "Oh, we know about CODE, right Jan? We sometimes write in code so the teachers can't read it if they find our notes!"

"Ya, along the same lines, if the Germans intercept their messages, they still don't know what it means!"

Oh, boy, this war is neat and Kamphuis is a neat source of information.

He knows everything and he takes the time to play with them. Great! What a guy! Now they get into how radio's really work, I mean REALLY work, not just "Plug it in, stretch the antenna and turn the knob," I mean REALLY work.

Mr. Kamphuis gets pencil and paper, draws radio waves, long and short, microphones and transmitters, receivers and speakers and when it's time to go home, their heads are spinning with all that neat new knowledge.

"Now straight home, boys!"

"Oh, yes, of course!" TJU, TJU, and hand in hand, they're on the way home.

Funny, they wouldn't think of diverting from their straight course home, when Mr. Kamphuis gives the order. Somehow, you just don't disobey that man.

Something is going on, Frits can smell it.

Yep, more German trucks than usual, more motorcycle activity! What's up?

Oh, yes, there's definitely something going on. They quicken their pace. There it is! Military cars parked halfway on the sidewalk, half in the street all over the place. In front of the restaurant, in front of the neighbor's houses, in the parking spaces of the "KOOLENBOER."

These vehicles are different though. These are "LUFTWAFFE" vehicles.

The kids have seen them before, but not in these quantities.

As they enter the Café through the front door, they encounter a room full of soldiers, hardly a civilian in sight.

They're occupying every table, sitting at the bar and playing billiards. The sliding glass doors to the "EETZAAL," the dining room are wide open even if nobody's sitting there.

Mama and Ellie are hustling back and forth with plates and Pappa is tapping beer as fast as he can pour it.

Mama passes the kids, breathlessly rushing a tray with plates to a table and shouts at them in passing, "Get out of those clothes and help Joop peel potatoes in the backyard!"

OOPS, this seems like emergency and for once they give no argument or hesitation.

As they're peeling as fast as they can, Paultje's learning too, with

91

Hedwig watching, clutching her doll, Joop explains what he knows so far.

"A search light battalion is going to be stationed here temporary permanent or something, at least for a while and they're setting up camp and equipment. Now they're having a break and it seems that the whole battalion wants to eat, "BRAT-KARTOFFELN UND SPIEGELEIER. Home fries with sunny side up fried eggs. And everyone wants to eat 'em here in Hof Van Holland."

Clasien comes out to collect the potatoes that are done and after a "THAT'S NOT VERY NEAT!" disappears into the kitchen with them.

A man from the AJAX grocery arrives with a flat of eggs while some of the soldiers come walking out to urinate behind the trees.

The bathrooms must be overcrowded inside.

The LUFTWAFFE guys look good in their pale blue uniforms with yellow epaulettes and yellow patches with silver little birds on their collars. The more little birds, the higher the rank, apparently.

The importance of the occasion grips them all and just like after the bombardment last month, Frits throws himself into his task with all the vigor he can muster.

This is serious business.

Hedwig is dispensed with a message, "We're thirsty!" and indeed, Clasien appears shortly there after with limonade.

Hey! This is teamwork and it doesn't stop until 6:30, when the soldiers have filed out of the Café, back to work.

The family kinda collapses around the round table in the bar, but not for long.

Pappa gives orders, "Ida, go feed the bunch, put the youngsters to bed while Ellie and I clean this mess. We don't have a clean glass or plate left in the house. Then we'll eat, you watch the store and meanwhile, you older ones, get back to peeling potatoes as soon as you've eaten.

They'll start piling in here again tomorrow afternoon at 3 O'clock, but we'll be ready for them this time! They'll be back for beer about eight, so let's get this joint ready! Let's go!"

Well, peeling potatoes in the kitchen is better than going to bed at least and they're making good progress. Mama has relieved Pappa in the Café and is now back, boiling potatoes in a big kettle on the electric stove. It's too warm to fire up the coal stove. Mama explains, as she's slicing up the boiled potatoes, "You can fry them faster when they've been cooked before and they also taste better. You'll see tomorrow, they'll love it!"

"Now, tomorrow, come straight home from school, because we'll have another madhouse on our hands!"

She wipes a stubborn curl from her forehead with her arm and she appears to be glowing in the lamplight. The kids can tell, she's loving it.

This is what it's all about, hard work, being busy, making money. She's in her glory now! This is what she came to Holland for!

The "BRAT-KARTOFFELN UND SPIEGELEIER" affair proves to be a very profitable venture.

Those Krauts must not have thought very highly of their outdoor kettle cousins or maybe they haven't had the luxury of "BRAT-KARTOFFELN AND SPIEGELEIER MIT SCHPECK" for a long time, because they come back in droves.

Then, at night, they come back for beer and song.

They sing along with the record player or with an accordion and they fill the joint with song and laughter.

All of a sudden, the amount of records with "SCHLAGER," Top Hits doubles, triples and quadruples. Ida does the buying and she knows what the soldiers like, so every week she buys the newest HIT records and the soldiers drink and sing their nights away.

A new girl has to be hired. A dark haired beauty from DOETICHEM, not far away. She has the best of dispositions and work habits and the girls rake in the tips. Whatever may be said about German soldier's bad habits, cheating on their bills is not one of them.

The system is simple. Each soldier has a "GROLSCH" coaster with his drink. The server marks a stripe along the edge for each drink served and at the end of the evening, the stripes are totaled, the tab paid, plus tip and off they go.

At the bar, Herman just marks a stripe on a pad for each drink he hands the server and at the end of the evening, the senior officer or "Unter-Offizier" checks with Herman, *"IST ALLES BEZAHLT, HERR WIRT?"* and if there's a discrepancy, he pays the difference and THAT'S THAT!"

Money is rolling in. Adjustments are being made. Heavy curtains are being installed, for by now there's a total BLACKOUT!

Out back, in the yard, a lot of construction is taking place.

The BIJ-KEUKEN is enlarged and restrooms are added, so the BEER-RELEASE can be handled more properly.

The financing for all this is worked out easily with the Landlord as Herman is willing to pick up his fair share of the improvements.

For the kids, life has changed. Life now mostly consists of school and KARTOFFELN. Peeling potatoes has become a daily routine and their hands have so much ground-in dirt and calluses that make their hands look as if they were eighty years old.

School is different too. After the RAES and KLOMPEN incident, Herman has gotten across the importance of good grades and Frits is buckling down and behaving himself. He's doing well.

The fact, that Herman has impressed upon him, that if his report card does not show marked improvements, he'll be restricted to the house all vacation long, may have been a contributing factor.

Another excitement has been added. Now, during an air raid, the powerful searchlights perform their fantastic dance patterns in the black sky and every so often the lights catch a plane or a flight of planes in their beam. Then other beams join it and the poor BOMBER becomes an open target for a German FIGHTER PLANE. The bomber, caught in that web of beams, dodges, turns and dives, but the grip of three or four beams is relentless. Many a night, as Herman and the Big Boys stand in the backyard, they'd see a Bomber get caught and shot at, burst into flame and start it's screaming dive toward earth.

The amazing thing is, the impression is always as if the falling aircraft is diving straight at them, although, when it does hit and explode, it may be as far as twenty miles away.

These are exciting interruptions of what might have been dull, normal nights otherwise.

Some nights, though nothing happens, no planes get caught in the lights, none are shot down, nothing.

One thing is the same story all the time. Up the stairs, three or four times, to knock on ANTOON's door, "ANTOON, ANTOON, FLIEGER-ALARM!" He could sleep through anything. Many a night, they would just sit and doze until the ALL-CLEAR and go back to bed.

One night, long after the ALL-CLEAR, a lone Bomber, crippled over Germany, is limping back to England and releases its bombs to lessen its weight. Result, a path of death and destruction, smack through the center of town.

The NAZI propaganda machine exploits that once again.

"DELIBERATE ATTACK ON INNOCENT WOMEN AND CHILDREN, etc, etc.."

It gets monotonous.

Of the three brothers BRUMMELSTROETE, only ANTOON is left. Gerrit has joined the WAFFEN-SS and has become a heavy machine gunner.

The other brother, WILLEM, is in a labor camp near HAMBURG.

Ida's youngest brother, KAREL, who'd been away in Seminary, has been sent to KIEL to work. It doesn't help the tension between the different factions of the KWAK family.

It is as if battle lines have been drawn forever between the FORRERS and the KWAKS.

Searchlights over Winterswijk

Fierling flak, aiming at a "Jabo"

Two LUFTWAFFE officers have now become BOARDERS, necessitating early EETZAAL hours for breakfast service.

Since the girls, Ellie and GERDA now occupy a room upstairs, Joop has been moved to KAMER ZES, with Frits and the BOER.

At popular request, DANCING has been re-activated, on Saturday nights this time, instead of Sundays, like before the war.

The work and the fun are about the same as Frits remembers, but now they receive allowances so they can buy an ice-cream cone on Sundays or go to the movies.

A lot of things are rationed and meat-eating customers have to provide stamps as well as money when they come in to eat. These stamps are pasted on sheets and thus Mama can get the meat at the butchers in turn.

Other items are getting short too; everything is going to the "WAR EFFORT," so other avenues have to be explored.

One Friday night, here's the scene, "To APELDOORN? By train? Woopie! Yes of course! You going too, Jopie?"

"I'm going."

"To MIJNHEER and MEVROUW van Zanten? What for?"

"You'll know tomorrow. Now don't say anything to your brothers and sisters, can I trust you?"

"Oh, Ya Mama! Oh, WOW!"

"On a real train, by ourselves, this will be fun!"

Frits is as excited as if he had received PRINCE VALIANT's "Singing Sword."

"Whaddaya mean, you've made the trip before? How come I don't know about this? This isn't fair! You promised? Well...right, Okay..I just promised too. I won't say anything either. Of course, I won't! What's so secretive anyway?"

The next morning he finds out.

In Mama's room, KAMER 7, they're being dressed. Over their under-shirts, suspended from strings tied around their bodies, are dozens of silk stockings. In little suit cases, underneath some neatly packed shirts of theirs, are dozens of bras and slips.

On Pappa's bike, Joop riding, Frits sits in back in his Sunday best, toting two little suitcases. Joop parks and locks the bike and buys two ONE-WAY tickets to APELDOORN.

"ONE-WAY? Aren't we coming back?"

"Shut up, stupid!"

They have to appear as two boys going to visit family for vacation. It's the first Saturday in August, the first Saturday of summer vacation.

This will be a great vacation, he can feel it in his bones.

While waiting for the train to come in from AALTEN, Joop explains in a husked voice, "Stupid, we're just a couple of young kids going on a vacation trip to OOM HANS and TANTE MARIE in APELDOORN and nobody makes that trip back and forth in one day, unless they're up to no good, you hear? So that's why we're traveling on a one-way ticket and we'll come back on a one-way ticket. Do you understand? Now act the part! We're going on vacation!"

Frits tries to get into it. "His first smuggling job, WOW."

"What if someone recognizes us when we come back?"

"No such problem. These people change shifts at 4 o'clock and we'll see different people on the train tonight,"

With that, the train pulls in, doors open, the boys pile into a 3rd class compartment, Joop puts the KOFFERTJES in the overhead net and they settle down across from one another, each with a window seat.

This is only the second time he's been on a train.

The first time was years ago when he went to ARNHEM with Clasien to spend some time with his Tante Paula and Tante Hetty.

It's fun to watch the landscape rolling by and chuck in and out of little towns and villages. He watches the power lines dip and rise, dip and rise with every pole they pass.

The train stops about every ten minutes it seems, as they pull into another station and passengers come and go.

Joop explains that this is a LOCAL train that stops just about everywhere and some other time, they'll try and catch an EXPRESS. An EXPRESS would only stop twice, in ZUTPHEN and DEVENTER and it would cut their travel time in half.

Frits doesn't mind, he wouldn't miss this for the world and he envies Joop for having done this more often.

The oldest one in the family always gets favored anyway and the oldest girl too.

Clasien is everybody's apple of the eye; Pappa's, Mama's, Mama's brothers, and sisters, they're always ooing and aahing over her; "she's so cute," "she's such a good girl!" and on and on and on. Sick, sick, sick.

He'd rather be a normal kid and be considered "bad," that's Okay.

It's more fun to be bad anyway.

A conductor, who's come to punch their tickets, rudely interrupts his thoughts. "TICKETS PLEASE!" Frits point to Joop, "He's got 'em!" He knows they're sunk. Now they're gonna get caught! They're gonna be searched, found guilty, and put in a dungeon.

Why are they smuggling stupid women's hose anyway? Why can't they buy them in a store in APELDOORN like normal people and..and... the conductor has left and his anxiety subsides. He lets out a deep breath, and sees Joop with a stupid grin on his face as if he's saying, "You got chicken, right?"

"That schmuck, I'll show him sometime, we'll see who's the toughest!"

"Why didn't we take an EXPRESS?" The fun has gone out of it a little bit, he wishes now that the trip was over with.

"There's no EXPRESS in the morning and the VAN ZANTEN's are expecting us at this time."

"OH!" he goes back to watching the scenery.

Twice more he gets a start. Once when a German soldier walks in and sits down, a German uniform with NEDERLAND on a patch on his shoulder. Then once more later on, after pulling out of ZUTPHEN, the same conductor comes in.

For a moment Frits thinks, "Now were sunk!" but he just waves at the boys as well as at the tickets that Joop holds out to him. He just addresses the other passengers, "Tickets please!"

After leaving Deventer the train clatters over the bridge across the IJSEL, right along the VERKEERSBRUG, the TRAFFIC bridge.

He's never seen a bridge like that, WOW, that's big. The steel girders rise at least 10 stories out of the water at this point. WOW!

They pass a neat windmill, a sawmill, because tree trunks, floating in a pond are guided into the gaping mouth of the windmill and come out on the other side as boards, being loaded on a horsedrawn wagon. Fascinating!

Ten minutes later, they pull into APELDOORN after following the IJSEL northward for a while and then disappearing into tree covered hills.

Mr. and Mrs. Van Zanten are waiting for them and they act like a long lost Uncle and Aunt. They hover over them. She hugs them, YECH, but they also buy them icecreams and that's good.

Sitting on the backs of their bikes, they're being pedaled home through beautiful, treelined streets.

A streetcar, canary yellow, comes clanging by with a bouncing antenna on top, riding along an overhead wire.

"This is a nice place!" Frits muses, "Wonder if we can live here sometime?"

The streets are busy with shoppers and strollers and bicycle traffic is very heavy. This town is very different from WINTERSWIJK and their speech is very different too! They sound more like Pappa does. This must be Holland.

He's wrong, he's still in the Province of GELDERLAND, but he doesn't know that, he might as well be in Timbuktu. He makes up his mind to look up APELDOORN on the map. He knows he's learned about it already, but he always confuses APELDOORN with AMERSFOORT, but he'll get it straight.

At the Van Zanten house, they're relieved of their treasures and get treated to cherry pie. Next stop; an amusement park, which turns out to be a disappointment, because all the wild rides and slides that Frits wants to ride, are off limits to him because he's in his Sunday clothes.

RATS, RATS, RATS..

Bread with real honey offsets the aggravation fast and before long, they're back on the bikes, off to the station.

This time, the KOFFERTJES they're holding onto have butter, covered by sheets. Loads of butter, heavy, heavy, heavy butter.

The return trip is as much fun as the trip over has been, except he doesn't startle as much, and they're back home just as darkness swallows the town. The first of many smuggling trips has been fun. He sleeps like a baby.

• • •

Summer vacation consists of the entire month of August and the Forrer-kids all have season passes to the swimming pool, which is actually a lake. It is right along the BEEK, a creek. Its official name is DE SLINGE, but no one knows that.

The lake is oval with a sandy beach at the near side and a dock built through the widest part of the oval.

Two perpendicular docks come straight from the center one to the beach and still another dock, paralleling the long one, cuts across the protruding docks, thus creating three swimming pools and three wading areas. The center one is HET DIEPE, it's an Olympic size pool for waterpolo and swim competition and it's ten to fifteen feet deep.

The two pools bordering it left and right, go from beach level to about four feet for beginners and the rear half of the oval is just a pond with water lilies and other plants.

The docks vary in width, with the widest ones around HET DIEPE for spectators to stand and sit during POLO matches.

The TOWER, a rugged wooden structure, has three spring boards; one, on it's right side at about 4 feet above the water, one on the second level, on the left, at about 15 feet and on the third level a short stubby board at about 25 feet.

Real heroes can still go higher by standing on the cornerpost, up another 4 feet, by holding on to the flagpole for support while steadying themselves for the dive.

The Forrer-kids love the pool. They're regarded as SINNERS for going there, because all "decent" Catholics go to GROLLE to the segregated pool. Two hours for girls, two hours for boys.

Mama was brought up that way, no wonder she can't swim.

Pappa says, the VROMEN, the pious, are nuts and if God wanted men and women to be segregated, he would have put EVE in a separate Paradise and the world would probably not have had as much trouble as we're having today.

So, guess what? Every morning, weather permitting, they're off at 8:45 for the pool. MASS at 8 o'clock first. That never stops, vacation or not.

They all like water and beaches and all five of them trot along, across the railroad tracks, direction BORKEN. It's only a twenty minute walk and once they veer off to the left towards BEKKENDELLE, they're on a sandy side road, lined with trees and blackberry bushes.

At the end of the month, these berries will be ripe for picking, but right now their only interest is getting to the pool.

They pass through the turnstiles, their passes dangling around their necks, the attendant waving them through, smiling at the familiar and eager faces. Two minutes later, they turn in their clothes on a numbered hanger and receive a penny on a string with a matching number to attach to their bathing suits. Frits is off in a flash, flying across the beach, up the perpendicular docks to the broader part that borders HET DIEPE and FLOP..in he dives at breakneck speed.

He comes up 50 feet further, near the ladder to the right of the diving tower. Up the ladder, onto the lower diving board and wham..a passable swandive. Under water to the ladder on the other side of the tower, up the stairs to the second level.. this time a good sustained swan dive, concentrating on keeping his legs together and straight. Under water again to the first ladder, up two flights of stairs to the upper level. Out of breath, leaning against the railing, he scans the pools and the beach area for his siblings. No point in diving off the high board without an audience.

Joop is his prime interest, 'cause the competition between the two is fierce and although Joop went off the high board before Frits ever did, Frits' style is better, maybe because Joop is so tall and gangly and his lower legs always seem to flap behind him when he dives.

Joop is not in sight. Clasien is straight ahead at the waters edge sitting in ankle deep water, facing Hedwig who happily slaps at the water with both hands as if she were still 6 months old.

Paultje? "Let me see, that white pig's hair should be sticking out like a sore thumb." "There he is!" He's making like a whale, disappearing under water while turning towards his sisters, then surfacing and spitting a stream of water at them.

Hedwig thinks it's hilarious, while Clasien seems to be saying as she waves him off; "Cut that out!" but Frits can't hear that from up on the tower.

There are very few people in HET ZWEMBAD so far. It's a bit cloudy today and it's still early. He checks out the corner post. One day this month he'll dive off it, but boy, oh boy, it's high. Why these extra 4 feet make so much difference, he doesn't know but it has been that way all along.

Every time you try a different height or a different style of dive, you're scared and apprehensive, but once you've done it, you're over it and then you can do it all the time. It's just that first time. That dreadful first time. He's going to come out one rainy morning before anyone else shows up and do it; just DO it, so no one will know if he goofs and then, one day, when they're all at the pool, he'll surprise them.

Yep, that's what he'll do!

As he continues to scan the pools for his brother Joop, he sees him sitting on a STIJGER, a dock, talking to a girl. Him and his girls...sick, sick,

sick. Joop is starting another school in September.

Having finished 6th grade, he'll be going to the Catholic M.U.L.O. Frits forgot what it stands for, but he'll be studying language and WISKUNDE, higher math. Good riddance; No more interference from him in school.

Unable to attract the attention of the rest of his siblings, Frits decides to dive without an audience. He's seen instructors tell the high school boys on the diving team how to do it and he's practiced the other guy's instructions. Inching just his toes over the edge of the board, this one is solid, fixed, no spring to it. He stands, heels high, body taught, arms stretched straight in front of him, quickly checking every muscle and position of his head and limbs, then a slow bending of the knees, body remaining erect and like a jack in the box, ejects himself upward and forward as high and as far as he can push himself. Temporarily horizontal, with his arms spread wide, back arched, he soars like a swan for a second. Then, as he approaches the water moves his hands together and hits the water vertically, head slightly tilted back and..pffft, he's in. He knows it was a good dive. The less splash you create, the better the entry. He grins to himself, "Too bad I couldn't get an audience."

He swims toward the beach, crosses underneath the dock between the pilings and joins Paultje, Hedwig and Clasien.

Hedwig wants to go for a ride on his back but Clasien thinks that's too dangerous, so Paultje and Frits make for the medium pool, where Paultje can't stand at the deep end and that's where they start their daily swimming lessons. DE BOER can swim underwater, but when he comes up for air, he sinks. Frits will have him swimming in one more week.

A six year old kid should know how to swim, he feels.

As a matter of fact, if they would just leave him alone with Hedwig for a few days, he would have her swimming too, he's sure.

He himself doesn't remember learning to swim. He feels he's known how all his life.

His dad has told the story many times, how he'd throw him in the waves at the beach of OOSTENDE before he was a year old. His Mama's protests did not make any difference. Pappa's attitude was, "All animals swim by instinct. It's the stupid human beings that screw it up by THINKING!"

Pappa was raised near the NORTH SEA in HAARLEM, and he tells about walking south along the beach some 8 to 10 miles, then swimming across the breakers to the deep water and then swimming all the way back with the current.

Frits can't wait to try that sometime, but first he's got to practice long distance swimming and there's no opportunity in this dry part of the country.

In the last few years, he's taken his swimming much more seriously, learned the backstroke, crawl, backcrawl, side stroke, treading water, life saving and has earned his diploma "A" last summer. This year or next year for sure, he'll be ready for diploma "B."

Teaching Paultje is getting boring and he says, "Let's go pester Joop!" Paul is always game, whatever Frits does, he does.

They can't see Joop from this vantagepoint, but they cruise underneath the dock until they see their legs dangling over the edge and they can hear Joop's voice. "Talking about himself of course!" Paultje nods. They slip into the "POND" part of the lake. It's about $2\frac{1}{2}$ feet deep at this point and they slowly crawl behind the unsuspecting couple.

Cupping their hands, they load them up and at Frits' nod, they splash the youngsters on their backs.

The girl shrieks and plunges forward off the dock, into the water, while Joop turns and curses the hell out of them.

If he weren't such a gentleman, he would have jumped after them and gladly drowned them, but as it is, he turns the other way and jumps after the girl to sooth her, giving him a perfect excuse to touch her.

He grins to himself, "Sometimes, these brothers come in handy." He might not have gotten this far with her for two more days, if it weren't for the splashing. He holds her, wipes her hair from her forehead and asks gently, "Are you alright?"

From a safe distance, the boys survey this scene, "He's sick, I swear, he's sick. Girls no less! How sick!"

The Kamphuis's, Jan and Henk have shown up meanwhile, (the lucky stinkers don't have to go to church during vacation.) and the four of them happily dogfight, wrestle and race in the water till the horn blows, 11:45. Time to go home for dinner.

"Man, oh man, this is the way to live!"

On the way back, Jan comes up with a great idea, a GRAND idea. "Remember the plane that was shot down, but didn't burn, 'member, the other night? Remember it stayed in the searchlight nearly all the way down? Remember I told you, we even saw parachutes in the searchlight, right?"

"Ya, I remember, we personally didn't see any parachutes, but the plane had most of its tail section shot off and came down in slow lazy circles, but didn't burn, Ya, I remember, what about it?"

"I know where it is!"

"You what?" They stop dead in their tracks. "Where?"

"Do you know where MEDDO is? I've never been there!"

"Oh yes, I know where MEDDO is. You go in the direction of GROLLE first, but then you bear right before the bus station. About three miles from there, where the road crosses from GROLLE to DEURNE there's an "AM-

STEL" CAFÉ on the corner where they sell ice-cream and..."

"Okay, Okay, you can get us to that CAFÉ. Then I'll make a map from my father's map and that way we find it. It's broken up, but it didn't burn like most of them. The Germans have already stripped it, but it may still have some neat stuff in it!"

"Alright, let's go!"

"NO, NO, first we go and eat. Then my father goes to sleep, (he always calls him Father, not Pappa or Dad, no, always, Father.) and then I can copy his map. He goes on duty at 8, so he'll leave a little after 6, so I can't "borrow" his map. We'll see you at your house a little after one! Okay?"

"Right on! Tju!" "Tju!"

Mama is surprised that only Joop wants to go back to the pool that afternoon, but after dinner, she puts Hedwig down for her nap and the boys disappear.

Disappear is right, the moment Jan and Henkie come into view, they're off.

They're making good progress and before long they're licking ice-cream under the AMSTEL sign in MEDDO. That was the last of Frits' earnings of last Sunday.

On the table out on the terrace, the map is being studied. The conclusion is to go about a half mile toward DEURNE, then turn left on the dirt road toward the border and after passing the fourth farm house, they should turn into the pasture on their left till they'd hit a wooded area and just beyond, in the next pasture lies most of the plane.

They don't' know how they're going to get to the plane, but they'll cross that bridge when they get to it.

They're confident that they'll get to the plane, one way or another.

Jan's map is very accurate, he must take after his father, the same insistence for detail. It takes more than a half-hour before they pass the fourth farm house and there they crawl underneath the barbed wire fence.

At the farmhouse, there's no sign of life, at this hour they're probably all in the field.

The wooded area is right where it's supposed to be and now it's time to make like Indians. Paultje and Frits take off their wooden shoes and socks and hide them under some leaves, continuing on bare feet.

They crawl the 40 to 50 feet along strips of trees and bushes and stop at the far side, hiding behind a blackberry bush with green berries.

They peer over the bush, but see absolutely nothing. NO PLANE, no guards. They're just about to bring out the map again when Henkie whispers, "Over there, I see him! Over there!"

It's the guard. He must have been sitting down. He's further off to the left than they expected and now, he's walking away from them, disappearing. He must have sat down again.

"The plane must be behind him, for it certainly isn't here!"

"Good point, Jan. Boys, this is what we do. We'll cross the pasture right along the fence here and behind those trees there and as long as we stay low, he won't see us and by the time we get to those trees, we're kinda behind him and then we can probably see the plane!"

No arguments from any of them and Frits does not expect a discussion, so as he finishes talking, he's on the way.

Some sight! Four of them, on hands and knees, crawling as fast as they can, every so often falling flat on their bellies, as Frits raises up, to scan the scene. All clear? Off again and before long, they're on the other side of the pasture, where a row of KNOTWILGEN, knotty willows, form a probable property boundary line. They can't see the guard from here, but by giving Paultje a lift onto his shoulder, where he steadies himself with the help of some tree branches, Paultje gets a better field of view.

"I see the plane!"

"Where?"

"Over there!"

That's a help, Frits can't see where Paul is pointing, because Paul's standing on his shoulders, facing the opposite way.

"Tell Jan, what you see and where!"

From his descriptions, the fuselage must be in fair shape.

"No other soldiers?"

"NO!"

"Come on down!"

Discussion time; if they go straight for the plane, the guard may see them, so it's best to go straight ahead through the field. It's a KORENVELD, wheatfield, recently harvested, and once across, they should turn left aiming for the nose of the plane.

It's still working for them, their luck stays with them.

The rough stubbles of the recently cut wheat are hard on the hands and knees and bare feet. It has been a warm spring and summer, so everything has been harvested earlier than usual. Normally this field would not have been ready till September.

They're fussing softly to themselves as they painfully make their way across. "Boy, if only the wheat was still here!"

They manage though, without incident and as they turn towards the aircraft remains they are upon it within three minutes.

It's a beauty. The fuselage is there nearly in its entirety.

The wings are ripped off and there's no sight of the motors. The mark-

Downed British bomber

ings of the R.A.F are still clearly visible and most window- panes are still intact in the cockpit.

Beyond the plane is a swampy area and a clump of trees beyond that. That's where the wings must have been left behind.

The boys edge closer along the trees, but at one point there is no more cover to protect them and they'd have to cross the clearing to get to the plane.

"Stay here till I call you!"

Down flat on his face, toes and elbows moving at the pace of a fast caterpillar, he jiggles across the field like a snake, his body an inch off the soil. At the wreck he lifts his head momentarily, peers around and satisfied, he's back on his belly jiggling to the far side of the plane, out of their line of sight.

They wait with baited breath and all of a sudden, "There he is!"

In the cockpit window, smiling from ear to ear, waving them on.

Like ducks in a row, they follow the same trail around the far side of the aircraft, where there's a gaping hole in the side, where a door used to be. Now they're standing in the aircraft, shaking hands.

Frits is thrilled. He has never before been close to an airplane, never touched one, and now he's inside of one. MY God, they seem big, much bigger inside than he'd imagined.

He goes, "SHHHS," putting his fingers across his lips and they split up. They spread themselves in different directions, Frits heading back for the cockpit.

He's wishing he was wearing shoes, jagged pieces of aluminum and Plexiglas are every where. The Germans have darn near stripped the plane; hardly a thing is left. The instruments have been taken out and the only things of value are pieces of Plexiglas, because people can make neat things from those.

He gets a good size square, well nearly square, out of one of the shattered windows, sticks it in back of his shirt and tucks his shirt back in. In the middle of the fuselage is a large gaping hole, manmade, that's where the bomb bay doors were, he supposes. The guns have been stripped out, but in the rear are about 7 or 8 "Point Fifties" attached with clips, in the bottom of the plane. They must have been overlooked.

They'll divide them later, but Henkie found them, so he gets to carry them. After standing in the cockpit once more, he pulls the wheel, turns it, pushes it, and imagines himself flying that monstrous thing.

There's nothing else to strip, so they decide to go. Paultje reaches into the ripped plastic of a seatback, and pulls out the foamrubber cushion.

That's a thought. Out comes the knife, the few remaining seat backs and bottoms are slit carefully and now they load themselves up with foam rubber. After tucking the stuff inside their shirts, they're off again, Frits first, still very careful and as he reaches the treeline, he waves them on. They follow like ducks, less carefully this time.

They retrace their tracks exactly, retrieve their wooden shoes and socks and head home.

Bounty hunters returning from a successful raid.

At the AMSTELBIER sign, they put all their pennies together and conclude they can get two more cones and will share them.

They lady proprietor, HOLLANDS GLORIE, Holland's pride, fat red cheeks, round head with a lace cap and a solid build, oversees all their hassles with the money and asks where they got all their "stuff."

After exchanging glances, they decide she's all Dutch herself, so they tell her their exciting tale.

Sometimes they exaggerate a little, they always interrupt one another, but she loves every bit of it and when she hears that they're the grandkids of the KWAKS, (Yes, she knew OMA!), they end up eating eight ice-cream cones amongst them even though they only had money for two.

It's a little late as they turn the last corner for home, but "What a day!" SURE AS TOOTING...THIS WAR IS FUN!!!

CHAPTER VI
April, 1942

Commotion in the middle of the night.

No "FLIEGER ALARM." No sounds of aircraft anywhere, yet loud commands, hysterical screaming, a child crying, no not crying, worse, screeching like a hurt bird, doors slamming, more loud male voices, car doors opening, slamming shut, it's pandemonium out there.

Frits is out of the window and on the EETZAAL, (DINING ROOM), roof. It's cold as hell out and foggy wet.

Mama and Papa's heads are sticking out of the window of KAMER VII, next to Frits'.

"What's going on out there?"...that's Pappa.

"Get inside, you'll catch cold!"...that's Mama.

He can now make out two trucks backed up to the row of little houses on the EELINKSTRAAT, he can see the little slits of light in the "black-out" type headlights.

"It's the WOHLSTEINS," he calls back at his folks "Pappa, they're arresting the WOHLSTEINS!"

More doors slam, more screams, more male voices cursing, then grinding gears and they're gone.

"Pappa, Pappa, they took the WOHLSTEINS, do something, Pappa. Aren't you going to do anything, Pappa? Pappa, you gotta do something!"

"Come inside!" It's Mama, whose face appears in Frits' window, "Come down stairs!" She's in her house coat hanging out of the KAMER VI window, "Come in here NOW!"

Frits crawls back in, dispirited, Mama wraps him in a blanket and dries his feet. "Boy, you're crazy to go out there like that in your pajamas. You'll catch cold again and you'll be down again with jaundice and you know..." Frits doesn't hear a word she's saying, he shivers terribly, but it's probably not from the cold.

As Mama goes on, even saying things like, "Go to Bed!" he just keeps walking, moving slowly down the stairs, across the cold granite floor of the hall into the kitchen. He seats himself on the chair near the pot stove, that's in place again for the winter, but is about as cold as he is now, since the fire has gone out long ago.

Pappa has preceded him down and is heating milk on the electric stove. Mama and Jopie file into the kitchen too and Mama begins again, "You should.." HUSH," Pappa interrupts softly, but sternly.

Mama gets cups down from the cupboard and puts cocoa mix in them, waiting for the milk to get warm.

"Why, Pappa, why? What have they done? And that little girl, what's her name? The granddaughter? They hurt her Pappa! Why? Why?, what did SHE do?"

Pappa stirs the chocolate milk, "Come sit at the table!"

Frits turns, Joop and Mama are deadly quiet.

"Drink your cocoa!, Watch it, it's hot, hold it…let me add some cold… here you go, stir it, O.K., O.K.!"

"Why Pappa, why? I know what you're gonna say, They're JEWISH, right? But what did they do? They're not rich Jews that ruin the world and all that other garbage. They're poor working people. He's been working for the County-Water-Department as long as we know him, he goes to work on his bike at 4 in the morning, EVERY morning, I know Pappa, he's not rich. I know! Why then, Pappa, why? They'll never come back, I know it, they'll kill 'em!"

Tears are running down his cheeks, Mama's not doing much better and Jopie is staring at his chocolate milk as if there's something fascinating in it.

"Drink your cocoa, Frits, here, dry your tears,"

"There is nothing I can say Frits, Nothing HOTDAMN!"

The last word shoots out with such vengeance that all three look up at him, startled.

"Sit down, Herman. Drink your cocoa too!"

She's worried that his ulcer will flare up. "Why don't we all drink up-up-up and go to bed? It's too cold here! Take your cocoa, if it's too hot and let's go, come boys!"

They rise. Frits is still crying uncontrollably.

"Come in bed with us!"

For the first time in years, he's in bed between his father and mother, his skinny body shaking with the sobs that won't stop.

Finally, with his head against his father's chest, he falls asleep, blissfully.

The WOHLSTEINS were the first.

Rumors had it that their son-in-law, who lived with them, had disappeared without a trace. Underground, possibly.

The WOHLSTEINS had denied any knowledge of his whereabouts and that's why they were whisked away; collaborating with the enemy! That's the story.

But then, other Jewish families disappear, the RAZZIA is on.

Strange things start to happen. Mama gets more and more uptight. It nearly gets to a breaking point one morning when she sends Frits to the cellar.

"Frits, get a bottle of milk and hurry, you'll be late for church!" God forbid!

Frits dashes out of the kitchen, through the hall into the café, around the pool table and into the slijterij.

As he jerks open the cellar door, he gasps! "WHAT THE HELL......?" A dozen pair of eyeballs glow in the dark and startle him right out of his socks. He slams the door, races back to the kitchen and grabs his Mama around the waste and whispers; " Mama, there are people in the cellar!" Mama jerks away from the stove, whispers; "Come" and dashes out of the door. In the deserted Café, she puts her nose right up to Frits' and with a voice full of panic, she hisses; "You didn't see anything! You hear? Forget what you saw! Don't say a word to anybody! You hear? Not a word. Just forget it. I'll get the milk. Go back to the kitchen! Not a word! Promise?"

"But Mama, what are those..."

"Shut up and go back to the kitchen!"

"But Mama, if you get caught..."

"Go to the kitchen! I'll be right there!"

"Papa and you could be arrest..."

"SHUT UP AND GO!"

"But Mama..."

"GO!"

He never did find out exactly what happened. Parents didn't talk to the kids about anything political. Kids talk too much and words slip out too easily. He never found out how often people spent the night in the cellar. Apparently they were smuggled in after dark, slept right under the bar, where German soldiers drank and ate and then slipped out again the following night. He wondered what they did about bathroom problems while the customers were still upstairs. He wondered about buckets and smell and how they coped with that, but true to his promise, he never said a word about it, not even to Paul.

The SYNAGOGE, that had suffered blast damage on that sunny Sunday afternoon of the first bombardment, burned down to the ground one night.

"TORCHED!" is the word. Then one night; All the remaining Jewish families are rounded up and their belongings are hauled out of their homes.

Good "STUFF" gets shipped off and all garbage lands on the sidewalk.

The "STUFF" on the sidewalk of GUTTERMANS's clothing store is interesting. There are some partial rolls of cloth that Mama can use, some spools of thread, half to three quarters full.

Frits and Paultje are busy. They'll be late for dinner, but with all this good stuff, they're sure Mama won't mind.

Here's a box, let me open it. The tape has already been cut, so Frits pulls up one lid, then another and..."GASP.".."What is it?"

Paultje, his arms full with rolls and spools, moves closer, nearly dropping his load.

Frits digs his hands into the box and pulls out HUNDREDS OF THOUSANDS OF "REICHSMARKS!" No, not Hundreds of thousands, no; MILLIONS AND MILLIONS, BILLIONS!

They're flabbergasted.

"Paultje, listen to me. Put that stuff down right here. I'll watch it.

Put these in your pocket!" He hands him some bills. "Now run home, show these to Pappa and get him over here immediately, fast! Tell him about this box, I'll watch it!"

He seats himself on top of the box with an attitude like, "You want this box, you'll have to kill me!"

Passersby aren't paying any attention to him, but he figures, "They don't know what's in the box!" He does.

500 million Mark note

In the distance he sees Paultje running back towards him with, of all people, Joop in pursuit.

"That SCHLEMIEL, I don't want HIM! Oh, well, Maybe Pappa's tied up!"

Joop is passing Paultje with his long legs. He reaches Frits, huffing and puffing.

"Pappa says, leave that junk here and get your ass to the dinner table!"

"Are you crazy?" He jumps up, opens the box and shows Joop all his BILLIONS. "Look at this; MONEY, MONEY, MONEY, lots of MONEY!"

"It's just worthless shitpapers, come on home!"

"WORTHLESS?" He nearly collapses. "WORTHLESS? But look here!"

EIN HUNDERT TAUSEND REICHS MARK! here; "EIN MIL-LIONE!"

"Come on! It's not worth two cents!"

"O God, really? Really?" "Come here BOER" he loads Paul up again with the rolls and spools, fills his pockets with millions and walks home with them. What a terrible, terrible letdown!

"But Joop, how come?"

The answer comes at the dinner table.

"About 1934, don't hold me to the exact date, the inflation..you know, when the prices keep going up and up all the time..?? Anyway, the inflation was so bad, that prices doubled everyday. A loaf of bread could cost 10,000 mark one week and 100,000 the next, week after week. The German REICH kept printing money, trillions of marks and Hitler, who accused Jews of GOUGING, socked it to everybody by one day declaring all money invalid. Everybody could go to the bank and receive 100 NEW MARKS, so everyone started on an equal footing.

He set the price of a loaf of bread at 10 pfenning and all other products followed suit. Then he declared that anybody and everybody could go to their bank and exchange their billions of worthless money at a rate of 100.000 for one penny or some ridiculous joke like that. All they had to do is provide proof of how they'd gotten their money, like from a salary or a legitimate profit in business, like selling beer.

Well, a lot of Germans traded their money, but a lot of people ended up with a lot of colorful toilet paper."

"We lived in Belgium at the time, so I didn't follow it all that closely, but the whole idea was, to stop a runaway inflation and to catch a lot of Jews with a lot of worthless money.

I think Hitler succeeded on both counts!"

"Y

113

Here lives a Jew's servant

a," says Mama, "I remember that when we were home in WINTERSWIJK on vacation one year, that OPA and OMA would only accept silver or gold coins from Germans that came here to eat and drink. They didn't want any worthless beautiful papers either."

"I'm keeping mine, though!" adds Frits, "'cause at least I was rich for a little while!"

The belly laughs all around are worth all the disappointment.

It is strange that all of a sudden, there's no more SLAGERY BAUMAN, or BAUMAN JUNIOR. The kids have never known their street without them.

Now another butcher appears in Juniors shop and a dress shop opens in Senior's old store.

The tension between the Germans and the Dutch increases daily as more and more men are rounded up for work in Germany.

Then to cap it off, Proclamations appear everywhere announcing that all radio's have to be surrendered to a warehouse and those caught with CLANDESTINE (a new word for the boys) radios will be punished severely.

Radios of all shapes and sizes are delivered to the warehouse by handcarts, bikes and baskets. It seems to the boys that there are at least a million of them.

The Germans don't want the "HOLLANDERS" to listen to the inflammatory speeches of RADIO HOLLAND or the BBC.

Besides, it is whispered, the BBC broadcasts secret codes to the underground.

Hof Van Holland is allowed to keep its radio because it's a public place that caters to the German Forces.

So the bar, with its radio, becomes even more popular than before, if only to catch the newscasts.

The war in AFRIKA is going backwards for the Germans, but judging from their broadcasts, they are still victorious everyday.

One Saturday afternoon, (only a half-day of school) the boys saunter over to the KAMPHUIS family and meet up with Jan and Henk in front of the lady's house with the hazel tree.

"I never did get one of those branches!" Frits is thinking while he and the boys watch the commotion across the street.

There's a staff car with it's top down and two covered trucks.

A house to house search for radio's is being conducted and people are being arrested and loaded on the first truck. The confiscated radios land in the second truck.

Apparently they just started at the beginning of the block, but a strange pattern is developing; in every house that is searched, a radio is found and the head of the household gets arrested.

Within a block, the truck is full of people and the strange possession is coming to OPA's block and Frits is expecting OPA to be arrested next.

He's sure, the old bugger has a radio hidden somewhere.

Now that the truck is full, a conference takes place in front of the staff car. After some discussion, an officer gets on the car radio and while a lot of people are sweating bullets, a break in the action takes place and everybody kinda hangs around. Then there it is, something people had been expecting, a civilian type car with 4 big horns mounted on top of it, back to back. The officer gets on the mike and the loud speakers blare out his message, "You have five minutes to come out with your radio's or face arrest, just look at the truck out front."

Just about every door produces a person with a radio, sometimes two and even OPA appears with his brand new BLAUPUNKT radio.

Inspite of the seriousness of the situation, that is comical!

Frits suggests, "OPA probably shit in his pants for fear of being arrested!" and the boys are starting to enjoy this show.

What is becoming obvious is that just about everybody, except the old lady with the hazel tree, conveniently turned in their old radios, just to be on record, and kept good ones.

The men that were arrested are released later that afternoon, but they must have had some anxious moments, being used for bait.

The boys mill around, hit Mama up for LIMONADE and just sit around the table and talk.

They've been quiet lately.

First of all, being in 5th grade made a big change.

Mr. Bruinsma, the 5th grade teacher is a tall man with a booming voice. He's the lead bass singer in the choir and he is good. He also knows Frits and his reputation as FOKKIE FLINK and must be a born psychologist.

When the boys walked into his classroom for the first time, they were all set to have a bang-up year torturing the teacher like they did Mr. Raes. WRONG! Within the first minute in the classroom, Mr. Bruinsma calls over the duo and says;

"Hey fellows, look here, I have this big tank of fish here. They need to be separated into different tanks, because these fish eat their own eggs when they lay them and the males even eat their babies, when they first spawn. Now what I need are a bottom full of round or roundish pebbles, so that their eggs will fall between them and the fish can't get at them. Now, I hear that you boys are the outdoors type and I wish you'd do me a favor! Walk along those railroad tracks where you hang out and gather up as many roundish pebbles as you can gather and then you can help me set up the aquarium and you guys can kinda look after it. What do you say?"

"Why, yes, of course, right Jan?"

"We'll do it, tonight, right after school, Okay?"

"Great!"

He, Mr. Bruisma, had those boys eating out of his hand from day one. Never a speck of trouble out of them.

Some drawbacks were developing, though...PIANO LESSONS!"

"I don't want to take piano lessons! Let Joop and Clasien take piano lessons if they want, I don't want piano lessons, I want to play drums and trumpet, but no piano!" "No PIANO!"

"Get me a trumpet and I'll take lessons, I promise or I'll make a drum again! But no piano, please!"

Pappa is adamant, "When you've learned the piano and you learn to read music, you can learn any instrument you want later, but you have to learn to read notes and learn the basics! Besides, it's only a half hour per week!"

What a pain; DING, DING, DING, with your right hand, DONG, DONG, DONG, with your left hand, practice a half-hour everyday, what a pain.

What an unbelievable pain! "It interrupts everything I want to do! I hate it, I hate it, what a pain!"

The sound of music brings them scurrying around the front of the building. It's the N.S.B. marching band. The N.S.B. (National Socialistische Beweging) is a part, apparently of the N.S.N.A.P., the Dutch NAZI's.

They're wearing their black uniforms with armbands, boots, German style, and carrying lots of flags and banners.

A group of thirty, carrying banners are out front with the HOOMPAH marching band behind them.

First the boys follow them a ways, while the band plays, *LAATJE-KUTZIENAZIENAZIEN, LAATJEKUTZIEN.* Now the boys fall in step behind the band, along with some other neighborhood boys, singing, *"LAATJEKUTZIENAZIENAZIEN, LAATJEKUTZIEN,"* while pitching balls of paper into the tuba. *ABOOMABOOMABOOMABOOM,* goes the drum, *APOOH APOOH APOOH* goes the tuba. The boys are having a ball marching behind them.

When the band strikes up the German SCHLAGER "ERIKA," they sing the Dutch version at the top of their lungs.

"BLONDE MIENTJE HEEFT EEN HART VAN PRIKKELDRAAD."

They wave at the people on the sidewalk who, smilingly, take in the scene. There goes a sharp, well disciplined, marching unit with a bunch of ragamuffins behind it, having a ball!

UNTIL THE NEXT DAY!"

When Frits reports upstairs in church to sing High Mass at 10 o'clock, he's informed that he's been dismissed from the choir for being guilty of sympathizing with the enemy.

He doesn't even stay for Mass.

"Can you believe that?" he asks his Pap.

Pappa is irate, "I'm pulling everyone out of Catholic school, that bunch of hypocrites! They preach, GOD LOVES EVERYBODY, but they can HATE when they please, that bunch of bastards. I'm telling you. What's the crime? A bunch of little kids having fun with a parade! That's sympathizing with the enemy? What kind of narrow-minded people run that show? Anyway, don't worry about it, go play! Change clothes first!"

"But Pappa, I don't wanna change schools, I.."

"We'll talk about it later, go change your clothes!"

"Darn, darn, darn! I really like to sing, darn it!"

He wanders off by himself. Paultje is still in church, so he meanders over to the garage just past the split in the road, BORKUM-BOCHOLT.

The garage used to be an active garage for WALHOF-TOURS repairing and maintaining busses, but the busses are long gone and the Germans are using it for a repair shop.

It being Sunday, everyone is taking it easy and in back of the building, a bunch of soldiers are lying in the grass. Two other ones are doing something out further in the yard and when he hears a loud bang, he investigates. Two fairly young airmen in greasy overalls are having some innocent fun and now they're teaching Frits.

"You need an ordinary round tin can with a push-in lid, knock a whole in the bottom with a small nail, you need carbide...Water...and matches, that's all."

"CARBIDE?"

"You know what that is. Carbide lamps? Welding torches?"

"Oh Ya!" He's seen the stuff, it comes in 55 gallon drums and it's actually nothing but soft grayish-white rock.

It's innocent and harmless, you can actually hold it in your hand, until it gets wet, then it starts boiling, it'll burn right through your hand. The important thing is that it releases a gas when wet. That gas is what gives that white, hot flame.

Oh, yes, he's seen those carbide lamps hanging on carriages instead of oil lamps that give a yellow light.

"Right, now come here! See that can?" It's a two-pound EGBERTS coffee can. "See, there's still a little left in it, but lets add some more carbide!" Two pieces, about $1^1/_2$ inches square, some water, put the lid on tight, "Right!" Frits hammers it tight with his wooden shoe. "GUT, Schön! Now lay it down, don't hold it. Put your foot on it, tight, hold it down tight. Aim it in a safe direction; See..the gas is starting to blow out. Okay! Here's a match, don't hold your hand in front of the hole, just the match. You'd burn your hand to a crisp. O.K. GO!"

Frits lights the match, lowers it toward the hole and...KABOOM! It's so instantaneous, so fast that Frits nearly jumps 5 feet high.

The soldiers just double up with laughter; "You should have seen that face!" "I didn't know anybody could jump that high!" HAHAHAHA!

Frits recovers fast. The lid landed against the fence, some 60 feet away and the can itself flew about 10 feet in the opposite direction.

"I told you to hold it down tight," laughs one soldiers, "you might hurt someone or yourself!"

"Okay! Okay!" "Lets do it again."

His heart rate had jumped a hundred beats a minute, but is getting back to normal. They shoot it a few more times and now Frits is controlling it better. This is fun. It sounds like shooting off a cannon; "KABOOM," it works every time.

Of course he can have some carbide; "But watch how you carry it.

Don't have it touch your clothes, even a little, little residue, like wiping your hands your pants, will burn holes in it, when your Mama puts 'em in the wash! And when you wanna keep carbide, you have to keep it in a dry, airtight container or otherwise it loses its PIZZAZ!"

"Here, take a paper bag, don't let it get wet. Ya! You can take the can, we've got more! Have fun!"

What swell guys! "DANKE SCHÖN, DANKE!"

"HAHAHA, you should have seen that face!"

"Boer, come here!" the voice comes from the corner of the yard, near the aviary. "Here, back here!"

"What are you doing back here? What's that? What are you doing?"

"Listen, don't be scared. When you hear a loud bang, don't be scared! Now listen! Get Joop. Tell 'em I need to see him, Okay? When you come back out, run off to the side somewhere, Okay? Go get him and Boer, keep a straight face!"

Paultje's off and Frits gets his cannon set up. He has a water pitcher with him. Good crystal, (Mama would kill him), and has himself all organized while the other Forrers were still in church, listening to the choir without Frits.

The match ready for striking, he watches the Boer running out and off to the side. The door opens again and here comes Joop the "dope."

"FRITS!" he hollers and "KABOOM!" Joop jumps back as if he was snakebit. "HE JUST GOT SHOT AT!"

Frits is rolling in the grass from laughing so hard and Paultje, after getting over his shock, starts laughing with him.

"You bastard! You damn bastard, you could have killed me, I'm telling Pappa!" Joop makes an about-face and still laughing, Frits retrieves his lid. It missed Joop by ten feet, but it scared the piss out of him! HAHAHA!

Here comes Pappa, but he doesn't look mad.

"Frits, let me see what you got!"

Frits explains how it works and Pap is going to try it.

"Hold it down tight with your foot! Don't get your hand in front of the hole, you'll burn it!"

"KABOOM" Pappa must have jumped six foot high, it was much louder than he expected and it happened so fast, he hardly got the match near the hole and KABOOM!

The boys are rolling in the grass, including Joop.

"YOU SHOULD HAVE SEEN HIM JUMP!"

Herman now sees the humor in it too and all four of them are laughing their heads off as they go find the lid so they can do it again and again.

"Ya Joop, you can do it too, but don't aim at anybody, promise?"

Herman disappears back into the Café and some of his customers come out to get a demonstration or try to it out themselves.

The "KABOOMS" don't stop until Mama hollers, "DINNER'S ON THE TABLE!"

"OUR FATHER, WHO ART IN HEAVEN…" it's a peaceful scene.

Life changes constantly.

Now, each morning, seven days a week, either Joop or Frits has to get on a bike with a two-liter milkcan dangling from the handlebars, cycle to a farm 12 kilometers out, to get fresh milk.

Everything is rationed and is harder to come by. Two liters of warm milk, directly from the cow is a delicious addition to their meals.

The farmer, Piet Bolding, is a big jovial guy who has inherited an immense property from his parents.

His old father still lives with them and can be seen making his way around the farm with a cane.

Frits learns how to milk, although he has to get up at 4 in the morning to get in on that, and that doesn't happen that often.

The one making the "milkrun" can't make church in the morning and normally, "missing" would have been considered a blessing. (Sounds sacrilegious, doesn't it?"), but Frits is being prepared for his confirmation next year and he needs to make Mass and Holy Communion at least on Fridays and definitely on the first Friday of the month. Friday is the day of the SACRED HEART and a novena, "Confession and Communion" on nine consecutive First Fridays, will guarantee him a permanent seat in HEAVEN on the right side of GOD. He's learning all this in Catechism, once a week for an hour.

"MIJNHEER KAPELAAN," (a different one) teaches Bible, Religion, Liturgy and Catechism, the interpretation of God's laws.

Frits is duly impressed, he commits fewer sins, that he never saw as sins and has a hard time accepting as sins.

To Mr. Bruinsma, he has become a star pupil, attentive, on time, eager to help, in good spirits at all times and an enthusiastic member of the class choir and the harmonica team.

He carries his little HOHNER harmonica in his pocket at all times along with his ever-present knife.

Some things, that some people frown upon as "sins," can easily be reasoned away if you're good at interpreting the Bible. For instance, "Stealing from the Germans is not really stealing, it's taking back what they stole from us in the first place."

His conscience is so clear on that subject that he doesn't even consider confessing it. All in all, he's being very good, probably the best he's been all his life.

Nightly bombardments happen infrequently, but the air raid alarm goes off nearly night after night. Most of the time bombers just cruise overhead on their way to the "RUHRGEBIET" that's getting a pounding on a near daily basis.

The SONDERMELDUNGS tell about planes being shot down by the droves and they do get to watch some shot down or burning with fair regularity during their nightly vigils.

"ANTOON, ANTOON, FLIEGER ALARM!" has become a standard phrase in the household and on this particular night, they're sitting in the kitchen, as Joop goes up for the second time to knock on the door of KAMER I, "ANTOON, ANTOON, FLIEGER ALARM!"

Antoon's parents are in the kitchen too. They're in their eighties and have been evacuated from their home, south of the tracks.

All homes within a half-mile from the tracks are now empty, because the "PRECISION BOMBING" is still not too precise.

Frits wonders if these people ever bathe. He doesn't think they've been out of their underwear in six months.

He's been in their dark little house and like most European homes of that time, there's no shower or bath and he thinks the house smells of death. He thinks their bodies are already dying even though they're still moving.

Now, they're all sitting in the kitchen, sipping cocoa-milk with not a sound in the sky. But...it will come...it always does.

The early warning system has become very efficient.

The monotonous roar of the airplanes starts with a soft HUMMM in the distance. "There they come!"

The powerful engines, four per aircraft, start droning with a thunderous kind of roar, that nearly makes the windows rattle.

"DOA KOMT ZE DAN!" Mevrouw Brummelstroete is telling her husband in her "PLATT" dialect that sounds like German.

"IK HEUR NIKS," he comes back. The aircraft are really loud now,

"HEUR DAN, HEUR DAN!"

"Ik heur niks!"

"OH, ie, ie, ie heurt nog niks als ie ne bom op'n kop kriegt!"

"You wouldn't hear a bomb when it hit you in the head!"

Uproarious laughter by everyone cut short by..."YEEET!"
"YEEEET!"

"Under the stairs, quick!"

"BOOM...BOOOM...KABOOM...YEEET..KABOOM..the explosions are further away now and the "MEN" dash into the backyard.

GOOD GOD!" There's fire all over, even close by, across the street somewhere.

"IT'S THE BAKERY, MAYBE BEHIND THE BAKERY!"

They rush out of the yard, across the street into the alley, Herman shouting over his shoulder, "Go back, Get buckets!"

Joop and Antoon turn around, Frits stays right on his Father's heels.

The baker is in his backyard, his wife standing in the doorway.

"Get out of here, go to Ida, GO, GO!"

The woman disappears, presumably to run out her front door to the Hof Van Holland.

The baker is spraying water with a garden hose on his burning shed and buckets are appearing from everywhere.

It's a hopeless process, buckets are filled at a neighbors faucet, passed along and thrown on the fire. It's like carrying water to the sea, it makes no difference.

"HOSE YOUR HOUSE DOWN! KEEP YOUR HOUSE WET!"

The baker obliges, he looks like he wants to cry.

The sky is aglow with fires all over and no fire truck is in sight.

There are two fire trucks in the district and there must be a hundred fires.

Otto and Herman are working side by side, passing buckets.

At a time like this, all animosity is forgotten for the good of the community cause.

The wooden fence around the baker's property is busted down on both sides, for easier access to the neighbor's water and the darn thing was burning anyway.

Another "drone" starts approaching from the west, More bombers..

"Frits, run home, stay there, tell Mama to make a lot of coffee! NOW, I said NOW!"

Frits takes off reluctantly. This is better than a BONFIRE.

A few men remain with the baker, who seems in a daze, alternately spraying his house and then the flames again. This time, the planes fly over without dropping anything and Frits reappears again and so do the others, one by one.

The ALL-CLEAR finally sounds as the sun tries to crawl up the horizon and the shed is finally burned down.

The baker cries without tears, "I'm ruined, all my stuff was in there, now I can't bake, I'm ruined."

The men lead him away, he's like a lamb. They're taking him to the Café for some coffee and Cognac and a reunion with his family.

He's still sobbing. Someone says, "He's in shock, get a Doctor!"

Frits is now the sole possessor of the hose and although the water pressure has dropped considerably, he's still enthusiastically dousing the smoldering ashes. It's fun, it makes steam shhhsshhsh, as he hits those glowing embers.

"Let me do it a while?" begs Joop, but not until the craving for hot cocoa out-craves the craving for playing with fire, does he hand Joop the hose and trots home.

He hits the sack exhausted, as the sun is high in the sky already.

He should be heading for the farm on his milkrun, but his folks don't even wake him till the noon dinner.

The bar is crowded and the conversation is about only one subject; the air raid. Now he learns the reasons why there were no bomb craters or busted windows at the bakers this morning.

The bombs that were dropped were incendiary bombs, "PHOSPHOR BOMBS," phosphor, as in matches, you expose it to the air and it starts burning. Very dangerous stuff. Invented by "NOBEL," Joop tells him, "Remember that Swedish scientist?" Doesn't mean a thing.

The center of attention is a bomb that one of the customers brought in. He's with the SIEGERHEIDDIENST, he works with the Germans.

Ida nearly got hysterical, "A bomb in the house was a bit much!"

They assured her it was O.K...

She's in the kitchen now, still shaking.

The bomb is a weird one, it doesn't look like a bomb at all.

It's about 14 inches long and about two inches wide. One half is black metal and the other, shiny brass.

"That's a bomb?" "Where are the fins, where's the detonator?"

The thing doesn't make any sense! The fact remains though, that it caused a lot of fires all over town, smoke is still hanging in the air. The newspapers estimate that 100 Thousand-pounders have been dropped and at least 1000 "BRANDBOMMEN," incendiaries.

Of course, no strategic target anywhere nearby, only "women and children!"

The good thing is, school is closed; one of the bombs landed in the school yard and burned down part of a Linden tree and the school is being searched for duds or time bombs. It's starting to hit close to home!

Frits still has to go "Melk halen" and as he gets out his mothers bike he asks Paul, "Boer, do you wanna come?" and as the Boer climbs aboard, Frits says, "We might as well make the most of it!"

Phosphor bombing by the British

CHAPTER VII
Spring 1943

It's been a bitter winter.

Not so much the total snowfalls and the freezing temperature, but the wet, bone-chilling winter storms coming off the NORTH SEA.

Mama has gotten hold of a roll of black corduroy and all the boys now have riding-britches made of corduroy. It sure beats bare knees in this kind of weather.

The worst storm was on Frits' birthday, November 14. It was a regular GALE and it knocked down the aviary and all the birds were gone, including the peacock and the gold pheasants.

That aviary had been there for thirty years. Gone, all gone.

If only there had been a hard frost, they could have gone skating, but no, some frost, some snow, but generally lousy, stinking conditions.

Making the daily trip to the farm for milk was a bone chilling, soaking chore. No fun at all, but they did it.

It also made them play at home more and they sat around and sang songs a lot. Piano lessons and practice were still a cross to bear for Frits and he managed to make no progress whatsoever.

Joop and Clasien were doing alright, but to just sit there and do finger practices all the time was a drag. He has been on page 7 for two months now. The teacher, Mr. Youngblood,(Jongbloed) only puts up with him because he gets paid and he'd lose three students if he kicked Frits out.

Spring is nearly as miserable as the fall, rain, rain and more rain. Bare trees and grayish landscapes, it's depressing.

Just one Sunday the sun is out and sure as hell, so are the bombers. Now they are Americans. They are not interested in Winterswijk; they fly way high, barely visible, mostly just contrails all over the sky.

Joop says they're B-17's. Heaven knows where he gets his intelligence.

The pattern has become: Yanks bombs during the day, Tommies at night.

That particular Sunday, the Yanks, while bombing the RUHR valley, flatten a luxurious suburb of ESSEN, called GELSENKIRCHEN and leave thousands homeless. Some will be housed in Winterswijk.

"Hey guys, have you seen the new neighbors?" "The ones that moved into young Bauman's house?"

The house had been empty since their unexpected trip.

Frits is clueing in Jan and Henkie. "They ate in the EETZAAL, this afternoon, I saw them myself. His name is Dr. Hans Stein and his son is also Hans Stein, he is nine and Ursula is ten. They're from Gelsenkirchen or someplace like that.

Pappa says they're famous for horse races and they have a little boy, I forgot his name and I forgot the mother's name and they don't speak any Dutch at all and they'll be going to the Deutsche SCHULE and they have a neat wagon and a real soccer ball."

"A real one?"

"Yeah, like in regular competition. And they have roller-skates, you should see them and an AUTOPED, a scooter, and..and...you wanna go over?"

How could anyone say no after such an introduction?

Off they go, the jolly foursome, two in wooden shoes, and two in high quarters.

At the STEIN house, they encounter Dr. Stein first. He's handing something through the front window. They're cleaning.

"WIE GEHTST, DOKTER STEIN? SIE MÜSSEN MAL ZUM DOK-TER GEHEN, HERR DOKTER!

DAS KANN YA SO NIGHT WEITER GEHEN, HERR DOKTER!" Frits sings him the first few lines of a popular German song. Which makes Dr. Stein break out in a hearty laugh.

"Können wir helfen?" The kids speak German as easily as their native tongue by now.

"Nee, danke!" He says; "NEE" instead of the proper German "NEIN." Must be his peculiar dialect.

"Kann Hans 'rausch kommen?"

"Doch!"

Apparently, young Hans can be spared and he comes out after his dad calls him. He's a lanky kid with the same dirty-blonde kind of hair as Joops and just as straight. Frits does the introductions and they're invited to the backyard, where they get to admire all the "stuff" Hans has received recently. They had been in a bombshelter when the bombs hit and their house was reduced to rubble. Apparently, in Germany people don't sit under the stairs during an air raid, they hide in shelters. Since they had nothing left, his

Frits   Hedwig Herman Joop   Ida   Clasien
Paul

daddy bought him all new "stuff" before leaving Germany because most of the items would be hard to come by in Holland.

He's very correct! This kid, Hans, has more toys all by himself than the two Dutch families combined. At least, Hans knows how to share.

"MUTTI" comes out back, recognizes Frits from the restaurant and gets introduced all around. She talks kinda funny and when asked, she explains; "Ich bin von BAYERN and mein Mann ist von NIEDER-SAXON. We speak in more melodious tones."

STEIN joins them in the backyard and asks if they would like something to drink and of course the boys will drink anything, hot or cold.

"Kommen Sie d'rin!"

In the kitchen there's no place to sit yet, but at least, it's warmer.

The other boys get to meet Ursula for the first time. She's younger than Frits or Jan, but she's taller and very pretty.

She could be a poster-girl for a typical "HEIDI" picture.

With her blue eyes and blonde braids, she could put a moviestar to shame.

Jan can't keep his eyes off her and he's not supposed to like girls!

She also has a very nice disposition and her warm smile makes the boys feel as if they've known her for years. "WOW"

Back outside, they get to try out the scooter (AUTOPED) and then into the meadow behind "WALHOF" for some soccer with a real SOCCERBALL!

Rain cuts it all short, so, exhausted but happy, everyone retreats to their respective homes.

The relationship with the STEINS is great, but Dr. Stein has returned to work in Germany and FRAU Stein wont let Hans go roaming far from home, like the foursome does, so the friendship with Hans becomes one of convenience. When they're around home they play with him and as such, Frits learns how to roller-skate.

"That's what I want for my birthday, Mam! Roller-skates!"

Clasien and Ursula become good buddies and they can nearly always be found together at the Stein or the Forrer house. They get along beautifully.

Because the weather is still much too cold for swimming, they climb the fence at the swimmingpool, just to check out the scenery.

It's not the same without the sun and all the leaves on the trees, but just strolling the docks gives them a feeling of getting a headstart on summer.

They circle the lake that makes up the swimmingpool and when they reach the creek, they follow the little "BEEK" downstream toward the castle and the BEKKENDELLE, the amusement park. The creek widens some because of the dam up ahead at the old watermill and the giant weeping willows line the banks on both sides. The water is pitch black and reflects the low hanging branches like a mirror. In another month, the willows will be green and the rhododendrons will add their luster to this beautiful garden spot. A little piece of paradise. The owner of the amusement park will again put out his rowboats and canoes and the scene will resemble the best of the RENOIR paintings.

Now, all is still quiet and peaceful until...."WHAT WAS THAT?"

"A SHOT?"

"No,that was not a shot,unless it was a small cannon or something. Be still a moment!"

"Boom!" There it goes again. "It's not a bomb! It' more of a BAM than a BOOM and it's behind the watermill!"

Off they are! As fast as their legs can carry them they race over, under and through bushes until they hit the trail, the lovers lane. Then by the restaurant and behind the watermill, where they stop. A LUFTWAFFE truck is parked by the side of the "KOLK," the pond that's formed by the falling waters of the dam and the watermill. A couple of soldiers are on both sides of the creek that flows out of the pond, scooping up fish. They're doing alright! The guy on the right already has seven or eight sizable fish at his side and is scooping up more. It's a very peaceful scene, so; what were the explosions?

They come out of hiding, start to close in on one of the fishermen, when the KRAUT on the other sides climbs the bank and hollers;

"ZURÜCK, ZURÜCK!" "Get back!"

They retreat behind the truck and peer underneath it to see what he's going to do.

He does nothing. His net and bucket is still down on the little beach and he just stands on the far bank. Nothing! Just stands there!

A little splash catches their attention as if somebody threw a fish back in the water or a rock or........."BOOM," a fountain rises out of the middle of the pond like a volcano and startles the hell out of the boys!

Fish are surfacing and start floating downstream. The Germans descend back down to the waters edge and start scooping up the fish with their nets and dump them in their buckets.

The boys approach the soldier on their side and ask;

"Is this the way you fish in Germany?"

He laughs, "Maybe not in Germany, but that's the way we do it here!"

His buddy on the other side is climbing the bank again and satisfied with the catch of the day, comes around the pond across the bridge over the waterfall, carrying his net and bucket of fish.

They whip out knives, expertly clean the fish and throw entrails and heads back into the water.

"How do you do that "BOOM?," they wanna know.

"Well, the explosion, the compression, kills the fish, they float to the top and we scoop 'em up!"

"But what do you explode in the water?"

"Oh...."HANDGRANATEN" he shows one.

"That's a handgrenade? I thought they were long! I've seen them on soldiers and I've seen them in the newsreels at the movies and they..."

"These are EIERGRANATEN"

They indeed look like eggs, but are even bigger than goose eggs.

"WOW! How do you work them? When they hit the water, they explode?"

"NO..NO, NO...you pull this pin and then it explodes in 7 seconds. So, I pull the pin, count 21, 22, throw it, 24, hits water, 26 and BOOM!"

Wow, this is awesome! "I can't wait till I'm big and become a soldier, this is living, this is the life!"

"Ya, das ist Ya ein schönes leben!"

The soldiers laugh at their enthusiasm, give them a fish each, not their big ones. They finish their cleaning and go down the bank to wash out their nets and buckets.

After they wash their hands, they come back up, load up and are off.

The boys just stand there staring after the truck, holding their fish, in awe of what they've just seen.

"LOOK WHAT I GOT!" Frits unzips his windbreaker.

"EIERGRANATEN" he says. He's got three of them.

"Oh, no!, how'd you get 'em? Throw 'em away! You're not gonna explode 'em, are you? Throw them away!"

Their reaction surprises him. Usually, they're not scaridy cats.

"What's the matter? They're harmless until you pull the pin! See?"

He reaches for one. Paultje's running, crying, "I'm going home, I'm scared!"

"BOER, come back!" but Paul stays where he is, half hidden behind the wall of the watermill house.

"We are not going fishing with these things?" Jan is resolute.

"Get rid of them. NOW! They may come back! I'm leaving, come Henk, let's get out of here!" He pulls his brother with him, although Henkie would rather have stayed and "FISHED," Frits can read it in his face.

"Okay..Okay.. you bunch of chickens, wait for me, I'll get rid of them!"

He walks in the direction in which the truck went, away from the boys, till he sees a drainpipe that empties out in the creek. He climbs down the bank, digs an opening underneath the pipe, hides his grenades and tucks them in with dirt.

After crawling up the bank, he catches up with his buddies, "I just put them in the water slowly, I didn't want to throw them!"

To himself, he says, "One day soon, I'm going fishing!!"

The chance came sooner than he thought.

At school, the next day during a break, Jan approaches him, "You didn't really throw those grenades away, did you?"

"How did you know?"

"I know you, you hid them, right?"

"Boy, you do know me!" They both burst out laughing!

Jan has him pegged to a tee; "I sure do and last night with Paultje panicking and crying, it just was not a good time to play with hand grenades. Besides that, if these kids ever, somehow would get a hold of one of these things, they might forget all instructions and blow themselves to bits. So I thought some older, wiser and more experienced people like you and I should go on a fishing expedition!" "Hahahahah!"

"Hahaha! You sound more and more like your old man, do you know that?" "When do we go?"

"I thought Saturday if the weather is lousy, like yesterday, cause then there won't be any people around there!"

"Alright, Saturday!"

On Saturday, the weather is absolutely stinko and they get soaked, just making it home from school.

After dinner, Jan shows up in old clothes, without Henkie, "Cause we have a job to do for Mr. Bruisma's aquarium!"

"You mean, Mr. Wolters, right?" Joop butts in.

"No, I mean Bruinsma, we still do things with him even if he's not our teacher anymore!" Joop is too nosy!

Out the door they go, direction; SCHOOL, but once out of sight, they detour back.

"Do you have your knife?" "Yep"

"Do you have towels?" "Yep," "Unfortunately, they're both good towels, but I couldn't get to anything old without arousing suspicion."

"We'll have to wash 'em somehow before we get them back home and into the laundry basket. Did you have any luck with nets?"

"No, I didn't know where to start looking!"

"I don't' know either, what'll we do?"

"We could cut some branches and tie our towels to them, somewhat like a net!"

"Tie them with what? Did you bring anything?"

They're marching along at a good clip. They're halfway there already.

"I'll tell you what, we throw the grenades in, one after the other, I'll stand in the water, pitch the fish to you and we're gone!"

"We better work from the other side then, because that has a little beach to work with!"

"Right, we'll need a 2 X 4 or a branch or something, cause it's probably deep on the far side and I'll need something to pull the fish toward me!"

"Next time, we need to bring a rope!"

"Wait a minute, I know where to get rope, let's go by Piet Streek and get some!"

"Who's STREEK?"

"How long have you been in this town? Nearly two years and you've never heard of Piet Streek? Come on?"

It's just a little detour and they're in front of "P.S. GRAAN nv"

"That's STREEK?"

"Yep, here's where they grind wheat into flour, and here we'll find what we came for!"

"Hi, Mr. Streek, can we have some rope?"

"SURE!" He has his hands full, he and his helper are holding a big 100 lb. bag under a chute. Streek steps on a lever, the chute vomits 100 pounds of flour into the bag, he folds over the top and slides it through a machine that throws staples into it and moves the bag over to a neat row of other full bags. He reaches for another empty bag, holds it under the chute, step on the lever and soon...

Frits and Jan stuff their pockets with pieces of string from a heap and with a "TJU," they're on their way again.

As they're marching along, Frits pulls out a few strings, that are all about 4 feet long, and starts tying them together, while explaining, "We have to tie these into a long rope!"

"Where do these come from and why are they cut so short and doesn't he need them?"

"When the farmers bring in their gunny sacks with grain..."

"What are gunny sacks?"

"JUTE, like those that potatoes come in!"

"OH!"

"Anyway, the farmers stitch those sacks closed with big crooked needles and these strings and they stitch 'em in such a way that both ends stick up like Mule's EARS, so they can carry those sacks! They grab those ears and swing the sack on their shoulders and they're off."

"Oh, ya, I've seen that!"

"Now, Mr. Streek pulls out the strings and, since he doesn't need them anymore, so he throws them in a pile, the farmers can pick 'em up and re-use them again instead of buying a new roll every time. But anyone is welcome to them!"

"How long should our ropes be?"

"Lets tie about 5 apiece, that'll give us about 15 foot lengths!"

"I still don't understand what we're going to do with all this rope!"

"You'll see, now we need some lumber!"

They're in luck. As they snoop around in back of the little amusement park behind the restaurant, they find some discarded old lumber and at Frits' direction, they select the three longest pieces.

They are soaking wet, Frits hopes that they'll still float.

"Hey, Jan, if they don't float, pull 'em to the surface when I tell you!"

"I still don't understand, what you're going to do!"

"You'll see! Let's tie these poles together end to end. Securely, Okay? Now, a rope at each end! Okay! Let's look for a good spot!"

"Here..the little tree..alright...I'm going down to tie this up. You hand me the BALKEN one by one, this one first!"

Streek's grain mill

He slides down the bank, ties the string that's attached to the first BALK, board, to the little tree. "Let her come slowly…!"

Jan lets it slide down easily and Frits lays it down and folds the second one on top of it and the third one on top of that in the same direction as the first one. They're stacked neatly along the water's edge.

"Don't let go of this string!" He crawls up the bank, ties another 60 additional feet of string to it and says, "I need a rock or a brick or something. That'll do…!" He found a half a brick and ties that to the end and orders, "Listen Jan, you run to the other side of the pond and I'll throw the brick to you on that little beach. Then wait till I'm down with my BALKEN again. Then I'll feed the boards as you pull them in slowly, so they won't get tangled. When you got them pulled tight you move over to that bottle, see it?…then we'll have the boards at an angle to the waterflow Okay? Then wait till I get there!"

"WAIT…WAIT," "I'm first going back to the restaurant, I'm gonna take my clothes off. Oh here, take these towels, one's for the fish and one's for me, keep 'em dry!"

"You're going to strip?"

"Sure am, I'll hide 'em in a dry spot and only put my raincoat on, then I'll run over, dig up the grenades and run over to your side!"

133

"We'll throw them in, one after the other, then we wait for the fish and if our barrier works right, the fish should be floating to our beach.

If necessary, I hit the water and grab the fish, toss 'em to you and we're off! Okay?" "GO!

Jan races to the other side of the KOLK and half falls, half stumbles down the bank and Frits throws him the brick with the string attached.

As soon as Frits is down by the water again, ready to handle the boards, Jan starts pulling in the string ever so slowly as Frits feeds in the boards one by one. The end result is a string of wooden boards angling across the creek at about 45 degrees.

Frits runs off to shed his clothes while Jan neatly rolls the string around the brick until it's real tight. With one hand he holds the brick, while digging a hole in the sand with the other. When it's deep enough he buries the brick and secures it with lots of sand, neatly compacted. It holds, great. He sees Frits streaking by, bare feet and raincoat flapping, he looks over his handy work and smiles with contentment.

He can see Frits go down the bank in the distance near a drainpipe and then racing back, disappearing briefly behind the old millhouse and presently sliding down to the beach, totally out of breath.

He looks at Jan's barrier, secured neatly and says, "Oh good, come up here!"

He's glad Jan has the barrier tied down, so he can be up here with him on the bank rather than down by the water, when those things explode.

It keeps right on drizzling, but that is good. No one is crazy enough to come out here on a day like this.

Frits asks, "You wanna do one?"

"No thanks, maybe later!"

"I'll throw the first one far, as soon as it goes KABOOM, I throw the next one in the DRAAIKOLK, the WHIRLPOOL, and the last one straight ahead. Are we ready? Where's the towel?"

"In my belt. Let's go!"

"No one around?? Here she goes!"

Frits pulls the pin, throws the grenade as far as he can, it goes down with a PLOEP and...and..NOTHING...NOTHING!

"What was that? Why doesn't it go BOOM? How long is 7 seconds? Why doesn't it KABOOM?"

"Do you know what I think?"

"Ya Jan, what do you think?"

"Remember the guy said, EIN UND ZWANZIG, ZWEI UND ZWAN-ZIG, he held it in his hand for two seconds before he threw it. I think that thing was in the water too many seconds and the water may have extinguished whatever makes it POP."

"Oh boy, Holy shit! I have to stand here with that thing in my hands for two whole seconds?"

His heart is already in his throat and his pulse is racing a mile a minute from the tension.

"Oh boy, I think you're right. How long is 7 seconds? Count it out for me!"

"Twenty-one, twenty-two, twenty-three, twenty-four, twenty-five, twenty-six, twenty-seven BOOM."

Frits sighs a sigh of relief. "That's pretty long, you're sure?"

"Okay, you get behind that tree!" Trembling, nearly chickening out. "Are those fish really worth it?"

"OH, HELL...GO!" He pulls the pin, "Een en twintig, twee en twintig," and heaves it, not quite as far this time. It hits the water and...KABOOM, there goes the water fountain! WOW! It's at least twenty feet high!

"Yippee!" "Here goes the other one!" Pull, EEN EN TWINTIG, TWEE EN TWINTIG..toss, ploomp, KABOOM, another fountain!!!!

FANTASTIC...FANTASTIC! "The towel!"

They rush to the water's edge. There comes the fish....Frits wades in... Too deep!!!! He gets back, throws off his coat and in his bare butt, he wades back in order to help steer the fish in Jan's direction.

The wind is cold, the rain is cold, but the water is freezing cold.

He can hardly catch his breath, the cold is like a giant pair of pliers squeezing his chest. But, they get most of the fish.

He rushes ashore, "The towel, the towel!" His teeth are shattering, a fast dry-down, towel around his waist, raincoat on...up the bank and they're gone.

Behind the restaurant, under the overhang of the shed, he dries his frozen body as best he can, gets back in his clothes and while his teeth are still clattering, they head for home. Grossly satisfied.

While Frits was drying himself, Jan took inventory, "We have eighteen!"

"Great catch, let's jog, so I can get warm. Eighteen, you said? Not bad!"

"Where are we going to clean them?"

"Wherever it's warm!" "How about the kitchen?"

"What about the towels?" He slows down. "Oh Jeez, the lousy towels! I forgot about them, what are we going to carry them home in and how do I get these towels clean, without anybody knowing it, damnit!"

Everything went so smooth, but now they're stuck with fishy smelling towels.

Jan has solutions, "I know. Don't worry, here, hold the other ends and lets carry them between us, they are getting heavy. We're going to my house!"

"Your house?"
"Yep!"

"Hi mother!" Hi, Mrs. Kamphuis!" "Hi boys!" "Oh, hi Henkie!"
"What do you boys have in that towel?"
"Mother, we have some fish, that we want to clean in the shed and.."
"No, no, no, bring them in here, we'll clean them in the sink. You boys are soaked, go sit by the hearth and dry out, I'll make some cocoa. You kids will catch colds, I swear. Here are some towels, dry yourself good, Frits hang your coat on the rack, it'll be dry by the time you have to go home!"
"Where'd you get the fish?"
"Oh Mrs. Kamphuis, they're actually my fish, but I told Jan he could have some!" (Jan never lies to his mother)
"You boys get warm in there, I'll clean the fish. Whose towels are these? Yours, Frits? You can't take them home like this, I'll soak them and then I'll wash 'em on Monday and on Tuesday you can take them back home, Okay?"
"Here's the cocoa, enjoy! I'll have them done in a jiffy, the head and guts I put on the bulbs I planted last week, It's good for them!"
"You have eighteen here, how many are yours? Jan? How about eight? Frits, then you have ten, you have a larger family. I'll wrap them up nice for you, these are nice fish…tatatatata " Boy, can she talk.

Jan and Frits are sitting in front of the hearth, soaking up the heat, both hands wrapped around their cocoa cups. They grin at one another, their eyes saying, "Do you believe this?"
Henkie, leaning over to them whispers, "YOU DID, DIDN'T YOU?"
"DID WHAT?"

As spring warms up, so do outdoor activities.
"DOELTRAPPEN" is one of them. Shooting goals by kicking the ball between "goalposts," consisting of some folded jackets or wooden shoes.
While the rest try to score on him, the "goalie" dives left and right, trying to prevent it. Regular soccer games can only be organized if there are enough guys, like four or five on each team.
Tennis balls are the usual balls available, but the addition of Hans Stein to the neighborhood, complete with soccer ball, has added real class to the sports. He's not available though. The stupid DEUTSCHE SCHULE that he attends gives "HOMEWORK!" real HOMEWORK! Who wants to go to a school like that?
One day after school, a hearty game of soccer is under way. Wooden shoes form the goalposts, the EELINKSTRAAT is the soccer field, and the sidelines are the fenced-in yards on both sides.

The game moves both on and off the sidewalk, it doesn't matter, and the boys are into the game, hot and heavy.

This type of activity can be found in every town and village in Europe. Where there are kids, there's soccer.

Every so often, the ball lands in someone's yard and one of the boys will clear the fence and retrieve it, carefully avoiding the flowerbeds, if at all possible. The ball is put back in play and on goes the kicking, the running, the screaming and the laughing...."YOUTH IN ACTION, TO THE HILT"

On one side, the whole length of the soccer field consists of a six foot high chicken wire fence. Behind the fence are chickens. OPA KWAK's chickens.

Sometimes, rarely, but sometimes, a ball will land in his chicken coop. Little feet, that fit right in the mesh of the chicken wire, are up, over and back with the ball in just seconds, no sweat. Until today.

At the height of some exciting action, a pass is returned across the "field." TOO high! Into the chicken coop.

OPA appears instantly, grabs the ball, walks out of the coop, locks the gate and disappears into the house.

"THAT OLD CREEP!" He must have been hiding in the henhouse.

The boys look at Frits. "Do something, he's your OPA!"

"ME?" Frits hasn't talked to him for months, maybe a year.

"He won't listen to me. You better try!"

"NO, no, Frits, get our ball back!"

Well, he gets an earful after ringing the doorbell.

About: how we damage his fence by climbing it, how he would gladly retrieve the ball, if we only asked, he was once young too. No, he was not giving the ball back, he was giving it to the Chief of Police, who lives down the street.

The deflated boys are sitting on the curb, cussing the old geezer in many different tones.

"Let's see if Hans can come out!"

Up come the "wooden-shoe-goalposts" and around the corner trots the group of ten "soccer-players" of the future.

Well, Hans is not home, so that ends that, nobody's home.

"Hell's bells!" they disperse. Jan and Frits climb the fence around the pasture, shortcutting toward the Kamphuis home.

As they cross a ditch at the end of the field, a big frog makes a jump away from them, but in a fast swoop, Frits has the frog by the leg, just as he becomes airborne again. It's a good size one and they wonder how KIK-KERBILLETJES, froglegs, would really taste.

OOPS, there's another one. And another, quick, another one. Pretty soon they have three each.

"What are we going to do with them, Frits?"

"Do you remember a certain tennis ball?"

A big grin spreads across his face, "SURE DO!"

"Let's go!" They're coming up on OPA's house from the rear. The kitchen windows are open and they can hear dishes rattling.

On hands and knees, they pass underneath the windows, past the front door to the parlor windows and ONE, TWO, THREE, FOUR, FIVE, SIX frogs are pitched into his living room.

They continue to crawl on hands and knees to the little gate, through it onto the sidewalk, straighten up and continue to walk home as if nothing had happened.

Mrs. Kamphuis has tears running down her cheeks from laughing so hard as the boys are busy fantasizing about what is going to happen. Probably!

"OPA sits down on the toilet and all of the sudden, "RIBBIT, RIBBIT!" right under his butt!"

She's holding her sides, can't stop laughing.

"He's ready for bed, pulls back the sheet and "RIBBIT," the frog jumps three feet high. He's so startled he makes in his pants!"

WHAT A GANG!

In the fall, they get involved in a play in the community center.

Frits loves plays. During his third and last year in Kindergarten, he had the lead role in a play about Angels, Saints and The Holy Family. Frits was the young Jesus. White gown, gold belt and slippers, a thousand blonde curls topped by a golden crown, holding a little blue orb with a golden cross on top. He looked soo saintly, it was touching.

This time, the play is about a fairy tale.

He's an elf in the chorus and they learn a new song for the occasion.

Rehearsing is fun and they're having a ball, clowning around a lot. Just one drawback; "Clasien." When they get home, Clasien tells everyone at the supper table, "Frits did this, Fokkie Flink did that!"

She's actually bragging about him, but his feeling is, "If I want my folks to know something, I'm perfectly capable of telling them myself!"

Other than that, he's having a ball. They come home late from rehearsals, so there is no time for the piano and that's great.

Something interesting happens that leaves him puzzled.

On the Saturday of the play, the players are getting ready for a final dress-rehearsal in the afternoon. Frits is dressed and Ursula, who's a good witch in white with a golden crown and magic wand, is gluing on his gray

A play about angels

beard. Frits is sitting on the edge of the stage and Ursula is standing in front of him. She's so tall, nearly a head taller, yet a year younger.

As she presses his beard to one cheek, "Turn your head now!" the other cheek, she stands so close that her body rests against his inner thigh and Frits feels a rush of hot blood racing to his face, making him blush so bad that it must have been obvious right through his beard and make-up.

Now, the rolls are reversed, she's sitting and he is standing. With a cotton ball, Frits applies gold dust to Ursula's face and ears, so that she will sparkle under the lights.

She's so pretty and with her golden hair combed out and hanging down her shoulders, instead of in pigtails, she does look like a heavenly creature and as Frits says, "Other cheek!" his face just inches from her face, he experiences an urge to kiss her. She's sooo beautiful! He's supposed to hate girls, but it feels so good, being so close to her, that he would like to wrap his arms around her.

It leaves him deeply puzzled about himself.

That winter, there is snow. Not consistently, but there's snow. Coal is harder to come by and more wood is being burned. But wood is hard to come by too. The boys now disappear into the woods and cut down dead trees. Fresh, live trees don't burn well and they smoke too much.

Transportation is a problem. How do you get it home?

Hans has a neat little wagon with iron bands around it's wheels, but they do so much damage to the beautiful red and green paint, that Frau Stein won't let them borrow it anymore. Carrying a fair sized log on their shoulders is fun and Paultje is so much shorter than Frits, that when they're carrying logs together, they look ridiculous, but Paul gets the bulk of the weight.

Hans' snazzy sled gives Pappa an idea. In Holland no sled can be bought for love or money, so Pappa builds two identical sleds.

It takes him days and days to get four 1"x 1" strips of wood bent in the same "sweep," but soaking them in hot water, lots of care and pressure and clamps get it done.

Having a blacksmith across the street comes in handy, because he forges 4 strips of metal into the same sweep, drills holes and countersinks them, so all Pappa has to do is install them. The final outcome is, two very sturdy big sleds. They wouldn't have won any beauty contest or won any races, but they are theirs and that's what counts.

Broomsticks are cut to size and metal points from the spools in the factory are heated till they're white hot in the smithy and then burned in place. Now they can sit on their sleds and propel themselves forward, backwards or turn, by sticking their PRIKKERS in the snow or ice and pushing away from their intended direction.

They're learning to pick up pretty good speed when the snow is hard packed. Steering with their PRIKKERS is becoming second nature fast.

Now, when they're rustling wood, they can tie their sleds together TANDEMSTYLE and pull their bounty home more easily.

Cutting logs with the big saw has replaced potato peeling and chopping wood after school has become routine.

The old acacia tree dies for some unknown reason and branch by branch, they're taking her down. That is the toughest wood in the world and to make it worse, it just won't burn. I takes a few months before the entire acacia is cut to pieces and on top of the old stump a round wooden table is mounted, which makes it "neat" looking and still the center of their traffic circle, their own private "ROUND-ABOUT."

The old shade tree will be dearly missed.

On a dreary day, no snow, no rain, no hail, just nasty clouds hanging in the streets that are lined with dirty mountains of snow, commotion near the "OUWE JACOB" gets their attention. Along with a quiet gathering of townspeople, they stand by and watch as workers, surrounded by soldiers, rifles at ready, are taking down the age-old church bells. A make-shift wooden crane system, somehow gets the massive bells outside the church tower and they are slowly lowered onto the flat horse wagons.

A total of four bells, the largest one weighing two tons, are hoisted out of the church. These will now be melted down for ammunition, according to the whispers in the crowd. They can read the words on the rim and top of the big one. Some that Frits will never forget.

"FOUNDRY's HERTOGENBOSCH VUGHT ANNO 1331"

Then some Latin words and "SANTO JACOBUS."

It tears at their hearts as if a little slice of their life is right on those flatbeds with the bells.

They're a half-hour late for dinner, but the news about the church bells has already reached the Hof Van Holland and a subdued group around the round table listens attentively to the boys as they give them their first hand accounting of the events.

The attitude of the town matches the weather and it's going to be a dull day.

Except for an unexpected event from an unexpected source, JOOP!

Joop has meanwhile moved up to the first year at the H.B.S., the school of higher learning. With the result that he has completely grown away from his younger siblings.

He now goes to school with the upper class and the girls he hangs out with are also too classy to have them associate with his "MIDDLE CLASS" family.

He's become a sharp dresser, and his homework takes up soo much time, they hardly see him anymore, just at meal times.

He doesn't go to early mass anymore, his school is in the opposite direction and he studies at the kitchen table as all the rest file out of the door at 7:40 AM.

Now he gets a hold of Frits after school and at the acacia table in the back yard, where no one can hear them, he confides in his younger brother, who's as flabbergasted as he is flattered.

Joop explains that in chemistry class, he has learned the ingredients of gunpowder and he wants to make his own, so they can blow up trees and other necessities!

"ARE YOU KIDDING?"

No, he's dead serious. As a matter of fact, he has already "ORGA-NIZED" (that's the new word for STEALING), a load of "potassium" and "powdered charcoal." (that sneaky devil).

Here he goes around with that shiny HALO on his head, but now that Halo seems a little tarnished and lopsided. But, oh boy, think of the possibilities. If they can make their own bombs, large or small, just imagine what they could do!

The bells of the ol' Saint Jacob

Frits' heart is going its mile a minute again, his whole skinny body is tight as a spring, ready to jump at this excitement.

"Now here's what we need; First, I need some more stuff out of that lab in school and I made a floor plan of the second floor and the lab and where the stuff is. If it's missing, they'll blame the underground! That makes sense! The underground gets blamed for everything anyway, so why not this?"

It also makes sense that Frits should do this alone, because Joop could be recognized. ALRIGHT. ALRIGHT! The thought of NOT doing it or even hesitating never even enters his mind. The fact that he's being used has not dawned on him either! He feels, he's the right man for the job.

Now the first thing they need is some container for the explosives to be packed in. Packed in tight, otherwise, the STUFF will just burn but not explode.

"Oh, just like the carbide?"

"Ya, just like the carbide! It has to be enclosed, what kind of container do you have?"

"Do I have? I have no container!"

"Drats, Anything, that's closed tight, in which we can make a hole for a "LONTJE," a fuse, anything that will burn slowly, like wool yarn or something."

"I don't have anything!"

"Aw, come on…Think..You always have all sorts of junk, it doesn't matter, big or small!"

"How small?"

"Oh, that doesn't matter, we're going to experiment with small amounts anyway!"

"Wait here!" He's back in a minute with a pocket full of little brown containers, about three inches long, flat, about an inch wide and half an inch thick.

"What are those?"

"That's some of that new stuff the Germans have invented, called PLAS-TIC, like that PLASTIC raincoat Mama got from that General, remember?"

"Ya, I remember, but what do they use these for?" He pulls off a top, "and where did you get 'em?"

"I got these from the mechanics at the WALHOF garage and they have flat mints in them. They're very tight and the mints stay really fresh in them especially, with tape around them and they don't break and they're very light!"

"Really? You never gave me any mints!"

"You're never around and most of the ones I get are empty, I get them out of the garbage!"

He wouldn't tell him now, while they're in the midst of this neat conspiracy, that he wouldn't have given him any if he'd begged for it.

"Now this is not exactly, what I had in mind, but it's a good place to start. We have to start somewhere. After we fill 'em up, we can tape them... do you have any tape?"

"No, but I'll get it!"

"All we need is a little hole in it to put a woolen thread through and we're in business. How do we make a hole? Can you get a hold of Pappa's drill?"

It still doesn't dawn on Frits that he's being used to do all the dirty work, he's too excited.

"Maybe, he keeps his tools locked up, but if I say I'm making something...Maybe! But let me see, what I can do with a knife."

He turns over the little container, looking at each side until the brand name on the bottom holds his attention. It's a little circle with a name in it and with the small blade of his pocketknife, he circles inside the spot, cutting a groove as he goes. He doesn't make much progress, it's too hard.

"WAIT!" he returns with two chunks of firewood.

"Here, Hold these on each side, tight!"

They put the little container down on the table, upside down, pressed between two pieces of wood. Frits fishes a nail out of his pocket, puts it on the little circle and with his wooden shoe "Whack," he cracks it into three pieces.

"That didn't work!" Somehow that was obvious.

"We're stupid, you know. Of course it would crack! Just a moment!"

He grabs another little box, cuts inside the circle again, walks over to the flowerbed, fills it with dirt and compacts it solidly.

Back at the table, he puts the top back on..."Hold it" it's clamped again between two chunks of wood, "Tight, real tight!" He puts the nail back on it, and "WHACK" again with his wooden shoe and ..they have the neatest round hole in their neat little bomb-to-be.

"All we need now is tape!"

"I'll get it, Electrical tape Okay?" "Okay?" "I'll get it!"

Now they're off to the H.B.S.

The teachers linger in the classrooms sometimes, maybe grading papers or preparing for tomorrow's class, but by 5:30 only the janitors are around usually and Joop cannot give him the slightest hint as to where they are in that building.

"We'll see!" Frits is in his blue "overall", "klompen" and brown corduroy windbreaker, that's tied very tight around the waist, so nothing can fall out. Joop slips into the alley by the factory, so he can see the front of the school and runs back to the waiting Frits with an "all clear."

144

"There are no more bikes in the racks, just a handcart out front, so it's all like we planned. I'll wait here and keep an eye out!"

Frits jogs down the alley that leads to the rear of the schoolyard.

Like most alleys in Holland, this one is in back of the houses that line the street on either side. The rear garden walls and their wooden gates form the alley and the ivy that covers the walls give it a rustic quiet look.

Many a romance is played out in these back alleys, but for now, Frits only thinks of reaching the pigwire fence around the schoolyard, that he's aiming for.

The fence looks imposing at least six feet of pigwire and then three more strands of barbed wire on top of that.

Piece o'cake! He takes off his wooden shoes, puts one against each opposing wall, upside down, and pulls some ivy down over them and starts to climb the fence. These fence makers must make these fences with kids like him in mind, 'cause each opening fits his feet like a stirrup on a horse and in no time, he's on top, scanning the scene on the other side, in the distance and below and lowers himself on the other side and races over to the backdoor of the school....LOCKED..."DARN"

Staying close and low, he stays under the windows as he skirts the wall to the side door. That door gives and he's inside. He's got to think a second.

Joop's directions were all from the back door and rather than trying to orientate himself or screw up, he decides to double back down the hallway to the back door.

His heart is pounding in his chest like it always does, when there's danger, but other than that, he's cool as a cucumber.

He's flat on his belly against the wall in the corridor, moving up noise-lessly, just far enough to peep around the corner with one eye. All's clear! As fast as his skinny legs can carry him, he's down the hall, ducking as he passes each windowed door, turns left at the end and stops. Nobody in sight! The stairs are off to his left. He edges over a few steps, peers up the stairs and runs up, two treads at the time. Again a left, then a right, again making sure he's clear and then into the second classroom on the left.

"WRONG!" "Let me see, let me see, didn't he say, "Second classroom on the left?" "This is no lab. This must be a history classroom. Ancient maps on the walls, an old harness from Prince Valiant's day and a magnificent CREST on one wall with two beautiful swords across it. Boy, this is like KING ARTHUR'S PALACE at CAMELOT and here comes PRINCE VALIANT, back from a CRUSADE to the HOLY LAND with his SING-ING SWORD in his hand, proudly saluting the crowd.

Standing on a chair, he tries to dislodge the sword by pushing the bot-tom tip upwards. He gets it to move up a little, but he's too short and looks around the room for help. The "Pointer!" from the blackboard. He picks up the pointer and now, by pushing up from the bottom, he gets the sword to slide up and out and he catches it by sticking the pointer into the protective guard around the grip. He lowers it into his hand and shivers, "WHAT A FEELING!" "Now, the HEATHENS, the MOORS, the MUSLIMS, they can all come; he's ready for them, he has the SINGING SWORD, and he'll.. he'll..he better get on with what he came for...

With a deep sigh, he gingerly puts down the saber(that's what it really is) and moves back to the door. It opens noiselessly and through the window in the door he checks CLEAR to the left, though the crack he checks CLEAR to the right and verifies the fact that he is indeed inside the second door. Something is screwy...maybe the first door is just a hall closet or something? If that's the case, he needs to move one more door down.

GO! BULLSEYE, he's in the lab. No more wasting time; the two containers are exactly where Joop said they would be. Down comes the zipper of his windbreaker, the two glass jars are pushed around to his back, up comes the zipper and he's out of the room.

As he passes CAMELOT, he hesitates, "Oh boy, that sword was the greatest...why not?"

Back into the classroom, back up on the desk, pointer in hand, he's going after the second sword. Paultje needs one too. There he goes with both sabers, back into the hallway. Not a sound is heard inside the cavernous halls. Not a soul is to be seen anywhere.

GREAT GOING! What's this? The door is locked, darn, no key in it either. Here goes that pulse rate again. He's gotta think and think fast.

He can't run around the school trying doors, that's an invitation to get caught. Okay.Okay, he knows what to do. He races toward the back of the school, ducks into the last classroom on the right and straight for the rear window.

The right window half cranks open easily and in no time he stands on the sill and jumps, clutching his precious swords. As he reaches the fence again, he hangs the sword on the barbed wire on top, the blade of one stuck through the grip of the other. He scales the fence, retrieves his swords, recovers his "klompen" and joins up with Joop, who gasps, "What the hell is this?"

"These are my swords and this is your stuff!"

He turns his back to him, saying "Let's go!"

He feels he's got a right to act indignant; HE ORGANIZED Joop's stuff and he ORGANIZED HIS stuff, so what's the difference? Sometimes Joop makes him sick. But Joop insists on hiding his loot, so now the swords are inside the pantlegs of his coveralls and the grips stick out right under his chin. Other than making it hard to walk, it's Okay and once they're home, the treasures end up under some boards in the shed until some other time when the coast will be clear to smuggle them into the house.

After dinner, they work on their project, but it gets dark too early and besides, Joop should study, so it's off until tomorrow.

"Good show, good show!" Joop is complimenting Frits on bringing in a spool of gray yarn (Mama's knitting a sweater) and a roll of tape. (It happened to lie on a truck fender in the WALHOF garage and the mechanic who was working under the hood didn't seem to need it anymore).

Joop has a whole bunch of little pewter measuring cups that he borrowed out of Papa's SLIJTERIJ, where Pappa sells drinks by the ounce, the pint or the liter, whatever they want.

"Whadda you do with those?"

"I need exact amounts to get the right mixture and actually, I should have a scale and weight, but I know what each one of these powders weigh, so I can calculate the right amount by volume!"

"You know how to do all this junk?"

"I attend the H.B.S., remember, little boy?"

"Don't you call me a little boy, or I'll have to challenge you to a duel with my..by the way, did you hear anything at school about my break-in?"

"No, but I have a chemistry class tomorrow, so maybe then I'll hear something, Okay, I'm ready for testing!"

They carefully fill one of the little packets with Joop's mixture, after feeding a piece of wool yarn through the little hole. They compact the STUFF carefully with their fingers and tape the cap on tight.

"Don't lick your fingers, wash 'em first!"

Joop leads the way with his "BOMB" hidden in the palm of his hand

"Where are you going to blow it, Joop?"

"I don't know, I was thinking; in the pasture in back, are there horses at the moment?"

"I don't know, I think Dr. Bos still has his ponies in the stable, but I'm not sure!"

They cross through the yard, by the fence and just a few paces into the dirt road and, "There's a horse!"

"Who's?"

"I don't know, but it's an old bugger, maybe Dr. Bos is treating it or something!"

"Oh, shit, whadda we do now?"

Back out to the street, thinking..."Hey how about that snowmount?"

All along the road, piles of snow are built into little mounds by street cleaners, who follow the snowplows and clear the sidewalk by piling the heaps on either side of people's doors.

"What about the "SNEEUWBERGEN," (snow mountains)?"

"Let's blow them up!" Joop looks up and down the street, it's close to the supper hour and as cold as it is, everyone is inside, huddled close to their stoves.

"Alright!" with a few swift moves, a hole is dug in this 4 X 4 foot pyramid. In goes the little brown box, the string is lit, they boys race behind the fence, just their heads showing and "BOOM," a muffled explosion and the pyramid is no more. The snow is back like before they shoveled it.

A close inspection proves that the BOMB didn't really shatter, it more or less split in half, but the result is an unqualified success.

They congratulate one another and start making BOMBS at a feverish pitch.

After the eleventh BOMB, they're out of boxes, so the ingredients are hidden in the shack and they divide the armament; Joop six, Frits five.

All done, they go in to do homework and eat supper.

The next day, eleven more "SNEEUWBERGEN" are mysteriously blown from the earth.

CHAPTER VIII
Spring 1944

By now everything is rationed or simply not available.

Clothing, furniture, and shoe stores have little to offer. Vegetables and fruits are not rationed, but not available that much.

Having known WIGGERS all of her life and having been a good customer all this time, Mama gets her veggies from the backdoor, rather than line up out front, like the rest of the townspeople.

Train trips to APELDOORN occur more often and Clasien comes along sometimes to make them seem even more "Harmless."

Frits doesn't understand the reason for all that smuggling, but it must make money. Mama now wears an expensive fur coat to church.

Pappa doesn't go anymore. He's had it with the "HYPOCRITES" and the "MONEYLENDERS" that should be "CHASED FROM THE TEMPLE!"

Milk runs are becoming milk-, potato- and wheat-runs and bottles of JENEVER are transported to the farm. More and more, money is becoming worthless and most things are being bartered.

As long as Hof Van Holland keeps getting it's supply of booze from SCHIEDAM, where the distilleries are, the FORRER family keeps eating reasonably well.

Air raids and bombardments are a near daily occurrence, but now in addition, they're being hit by American Fighter-Bombers, everyday that the sun shines. Everyday in school, oranges from Spain are distributed as a food-supplement plus something new: VITAMINS, Vitamin C, 2 a day, 6 days a week.

The teachers talk about this new discovery and it all makes good sense to the kids, when they just think back in history, when SCURVY would hit the ships' crews after they ran out of fresh fruit.

In the attic, sides of pickled HAM and BACON are stored, hung from the rafters, because they'll last forever like that. Food and supplies are being hoarded in every nook and cranny for rougher days to come.

Everyone talks about the invasion that is going to come any day now and as if the Germans want to confirm that point, they evacuate hundreds of families from the coast.

All along the NORTH SEA coast, bunkers are being added to existing bunkers and existing bunkers are being reinforced and modernized.

WINTERSWIJK has the dubious pleasure of getting hundreds of EVACUEES. (another new word for the boys) from SCHEVENINGEN.

As most of them are protestant, the Catholic school is hardly affected. Just two lanky brothers, a 5th and a 6th grader, that's all.

They're tall, skinny and mouthy, but that'll change. You just don't walk into a farm community and put on a superior act. That doesn't fly. They'll learn, just stand by. The opportunity to shut their mouths will come.

Today, as Frits makes his way back from JONGBLOED and his piano lessons, those damn piano lessons, he detours just a "little bit" and is kinda caught by an "AIR RAID" alarm. Instead of heading for the nearest shelter or a convenient home, he dives into the nearest alley between the houses.

He moves away from the houses as far as he can to improve his "view" and, "MY OH MY!" is he rewarded.

"JABO" is a German abbreviation for "JACHTBOMBER," fighter-bomber and as they come in, in a loose "IN-LINE" formation, the ACK-ACK starts firing ferociously from all directions.

They're coming in very fast. Frits figures, 1000 kilometers per hour.

The flight kinda passes him on the right, turns left in formation and now the leader breaks off to the left again and for a moment he thinks, "He saw me and he's coming right at me!"

He hits the dirt and covers his head as the plane comes screaming down at him. The pitch and the roar of the engine increases unbelievably and when he hears, TATATATATATAT, he knows he's had it, he's dead!

The fighter pulls off with the engine screaming and then, KABOOM, the bomb hits.

As the next plane comes screeching down, Frits realizes he's still in one piece and the bomb blast was at least a hundred yards away, he slowly gets up as the TATATATAAATAT of the second fighter starts hammering in his ears.

He can actually see the flashes of the machine guns as the plane comes thundering by. They're shooting at the rail yard, KABOOM, and whatever is out there. The second bomb has hit, the third plane is barreling on down and he can hear the steady staccato of a "FIERLING FLAK" and it looks like the ACK-ACK and the fighter are shooting at one another, just like GUNSLINGERS facing each other in DODGE!

P-51's carrying 1,000 pounders

Once he's sure, he's not the target, he relaxes and takes in the show. The second flight is now peeling off and with about 15 seconds intervals, they come down, ROARING, SPITTING FIRE, then a pull-out and...KABOOM.

What a sight!!! They're Americans and he can clearly see the pilots in their cockpits and they're so close, he can read the numbers on the tails.

They each make one pass and drop one bomb, so in spite of the fact that they have another bomb as yet hanging under their wing, they continue on, instead of coming back for another run, like they do most of the time. They must be hunting for another target, somewhere else.

He heaves a big sigh. "Boy, if I were only big enough, that's what I would do. No more PRINCE VALIANT or TARZAN, no, a FIGHTER PILOT is what I'm going to be."

Then people would talk about me too, like the Germans do about the fighters, "DA SIND SIE WIEDER, DIE TREUE ACHT, DIE HALTEN HIER BEI UNS DER WACHT" (there they are, the loyal eight, they're standing guard over us)

He moves his hand like a fighter coming in, "WOOOOO, TATATATAT-TAT, WOOOOO, KABOOM." Oh, he's into it now!

He's tempted to go and check out what they've hit, but he's supposed to go home and Sunday is his CONFIRMATION day and right now, he's being as SAINTLY as he's ever been in his life. So he trots on home to relive his experience with his siblings.

On the way back, when he's nearly home, he stops in his tracks as a convoy catches up with him.

A convoy is nothing unusual anymore, although anything military is attractive to him, but this one is unusual.

The convoy includes: half-tracks with soldiers lined on each side, rifles at ready, (he has not seen this kind of scene since the invasion 4 years ago), followed by several flatbeds with railroad tracks and ties, (that's not too unusual), and then three of the biggest bombs he has ever seen or imagined.

Another, soldier loaded, half-track, more supply trucks, a staffcar and one more half-track bringing up the rear.

He forgets all about his fighter story. These bombs, that just passed by, were larger and longer than the biggest flatbed, they had to be 40 feet long or more. There isn't an aircraft in the world that could carry a bomb that big.

"Or is there?" Joop has already told him about new inventions like, radar, microwaves, heavy water, and splitting atoms, but never about a giant bomber. Racing home, he arrives out of breath at the front door where Pappa, Mama and a bunch of the kids and customers are still looking in the directions of Borken, where the convoy is disappearing.

"Pappa, Pappa!" he tugging at his vest, "What was that, did you see that? What was that?"

"A VAU EINZ!"

"A what?" Pappa is so busy rapping with his customers, that Frits turns to Joop, "A what?"

"A VAU EINZ!" "A VEE ONE! they call it." "It's a rocket," one of the gentlemen said! "I understand," Joop continues, "that those wings on the other trucks get attached to the big bomb and the STOVE PIPE that you saw, they are the actual rockets, that push that VAU EINZ at great speed. So they're actually huge FLYING BOMBS and they fly all the way to LONDON."

"Holy Moses!"

"They've been firing them from the coast already, the radio has been talking about them, and Hitler said in a speech, that this was just the first in a series, that's why he calls it the V-1. V-1, I believe stands for "VERGEL-DIGUNG" or some word like that, but I know it means he's repaying the British for all the bombs they've dropped on the "FRAUEN UND KINDER" in the HEIMAT. You know how he carries on. Plus he said that shortly they will have a flying bomb that flies all the way to AMERIKA, also because

152

of his VENGEANCE thing. To punish Americans for bombing his people."

"Mr. Olthof, over there, says they're going to launch these things from right across the border. Something about SABOTAGE and trouble with the Dutch UNDERGROUND."

Leave it to Joop if you want some information, he must stick his nose in everything.

"How can a thing like that fly by itself and know the way to LONDON?"

"It has a guidance system!"

"HUH?"

"What can I call it? It's an automatic pilot that's controlled by gyros!"

"HUH?"

"They set the course before launch and the GYROS keep it on course"

"HUH?" That was over his head, just like "microwave" and "radar."

Right then, the ALL CLEAR is sounded and it reminds him of the story he wants to tell about his JABO's, but he can't find anybody who wants to listen to him. All the conversation is about the VAU EINZ.

On Sunday he is CONFIRMED along with the other ANGELS in his class.

He is dressed in a brand new gray suit, not a "hand-me-down" from Joop, nor "hand-made" by Mama, a REAL new suit, the first one of his life.

A grey "PLUS-FOUR," knickerbockers, complete with NEW shirt, NEW shoes, NEW tie, and NEW socks. A new belt and white gloves complete his beautiful appearance.

He receives a new MISSAL and he hands out BID-PRENTJES," PRAYER-CARDS, with all the events of his important day recorded on them.

He chose the name "BONIFATIUS" as his confirmation name and as he renews his baptismal vows along with the rest of his class, he's impressed enough to vow, that he'll never sin anymore. (He doesn't remember too many sins anyway).

When the Pastor preaches in his Sermon about following the lead of their "PATRON SAINTS," he knows just what he's going to be, a MISSIONARY!!

St.Bonifatius had come to Holland in the eleventh or twelfth century, had converted many heathens to Christianity, started the Diocese of Utrecht and was murdered by Norsemen. (He thinks)

"Yes, that's what I'm gonna do! I'm going to become a Missionary, go to Africa, save souls and die for my God. Yep, that's what I'm gonna do!"

A nice dinner, a nice party, wearing his good suit all day, sunshine, no bombs, (just one scare as German fighters roared over at tree top level) and a lot of happy relatives. The feud is forgotten for the day, as the Uncles and

Aunts corner him outside the church to congratulate him. Even OPA adds his grumpy good wishes and all his cousins beam their approval.

It's a perfect day; a clean white soul in a healthy skinny body with a pure mind. The folks are proud; "Their own little SAINT FRITS."

As talk continues about an impending invasion, the bombing intensifies, not so much in WINTERSWIJK, but beyond in Germany. Winterswijk gets its share, but the vaportrails of the B-17's seem to multiply everyday. They must be bombing the hell out of Germany. The radio keeps bragging about "Victories," especially at sea, but they never talk about AFRICA anymore.

At the "OST-FRONT" everything seems "honky-dory," but more and more troops are being stationed around town. Lots of FLAK, FIERLING FLAK, light four-gun pieces, firing 20 and 30 mm shells and heavy FLAK, going after the high flying B-17's. Those big guns have long, long barrels and are noisy as hell.

Trucks now drive on "HOUTGAS," WOOD-GAS.

They have great big barrels attached behind their cabs that burn wood and somehow keep the engines running.

All along the roads, "SPLITTERGRABEN" are dug. "Z" shaped trenches that the drivers can dive into, when their trucks are being shot at.

Around all garages, factories and public buildings, railroad stations, "SPLITTERGRABEN" begin to appear.

Truck-shelters are built along the highways, about a quarter mile apart.

They consist of earthen walls, about six feet high on three sides, topped with a frame of rough pine stalks, forming a roof covered by branches and camouflage netting.

All men, between the ages of 16 and 40, who cannot prove that their jobs are essential for National Security or the war effort are called to report to labor camps for DEFENSE construction. Pappa is 48 and Joop is 14. It's getting close!

At one of these construction sites, Frits "organizes" a beautiful "Ha-Jot" knife, with a leather-on-metal sheath and a "H.J., in German pronounced HA-YOT, stands for HITLER JUGEND.(Hitlers Youth)

He also "finds" a piece of camouflaged parachute silk. Mama convinces him that there's not enough to make a pair of camouflaged coveralls, but she would like a piece for herself for a "shawl." "Of course Mama, I'll get more some day!" From the remainder he makes an ingenious belt for Paultje and himself.(Paul thinks it's ingenious too.)

The piece is cut in two, each piece rolled up tightly. A big, one inch

B-17's   Daylight raid

glass marble is knotted in each end, fitted around the waist and then belted by twisting the marbles around each other. "Voila," now they have a belt. They can roll their knife or money in it, that's storage. They can swing it at somebody with the marble at the end and now it's a weapon. When they stretch it tightly at an angle, it's a rainshelter and when draped over their heads while sitting on their haunches, it's a camouflage net.

"GREATEST LITTLE BELT IN THE UNIVERSE."

And it happens...."INVASION!"

The little town just vibrates with anticipation, "It'll be over soon!"

It's early June and the weather is glorious. The train and convoy activity picks up, but not the JABO's. They must be busy at the front.

The men have a map of France on the round table and they plot the German victories. That's all they hear, one "victory" after another. As they study the map, they have plenty of reason to worry, the Allied advance is mostly slow and sometimes stagnant. The happy vibrations stop. Could these Krauts really be that strong that they can hold the advance in France and Italy and still hold their own in Russia? "Inconceivable!" Even push them back? "No, God please NO!"

One night...no warning...no alarm...the whole town is rocked out of bed by an enormous roar, that grows and grows to an unbearable level and seems intent on descending right into their house and obliterating them. Thank goodness, it roars over and the noise subsides.

"WHAT IN THE HELL WAS THAT?"

The girls, in their nightclothes, cling to Mama, crying in hysterics. This time it would have woken Antoon for sure, but he's not here anymore.

"Pappa, what was that?"

"Go down to the kitchen, Ida make some cocoa, I'll get my clothes on!"

With his pants and jacket over his pajamas, he scoots down the stairs and out the front door, Frits, his coveralls over his pajamas, right on his heels.

Otto and Pecht are standing on the corner in front of Otto's shop and Wiggers is on his way over to join them. Other people start appearing and listen to Otto, who's got everyone's attention.

His bedroom, right over his store window, faces East and at the first noise, he'd opened his curtains and saw this huge fireball climbing from the East. It's was the V-1, he's sure of it, (Pappa forgets that he's supposed to be mad at him) although he doesn't understand it. The whole thing was ONE BIG FIREBALL, accelerating into the darkness. Lots of questions and a lot of repetition sends Frits to the cocoa in the kitchen and a chance to show off his newfound knowledge.

"Hey, guys! We gotta check that out!"

"They say it's across the border!"

"So what?" "We've been across the border before, right Boer?"

"Whadda ya wanna find out?"

"I wanna see how they shoot 'em off!"

"You'll never get close enough, they'll have that place guarded tighter than a drum!"

"Oh, we can get into most anything, can't we Boer?"

Paultje nods sleepily, "I wanna go to bed!"

"Alright, it's all over with, come on kids, back to bed. Frits, you have your clothes on, go tell your Father to come in and that we're going to bed and...." "THERE'S ANOTHER ONE!" he's out the front door as the thunder of the rocket starts building. There it is...an orange ball, totally aglow, thundering overhead into the night sky with an earsplitting noise. Everybody covers their ears with their hands and follows the fiery ball as it disappears on the far horizon in the West. The conversation that had completely died down starts up with renewed vigor and enthusiasm. Joop, out in his pajamas to witness the event first hand, returns with Frits to the kitchen, where the girls are crying again, holding onto Mama and Paultje with a look on his face as if he would like to join them.

Joop is analyzing, "I don't understand it. If it has a rocket motor at the tail, how come the whole thing is aglow? I don't understand it!"

"Let's go to bed!" Mama's thinking about school.

"We're sleeping with you, Mama!"

"Okay, Okay. Let's just hope, there won't be anymore tonight!"

THERE ARE...all night long...every hour and fifteen minutes...

"WHAT A MESS...HOW CAN ANYONE GET ANY SLEEP THIS WAY?"

All the wagging tongues in town and all the newspapers have ONE topic...Vee One.   VAU EINZ

A lot of different opinions are offered, contradicted and reversed.

The launches continue during the day and now they can get a clear look at that new scientific marvel.

"See that thing on top that I call the stove pipe? That's the actual engine that pushes that flying bomb. The newspaper this morning had a good point; that stove engine has enough power to keep it flying at a high rate of speed, but does it have enough power to get off the ground?

There must be another source of propulsion to blast it into the air!"

"PROPULSION?"

"Yes, Push-Power, to push it off the ground!"

"You guys better get to school!"

The family science editor says, "I'll probably have more information later during dinner!"

Sometimes Joop does have some values.

The newspapers report other interesting facts: within a radius of many, many miles, horses and cattle get so startled by the noise that they take off in complete panic, like a stampede in cowboy books, and break out of stalls, run through barbed wire fences and in many cases severely hurt themselves or even get killed. Farmers are pulling their hair out.

Another thing the newspaper tells is the approximate location of the launch sites and of course Jan has already plotted the exact location with the help of his Dad, who patrols that area near the border.

It is indeed within the Dutch border and the boys are familiar with the area, so a decision is reached within minutes; "Saturday is the day!"

"We'll be out by noon, we'll meet at one, study the map, and we're off!"

Everything goes according to schedule and complete with new belts, coveralls and bare feet, the Forrers are dressed for the occasion and the Kamphuises are also in their Saturday-best; old clothes and old sneakers.

V-1

They're happily chatting away with a farmer, who's giving them a ride on his horse wagon with empty milkcans. After a few miles on the main road, their route becomes a ZIG-ZAG through the fields on dirt roads that are actually mere wagon tracks. They help put down the empty cans at the appropriate farmhouses, two here, five there, until they're down to the last few, which are his. The farmer personally has not had any cattle losses, although the cows were terribly spooked and ran around the pasture like idiots and as a result gave less milk that first morning and they're still not back to regular production, but they're not reacting as badly anymore, so he hopes for the best.

At the farmhouse, they enjoy some fresh milk and a front row seat at the next launching.

IT IS AWESOME!!!!! They see it, before they can hear it, "THERE IT IS!"

They're sitting on the wagon facing in the direction from where it should be coming according to the farmer and indeed, there it comes..noiselessly at first. It's about the size of a fighter plane, with short stubby wings and a stovepipe mounted on the rear, sticking up and backwards, spewing fire. It's just gliding it seems until the noise hits, like a sledgehammer.

The farmer had told them to open their mouths, to equalize the pressure on the eardrums and it's too bad that there's no one to take a picture of them; four monkeys with their mouths wide open and their hands on their ears. Too bad. They're too intrigued to see the fun of it!

After thanking the farmer, (he can't talk 'em out of it,) they trot off in the direction of the launch. It should be two, maybe two and a half kilometers from the farm. The farmer has told them that the area is crawling with soldiers and Secret Police and he doubts very much that they'll even get close. The farmers wife has made them small plugs of cotton and now,

158

their ears plugged expertly, they march down dirt roads, across pastures, jump ditches and climb fences.

This part of Holland is flat as a board and the only obstacle that they encounter is a creek that's too wide to jump, so Jan and Henkie are forced to take their shoes and socks off. Paul and Frits don't' have that problem, they simply pull up their pants legs.

Things couldn't be better, the weather, the scenery, the progress they're making, the timing, everything is just great. They feel like singing....

"HALT, HÄNDE HOCH!"

"What the hell is that?"

Of course, they stop. Henkie hits the deck. They look flustered, wondering whether to fall like Henkie or run, but they don't get to choose.

"AUF, HÄNDE HOCH!" it's a loudspeaker. They're on a dirt road between two pastures approaching a wooded area and that's where the loudspeaker must be.

"LET'S DO IT" Paultje is panicking, "PLEASE, LET'S DO IT!" he raises his hands.

Boy, this is a like a cowboy movie.

"AUF, HÄNDE HOGH," "AUF" "Henkie, get up!" Jan orders while he raises his hands. Frits considers running, but where?

There are our heroes! What a sight! Dangerous war criminals, 9, 10, 12 and 13 years old. They must have looked like the ultimate threat to the THIRD REICH. They are still baffled as to where the sound comes from. "What are we going to do?" Paultje sounds like he's going to cry any minute now.

"Oh, quit bawling, nothing is going to happen. The worst that can happen is that we wont' get to see the launch today, so we'll have to do it differently next time, that's all! Next time we won't come up walking out in the open!"

"I'm not coming next time!"

"Shut up!"

"What shall we do now?"

"Shall we start walking?" Hands high over his head, Frits starts walking in the direction of the speakers.

"HALT" Oops!

Just then an open car appears, it's one of these amphibious Volkswagens with two soldiers in it. The passenger is sitting on top of the seatback, steadying himself with one hand on the windshield and holding a submachine gun with the other. They approach fast in a cloud of dust and stop smack in front of the boys.

"Was machen sie hier?"

After four years of German occupation, Frits speaks German as easily as his native tongue and he does the talking,

"I'm Frits, this is my brother Paul and these are Jan and Henk Kamphuis. Their father is a border guard in this area and we're looking him up!"

"GLAUB ICH NICHT" "I don't believe that!"

"And we want to see the launch of the VAU EINZ!"

"Ah, now we're getting closer to the truth. Lower your hands. Where do you live?"

"In WINTERSWIJK, in't HOF VAN HOLLAND and they," he waves in the direction of Jan and Henk, "live in the EELINKSTRAAT."

"Hof Van Holland? "The café? With Ellie, the waitress?"

"Ya, you know Ellie? We now have a new one too, you should see her, she's cute, she's younger and can we see the launch?"

"How old are you guys?"

"Jan is the oldest, he's 13 already. I'll be 13 in November, Henk is 10 and Paultje is 9." Paul smiles at him as to confirm it and in spite of himself the soldier smiles back. He looks over his shoulder at his mate behind the wheel. The chauffeur kinda grins and nods.

Soldier #1, an OBERGEFREITER in the LUFTWAFFE, checks his watch and says,

"The area up ahead is restricted, so you can't go there. You must turn around. But what I'll do, I'll escort you out of this area and put you on the highway toward home, so you won't get into further trouble or endanger yourself! Get in the car!"

All four of them pile into the back seat and it takes off.

It has to travel a quarter of a mile before it can turn around and now they're heading back in a direction of the launch area.

The OBERGEFREITER talks into his radio and they pass the point where they were first picked up and after turning past a cluster of trees, they stop at a tent with the flaps thrown up.

There's a radio on a table inside the tent and a Lieutenant stands on top of a platform, binoculars in one hand and a mike in the other. He must be the guy, who spotted them.

The Obergefreiter gets on the platform with him and they throw glances again.

"What are they gonna do to us?"

"Nothing! Quit whining!"

Frits surveys the area and he realizes that with that platform behind the tree, the Germans are in a position to see for miles in three different directions, but there's no sign of a rocket anywhere.

The conversation on the platform comes to an end, the Obergefreiter gets back in his seat and says something to his driver, checks his watch and turns to the boys, "I'm taking you to the highway. Keep your eyes focused on your right, while we're driving!"

They bump along on a dirt road that follows the edge of the woods to the East and after about 5 minutes, they stop as they get to a clearing.

"Just a moment, I must get clearance to cross!"

He talks into his radio and points to his right in the distance.

They're too far out, but it looks like, way out, way, way out in the distance there's a V-1 and a locomotive. It's too far to see anything clearly, but that's what it's gotta be; a locomotive with a V-1 on top.

Yes, that's what it is. It's moving now and the closer it gets the more clearly they can tell; the "V-1" is mounted on top of the train and they're racing in their direction, the rocket engine burning, sending a plume of smoke the opposite way like a twirling tornado.

The train stops very suddenly, way back there, but the bomb continues, now flying on it's own. It sinks a little lower to the ground and then starts a slow climb as it accelerates. In a few seconds, it's right in front of them and it's awesome.

As big as it is, it's kinda elegant and gracious, but boy, is it big! The flame must be 20 feet long and the smoke at least a mile.

And then it hits. Like a thunderclap..Louder than the loudest thunderclap they've ever heard.

With their mouths wide open, they stare after the machine as it roars into the heavens.

The cars starts up and crosses the path THAT THE ROCKET JUST TOOK and Frits asks, "Why the train?"

"The train gets it up to flying speed. It flies at about 100 MPH, you see, the wings are so short, they don't provide a lot of lift, but once they reach 100 miles, the train stops and the "V-1" continues by itself. The tracks are regular railroad tracks, but that little locomotive is a very fast electrical train.

Now, we can disassemble the whole thing in a few hours and put it up somewhere else in half a day and launch again, one every hour to an hour and a half."

"You move it a lot because of sabotage, right?"

"No, we've had no sabotage yet. Could happen though. No the reason for us to move it frequently is that through air reconnaissance or intelligence provided by the underground, the enemy may pin-point it's location and come out to bomb it. That's why we move it!"

They've come to the highway and with a handshake, "DANKE SCHÖN" and "GRÜSZ GOTT," they part ways, the car is gone and the boys head home.

Boy, do they have some stories to tell, wait till Joop hears this, it'll make his ears flap.

They carefully take the cotton out of their ears and decide to save it, the next one is due again shortly.

It's a long way home, but they're practically floating.

The launches continue for two more days, but in the meantime a new fear arises. One of the rockets, after reaching about 5,000 feet, starts a slow circle to the right and descends in a wide turn until it hits the ground with an explosion, that sounds like a hundred ten-thousand-pound bombs and creates a crater that would have swallowed a city block.

It landed in the cemetery and all of the population goes to inspect and admire the hole. It's big enough to swallow an entire church building!

"It's the gyro's" Joop explains. "Sometimes the gyros lose speed and that throws off the guidance system and then it may fall any place. Back at the launch site, right on our heads, any place!"

"Huh?" "You're kidding?" "OH Boy!"

Another reason to follow each launch carefully!

CHAPTER IX
Dolle Dinsdag

The war effort in France is not at all going according to the hopes and wishes of the people of the occupied countries.

Here it is AUGUST and the Allies are still bogged down in northern France.

"WHAT'S HAPPENING?" "What's happening in Holland is that things get tougher yet. More people are being shipped off to labor camps, more people disappear into the UNDERGROUND, more bridges are being blown up, more people are arrested and more people are executed, guilty or not.

Less and less food and clothing is available and daytime bombardments intensify.

The "Foursome" is off from school for their month long summer vacation and today they're hanging out at the "HOUTLADING," the lumberyard at the railroad switching "EMPLACEMENT," (French for R.R.Yard.)

Jan and Frits have already sent the "Little Ones" home once, loaded down with soaps. Bars of soap, good soap, regular foaming soap, no sandsoap! They "found" it in the "lived-in" railroad car that houses the gunnery group.

Now, they're on top of the flatbed car which has a "FIERLING FLAK" mounted on it and are getting practice sitting in the gunner's seat moving the cannon around.

"JEEZ, that thing is fast!"

Turning one wheel with one hand makes the whole thing, all 4 barrels included, swing around with blinding speed and turning the other wheel with the other hand makes all four barrels move up and down with unbelievable ease.

The gunner explains, "These new guns can go down as low as 10 degrees above the horizon and as erect as 85 degrees up, nearly straight up." That's fantastic. "Americans don't have anything like this." He says. It fires

30 millimeter exploding bullets!"

"30 MM?" I thought these fired 20 MM?"

"No, we fire 30 MM nowadays, the British shoot with 20MM and the Americans with point 50's. The 20 MM's are exploding too, the point 50's are solid."

The guns are fed with canisters, oversized magazines and while one man fires, two others stand on each side of the cannons, ready with two canisters each, filled with 20 rounds apiece. They slap them into place as soon as a canister empties out and the cannons keep right on firing!"

"How long does it takes to exchange one?"

"Show 'em!" "CLICK-CLACK," it's in. One second, that's all. "WOW!"

"Can I try it now?"

Everyone gets to swing the platform and raise and lower the guns.

"What a sport!" You'd have to really be coordinated to look through the metal sight, turn both wheels, follow a passing or incoming aircraft, push the firing pin with your foot, stop a second for reloading and swing again.

"It's something!"

Heinz, a GEFREITER, shows off the ribbons he's won for marksmanship and a ribbon through his buttonhole indicates that he has won the "RITTERKREUZ."

He earned that in Russia by having two confirmed "KILLS" in one day.

He's only been in the service two years and spent most of his time AM OSTFRONT. He really had wanted to be a pilot, flying the planes, rather than shoot at them and even though he passed the physical he failed, what he called, the Psycho-Technical-test, whatever that means.

He's only twenty and looking back, he says, "Maybe it's better this way. Ever since the Americans got into this mess, we've lost pilots by the dozens and we hardly have any planes left.

At least I'm still alive and this will always be kind of a soft job.

One of these days it will be over, soon I hope and I'll go home and back to school, marry my girlfriend an have kids, "LAUSCHBUBES" like yourselves!"

"Where are you from?"

"I'm from HEIDELBERG. Ever heard of it?"

"Oh, Ya, ICH HAB MEIN HERZ IN HEIDELBERG VERLOHREN!" Frits knows all the popular songs.

Heinz laughs, "Hahahah, Ya, that's the one!"

"Where is HEIDELBERG?"

"South, down the Neckar."

"Near Bocholt?" Heinz laughs again, "No, much further south, and old city like your MAASTRICHT or NIJMEGEN. Beautiful castles, a beautiful RATHAUSE, a town hall, gorgeous in the moonlight along the river. You ought to come and visit sometimes!"

"Hey, that sounds good, when do you wanna go, guys?" All around laughter.

"Can we walk it?"

"No, not hardly, it takes a day by train, but it's a beautiful ride along the Rhine river valley with its vineyards, castles and picturesque villages. You'd love it, I know."

It sounds mouthwatering good.

Just as Henkie says, "I'm hungry, let's go eat!" The airraid sirens go off.

"Okay, guys! Off! Get under cover!"

As the boys scramble down, Frits observes, "Probably just bombers, flying over!" He makes no attempt to leave. "And maybe NOT!"

"One way or the other, we'll be ready. Load 'em up boys!"

The soldiers slap the magazines into place and HEINZ smoothly moves his guns back and forth, up and down.

"Come on!" he shouts, "I'm ready for you, you SCHWEINHUNDEN, come show your faces, you bastards!"

They must have heard him, cause there they are....JABO's in echelon formation, one wingman on the left, two on the right of the leader. There's one flight...two...three....four...God...six flights....twenty-four "P-51's "MUSTANGS, wild horses!" Shouts HEINZ. "Hey you, you better get out of here!"

"No, I wanna help!"

"Suit yourself!" Heinz swings his guns in their direction although the planes are still well out of his range and give no indication where they're going to attack.

Frits is holding a magazine, ready to hand it up to the loaders, staring at the planes. He remembers how, in the alley, it looked like the planes were coming straight at him, well, they turn and by God, they're coming straight at him. The lead plane starts spitting fire and Heinz has his quadruple barrels spitting right back. That does it. Frits jumps from the train and as fast as his little legs can carry him, he crosses the tracks, the fence, a ditch, the street, another ditch and he falls flat on his face against a warehouse wall covering his head with his arms.

As soon as the TATATATAT of the first plane stops, he jumps and runs again...KABOOM....the concussion throws him to the ground...

"Damn, that's close." Up again and running and by the time the next TATATATATA begins, he's behind the warehouse, protected from the concussion from the next KABOOM by the building.

P-51 Bombs Away!

"VERDOMME! they may plan to knock out these warehouses!" UP again, racing further away from the tracks.

The TOTOTOTOT of HEINZ's guns hasn't stopped and the barrels must be red hot by now.

There it is...A SPLITTERGRABEN, he dives in head first and after a while peeks out as all twenty-four planes make a pass at the yard.

They're dropping both bombs this time. The moment the TATATATA stops, they release the bombs and they, almost gracefully, glide to earth.

They explode very UN-gracefully! Debris flies everywhere, smoke fills the air and HEINZ stopped firing. Frits lifts his head to investigate, but he can't see much from this angle, one building's in the way. He stares in amazement at little sandspirals that jump out of the ground like tornadoes in the dessert. "CUTE!" "CUTE?"

"BULLETS!" "FLOP," flat on his face on the bottom of the SPLIT-TERGRABEN.

It's muddy and the moisture soon reaches his skin. He shivers, but not only from the cold.

"VERDOMMETJE!"...that was too damn close. He doesn't raise his head until the sound of the engines fades in the distance.

He finally gets up. Everywhere, fire and smoke. Stacks of wood burning ferociously, boxcars and passenger cars spewing flames into the air. In the distance the railroad station building is smoking.

After crawling out of the muddy hole, he looks around, "JAN!"... "BOER"

He shouts at the top of his lungs....NOTHING!

Too much noise, ambulances and fire trucks are racing to the scene of destruction, sirens screaming. He sticks two fingers in his mouth, "ZEEEUUUUIIIT" He whistles their signal, "ZEEEEUUUIIIT"...NOTH-ING.

Slowly, he makes his way back to the street.

"JAN," "JAN!" "BOER!" The street is one big mess, junk and holes all over the place. He's totally unaware of the mud that covers him. He feels like sitting down, deflated.

"Where's the gun?" he wonders. He crosses the street, but doesn't have the energy to climb the fence. The gun is gone...HEINZ is gone...twisted steel...that's it! "Hope the boys are all right!" They had plenty of time to get away. They know how to find shelter, we've been doing this for years.

He should be worried about Paultje but he's not. That kid is alright. He may look dumb, but he isn't.

He takes in all the activity of ambulances, trucks, cars and fire engines racing by, bouncing through the potholes.

It's mostly German Military equipment and he watches with fascination, as their efforts to douse the flames are nearly futile.

"FRITS!" F R I T S !" It's Jan, running his way. Frits turns towards him and before they even meet he hollers, "Where are the boys?"

"Home...probably, they kept running. Look at yourself, what happened to you?"

Frits starts to tell him what happened, when he spots a body, crushed into the wall of the warehouse, about six feet above the ground.

"He's SPLASHED! Oh God, it's HEINZ!" He vomits in the ditch until he thinks his guts are coming out...God he's sick..."What a sight!"

That body must have traveled 150 yards in the air before being com-pacted in that wall.

Jan holds him around the shoulders and that's how they arrive in their backyard.

A MUDPIE, with an arm around it.

"NO MORE HOUTLADING"

Pappa's screaming as he's hosing him down. "NOW STRIP!"

More hosing...

"No more houtlading!" he repeats.

Splittergraben

All he gets for an answer is just a nod and a whisper; "No more HOUT-LADING!"

The following day, they're far away from tracks and other possible targets. They're working hard at a labor camp, where Dutch laborers are building bunkers. They're civilians, pressed into action, moving dirt, pouring concrete and hammering away.

In a clearing is a big stainless steel kettle, (they haven't changed in 4 years) and a big fat cook, wrapped in a big white apron. He's cooking KARTOFFELN SUPPE!"

The boys are splitting logs and washing and cutting potatoes. They don't peel 'em here, they eat 'em skin and all.

"OPA would be proud!" Frits is thinking as he overlooks the situation.

The laborers are nearly out of sight, building their defenses facing west, from where the Allies are supposed to come. The soldiers that are guarding them, he can't see either. Probably sitting down or leaning against a tree.

No one here but them, the "foursome" and the cook.

The axe, he's swinging is a beauty, bigger than Pappa's and probably stainless steel, it looks so good. The cook carries a bayonet on his hip and that's it. His rifle stands up against a tree, but other than that, it seems very "peaceful."

He brings an armload of wood to the kettle, picks up the axe and moves it back to the woodpile, grabs the rifle on the way and behind a big tree, very quietly unloads it. He has never fired a rifle yet, but he knows how they work and without a sound, removes all five bullets.

It's an old MAUSER and each individual bullet has to be removed by sliding the ACTION back and forth, moving the bolt.

He grinds his teeth, it seems so loud, but the cook doesn't hear a thing. Thank God for well-oiled weapons.

He puts the gun back in it's place and nods at Jan, who in turn prods the other boys with his elbows as they sit around the "KARTOFFELN" pot.

Frits and Jan pick up the pot with the potatoes and carry it over to the kettle, where the cook accepts it with a joke.

The cook starts pouring the potatoes in his kettle while the three boys in back gather their loot and ease into the woods. Frits picks up the axe and quietly follows them. When the cook turns around with the empty pot in his hands, the kids are at full speed, quickly disappearing from view. He drops his pot, grabs his rifle, snaps off the safety and hears nothing but "CLICK" as he pulls the trigger. Frits is waving the axe at him, smiling from ear to ear. "See you, sucker!"

They hear him hollering, "Halt, halt!" as they're speeding along.

"DUMB, FAT ASS!"

When they're safely out of range, they sit down and check out their treasures.

Paul has a neat little cleaver, like butcher's use, smaller maybe, but high quality and he has half a loaf of sour bread.

Jan has a quarter side of boiled ham and two carving knives and Henkie has four cans of "SCHWEINEFLEIS', pork.

As they have no can opener, they slice some ham and bread and dine out like gentlemen at Sunday picnic.

Frits produces a pack of cigarettes, their latest experiment and they light up, enjoying the quiet of the woods.

When they get home that afternoon, the town is in an uproar.

"WHAT HAPPENED?" "What's happening?"

"WE'RE FREE!" someone shouts. A Dutch flag hangs out of an upstairs window. They haven't seen one of those for years.

People are all over the street, singing, "ORANJE BOVEN!" "ORANJE BOVEN!" They're singing about the House of Orange, Queen Wilhelmina. etc.

"WHAT HAPPENED!?" Jan's father isn't home and his mother doesn't know much, so after depositing their loot at the Kamphuis house, they race to the Hof Van Holland, straight into the crowded bar. "What?? "SSHH," SSHHH"

They're listening to a crackly broadcast in Dutch. (For God's sake, Pappa has the BBC on) There must be 40 people in the Café, all people without radios.

The radio is making statements like, "Prince Bernard is in BRUSSELS, leading the Dutch Brigade of the British Army under MONTGOMERY.

ANTWERPEN is in British hands and the TOMMIES are entering the NETHERLANDS at the southern Province of ZEELAND.

MAASTRICHT is controlled by the YANKS and other Tommies are entering EINDOVEN. We expect to be in ARNHEM by tonight and in AMSTERDAM tomorrow."

"WHAT HAPPENED?" "SSHHHH!"

"Paris is in American hands, without a shot being fired. We'll be back with another report shortly and Her Majesty will be on the air momentarily!"

Everyone shouts, hoops and hollers, "ORANJE BOVEN, LEVE DE KONINGIN!"

"Long live the Queen!"

Folks file into the street and arm in arm, head for the center of town, laughing and singing.

People, men especially, who haven't been seen for years, (must have disappeared underground) are now dancing and singing in the streets.

"J O O P !" They spot Joop. "Joop, what happened? Did the Germans surrender?"

"No, but the whole front collapsed, the GERMANS are surrendering by thousands and the Allies are racing forward as fast as their supply columns can move with them."

"Radio Holland has asked for all personnel to go on strike in order to hamper GERMAN resistance as much as possible. All trains have stopped running already, gas and electric will probably go off too shortly and all we do now is wait for the liberation to arrive and that will be tomorrow!"

The day will go down in history as "MAD TUESDAY," DOLLE DINSDAG.

Pappa switches the radio back to "Frankfurt" and the German radio confirms some of those claims, like, "HEAVY FIGHTING AT ANTVERP" At least that confirms a hundred mile breakthrough. They don't mention

Soup kettle, Kartoffeln suppe

Germans, loaded with hand grenades

PARIS OR MAASTRICHT.

Risking arrest, Pappa goes back to the BBC and listens to the Queen, hoping "VOET AAN LAND TE ZETTEN IN "NEDERLAND." She's talking about coming ashore in Holland soon and she compliments her people on their courage and loyalty and begs them to aid the Allied forces by resisting all German war effort.

There are very few people left in the bar as Herman turns back to "Frankfurt." Fighting at the "MEUSE" near Charleroy, Belgium, and places in France confirm a considerable advance in one day and indeed, similar progress tomorrow would put the ALLIES in Winterswijk by nightfall tomorrow or the day there after.

"WELL," Herman says, "Ida, it may all be over soon. Heaven knows what the future will bring. At least we haven't lost any loved ones in our family as so many other ones have!"

"Thank God for that. I often wonder how my brother PAUL and MIENTJE and kids are making out in INDIE!" "We haven't heard from them in years."

"They'll be alright. If Germany gives up, Japan will follow shortly thereafter, you'll see. Go fix supper."

Back to "Frankfurt." The Germans are hitting the Tommies with V-Ones near Antverp. "Can you believe that?" Back to the BBC "MAASTRICHT and EINDHOVEN are in our hands!"

"Frankfurt again, "Heavy fighting at the Albert Canal!"

That's in Belgium, if the Germans hold them at the Albert canal, then they can't be in Holland yet! "Weird!"

The party in town is getting in high gear. Flags are popping out of every building now and the market place is full of people, singing, dancing, marching arm in arm, while someone with a tuba is adding a lot of "HOOMPAH-HOOMPAH" to the merriment. In the Market-Restaurant, glasses of beer keep lining up on the bar and people keep walking in, scoop up a glass and disappear back out the door again, back to the merriment.

The BBC is blaring soo loud, you can't hear yourself think and our "FOURSOME" files right in with the rest of the crowd. Frits passes beer back to the young ones while Jan grabs his own and out the door again, singing with the rest, "WIE GOAT NOG NEET NOA HUUS, NOG LANGE NEET!" "We're not going home, long time yet, a long time yet!" Frits finishes Pautlje's beer too. Paul makes a sour face; Next time, get LIMON-ADE! Back to the bar for more beer.

"NOG LANGE NEET, NOG LANGE NEET!" What a party! The churchbells would have chimed in, had they not been stolen, but more and more instruments appear to add to the noise and they're highly successful; at making noise.

"Boy, they're noisy, not good, but noisy. That's what everybody cares about anyway, more noise."

Not a German or Dutch Nazi in sight!

A few guys in blue overalls carrying rifles, identified by their orange armbands as "BINNENLANDSE STRIJDKRACHTEN" (Internal Fighting Forces), lovingly known as "B.S.ers." They get a lot of attention and a lot of backslapping and hugs. It's a blast! Holland is finally free!

Exhausted and hungry, the foursome gets home just in time for, "Wash hands and knees and join the table!"

"Holy Father, who art in heaven..."

Funny, Mama is very subdued and Pappa is in the Café, he'll eat later, so the kids kinda have the floor.

They laugh themselves silly about Paultjes first beer-drinking attempt. It's been a great day!

"Oh, Mama, do I have to go to bed?"

"It's eight o'clock!"

"Ya, but Mama, it's vacation!"

"I know, but you'll be up early again, so brush your teeth and say good night to PAPPA, LET'S GO!"

"Darn, they treat me like a little kid around here!"

Clasien is brushing teeth already and the little ones are asleep.

"WHAT'S THAT? WHAT'S THAT?" He drops his toothbrush and heads for the window.

Just as the sun is setting in the west, truck after truck piles into town from all directions. Staff cars with S.D.-men, screech around corners, people cry and scream and an occasional shot is fired. Dutchmen race into houses, the first ones they come to. Crying women try to stop invading soldiers. More screams and more shots. Flags disappear instantly. More trucks, belching out more soldiers with rifles and sub-machine guns.

Trucks, loaded with men huddled together, rifle barrels trained at their chests, pull out and disappear.

The scene at the market place must be a mess; they can hear the screams from here. A staff car with a loudspeaker passes slowly through the street, announcing an immediate curfew. Anybody seen outside will be shot on the spot.

The customers rush out the backdoor, hoping to make it home through the back alleys. Pappa locks the front door.

Frits is hanging out the window, checking out the action.

Mam, Joop and Clasien are sitting by the radio, Mama and Clasien holding hands and sobbing softly. The streets are quiet now with just an occasional car or soldier patrolling and every so often a passing truck.

The whole "RAZZIA" took less than a half-hour.

The scene in the Café is somber. Ellie is cleaning glasses behind the bar, Pappa's going from table to table collecting them and depositing them on the bar for Ellie. He's wiping ashtrays and tables and all that time his mouth keeps going.

"I told them. It was impossible to maintain that type of pace. If nothing else, you've got to wait for your fuel trucks to catch up, plus your food and ammo. And the guys have to sleep. You can't make that kind of progress without running short of something. Remember the Germans and their BLITZKRIEG? In France, Poland and Russia?

Well, they're the inventors of this type of warfare and they moved fast, but they didn't outrun their supply-lines and I bet you, these Tommies won't outrun their tea-supply either.

And that Goddamn "Radio Holland"; do you know how many Dutch lives this stupid joke is gonna cost? All these guys that were rounded up today, that had gone underground, "POOF!" Gone! LABORCAMPS! GONE!

The ones with the orange armbands, tomorrow morning, "POW, POW!" shot as examples.

Those dumb bastards there in LONDON and that Queen. He starts imitating her; "Tomorrow, I'll...no, wait a minute, she doesn't say, "I'll," she says, "WE'LL" put our feet on Dutch soil!" Shit, there won't be any Allied foot on Dutch soil for another year, if they keep screwing up like this.

Those dumb Britishers got stopped at the ALBERT CANAL in BEL-

GIUM, they did not get into EINDHOVEN, MAASTRICHT or ZEELAND, well maybe into ZEELAND up to the river SCHELDE, but the BBC and the Queen should not have stated or implied any different.

I know the Germans propaganda machine, Mr. Joepie Gobels, would pull shit like that, but the Queen of Orange??, that stinks!!"

Oh Wow! "What is this?" The lights go off and the radio falls quiet. "Ellie, you have candles there, right?"

NO LIGHTS is a routine drill, nothing to worry about.

"Sit still," Pappa flicks his lighter. "Joop, get the petroleum lamp from the BIJ-KEUKEN. Oh Hell, wait, we may as well go to the kitchen, that radio won't come on anymore tonight!" He turns the knob to "off" and they file out on their way to the kitchen.

It's like a mini-procession with those candles.

THE ELECTRICITY DOES NOT COME BACK ON!!! NOT TO-DAY... NOT TOMORROW... NOT AT ALL FOR THE REMAINDER OF THE WAR!!!

The proclamations are all over town, proclaiming a state of emergency. Curfew at eight at night till six in the morning. Violators will be shot!

If striking railroad workers, electrical and gas workers, civil servants, do not return to work today, no more service will be supplied including no garbage collection or police protection. Food supplies will be halted and coal supplies will be stopped. Factories will only produce essentials for the WAR EFFORT, etc, etc.

"LET'S TALK!" The café is empty, it's two o'clock. One newspaper has arrived, all bad news. Only "BRAM" was in for his two "BRANDEWIJNTJES," no one else, all day. The whole family sits around the reading table. Mama removes the long reading lamp, so the kids can look across.

Pappa looks at his brood, "It's going to be rough!

"The way I see it, from here on in, we have one common goal; SUR-VIVAL!

Everyone, young and old, we're going to work together for one purpose; SURVIVAL. Until this is over, we won't have time for play anymore. We need food, first of all, fuel second, light third and clothes next. Your Mama is going to get on her bike and contact farmers, negotiate for potatoes, meat, wheat and vegetables. We don't expect her to carry it home boys, you're going to need a wagon. HOLD-IT, HOLD-IT! I'm not finished! The milkruns have to double if we can't get twice as much from our BOER, no, not you, we'll have to find another. Thank God, we have things to negotiate with, liquor and wine, pots and pans. We're more fortunate than most.

Boys, every minute, every spare minute, gather wood, compile lots of it before the snows come. Frits, I need two car-batteries, can you get those? Negotiate with booze, if necessary!"

"What are you going to do with batteries, Pap?"

"I'm going to rig up the radio, that's what!

Frits, how much carbide can you get a hold of and we need two more carbide lamps, they give excellent white light. Candles, Ida, you can get wax, right? Joop, figure out how to make candles."

"What else?" More discussions, but the basic idea is clear.

Frits feels that he will have to shoulder the responsibility for his families survival. Twelve years old? He can handle it!

Within a half-hour he is back. Sometimes, you need a little luck.

On his way to the WALHOF garage, he stops by the STEIN's. Panic, sheer PANIC.

Ursula is crying and Mutti looks as if she just quit.

"What's going on?"

"We're going back to Germany. Yesterday people knocked the door down and threatened to kill us, they had guns and they wanted Dr. Stein. They searched the house and punched Hans, it was terrible! Dr. Stein is coming with the car, we're packed to go. Is there anything you want?

Might your parents want to buy any of our furniture? It's brand new, you know. Sure, you can have the wagon, Hans, give Frits all your things. You can't take it with you anyway. At least, you people have always treated us decently!" She starts crying again, it's time to get out.

Back home again, he opens the backdoor, and hollers, "COME HERE, COME OUT, SEE WHAT I GOT!" As they come out, he puts it all on display, "Wagon, Autoped, Roller skates, soccerball, chess-set." And "Mam, Pap, you gotta get over there. They wanna sell everything cheap!"

"Who?"

"The Stein's of course, they're going back to Germany today, you gotta go now!"

Two 12 volt batteries and a ten liter drum of carbide is more than Pappa bargained for. "I need 2 six volt batteries, but I guess, I can make it work!"

"Two 12 volts batteries gotta be better than two 6 volts ones, right? It should make the radio play louder, right?" "NO?" He couldn't get another carbide lamp at the garage, but the total cost of his purchase so far, "one bottle of rum," not bad.

He puts his little wagon to good use for the first time, cause boy, those batteries are heavy! He wants to put an old blanket over them, for the trip home, but is told something about "acid," that eats cloth. He understands no more about acid and cloth than he understands about 12 or 6 volt batteries. He doesn't care anyway.

After DOLLE DINSDAG a lot more troops are stationed around WIN-TERSWIJK, lots of them at farmhouses.

"Kamp VOSSEVELD," that used to be a labor camp is being converted to a military post and then one day, here comes the sorriest sight, they have ever seen.

The "DEUTSCHE VOLKSSTURM," they're called. Walking west, out of Germany, comes the most RAG-TAG bunch of people, since the "SANS-SOUCI" troops of Napoleon after their defeat in RUSSIA.

Old men and young boys in all sorts of uniforms, color and sizes, come walking, no...STUMBLING....down the road in three columns. They're tired, hungry, sore and listless. They look like they'd rather lay down and die, than go to war and fight!

The foursome falls in with them and share sad tales of 15 years old boys, taken out of school and away from their families for the first time. Or the 55 years old Grandfather, who's been taken away from the family business, leaving it to the women to run. He has already lost one son and two grandsons, has a daughter on the Russian front as a nurse and a son in France somewhere. It's a pathetic bunch.

At "KAMP VOSSEVELD," the boys help out around the barracks and Frits has a job in supply, handing out mattress covers that are to be filled with straw, sheets, pillow cases and blankets.

Later on, the little ones get to work in the kitchen and when Paultje brings Frits an apple in the supply room, Frits whispers to him, "Hey Boer, don't' organize anything yet, you hear!" Paultje nods and gets back to work.

Jan is nowhere in sight. Heaven knows what he is doing!

The job turns out to be a whole day affair and when they leave in the evening, they each carry a loaf of sour gray bread and a request to come back tomorrow. They walk home, dead tired.

During the following days, the "VOLKSTURM" people get issued uniforms, so now, at least, they look like they belong to the same army. They also receive their backpacks, rifles and helmets, but no ammo yet.

Pappa suggests, "That's so they won't shoot their officers!"

Jan has been "filing" papers in the office.

"Do you understand that stuff?"

"Nothing to it."

The camp has not become a target for the JABO's yet, maybe they're not aware yet of its military value.

Now, after a lot of drilling, marching up and down the camp, the new recruits go out for WAR-TRAINING. About 5 miles from the camp is the old "STEENGROEVE," an old claypit, where mortar was mined for years. About a quarter of the pit is filled with water, the rest is for exploring for "FOOLS GOLD."

The Germans, however, use it for target practice. At one point the pit is about a hundred yards wide and two hundred at the far end. Perfect rifle ranges. At the 100 yard range, soldiers lower targets down the cliff, about ten feet, secured by ropes, and raise them for scoring, after the Volkssturmers have fired.

The boys are helping out with the instructions across the pit. German instructors are teaching the old and young recruits how to shoot from the prone, kneeling and standing positions.

The way the boys are helping out; they pick up the ejected shells and throw them in buckets. Some end up in their pockets.

After four year of living under wartime conditions, they have never had a chance to fire anything, but today is the day. They have been exposed to all sorts of weapons, but their experience with the EIERGRANATEN is their only real war-like encounter. Now is their chance. As one platoon finishes and marches off and the next platoon has not arrived yet, the instructors get a break and that's when Frits asks the supervising "OBERLIEUTNANT," "DARF ICH MAHL SCHIESEN?"

"NATURLICH, MEIN KLEINER MANN!" and he's advised to try the prone position first. He's on his belly, at an angle, feet spread apart, toes dug into the dirt, elbow firmly on the ground and the rifle tightly pulled against the right shoulder with his left hand.

"Pull that butt into your shoulder, open the action, put in the bullet, close that bolt; down all the way, you're ready to fire. Don't put that finger on the trigger until your sights are lined up with the target."

He's heard it a hundred times in the last few hours, but this is different. Now he's doing it himself. His arms are a little short, but he manages, he's controlling it. "Okay!" the sights of the 7 MM Mauser are lined up right under the black bulls-eye, his finger moves to the trigger, "APPLY SOFT PRESSURE!" he's telling himself and...."BANG.".the damn rifle knocks him in the cheek so hard, it makes him yelp. The barrel jumps up and his shoulder gets a knock, he had not expected. The soldiers and the boys think his reaction is hilarious; "I told you to pull it hard into your shoulder!" The corporal thinks it's funny! "Wanna shoot some more?" "hahaha"

"No thanks, how about you guys? It's fun!"

"We'll take your word for it!"

Another fun part of the training is the "hand grenade" exercise.

The soldiers lie on their bellies, take a hand grenade from their belt, pull the pin, jump up and run, throwing the grenade as far as possible and then hit the dirt again.

They're practicing with the long stick-like grenades, not the round "EIERGRANATEN" from the fishing days.

Of course, they're duds, just practice grenades and the boys are having a great time, throwing them back to the recruits.

On the average, all the boys get out of their long days is a few meals and a loaf of bread each. That's not too bad though. The sour bread can be kept for a long time and they're being stored in the cellar. The mildew that develops can just be sliced off and the rest of the bread remains for consumption.

After a few weeks, the new recruits are considered ready to save Germany.

The "VOLKSSTURM," old men and young boys are off to the front to beat the "ALLIES" and save the "THIRD REICH!"

"PATHETIC!"

SEPTEMBER 19, 1944

9:30 A.M. A BRIGHT DAY! They always come on bright days....AIR RAID!!!!!

Whenever it's clear, the JABO's come and shoot at anything that moves nowadays!!!

They have the sky to themselves. Hardly ever do the German fighters make an appearance and the exciting dogfights that they could follow from the ground have all but vanished. Too bad. To see one fighter swoop down to tree-top level with a pursuing enemy on it's tail, sometimes two, to hear the TATATATATAT of the machine guns and "YEEEEEEEE," the painful scream of the planes, pulling straight up to the sky, like a homesick angel, then turning and diving again in order to lose the fighter on their tail and the "TATATATATAT" once more, ripping into the splintering aluminum and scattering smoke over the sky. "FANTASTIC SPORT" "GONE!" What used to be a routine show,"GONE!"

This time it's different. The students from M.U.L.O., (Frits and Jan have moved up in the world,) are rushed out of the school and herded towards a bomb shelter. Jan and Frits have graduated from grammar school and are in their first year of the Middelbaar Uitgebreid Lager Onderwijs, the "MULO," and are on their way to the shelter, but trying to avoid going there. There is no aircraft engine noise anywhere, so they just hang around, waiting for the action to start. They don't like shelters anyway. A direct hit would kill everyone inside anyway and sitting under a classroom bench is probably the safest place, even if the building collapses right on top of them.

Middle school

As the boys are shooting the breeze in the schoolyard, a distant hum interrupts them and they try to figure out, where to look and where the noise is coming from. The soft, monotonous, hummmmm, seems to come from the South, maybe even from the East. Strange!!! If they're Allies, the noise should be coming from the West, Germans would be coming from the East, but Germany doesn't have many heavy aircraft left over. Weird!! Now the steady drone of the engines is starting to make the earth vibrate a little and the noise keeps building as the aircraft come closer. The "HUMMM" is building into a roar, a tremendous "ROAR," but yet there are no aircraft in sight. They must be really low, and.....

"THERE THEY ARE!!!!!" OVER THERE!!!! "THERE!!!

People dive into ditches, gutters, shelters and up against walls, flat on their face.

Now they're roaring overhead, "PLANES, PLANES, PLANES AND MORE PLANES!!!"

"Hey, hey, look at that! What are those???? "Gliders..." Those are GLIDERS!!!!

No bombs are being dropped, so everybody's getting up, dusting themselves off. The shelters are emptying out and soon the whole school population is standing in awe, staring up with their mouths open, many clutching one another in fear.

They are seeing the "grandest airborne spectacle" that the world has ever seen. Thousands, (maybe hundreds, but it seems like thousands) of planes, formation after formation of aircraft, towing gliders.

The flights are stacked down; each flight a little lower than the flight in front of it. The "GLIDERS" hang behind and below their "TUGS," so as the flights pass over, the planes get lower and lower till it seems like the gliders must have leaves caught in their fuselages.

For a while the sky is darkened by a massive amount of planes and the reverberations of the engines make the windows rattle!

They are so low, the students can clearly read the serial numbers and the markings tell them that most of them are Americans and the rest Canadian.

When they finally drone away over the horizon, excited conversation breaks out all over the yard, like a bunch of cackling chickens. Everyone wants to talk at the same time.

"LET'S GET BACK INSIDE," it's the principal, "WE'LL DISCUSS IT INSIDE."

"WE'LL SEE WHAT WE CAN FIND OUT AND WE'LL KEEP YOU POSTED! INSIDE PLEASE!"

He must know somebody with a radio, maybe he'll call Pappa, who's still allowed to keep his radio and he's got it going on the batteries.

School had started as usual on September one, in spite of the lack of electricity, classes are conducted at their regular pace and now Jan and Frits get lots of homework too.

Back in the classrooms, maps are produced, the flight direction of the planes is being plotted and the amateur strategists are guessing where the planes came from and what their target might be.

Some opinions prove to be correct: the formation has flown East from England until they crossed the Rhine, then swung to the North-West, crossing the border into Holland for a landing, north of the rivers near ARNHEM.

The headmaster makes a brief appearance with the following announcement:

"After dawn this morning, British paratrooper have landed at DEELEN, north of ARNHEM, Americans have landed at GRAVE and are moving toward NIJMEGEN. The Brits have successfully crossed the ALBERT CANAL in BELGIUM and are in HOLLAND, approaching EINDHOVEN to the north. Unconfirmed as yet, "The crossing of the MAAS, (MEUSE) near MAASTRICHT, but paratroopers have been confirmed at SON in BRABANT, to the north of EINDHOVEN. I'll be back, when I have more information."

"HURRAH...HURRAH...!!!! ORANJE BOVEN!!! It's like "DOLLE

DINSDAG" all over again!

The national map is pulled down and marks are made all over the map, plotting where activity has been reported and it becomes a puzzle of seemingly unrelated dots, without any sensible pattern to them. But then it slowly becomes a broken line from South to North and all the dots are near canal- and river crossings.

The kids are shaking hands, hugging or huddling around the map in front of the room and the whole place is humming with excitement. This time it's different from "DOLLE DINSDAG." This time, they've seen an armada of war-machines for themselves and they know that these gliders are not going back to England, they're in Holland to stay, somewhere not too far to the north of them.

If the allied forces are to the north of them and also to the south of them, how long could it possibly be till they get to WINTERSWIJK to liberate this little town?

A guessing game starts up about gliders, "What's in them?" "Men or equipment?" "Is somebody flying them?" They've never heard of a glider that's as big as a bomber or that can be used as a strategic weapon.

The only significant update that they receive is that the bridge at GRAVE is in American hands and heavy fighting is reported everywhere.

"Okay!!Okay!" Let's settle down and continue with our lesson. You may need it shortly.

"AH, come on, teach!"

"Cut it out, Fokkie Flink, conjugate the verb, "ZIJN" in English, please and class, settle down. Go ahead, Frits!"

"I am, you are, he is, we are, you are, they are. I was, you were, he was, we were, you were, they were!" CRAZY LANGUAGE, but he's right, "we may need it shortly!"

Again, radio Orange announces victories all over the place and the German radio confirms the locations where fighting is taking place, so that checks. The Germans claim a lot of victories, as if they're cutting off many of the air-born Allies.

No more AIR-ARMADAS come over, but the JABO activity is intense.

WINTERSWIJK itself is not getting the brunt of it yet, but the supply lines of the Germans must be getting a beating.

After school, everyone huddles around the radio and since there are no customers in the bar, the BBC can be switched to on occasion. This way they get both sides of the story. This time, EINDHOVEN and MAASTRICTH are definitely in ALLIED hands and bitter fighting continues near ARNHEM and NIJMEGEN.

The exercise is called, "MARKET-GARDEN" and a pattern is definitely evolving, "THEY WANT THE BRIDGES!" They are not advancing over a broad front, they have created a stretch, a hundred kilometers long, of little individual battlefields, created by some 10 aerial drops in different locations and now, they're pushing up from the south to connect all the dots and secure all the bridges.

It's starting to make sense.

Radio Orange repeatedly asks for "RESISTANCE," for the UNDER-GROUND to sabotage the German supply effort in order to aid the Allied cause.

Even though the whole town seems electrified by the events, no public repeat of "DOLLE DINSDAG" celebration is seen anywhere.

"Maybe tomorrow! Maybe tomorrow we'll have a nice surprise. Maybe tomorrow we'll be liberated!"

THERE'S A SURPRISE ALRIGHT!!!! NICE SURPRISE!!!!
PROCLAMATIONS EVERYWHERE.....

"STAY INDOORS...ALL PUBLIC BUILDINGS ARE NOW TAKEN OVER BY THE "WEHRMACHT!" and are "OFF LIMITS" to civilians.

"Public buildings?" "Are schools public buildings?"

"YOO HOO, HALLELUIA! "NO SCHOOL!" "YOO HOO!"

"You've gotta stay indoors though!"

"That's alright! But NO SCHOOL!"

"THERE'S NO SCHOOL, TILL THE END OF THE WAR!!!!"

The radio remains the center of attention. The story remains about the same; "Heavy fighting and heavy losses by the Allies!"

That's the German viewpoint!

Victories of adjoining forces are reported at all points along the thin line that stretches from BELGIUM to NIJMEGEN, then a 15 mile break in the thin line and then THE BRITISH in ARNHEM on the other side of the RHINE!

The TOMMIES are up against a "SWARTZE PANZER" division, according to the German broadcasts and Pappa cynically wonders where the "SWARTZE SS" so suddenly got their tanks that they're deploying near ARNHEM. There's no way they could have gotten back that fast from the French or Belgian fronts. Certainly not back from RUSSIA.

The "WAFFEN SS" is an all volunteer outfit, dedicated and sworn to Hitler. The "SWARTZE SS" is the ELITE of the ELITE of the WAFFEN SS. In their black uniforms with the SKULL and CROSSBONES as their silver emblem, they look impressive and scary and have earned a reputation as tenacious fighters.

Military activity around WINTERSWIJK increases rapidly.

Fighting is taking place within a 50 mile radius in many directions; to the NORTHWEST is ARNHEM, due WEST is NIJMEGEN and GRAVE, SOUTHWEST; SON and EINDHOVEN. So supplies for any of those battlefields are routed through WINTERSWIJK by rail or truck.

The only newcomer on the scene is the Russian PONY-CART!

They are four-wheel wooden carts, smaller than the Dutch milk wagons and drawn by two small horses. They're called RUSSIAN PONIES, but they look exactly like SHETLAND PONIES, bigger than Dutch ponies, yet smaller than a horse.

The ponies and the wagons look like a smaller version of the covered wagons in the COWBOY books by Max Brandt or Zane Grey, only without the covers.

The "MARKET-GARDEN" operation is progressing strangely. The successes in the south, right up to the WAAL at NIJMEGEN, seem real and substantiated, but the occupation of ARNHEM and the RHINE bridges sound like a "see-saw" battle. One time the TOMMIES seem to have control and the next moment the Germans are clobbering them.

Ida's sisters, PAULA, HETTY and NEL live dead-smack in the middle of that warzone with their families. Paula and Nel in ARNHEM and Hetty in VELP. Most of that is in British hands, but heavily challenged by German troops.

Both sides, the BBC as well as Frankfurt report heavy artillery, street fighting, hand-to-hand-combat and heavy destruction.

There is no communication possible at all and obviously, Ida is very worried about her relatives out there and is caught weeping silently from time to time.

Unfortunately, there is not much change in the news, even the next day. It is incredible that the forces are that close and yet cannot bridge that gap between Arnhem and Nijmegen.

Joop was born in NIJMEGEN and Ida and Herman met in ARNHEM, so this is their old stomping-ground and Herman keeps saying, "When I was courting your Mama, I would cycle to ARNHEM to see her, just 19 kilometers from NIJMEGEN, door to door.

We'd go out and I would ride back and I'd be home in forty-five, maybe fifty minutes. And now those TOMMIES can't do that by tank and truck in three days?"

The spirits dampen again. The Germans continue their build-up. Celebrations and enthusiasm fade into history, it doesn't look good.

The southern part of Holland is liberated alright, but the BEACH HEAD at ARNHEM collapses, the progress of the Allies is halted and while the LIBERATORS are within a days walk away, the Dutch people of the "ACHTERHOEK" and the rest of Holland are trapped.

No food, no trains, no coal, no trucks, no clothes, no electricity, no gas and winter on the doorstep. It looks bleak, VERY BLEAK!"
GLOOM SETTLES OVER HOLLAND!!!

CHAPTER X
October 1944

NO SCHOOL!....the ultimate of all blessings...NO SCHOOL!!!
"FULL-TIME GOOF-OFF TIME!" "WHAT A WAY TO LIVE!"

Of course, there are always lots of chores and some are repetitious, "CUT WOOD! GET MILK!" Other chores are more exciting. Digging potatoes with another 100 young kids.

All the foursome is doing is smoking ERZATZ cigarettes or negotiating with the Germans for merchandise.

Pappa has oodles of tobacco leaves hanging in the attic, waiting for Pappa to shred them with his new machine that creates cigarette tobacco.

He rolls his cigarettes like a COWBOY, tip closed with a twist and very thin at the end, so as to waste as little tobacco as possible.

Most of the leaves are "ORGANIZED" by crawling into somebody's yard, flat on their bellies, cutting off just the bottom leaves that are brown already and dragging on the soil.

The boys are heavy into smoking themselves, either Pappa's homegrown "SHAG," stolen cigarettes, Lindentree blossoms, Surrogate or Ersatz cigarettes, called "BLAZERTJES."

Most of that stuff tastes terrible, but smoking is the manly thing to do, sooo...they smoke!"

At one of the visits to their school, now a warehouse, they come upon gasmask cans and gas suits.

These rubberized suits with gasmasks should protect a person 100% against "MUSTARDGAS" attacks. The suit is slipped on over the regular uniforms, so it's bulky and the pants, complete with attached boots, look like a fisherman's wading coveralls.

With the hood up and the gas mask on they look like they're from outer space. Of course, they "need" a fair supply of them for "home-use!" Sure!!

The first water test proves to be a disappointment, because the boots leak like a sieve through the stitches, but the rubberized jackets with the hood make for pretty good rain gear.

Their roving brings them to many of the encampments of the "NEW" RUSSIAN PONY detachments and that accounts for a new experiment or two.

The ponies are in size, halfway between a pony as they know it and a regular horse, but they are unusually spirited. They never walk. They always trot or run. To keep up with them, pulling a wagon requires a steady jogging speed.

Riding them is different altogether. Most of them have never been saddle broken, so trying to ride them becomes an experience.

First, they're lured to the fence with some grass or oats. One person grabs the halter, another climbs on top with the help of the fence or the gate, the halter is turned loose, the pony gets a swat on the ass, the pony goes flying down the pasture, the young rider hanging on for dear life.

By hanging on to the manes, they sometimes manage to stay on top. Most times they go flying off as in a rodeo.

If all goes well, the pony stops at the end of the pasture, so our young COWBOY can slide off and walk back, with or without the pony, mostly without!

That's when things go well. Sometimes things are different. Sometimes the horse bucks so wildly, that our young hero goes flying within 2 seconds. Sometimes the horse turns so fast that the young rider gets shot off the horse like a bullet.

All in all, it's a lot of fun and the German soldiers, lining the fence, taking in the action whoop and holler as if it were a real rodeo!

Riding the little wagons is also an interesting challenge. These little horses have minds of their own and they just feel it when an inexperienced hand takes over the reins. They take it as their chance to do their own thing and go their own way. The strong hand of a soldier is often required to get things back under control and then the lessons can start up again.

By night-time, when the foursome gets home, they're convinced that they could take a wagon train from Virginia to Texas, across mountains, valleys and rivers. Their confidence is boundless!!!

One sunny day, there aren't many anymore, they're eating at the pony bivouac around noon, when the distant wail of an air raid siren tells them "HIER SIND SIE WIEDER, DIE TREUE ACHT," the JABO's again!"

Sure as the dickens, there comes that familiar sound in their direction. Building up fast is that deep growl of powerful engines. Canteens and sandwiches in hand, everyone races for the "SPLITTERGRABEN," away from the farmhouse and the barns.

In a way, it's comical to see the farm family and the soldiers scramble in all directions for their foxholes.

The farmer, ARNOLD DRIESSEN, has never bothered to build any kind of shelter because he is so far removed from any strategic point, that he doesn't have to worry.

UNTIL NOW! The strategic point has moved to HIM!

NOW, he has a complete supply-detachment, complete with hundreds of horses, dozens of trucks and cars, numerous storage tents and a hundred-plus soldiers.

But, he shouldn't have worried, the attack is not meant for them.

The P-51 MUSTANGS come just about dead-over, but then peel off to their right 90 degrees, and dive down onto an unseen target.

"UNSEEN" from the pony bivouac that is, cause just as the first P-51 starts it's staccato TATATATATAT, a FIERLING FLAK and a heavy FLAK piece open up at him.

"MUSIC OF WAR" TATATATATAT, interspersed with an equally fast DUMDUDMDUDMDUM and a slower POPPOPPOPPOPPOP, could make the basis for another "WARSAW CONCERTO." Chopin would have had a ball with this.

One after the other, the planes go in on the target about a mile away from them and as the last one goes in, the first one has completed three-quarters of a circle and goes in again with his TATATATTA and this time also releasing his bombs. Ten seconds after the start of the groan of the pull-up, they hear the familiar KABOOM.

"Five-hundred-pounders," war-expert Frits informs the Sergeant next to him in the GRABEN, watching the spectacle.

Then SUDDENLY!!! It's as if a hundred heavy ACK-ACK guns join the music.

All sorts of explosions, big and small, seem to blast up at the aircraft and huge fireballs appear on the horizon.

"What are they shooting with, Sarge?"

"WRONG, WRONG, SOMETHING WRONG...THEY'RE NOT SHOOTING BACK! The railroad is over there....They've hit an ammo dump or an ammo-supply train...let's GO! LET'S GO! SCHNELL... EVERYBODY LET'S GO!"

As the JABO's disappear, mission accomplished, the Germans fever-ishly harness their horses, start up trucks and race in the direction of the continuing explosions. The explosions try to outdo one another for noise and ferociousness and intensity that would have pleased CHOPIN!

On the little wagons they carry firefighting equipment, that is worth a study in itself. Some old, some new, some small, some big, and it bounces all over these carts as they're racing from the dirt track to the road and back onto another dirt track. Left, right, left again, just following the fireworks until they come to a railroad crossing and…THERE IT IS!!!

Off to their left, a quarter of a mile down the track, stands a train, steam from the engine shooting a hundred feet into the air and behind that tall fountain is a huge fireball, that envelopes a thousand little explosions.

The pony caravan gets off the road onto the dirt path along the tracks, but can't do much, other than just, TAKE IN THE SHOW!

In two of the boxcars is a fireworks exposition, uniquely limited to war. A huge fire is burning and it sets off all sorts of explosions as it heats up the primers of all sorts of ammunition that are stored in the cars.

Riffle cartridges explode singularly or boxes at the time, sending bullets and casings 1000 feet in every direction.

Bigger rounds explode with great regularity and one heavy shell lands in the field to the right of them. One of the soldiers, reacting faster than the boys, is over there in a flash, scoops it up and drops it with a scream. The thing is bloody hot. So now he sticks his hands in the dirt of this freshly plowed field and picks the shells up again. This time resting on a bed of protective dirt.

"A 105" he announces.

"What'a a 105?"

"A ONE-0-FIVE is an artillery shell, that is used by the heavy TIGER tanks and by the 105 HOWITZER cannons, that you see being pulled behind those heavy trucks!"

"Can I have it?"

"Sure. This one is in good shape and there'll be plenty more of them, although a lot of them will be split and mutilated!

You see, the explosion goes to the area of the least resistance, so when a cartridge is chambered inside a gun, the pressure can only go one way, out the barrel, behind the bullet. But on the train over there, the weaker spot may be a seam on the side of the shell and it may split open at that point."

"You come back here in a few days, when that thing is burned out and you'll find thousands of them in a mile radius." Another soldier adds.

"A FEW DAYS?" THESE FIREWORKS ARE GONNA GO ON FOR A FEW DAYS?"

"Oh maybe more. If the fire ignites the next boxcar and the next, it could go on for weeks, if the other cars are also loaded with ammo!"

"WOW! We're going to come back tomorrow with the whole family and a picnic basket and we can make a day of it, watching the fireworks!"

Jan wants to know, "Aren't you guys going to try to extinguish that fire?"

"You crazy?" "Would you go within 50 feet of that fire with a hose,

Shot-up locomotive, fall of 1944

while being fired at by a dozen "105" cannons?" "You're nuts!"

"WHAT IS THAT IDIOT DOING OVER THERE?" "THERE!!! He's pointing, "THERE, TO THE LEFT OF THE LOCOMOTIVE! See him?"

A soldier is running along side the train towards the fire and explosions as fast as his legs can carry him!

"He's trying to kill himself, he's gotta be nuts!"

They see him duck underneath the boxcars and disappear from view.

Jan suggest, "He must want one of those shells pretty bad!"

Laughingly, all sorts of other cracks are being made about the "NUT" and then they see him running again, but this time away from the fireworks.

"Maybe he is part of the train crew and lost a pack of cigarettes back there"

Laughter all around, "Or maybe a pack of rubbers!" more laughter.

The answer comes soon enough. A locomotive comes steaming in from town, passes them, brakes hard, backs up to the spewing locomotives, the same man comes running up again, ducks underneath, reappears and races away as if the devil is on his heels.

Immediately, the train starts pulling backwards and now, as it passes them again, it's pulling eight boxcars and a disabled engine away from the destruction fireball.

"WOW!" "NOW WE KNOW, WHAT THE IDIOT WAS DOING!"

He unhooked the cars and that way saved eight boxcars.

"How clever and how courageous! WOW!"

As they continue to watch the fireworks, a repeat of the same stunt takes place on the far side, away from them.

A half-hour later, all that's left are five boxcars, two in the middle belching fire, bullets and smoke. There are two more boxcars at the far end and one more on this end, patiently waiting to be ignited or maybe not.

The pony caravan starts to return to camp, there's nothing that anyone can do here but enjoy the show, so they pull out.

The boys decide to stay a little while longer, hoping for more HOWITZER shells to blow in their direction, but their stomachs finally send them home with their trophy.

It's a beauty! About 12 inches tall and 4 inches across, it's the shiniest brass they've ever seen. They're wondering if this is maybe a part of the "OLD ST. JACOB's bells, that were carted off a while ago.

The family's in awe at the supper table, about the news the boys are enthusiastically reporting. Their enthusiasm is contagious to the point that Herman really considers taking the family out there for the show.

Mama objects, "What if the thing explodes really big? And what if the JABO'S come back to shoot up the rest?" "and..."

"Oh boy, can she dream up problems!"

Pap finally, with a sigh, backs off, "We'll see tomorrow, maybe it won't even be burning anymore!"

The boys realize, "That just killed it!" but they're not worried, they're gonna go anyway!

With one CARBIDE lamp on the table and one over the sink, they have very white lights, that throw immense shadows across the kitchen, making it feel warm and cozy.

After the dishes are done, there's only one place to go in the house, right there, around the kitchen table, where now the lamp is the only light in the whole house.

Not having any homework to do, the family sits and talks and before long, they sing.

Songs of the countryside, songs of love, songs of happiness, and songs of sadness. Pappa knows an endless array of old, old sad songs, some going back to his grandfather's time.

Also a more modern song, that the kids love. It's World War I vintage, about a little girl, "LIENTJE," who's father was a K.L.M. pilot and somehow died as a result of the war, near or over "Indie," the Dutch East Indies, Indonesia.

The song is a tear jerker, but beautiful so every night he's got to sing it for them, "Linda's Daddy was a pilot!!!!"

LINDA'S DADDY WAS A PILOT

Frits Forrer

LINDA'S DADDY WAS A PILOT

LINDA's Daddy was a pilot, for that airline K.L.M.
MAM and LINDA dearly missed him, when he was away from them!
When he'd take off in his airplane, they would search the sky above.
Though they'd wave, he couldn't see them, but he'd always sense their love.

And staring in the ev'ning sky, her MAMA'd whisper with a sigh,
"Your DaddyDear flies by the Heavens, so bow your head and let us pray;
Good Lord, oh Lord, please bless our Daddy, help him safely land today!"

He'd bring presents when he's homebound, from the tropics far away.
Little monkeys, satin dresses and a bird that made her day!
And he'd tell exciting stories, 'bout an era, long before.
But one day, he brought some bad news; He'll be flying in a war!

And staring in the ev'ning sky, her MAMA'd whisper with a sigh,
"Your DaddyDear flies by the Heavens, so bow your head and let us pray;
Good Lord, oh Lord, please bless our Daddy, help him safely land each day!"

One bright morning, LIN's still sleeping, MAM is woken by the phone.
And a man's voice from the Air Base, whispers in a somber tone.
"Tell the truth, please!" hollers MAMA, "Oh, please tell me, it's not true!"
But the voice says; "Sorry, Madam! Is there something we can do?"

Our LINDA wakes by MAMA's scream and MAM is sobbing: "It's no dream! Your
Daddy-Dear is now in Heaven, so bow your head and let us pray!
Oh Dear Lord, Who art in Heaven and with you, Lord, Dad will stay!"

One year later, we find LINDA, flying east with K.L.M.
Daddy's grave! her destination, with Dad's brothers, two of them.
"Are you going by the Heavens?" LINDA asks the Engineer,
"Oh, kind Sir, please take me with you! Yes, I know, it's far from here!

And please, Sir, let my MAMMIE know. She'll understand I *have* to go!
Cause Daddy-Dear is up in Heaven, I beg you Sir, with all I'm worth!
For my MAMMIE's always crying! I'll bring Daddy back to earth!"

LIENTJE'S PAPPIE WAS EEN VLIEGER

Lientje's Pappie was een Vlieger bij de grote K.L.M.
Mammie and het lieve kindje, hielden, oh zo veel van hem.
Als hij eens een reis ging maken, vloog hij over hun huisje heen
En dan wuifden Mam en Lientje, tot hij heel, heel ver verdween.

En turend in de eile lucht, sprak Mammie met een diepe zucht;
"Je Vadertje vliegt langs den Hemel, kom buig nog even je knietjes krom
En laat ons bidden; "Lieve Heertje, breng onze Pappie gauw weer om!"

Wat een vreugd als Pappie thuis kwam, met cadeautjes, oh, zo fraai,
Mooie poppen, een klein aapje en ook eens een papagaai.
En dan kon hij mooi vertellen van het land vol toverpracht,
Maar een week in hunne vreugde, was helaas gauw doorgebracht.

En turend in de eile lucht, sprak Mammie met een diepe zucht;
"Je Vadertje vliegt langs den Hemel, kom buig nog even je knietjes krom
En laat ons bidden; "Lieve Heertje, breng onze Pappie gauw weer om!

Op een ochtend, Lientje sliep nog, rinkelde de telefoon
En een mannen stem van Schiphol, sprak op smartelijke toon.
"Spreek de waarheid!" gilde Mammie, "ik kan niet tweifelen, Meneer!"
Maar de stem sprak droef, "Mevrouwtje, hij viel op het veld van eer!"

En Lientj' ontwaakte door een gil . En Mammie snikte; "'t is Gods wil!"
"Je Vadertje is in den Hemel, kom buig nog even je knietjes krom
En laat ons bidden; "Lieve Heertje, want ons Pappie komt nooit meer om!"

Maanden later mocht klein Lientje met een Oom naar Schiphol mee.
'N grote Douglas zou vertrekken, naar het land ver over zee.
"Gaat U aanstonds langs de Hemel?" vroeg ze aan de Vliegenier,
"Och Meneer, laat mij dan meegaan, al is het zo ver van hier!"

"En Oompje, zegt U dan aan Moe, 'k ben eventjes naar Pappie toe!"
"Want Vadertje is in den Hemel,. Meneertje, laat mij meegaan, kom!"
"Want Mammie zit steeds zo te huilen. Misschien breng'k Pappie wel weer om !"

It's very touching and those evenings in that family kitchen, the stove burning their own logs, the single lamp on the big table, a closeness grows that supercedes all threats of war, all cold weather and all worries. They have one another and that's all that counts!

The following day, the party is still on, but the performance has changed. The two cars that performed yesterday have totally burned out and are twisted pieces of steel, like modern sculptures, stretching their skinny arms into the sky. The frame of one of the cars is so twisted by the intense heat, that one wheel is lifted off the ground about three feet.

Paultje comments, "Looks like a doggy talking a piss!" and roaring with laughter they admit that IT DOES LOOK A DOG WITH IT'S HIND LEG UP!"

The particular car that's now burning seems to have smaller caliber ammo aboard, because the exploding bullets don't sound very loud.

Probably pistol, rifle or machine gun bullets, like point 50's. Just the same, the bullets are flying all over, so they stay a safe distance away.

"Let's check the woods, see what's out there!"

"Not me, not till that thing stops burning. If there's an explosion, half that train may end up in the woods on top of us!"

"Oh, Boer, come on! Any bullets flying in our direction are gonna hit the trees first before they can hit us, but let's go back to the other side of the woods, away from the road, that way we'll have all those trees between us and the fireworks!"

"Alright" and they're now proceeding slowly through the trees toward the boxcars and don't have much luck finding anything. The stuff must have blasted in the other directions. Now they're getting too close, they can see the boxcars burning through the trees.

"We better back up and come back when the fire is out. Let's go!"

"WAIT!"..."OVER HERE!!!" It's Henkie.

They rush to the spot. This is how treasure hunters must feel, their hearts jumping with anticipation.

A broken crate, slit wide open, holding about 15 rounds of "105;s." They're mostly intact, but some have dents and scratches. One is slightly bent.

"WOW, look at that!" Frits bends over to pick up one up.

"Don't, don't touch them, they may go off!"

"Would you stop your whining. This crate was blown into the sky several hundreds of feet, landed here with a thud, so hard, that it cracked open the case and you think my tender hands will make this thing go off? Come on!" Be real, "use that gray stuff God gave you and stop quivering!"

As he stoops over to take one out, the other boys step backward anyway and Paultje hides behind a tree, just some pig-hair and blue eyes sticking out. Frits picks one up gingerly and cradles it in his arms as if he were holding a baby.

Now the boys move in closer, "Is it heavy?" "Let me feel!"

"Me too!"

"Don't drop it!"

"Aw, shut up! The only way this thing can go off is, turn it over Jan, when a pin hits this primer, just like a rifle bullet that we shot at the STEEN-GROEVE. The primer starts a flash when hit, the flash ignites the powder and the powder explodes, sending the bullet, bye, bye. That's the only way it will work, that's the only way it will explode, so stop your miauwing!"

After everyone has had their chance to hold it and admire it, the question comes up, what are we going to do with them?"

"Keep 'em of course! We'll take the bullets out, take out the powder so we can make more snow mountain-bombs and we'll sell or trade the shells!"

"Ya, we outta be able to get some nice stuff for these things!"

"But we can't go down the streets, carrying these big bullets!"

"True! Let's see! We bury them, come back with the wagon and take them home!"

"Let's find a spot!"

"But how are we gonna take these bullets out? They're in there tight!"

"Ya, you're right, true, Tell you what, let's bury the rest and we'll work on this one…let's find a spot under a bush or some place, where nobody is just gonna stumble on them when they come walking through here!"

Under a young Christmas tree, they find the perfect place. They clean away the leaves and some of the dirt. The crate is disassembled completely, the planks are laid on the dirt with the rounds on top, the rest of the planks on top of the ammo, then dirt over it and the leaves make it all look undisturbed underneath the evergreen branches.

"Let's mark the spot. Chip a piece of bark off that oak, Jan, eye level. Boer, that birch over there. Henkie, that oak straight behind me. Great, that puts this right in the center."

"Now, Jan, walk straight to the road, make a mark and come back for us. See if there may be glitches!"

Jan comes back, "Simple, no problem finding you!"

"Great!"

"Now let's see how we get this bullet out. Any idea, Jan?"

"Hold it tightly, Henkie, give me a hand trying to turn this thing! MY God, this is tight! Just No Way!"

"Does anybody else have any ideas?"

"This thing won't budge, I'd hate to think, that we might have to saw it off, that would ruin the shell."

"Well we could put this in Otto's vise and maybe he has large pliers and..."

"Are you crazy?" "Oom Otto would throw you out on your ear. He wouldn't be caught dead with anything German in the house. You remember the Easter Sunday, when they arrested him and tore up his whole house looking for weapons. NO way! He won't touch this!"

"What if we gently drop the shell on something solid with its neck, so the weight of the bullet will stretch the metal and loosen it some?"

"HUH?"

"Let me see!" Jan is thinking, they can hear the gears in his brain grinding away. "I need something hard, like a rock or a..., here we go! This may be perfect and it probably won't scratch the brass."

"I still don't know what you're talking about!"

Jan is unperturbed. "Who has a handkerchief? Okay, great, your belt will do fine!"

Frits hands him his camouflage specialty belt and Jan spreads it gently over a protruding root that sticks up about 3 inches above the soil and is maybe an inch and a half wide.

He carefully lays the cartridge on the stump, with the bullet sticking out over the root. He lifts the cartridge by the bullet about 4 inches above the root and drops it. Paultje disappears behind a tree like a shot and Henkie and Frits jump back quickly.

Jan laughs, "You said yourself, there's only one way to make this thing go off and this is not the way!"

He picks it up again, turns it a quarter of a turn and drops it again. He repeats that procedures a few more times and says, "Let's try it!"

The boys bend down, clamp their hands around the shell as Jan tries to turn the bullet. It wants to budge, it's a little loose, but can't come out yet. It does wiggle a little, so that's encouraging. They can actually see about a millimeter space between the bullet and the shell, where a minute ago there was none.

"You're a genius Jan, a damn genius!"

"I know, I know!" Jan is so modest. He repeats his procedure a few more times and the millimeter grows to THREE and with a little effort, the bullet comes out. "HURRAH...HURRAH...!"

"Pautlje, bury the bullet, let's see the powder!"

"What powder?" All they can see is some white cloth with black print, surrounded by, what looks like green macaroni.

"This is not gunpowder!"

"It's gotta be, how else would it fire?"

"I don't know, let me pull it out!"

"By God, this is in here tight!"

"Jan, turn it over and bang it softly on that root, wait, wait a minute, my belt! You'll cut my belt!"

While Frits is retying his belt, Jan softly bounces the shell up and down.

"It's coming a little" he bounces it some more and pulls one of the macaroni out. It really looks like a 9 inch piece of green macaroni, ready for cooking.

After the first one, the rest comes more easily until finally the piece of cloth comes out. It turns out that it is the same macaroni, packaged in the cloth.

They're flabbergasted. This is not at all what they expected.

"Whatta we gonna do with this?"

"Joop will know! If that green stuff can make that bullet fire ten miles, then there must be something we can do with it. Stick the stuff in your shirts."

"Jan the shell is yours!" "Let's go!"

There is excitement in their step as they make their way home.

Mrs. Kamphuis loves the shell. "I'll shine it up nice and I'll put flowers in it!" .

"Aw, MAM! Flowers?" "Please!" "Women!" "Flowers in a gunshell?" A 105 shell?"

Joop has his advantages. He's smart. Book smart, but smart.

Right now, he's looking at a piece of macaroni, straight macaroni. It's about the same thickness as real MACARONI and also hollow.

"I must admit, I had never thought of gunpowder in any other color than black, and this is certainly no powder! This may have a different composition and there maybe dynamite blended in with it or maybe some other explosive, but it certainly provides a hell of a bang. It throws a ten pound projectile more than ten miles and it can blow up a tank with one hit! So this MACARONI as you call it, may have some potential, let me think!"

They're sitting in the shed, because it started to rain again, and it is a little crowded, because the shed was not designed for conferences, just for tools.

Joop is still in control, "I'm going to try something, I need to do some testing as soon as the rain lets up. How much of this stuff do you have?"

"How much do you need"

Joop laughs heartily; "You mean you have a trainload of this pasta?"

"We may!" Now it's everybody's turn to laugh.

The rain cooperates and they mosey outside, macaroni inside their wind breakers.

"Let's go to the pasture out back, who's got matches?" "Okay"

At the pasture, Joop clamps one of the 9 inch pieces between the crossbars of the gate. "First I've got to see how this stuff burns and then I'll try something else. Hold that gate still!"

He lights a match, holds it to the end of the tube and jumps back. NO problem. It just burns slowly with about a one-inch flame and a lot of smoke.

"Alright, we can work with this. You see, not knowing what this stuff is made of, I had no idea if this would singe away in a split second or would explode or what.

Now, at least, we know that nobody is going to be burned badly by mistake. Now for my next test I need your KLOMP. ("MIJNHEER JOOP wears regular shoes, not wooden ones)."

He puts a piece on the ground, lights it, extinguishes the flame with Frits' KLOMP and the green macaroni shoots forward into the pasture, slithering like a snake, doing about 20 M.P.H. until it's burnt out.

The boys are whooping, "YEAH," let me shoot one!"

"Lemme do it too!" Everyone has to have a try and they never fail; the moment the flame is squashed, the darn thing starts smoking and chasing along the ground, trailing smoke.

"Okay, that's enough, that's what I hoped for and it's working. Let's go back to the shed!"

"Whatta you talking about? What are you going to make? How come it shoots like that when you step on it? And how come it doesn't do that when it's burning, only when you step on it?"

The questions from these eager kids flatter the hell out of Joop and he's feeling mighty important right now!

In the shed, he says, "I need a long thin stick, I need tape and do we have an old rag?" "Okay!" Give me about 8 macaroni's. Hold it, wait, let me tape these together first."

He holds two of them together, overlapping about two inches, tapes them, then adds the others, bundled together tightly and tapes them at the top, careful to put the tape across the tops as to seal them off. The end result, a bundle of green macaroni with one piece dangling down by few inches.

"Sharpen that stick on both ends, please...NO..NO...wait, I need a longer one, at least three feet, ja, that's it Boer, sharpen it, Frits, wet the rag for me, let's go, let's go!"

There they go, all their questions unanswered. This time they trudge into the pasture as far from any homes as they can get.

Joop puts the stick in the ground and plants his contraption on top of it. The longer piece is hanging down, about two inches below the other pieces. He pushes down, so it sets itself well onto the pointed stick, hollers,

"Have that wet rag ready!" strikes a match and pitches the matchbox at somebody, grabs the rag and lights the piece, hanging down. As soon as it burns, he squelches the flame with the rag and jumps back a safe distance. The smoking piece shrinks fast as it's smoldering and now it reaches the other pieces, bundled together. They start to smoke too and PFFFT, it sizzles a second and shshshooooo, it shoots up in sky at least three times as high as the treetops of the tall willows that line the pasture.

The boys cheer and applaud wildly, but Joop grabs the stick and starts running.

"Let's get back to the shed!" They all race after him, but back in the yard they want to know, "Why did we have to run?"

"Well, someone might think that we're sending signals of sorts, so let's wait a while and see if we draw any attention!"

"Joop, Joop, how does all that work?"

He's about to start answering when Mama's voice interrupts them;

"Boys, Boys, I need some wood in the BIJKEUKEN, do you hear me, boys?"

"Ya, Mama, we're coming!"

"Shall we get Pappa in on this?"

"I don't care!"

"I don't either, just don't tell 'em how we got these exactly, let me answer, if he asks!"

In the kitchen, over cocoa and home made cookies, Joop "EINSTEIN" explains the principals behind the "VAU ZWEI!"

"VEE TWO? Never heard of it!"

"You will!" Anyway, it's based on the theory of propulsion...." most of it is over their heads, but they eat it up every word of it.

"THEY ARE NOW INTO ROCKETRY!"

The weather has it pros and cons. Typical fall weather, rainy and sunny, mostly rainy. That chilly, constant rain that covers the lowlands at least 150 days of the year.

The "PRO'S" are: no bombing! Day or night!

For the boys, that is no known advantage, but grown-ups appreciate the relief.

The disadvantage is, it puts a crimp on their activities.

Pappa has concluded that the war will last at least till next summer and that they must plan for a long hard winter.

"MARKET-GARDEN!" the exercise that had brought so much hope to all of Holland did very little as far as the advancement of the Allies is concerned. Instead, it bolstered the Germans confidence and the resolve to hold on.

Hitler refuses to see the danger of his situation and after another attempt on his life, seems willing to sacrifice the life of every man, woman and child, Foreign or German, to satisfy his own hollow, stupid ego.

Pappa seems to understand the consequences.

"We have to have enough wood stashed, enough potatoes in the attic, enough sides of ham and bacon and enough carbide, to make it through the winter, so, let's go!"

Most every day, as the boys do their thing, the wagon, inherited from HANS comes with them and returns, loaded with dead wood of all shapes and sizes.

Every now and then, their load is a 100 pound sack of potatoes or a 50 pound bag of flour.

The milk runs continue every morning and by 8 o'clock, there's always fresh warm milk on the table.

They're into making butter and yogurt now too and a couple of wide-neck bottles stand behind the stove, day and night, fermenting away!

Mama skims the cream off the milk, puts it in the bottles, corks them up and lets them get hot behind the stove. Whatever "fermenting" may mean, the kids don't understand, but they do enjoy the loud "POPS," when the gases inside the bottle blow the big cork to the ceiling. "TADAH!" Round of applause.

On one of their trips, the boys hang around one of the many "LAGERS," the camps with the Russian ponies.

The atmosphere is relaxed and the soldiers that are not on duty, leisurely hang around and amuse themselves with the boys.

The clouds drift by at tree top levels, so there's no chance of JABO's so, with cups of "ERZATZ COFFEE" in their hands, the boys and the soldiers sit, hang or lie around an accordion player and they sing along with fervor.

After 4 years of German occupation, they know as many German songs as they know Dutch ones, so they're singing their hearts out!"

After a while, Frits strolls away from the group, visits with the farmer, the cook, checks things out in the barn, pets the horses and calves, chooses not to pet the pigs and finds a friend in the farmers dog, who follows him everywhere.

The dog's a mutt-of-sorts with sad loving eyes and a little scratching behind the ears has earned Frits his undying loyalty.

One of the farmer's sons is of Joop's age and knows him from way back when, so this leads to a visit in the kitchen, a glass of milk and a piece of cake. The dog too!

The tour continues. The stalls inside the farmhouse are called the "DEHLE."

It's actually a covered court yard, lined with stalls at two sides, huge doors on the far side and the living quarters on the near side, all under one roof. The cows stay inside during the winter and hay is stacked to the rafters, right over the stalls to ensure they'll live through the long nasty, cold winters.

He meanders outside again, checking out the trucks, the staffcar and.... OOOOH wait a minute, back to the staffcar.

"WHAT IS THAT?" On the back seat, on top of a blanket is a beautiful sub-machine gun. He opens the passenger door carefully, looks around once more, and glides into the backseat, next to the gun. He picks it up lovingly; it's a beauty! It has an outer barrel around the inner barrel, about an inch and a half around with dozens of $1/2$ inch holes in it at regular intervals. It has a highly polished wooden stock and wooden handgrip, sticking down in front.

It is in immaculate condition and it must be Russian. The lettering looks somewhat like Greek, yet it isn't. So, it must be a MACHINE-PISTOL that the commandant has brought back from the "OST-FRONT."

Two round drums with a bullet sticking out of each one are lying on the blanket, next to the gun. The bullets are about like a 9 MM round, but the shells are bigger and have the same crimp in them as a rifle cartridge.

"Boy, this is a beauty! But how do I get it out of here?"

He leaves the car and continues his stroll, but now he's looking for a hiding place.

An old barn, off to the side, looks like a good place for his purposes. It's full of old rusted plows, a tractor that looks like it will never run again, generally, it's full of junk that's too good to throw away as yet. It also has a half loft at the rear, stacked with paper and jute sacks.

He selects the cleanest paper sack, turns it inside out, stuffs it inside a jute 100 pound potato sack and walks back to the car. Casually he drops the bundle underneath the nearest truck and strolls back around the farmhouse, back to the singers and the accordion. He winks at his buddies and turns back around the big barn, talking to and looking at the soldiers as he strolls by.

No sign of "HERR COMMANDANT." "I wonder if he can see me from the house?" "Which would be his room? Wonder if he can see the car from there?"

He's sure that the commander of this outfit does not sleep in the barn or in a tent, he probably requisitioned the best room in the house.

After making sure, that the car cannot be seen from the living quarters, he makes it slowly back to the truck.

Suddenly, he's in high gear. Everything happens in seconds.

He grabs the sacks, open the car door, slides in back and in three quick moves has the gun and the magazines inside the sacks. He swings out of the car, closes the door and slings the sack over his shoulder and casually walks over to the old barn as if he's carrying a sack of potatoes.

In the shack, standing on top of the old rusted seat of the tractor, he swings the sack onto the loft, covers it with other sacks and is out of the barn.

'Round back he moves, behind the trees, behind the big barn and joins the singers, coming from the opposite direction, away from the gun.

They stay a while longer until it's time to suggest, "If we don't gather up some wood today, Pappa's gonna be real mad!"

The soldiers can relate to that with a lot of "GRÜSZ GOTT" and "AUF WIEDERSEHN," they walk off, pulling an empty wagon.

There must have been twenty soldiers that could attest to the fact that they had nothing in the wagon.

The boys jump all over him, as soon as they're out of earshot;

"What have you got?" "Are we picking it up now? C'mon, what is it? Tell us!"

All they get out of him is, "You'll see!" and "We'll have to time it carefully when we go for it."

That makes it worse, the suspense is killing them and when they're taking a break along the roadside, he clues them in.

"REALLY??? A RUSSIAN SUB MACHINE GUN???? WOW, WOW, I've seen them in the newsreels when we still had movies, WOW, when are we going after it?"

"In a few days!"

"A few days? Why not now? Or why not tomorrow?"

"NO, NO, that commandant is going to be madder than a pistol and probably mad enough to kill us!"

"What if it's gone in a few days?"

"Possible, but not likely. The word is, A FEW DAYS AND THAT'S IT!"

A few days later, they visit again with half a load of dead trees and again ride the ponies, eat some soup and leave.

"Are we getting it now?"

"No way!"

"Why not?"

"Why not? Because I walked to the far side of the house so I could see behind it and his car is still there!"

"Ya, but that car could be there for the rest of the war!"

"Tough! But our chance will come, let's go in the other direction today and see if we can see the car from that angle on that backroad!"

Turning left this time, coming off the farm path and left again on a dirt road, they can now see the far side of the farmhouse and through the trees and vaguely make out the car and the trucks.

"Whadda ya gonna do?" "You gonna get it now?"

"No, not now. Someday, when that car's not there! Let's follow this road and see where it leads, so we can come back from this direction, next time!"

The next time comes two days later. The car is not in sight this time and they have not passed the bivouac, coming from the opposite direction.

"Let's get some wood first!"

They retrace their steps till they get to a wooden patch, surrounded by pastures and plowed fields. In the woods, they gather enough dead wood to load up half the wagon and return to the spot from where they can see the farm.

"Good, still no car, turn the wagon around!"

With that, he's across the ditch, under the barbed wire and now saunters through the field, his hands in his pockets, resembling a farmboy in his wooden shoes and blue coveralls. He carefully keeps himself lined up with the old barn and the farmhouse, keeping the barn between himself and the main house.

Nobody stirs on this side of the farm and he arrives at the barn undetected. Standing on the metal seat of the rusty tractor again, he feels for his gun underneath the potato sacks, pulls it toward him, grabs the top of the sack, bunches the top together and swings the sack over his shoulder. He jumps down, the gun hitting him hard on the hipbone. He stifles a "YIKES," stops at the door and not seeing anything, he sneaks around the corner and sets off across the field. Carefully keeping the barn again between himself and the farmhouse, he heads back to the boys.

This is the worst part, "WALKING SLOWLY!" ...All his instincts scream,

"RUN..RUN!!" but his brain says, "slowly...slowly..."

All during the "ACTION," he was cool as a cucumber and his reactions were very natural, but now that he has to walk the length of the field without haste, his heart is racing and cold sweat runs down his spine.

Yet, he controls himself and when he's back with the boys, they holler at him, "WHAT DO YOU THINK YOU'RE DOING?" "ARE YOU ON VACATION OR SOMETHING? COULDN'T YOU HURRY A LITTLE BIT??"

"SHUT UP! MOVE THOSE BRANCHES A LITTLE BIT!!!GOOD!!!

Now let's move out slowly...slowly. normal pace!"

Though nervous, they follow directions and they don't breath easily until they've made two right turns and are on a paved country road, moving away from the ponies.

"What's it like?" "When can we see it?"

"Let's go to 't BEUKENBOS and then we'll look at it!"

The BEUKENBOS, named for it's many huge beech trees, is like a country park with winding paths, ferns, toadstools, big red squirrels and flowers. The creek, THE SLINGE, cuts the park in half; the same creek that meanders past the swimming pool, through the BEKKENDELLE, over the waterfall then forms the KOLK, the pond where certain kids go GRENADE fishing.

There is an uncultivated section to the park, where no one ever goes, especially not now, in wartime and fall.

The creek makes a 120 degree turn there, forming a deep swimming hole on the outside of the curve and a natural beach on the inside.

Right there, on the bank, 12 feet above the beach, is an open spot, here they're going to build their LOG CABIN and a FLOAT.

They have already "ORGANIZED" 50 nice straight pine posts from the truck shelters along the roads. They're going to need a lot more of them before they can start construction, but it'll happen soon.

The little path that leads there is virtually non-existent, so Frits slings the bag with his gun over his shoulder and each one picks up a corner of the wagon. They ease themselves down the bank along the road, across the ditch and after about 20 paces into the woods, they deposit the cart and walk on.

Nobody is gonna spot their cart there, so it's a safe place to leave it.

They march on to their "secret" spot, high above the little beach and sit down in a little circle like Indians and start unwrapping their treasure.

The "OOH's and AAAH's don't want to cease.

It's indeed a beauty! It is fairly heavy, about the weight of a rifle, but it's much shorter and more dangerous looking.

They agree that the cartridges are different from anything they've ever seen and that the caliber is about 9 MM. They have no screw driver, so they can't open the magazine and find out how many rounds it holds, but judging from the size of the cartridge and guessing at the size of the spring inside, they estimate between 70 and 100 rounds.

After carefully checking the mechanics of the gun, sliding the action back and forth, testing the safety and feeling the restriction of the trigger when it's on, they're ready to try it.

"What shall we shoot at?"

Glancing around, Frits asks, "How would you like DOVE for supper?"

Behind and above them are hundreds of wood-doves, sitting on bare branches, singing their "ROO-COO, ROOC, ROO-COO!" "ROO-COO, ROOC, ROO-COO!"

"ALL-RIGHT!" Frits slides back the action, latches it, slams in the

Russian submachine gun

magazine, carefully unlatches the action, slides it forward and is ready to shoot.

He stands up, puts the gun to his shoulder, moves over the safety with his thumb and ......TETETETETET, he fires about 15 round that sets the birds scattering in all directions.

"Did I get any? Did you see any fall?" Nothing?" "Damn, not a one?" not one?"

Nobody saw anything fall, but branches.

"That's impossible, there must have been a hundred of them!" ... NOTHING! Not a single one!"

"Can I shoot now?" "Me too! Me too!"

"Okay! Okay! But wait a minute. These bullets are going to be hard to replace. Let's pick up the empties and let me see a moment, Okay?"

"We'll shoot at that stump across the water. That way we can see where our bullets hit!"

They set up. They're shooting from a sitting position at a little stump, about 5 inches tall and 4 inches wide.

All around it is the yellow sand from the vertical bank, carved out by the strong spring currents that make their turn here every year.

Frits lines up the sights, his left elbow on his left knee, his left hand firmly on the front grip, pulling the butt hard into his shoulder. His right thumb flips the safety, he holds his breath, squeezes the trigger and... TETETE three rounds fly out. The first one hitting the target, the second one too high and the third one at least six inches above the stump.

"DAMN! That thing kicks up! It's powerful!"

"Now remember, JUST SQUEEZE THAT TRIGGER FOR ONE SECOND!"

"DON'T HOLD IT DOWN! Three rounds will be gone in a second!"

He flips the safety back on, hands the guns to Henkie and helps him set up.

"Henk, pull it into your shoulder hard. Do you have the stump lined up in your sights?" "Okay, here goes the safety, fire when you're ready, hold yo....." TETETETETET "OH SHIT!"

Some seven or eight rounds spit out of the barrel, each one hitting a foot higher than the other, the last few flying away over the bank.

"Oh shit, Henkie, I said...wait...watch that gun!.. put that safety on... keep pointing it over there! Henk, I said; touch that trigger just a second, JEEZ, how many bullets did you pump out-o-there?"

"We're gonna be outta ammo in two minutes."

Henkie tries to say, "But...but...!" but Jan interrupts, "Oh hell, do you know what I think? I think you've gotta shoot this differently than a rifle. With a rifle you squeeze the trigger gently till the shot goes off, but here, if you do the same thing, 10 rounds are gone before you even move your trigger finger back!" Jan goes on, not about to be interrupted; "WAIT, WAIT, listen to me, listen! Instead of PULLING the trigger, you BANG the trigger. You lean your finger against the trigger and "BLAM," just slam it and come right back, like this!" He gestures with his index finger.

"Try it Jan, try it!"

Jan gets himself into position...aims..."Your safety is still on!"

"Right!" his thumb moves and TETETET, all three hit the stump.

"ATTA BOY!"

"That's the way, Boer, are you ready?"

He's ready, he fires, results....same as Frits. One right on, two above.

"Okay..THAT'S Okay!" "My turn!"

They each get a few more turns and as Henkie's firing, "CLICK," no more! The action stays open and the barrel magazine is obviously empty.

"Set the safety and hand it to me, please! How many did we shoot? Let's figure it out a second."

Frits detaches the round magazine and replaces the gun in the paperbag, then into the potato sack and now into the pants leg of a rubberized "GAS-PAK," a gasoutfit. He cuts the pants in half, "72," sticks the one pantsleg holding the gun into the other. "72?" "You sure?" "Rope please!" "Yep, 72" "Gee, that's less than we thought."

"Well, that means we have 72 left in the other magazine. Thanks!" He's folding over the ends of the pantslegs, ties them up tightly and says, "Let's bury it!"

"You're not gonna take it home?"

"No, this baby stays here for future use!"

LIFE IS GOOD.

They gather some more wood as they go and after lifting their wagon back on the road, they make for home.

Some of it gets unloaded at the KAMPHUIS family where they get to drink their last cocoa. There is no more available.

The drizzle starts up again as they head for home, but it doesn't bother them, they're feeling good about themselves, looking like the hardworking good little boys that they are.

(Never mind the little tarnish on their HALO's)

```
O.T.Einheit Wilhelm Wissel                    Winterswijk,den 26.2.45.
Hotel "Hof van Holland"
W i n t e r s w i i k

            Liste der Gefolgschaftsmitglieder der Baustelle Winterswijk

    Name:        Vorname:      Geboren:     Beruf:              Wohnhaft:
Reichsdeutsche:
1. Kiefer      Ludwig         29.3.08      Hptbauführer        Weurden 41          Wint.
2. Weitemeyer Friedrich       28.4.98      Bauführer           Weurden 41            "
3. Lüdeke      Doris          10.7.27      Büroangest.         Weurden 41            "

Gleichgest. Stammpersonal.
4.  Haffnero Antoon           15.6.01      Lohnbuchhalter      Groenloschew.65       "
5.  Haffnero Antonia H        13.9.28      Steno-Typistin      Groenloschew.65       "
6.  Ophoff   Jacobus          12.8.23      Büroangest.         Kottenseweg  58  I    "
7.  de By    Richard          21.1.06      Küchenverwalter     Kottenseweg  58  I    "
8.  Sterenbergo Hendrik W.    10.6.20      Schachtmeister      Morgenzonw.  8        "
9.  Groeneweg Nieske H        18.9.98      Köchin              Muliersweg 15
10. Perier   Maria            20.2.09      Zimmermädchen       Weurden 41            "
11. ernaczinski Stanisl.      24.4.03      Schachtmeister      Weurden 41            "
12. itnehofski Walczak        30.8.08      Schachtmeister          "                "
13. Lepzy   Stanisl           8.11.13      Vorarbeiter             "                "
14. Marcioszek Valentin        7.1.14          "                   "                "
15. Marcioszek Vincent        10.3.11          "                   "                "
16. Sobanski h Stanisl.       14.4.95          "                   "                "
17. Crame Franz                9.10.87         "                   "                "
18. Mnich Stefan               3.8.22          "                   "                "
19. Schott Jakob              29.8.94          "                   "                "
20. Memot Jakob                7.5.03          "                   "                "
21. Sledzj Josef              24.2.98          "                   "                "
22. Werner Josef              11.7.97      Stammarbeiter           "                "
23. Szebka Josef              20.1.87      Stammarbeiter           "                "
24. Krenalkowa Josef           2.2.25      Vorarbeiter             "                "
25. Widrich Stanisl.           1.6.26      Vorarbeiter             "                "
26. Kasperczak Lorenz          9.7.04      Stammarbeiter           "                "
27. Marchewska Martin          4.6.22      Stammarbeiter           "                "
28. Basanella Angelo          27.12.14     Stammarbeiter           "                "
29. Oasemer Guiaeppe           9.1.15      Stammarbeiter           "                "
30. Dellai Marion              4.12.12     Stammarbeiter           "                "
31. bser Igenio                8.12.09     Stammarbeiter           "                "
```

Stand vom 26-2-1945.

Der Einsatzleiter

Wilhelm Wissel

Germans and Prisoners of War at 41 Weurden

CHAPTER XI
November 1944

Just one month before Frits' 13th birthday on November 14, a drastic change takes place in their lives.

A German officer, HERR HAUPTMANN, of the "ORGANISAZION TODT" appears in a staffcar, accompanied by a beautiful dark-haired girl of about 25, an "OBER GEFREITER" and a chauffeur.

Three of them sit down, but HERR HAUPTMAN remains standing.

"KAFFEE, BITTE!" sends Herman scurrying to the kitchen, orders 4 coffee and runs back to face Herr Hauptmann, who's pacing the floor.

"WIEFIEL ZIMMER HABEN SIE HIER?"

"Moment, mein Frau...ja?"

Herman still hasn't picked up on the German language. He takes over the brewing of the coffee and Ida appears in the Café.

"Jawohl, Herr Hauptmann, womit kann ich ihnen dienen?" Her German is fluent.

He drops a bomb on her, "We, the "ORGANIZATION TODT" are taking over your establishment!" "Don't worry," he raises his hand to shut off Ida's wordflow, "Take it easy Lady," Ida has turned white as a ghost. "We're not throwing you out!" He smiles at her and pats her hand. Ida had to lean on the table to steady herself, "We're moving in with you! Sit down, sit down, genädige Frau, sit down!"

Herman enters with the coffee, three at the front table, one in front of the HAUPTMANN at the round table.

"Setzen sie sich auch, bitte!"

That Herman understands and he obediently sits down next to Ida at the round table and so does Herr Hauptmann.

"Now don't panic and hear me out! Please!"

"We, the O.T. will rent your premises and hire you and your staff, if you have any. We will pay and we will pay well! We will need all the rooms you can spare upstairs and they'll be inhabited by soldiers.

Your place will be closed to the public!"

He talks in short, clipped sentences. "He must be PRUSSIAN." Ida thinks, "He must be hard to deal with." Herman already dislikes him intensely.

"Downstairs here, will be converted to a SCHLAF-LAGER, a ward, dormitory like thing. We will house Russian and Polish prisoners of war down here.

You will not serve them anything, certainly not alcohol. They have no money. They are prisoners. We will provide all the food and coal, including for your family, so you will not starve. The P.O.W.'s sleep and relax during the day and repair railroad tracks and roads at night. We will bring a generator and you'll have electricity again.

We will now inspect your premises and establish a fair price!"

"Come!" he signals to the front table and the Lady and the OBERGE-FREITER jump up. He rises himself and Herman and Ida rise with him. He leads the way as if he owns the place.

He dictates a steady stream of words to the Obergefreiter as he walks, and the Sergeant writes as fast as he can, barely able to keep up.

"The front room, 15 by 30 meters. Billiard space, 6 by 10 meters. Dining room, good, nice size dining room!"

Then outside, checks the yard, the bathroom, the BIJKEUKEN, the kitchen, under the stairs, stops in the Parlor door and turns to the lady, "We eat here!" Up the stairs. "Who sleeps here?" "How many in your family?"

"Big rooms.....good!" "Only one bathroom up here?" "No tub, no shower?"

The look on his face says it all, "Backward, dumb Hollanders!" but his mouth goes on, "Your girls room?" "Ya?" "They'll move in with you!"

To the lady, "This is our room!" she just nods.

Frits is staring at her, "My, she's pretty!" He's following the procession. They're heading back down. "Let's look at that kitchen once more!" Herr Hauptmann is still leading.

"Electric stove..good! Total 3 ovens...we'll make some changes... Let's sit down!"

Back at the round table, he reviews the Sergeants notes and calculations and mentions a figure. He's not negotiating, he's telling them.

He's up in a few seconds, out to the car and they're gone, leaving Ida and Herman at the table STUNNED.

It's as they've been picked up by a violent whirlwind, sucked into the air, twisted and dumped again! Herman's whole being revolts against it!

"That arrogant son-of-a-bitch, that lousy bastard!"

"Herman, Herman, calm down, let's look at it a moment; it may not be so bad after all. We hardly had any more business with that curfew at eight. We can hardly get any liquor anymore and I don't know how we would make it through the winter. Now we'll have food, we'll have heat, we'll have electricity, think about it! We'll have to cook for all these people, but that's Okay, we're being paid for that and we'll have plenty to eat for our selves. Think about that!

Just think of all these poor people that don't have any food, especially in the cities. Most of them don't know where tomorrow's meals are gonna come from. Pappa, this may be a blessing in disguise.

Besides that, there's nothing you can do about it, and if you stand up against them, you'll end up in a concentration camp and then what?

The "O.T." is going to take over our place anyway, whether you're here or not, so let's calm down!"

"When did he say they're coming?" "How many?"

The kids have all filed into the bar and are sitting at the round table with their parents or standing around it. The questions are coming fast and furious, like machinegun fire.

"What's the "OT?" "When are they coming?" "How many are there?" "Will the Russians try to kill us?" "What do we do?" "How about BRAM?" "What's he gonna drink?" "Can we help?" "Am I going to sleep in your room?" "Really Mam?" "No more customers?" "Can we keep the radio?" "What's that lady gonna do?" "Is she the cook?" ???

"Kids, KIDS!!!! Slow, slow down!!"

"Let's go the kitchen and talk about it. It's warmer there!"

In the kitchen, all questions are answered but a few, How long will they stay?" "What are the P.O.W.'s going to sleep on?"

"How many are there going to be?"

"We'll see!" Mama is in solid control. "We better vacate KAMER V and put the girl's stuff in our room!"

"Goody, we'll have power again!" "Ya, that's right!" "Maybe, indeed, it will all be for the better!" "Let's do it!"

Two days later, they start coming in. First only eight....the original four and four more soldiers, including a LIEUTENANT who gets a room by himself. The Hauptmann and the Lady set up quarters in room V.

After Mama has been there to bring fresh flowers, she comes down, bristling, out of breath. "They should be ashamed of themselves. She's nothing but his mistress, the slut. There's a picture of his wife and his children right on the dresser, as if she has no shame! His family is back home some place and he's off to war, whoring around and she...she...she.."

Ida is exasperated. Joop says, "She's very pretty, I don't blame him!"

213

"You...you....men...you...!"

The kids laugh at her frustration....

As it turns out, Mama may as well get to like "INGRID," because she's in charge of the food. She displays a lot of charm and tact, letting Mama feel like she's still in charge of her own kitchen, even in charge of the soldier who is the "chief cook."

Ingrid inquires from Mama, "What do we have?" "What do we need and was it satisfactory?"

Ingrid orders stuff and things run rather smoothly. Mama kinda likes her. One thing that bugs Mama is them sleeping together and another thing is that Ingrid wears the most form fitting slacks that really accentuate her figure.

Mama has never worn slacks in her life and maybe she is a little jealous??

For days, all they do is get things organized.

Tables stacked on top of tables. Rugs rolled up. The billiard table is moved the "EETZAAL," paintings are taken off the walls, clocks go the same route, UP INTO THE ATTIC!

The place looks different and it IS different.

Bram and the other steady customers come to the side door for their "NIPS" and besides the morning MILKRUN, their whole routine is changed and will remain quite different.

They start to arrive....The P.O.W.'s. A rag-tag bunch of men between the ages of 20 and 40. They look disheveled with growth of days on their faces. They're mostly dressed in large military overcoats without markings or insignia.

They carry their own strawfilled mattresses and blankets and clutch some sort of canteen.

Forty-eight of them line their mattresses against the far wall and lie down immediately, covering themselves with their blankets right over their fully clothed bodies. Only some of them took their boots off, they must be dead tired.

Most of them sleep until "CHOW-TIME," then file outside to the bathrooms and tidy up a bit. All of this, under guard. They're sloppy, they're relaxed, but under guard just the same! A soldier with a rifle slung over his shoulder watches them at all times.

One guard at the front door, one in the backyard, and two inside the restaurant.

That first day, there isn't much to do for the prisoners so they receive soap, ANTI-LICE soap (the kids have never heard of that before), shaving cream and underwear. They spend the day washing, cleaning up and doing laundry.

After all the terrible propaganda that they're heard about the Russians, these POWs seem like regular human beings by the time the day is over. Only a few speak a little German, but they manage to teach the kids some of the most basic words in Russian and Polish.

One of the soldiers has a dog called "SPITZ." He looks just like a KEESHOND but the soldier has a Russian name for his breed, that the kids cannot pronounce nor remember, but they can remember SPITZ.

It's a magnificent animal with the purest white hair and the blue-est blue eyes. The boys are immediately infatuated with the dog, especially since they lost their Shepherd a few years back, due to old age.

Now they have a new enthusiastic playmate.

Their family life is shattered. They're never alone anymore as a family and even the radio is denied them, because it remains turned off, when the prisoners sleep.

After two days, they're called into action.

The JABO's bombed the switching yard as soon as the sun came out, (there hasn't been any sunshine for two weeks) and after dark, all but three P.O.W's are marched out and return at 2:30 in the morning. As they come in, they're fed again. Mama's been called down at about ONE to run the kitchen, but Pappa stays in bed. His ulcers are acting up badly.

The next day, the boys listen with their mouths open, how by 11 o'clock, the first trains started rolling again and by one, everything was back to normal.

"But where did you get the dirt to fill the holes? And the gravel? And the rails and the ties?"

"Oh, it's all stored out there and it's brought out by truck or rail. Nothing to it!"

That's amazing. The Yanks come and blast away the tracks. The Russians repair them in the evening and the Germans run their trains again all night. It's a strange war out there.

While everything has become routine at HOF VAN HOLLAND (different, but routine) a sad episode touches their lives.

PROCLAMATIONS appear all over town.

"ALL ABLE-BODIED MEN, WHOSE WORK IS NOT ESSENTIAL TO THE "WAR-EFFORT," BETWEEN THE AGE OF 16 AND 45, will report to the marketsquare with shovels and pickaxes. Lodging and food will be provided. Anyone not reporting for this important DEFENSE EFFORT will be arrested and BLAH, BLAH, BLAH.

They've heard it all before, but it's getting closer to them. Joop will be 15 next FEBRUARY 11 and Pappa turned 49 in July.

"Joop, you don't stick your nose out of that door anymore, you hear!

For the remainder of the war! You look 17, so they may grab you, so stay in, don't even go across the street, you hear?"

"Ya Pappa!"

"They won't grab me, even if they raise it to 50, because of my ulcers and because I'm running this joint which is certainly essential to the WAR EFFORT!"

THREE people show up. A total of THREE.

There is a big and ominous cloud of silence hanging over the town for the next day.

Then, at 6 AM, a wail rises from the entire population!!!

A PROCLAMATION now announces the arrest of the following people,

The PASTOR, Catholic. The MINISTER, Protestant. The PASTOR, Reformed. Mr. WILLINK, the manufacturer, Dr. MEYERINK and so on, TWENTY THREE in all. The most prominent people in town.

They will be EXECUTED Sunday at noon unless at 8 AM on Saturday morning 600 men between the ages of 16 and 60, report to the same market square. No repercussions will be applied to those men, that should have duly reported yesterday, but failed to do so, IF they appear Saturday at 8 AM.

The whole town is in a quiet uproar.

"Uproar, because they're upset and "Quiet" because there are no public demonstrations, except ONE.

At about noon, Mrs. WILLINK, the wife, (the very rich wife) of the owner of most of the factories and the number ONE employer in town, comes walking through the street, ringing a handbell and crying.

"PLEASE, REPORT TOMORROW AND SAVE MY HUSBAND. PLEASE, I BEG YOU. PLEASE REPORT!"

Crying, screaming, at the top of her lungs, all the time ringing the bell.

Mama runs out to her and tries to calm her, to come in and have some coffee, telling her, "Everything will be alright, please, come have some milk!" but she gets shoved aside and Mrs. Willink continues down the street."

"PLEASE, REPORT TOMORROW...."

Mama's crying openly in the street, her body just heaving with sobs and as a neighbor and Herman put their arms around her, all she can do is sob.

"What has this world come to???" SOB.

EIGHTEEN HUNDRED men and boys show up that Saturday morning. The youngest one is 12 and the oldest one, 81.

It's an emotional scene. Six hundred are selected and by 2 in the afternoon, they're loaded in trucks and horse wagons and carted off.

The prisoners are released.

On Sunday, the churches are filled to the rafters.

PROCLAMATIE

Reeds herhaaldelijk heb ik mij per oproep tot de bevolking gericht om zich te melden voor den arbeidsinzet te Zevenaar en Bocholt. Aangezien hieraan niet het noodige gevolg is gegeven, moet ik U in opdracht van het S.S. commando te Zevenaar het volgende mededeelen :

1e. Heden zijn als strafmaatregel de volgende personen in verzekerde bewaring gesteld en naar Zevenaar overgebracht :

Blaauw, G. J.	Holders, H. W.	Smit, H. M.
Broer, M.	Klein Bussink, G.	Stemerdink, G. W.
Bijlsma, K.	Klumpers, H. J.	te Strake, G. J.
Colenbrander, J. H.	Leurdijk, J. H.	Wassink, J. W.
Colenbrander, G. J.	Meijerink, G. H.	Willink, H. C. J.
Diepeveen, N.	Nuijs, H. J.	Woordes, G. J.
Flach, A.	Overweg, J. F.	Bruynsteen, J. G.
te Gussinklo, R.	Ruepert, F. A.	

2e. Alle manlijke personen van 16 tot 60 jaar dienen zich op Zaterdag 28 October a.s. vanaf 9 uur tot 2 uur aan het raadhuis te melden voor tewerkstelling, met 1 deken, eetgerei en schop

3e. Zij, die hieraan geen gevolg geven stellen zich bloot aan de zwaarste straf.

4e. Alle vrijstellingen door mij of andere instanties afgegeven komen hiermede te vervallen en alleen geldig zijn de vrijstellingen afgegeven door het S.S. Commando te Zevenaar en door den Beauftragten van den Rijkscommissaris voor de Provincie Gelderland.

5e. Indien zich niet voldoende personen aan het raadhuis hebben gemeld, zullen bovengenoemde in verzekerde bewaring gestelde personen Zondagmiddag 12 uur in Zevenaar worden gefusilleerd.

Ik vertrouw en reken er op dat de bevolking al het mogelijke zal doen om het leven van deze personen te sparen.

Winterswijk, 28 October 1944

De Burgemeester van Winterswijk
Dr. Bos.

Sunday at twelve noon, these people will be shot

217

"Volunteers" on their way to build defense works, 1944

Never in the history of WINTERSWIJK have so many people attended church in one day. It seems like the experiences of the last few days have unified the people and strengthened their resolve.

Mrs. Willink is hospitalized and is under psychiatric care.

First reports are, "She's completely lost her mind and will probably not recover!"

Snowfall comes early in December and it keeps falling steadily.

Hardly a plane is seen or heard during those days and the POWs are put to work on road cleaning details and defense works. Instead of marching to the rail yards at night in all sorts of weather, they ride back and forth to their assignments in trucks and they're not complaining. They have to work, but that beats being shot at some front. They eat well, sleep warm and generally receive good care. They can tell that the German victories in Russia keep moving Westward according to the radio, so in other words, the Russians are advancing. Their attitude is, "All we have to do, is survive a few more months and we'll be free!"

It inspires them and they go through the day with reborn enthusiasm.

The progress by the Allies in Western Europe is non-existent and even though Italy has surrendered, the Germans are holding back the Allies in Italy.

In Southern Belgium, in the Ardennes, the Germans are beating back PATTON and his tanks and CHRISTMAS is therefore very subdued. It's white alright and kinda pleasant, but very quiet and very solemn.

Somewhere during the late evening, while the kids are fast asleep, the radio reports heavy bombing of BERLIN and the RUHRTAL. "Have they no respect even for the day of the Lord?" The Hauptmann is irate!

But when the radio announces that a massive "TANK OFFENSIVE" has been launched near BASTOGNE, he shouts, "Boy, we caught the Yankees napping, didn't we?" Same Hauptmann, 5 minutes later.."MERRY CHRISTMAS!"

The boys are having fun with the snow.

The roads are hard packed after snowstorms that lasted for days. It's ideal for the "PRIKSLEE"'s, the sleds that Pappa built last year. They make it all around town, propelling themselves with their sticks.

They have attached long ropes to the front of the sleds and when a pony-cart comes trotting by, they chase it, double time, swing their rope over the wagon's rear chain, jump on their sled and fly down the street, pulled by two Russian ponies.

If the pony cart makes a turn in a direction in which they don't want to go, they turn loose of the rope, haul it in and continue on their way with their PRIKKERS.

It's a ball out there. No school, plenty of food, a warm place to sleep and plenty of snow!! "What can be better?"

"WHAT COULD GO WRONG???"

Something does! SUDDENLY, very suddenly!!! The early morning hours of February fourth. Out of a clear blue sky.

The "HAUPTMANN" spends a lot of his daytime hours on the road. At night, he spends much time with Ingrid, so the family doesn't see him all that much and doesn't hear much from him either.

Until this morning..."HYSTERICS...SCREAMING....YELLING..."

"STAY IN THE KITCHEN!!! STAY OUT OF IT!!!"

Mama's crying and screaming...Men's voices are bellowing....

Doors slam and finally Mama comes back to the kitchen, in complete hysterics. The girls start crying with her. "What happened Mama, what happened??

"Where's Pappa??"

"Pappa has been arrested!"

"WHAT??? I'll kill the bastards!"

"Why was he arrested, Mama?" "Why?"

"Calm down Mammie, calm down, tell us what happened!"

"He was arguing with the Hauptmann over something. I could hear them shouting. That's when I ran in there and the Hauptmann had pulled his pistol and hollered things like "SCHWEINHUND," "I'll kill you" and he would have shot Pappa, but I jumped in between and I got them to quiet down. He did put his pistol back, but he told the Sergeant to arrest Pappa and they took him away!"

"Where?" "They took him where?"

"What were they fighting over?"

"What are they going to do to him?" "Are they going to kill him?"

"I don't know, I don't know!"

"Oh Ingrid, Ingrid, what happened?"

"Kids be quiet, be quiet!!! Ingrid, what happened?"

Ingrid doesn't know for sure, but Herman and "Herr Hauptmann" have never hit it off and this time they argued over the radio.

Herman got real mad, called him some names and said things like, "The Americans crossed the Rhine already and they'll have your ass pretty soon!" and things like that and the Hauptmann said, "You won't live to enjoy it!" and pulled his pistol. You know the rest."

"Where is he now?"

"Oh my God, with his ulcers, he will die for sure, where do you suppose they've taken him?"

"To the jail at the police station, I'm sure!"

"Kids, stay here. Work with Ingrid. I'm going to bring him back! Stay inside please, don't start trouble, behave yourself till I get back!"

Her tears stop, a determined look burns in her eyes, she grabs her coat and disappears.

It turns out to be the longest day of their lives. All day long, they work and wait, wait and work and finally the youngest four crawl in bed together in room seven, the room now shared by Pappa, Mama and the girls.

Joop stays up to wait. There's little to be done.

Frits has told Paul that if Pappa does not get released soon, he'll get his submachinegun from the woods and ambush HERR HAUPTMANN. Paultje, through lots of tears, got Frits to wait till Mama returns tomorrow and see what she has to say.

Mama arrives at ONE AM. In spite of the curfew, nobody has stopped her. Sitting on the bed, she tells her tale;

"Pappa's alright!" "Pappa's coming home tomorrow!"

"Where have you been all day, Mam?"

"Well, from the Police station at Cityhall, where I saw Pappa, I had to walk to the ORTSCOMMANDANTUR, because this is considered a political matter, not a criminal matter, since the O.T. is basically a civilian engineering outfit!"

"It is?"

"That's what they say. So then I had to wait for "HERR ORTSCOM-MANDANT," the civilian German town commander. He finally saw me in the afternoon and was very encouraging, but then he talked to the Hauptmann and then he said, it was more serious, than he originally thought and it was over his head.

So I had to see the "GAULEITER," the district commander. When I got there, I was told, that he could not see me today. It was six o'clock by then, and it's a good thing I speak DEUTSCH, because I told them I was not leaving till I got to see him, "If I have to stay all week!"

"Hurrah for Mama!!!, and then??"

"He finally saw me at midnight, he will hear us again tomorrow, but he will release Pappa! The only thing is, we will probably have to leave this house!"

"LEAVE THIS HOUSE??"" "GO WHERE?"

"SLEEP IN THE STREET AND FREEZE??"" "WHAT WILL WE EAT?"

"I'm gonna kill him, I swear, I'll kill 'em!"

"Kids, Kids, let's get some rest. Things may work out alright tomorrow.

"At least, we'll have Pappa back, let's get some sleep! Tomorrow it's going to be a lot better. Don't cry…please…don't cry…let's get some sleep."

"Tomorrow…Mam? It's 2:30. It's already tomorrow. It's February 5th. It's Paultje's birthday. He's NINE today, Mam!"

SOME BIRTHDAY!!!

In the morning, Mama leaves again and around noon she reappears, proudly hanging on to Pappa.

The old man hasn't had that much hugging and kissing in his lifetime and the tears are running freely.

"How was it Pappa?" "Did you get any food?" "Where did they take you, Pappa?" "Did you tell off the Hauptmann, Pap?" "Did they beat you up?" "Did they drop water drops on your head until you confessed?" "Were you torched? Do you want me to kill the bastard, Pap?" "I'll kill 'em for you, I will!"

"What's going to happen now, Pap?"

Everyone is talking at the same time. They're sitting in the parlor, because there's no privacy for them in the kitchen or the Café anymore. Kamer VII or the parlor are the only places left them with some privacy.

Herr Ortskommandant

"Hold it, Hold it! Let me talk please..Hold it." He holds up his hand like a cop stopping traffic.

"I'm alright! Yes, I've been fed and no, we're not going to kill anybody, though I can relate to that sentiment!

We've made a deal with the GAULEITER, Herr Mueller! I am free to go, but we must leave this house, as it might lead to a killing after all. We can…Hold it, Hold it…I'm still talking!" Here he goes again with that hand. "We can take with us, just what we need….. enough beds to sleep on, enough chairs to sit on, enough pots to cook in and so on…"

"But where are we going?" Pap?"

"I said, "HOLD IT!" now would you shut up?"

He's getting louder, agitated. Ulcer time. Time to back off.

"We'll only be allowed to take food for three days, that's it. And that's the worst. Where every Hollander has been starving or struggling like hell, we've been living like kings because of the Ruskies and the O.T."

"Now listen, we have three days to get out and this day is already half-way shot. So today, we pack. We'll get together with the neighbors, and see how much booze and food we can smuggle out of this house and store with them. Booze means food and food means survival. We need to survive for a few more months. Italy is in Allied hands, France practically, and Belgium and Luxembourg have been liberated and the Yanks have already crossed the Rhine. If this winter weren't so bitter cold, it might already have been over. The cold is our worst enemy at the moment. We have stacks of wood out back and we're going to need that. By the way, thinking of cold, the Russians are into Poland already and are ready to jump on Germany's back from the other side, so the pressure is really on. One..two..maybe three months and we'll be back here!

NOW FIRST! No fighting or crying amongst ourselves. This is survival.

Frits, Boer, go down the street and check out the empty houses and find some that require the least repair and report back!

Joop, go next door to Van Duren. Stay in the alley, don't show your face in the street. Ask him if we can borrow his handcart.

Clasien, Hedwig, go upstairs...."

The boys are off! Down the street they go on ONE "prinkslee" in tandem, prikking away. More than half the houses are deserted. People having moved out to a farm somewhere, where they're safe from bombing. Some were Jewish homes that were temporarily occupied by EVACUEES, like the STEIN family.

All houses have their windows blown out or boarded up. Most have window panes made of cardboard with little 2 inch round windows in them, about 4 inches apart, set at regular intervals. A lot of the houses nearby are small, some have severe roof damage and in some the walls are partially collapsed.

In the second block, past BAUMAN'S JR old store and the GAPER, the druggist, the houses are attached, but three stories high, with nice yards in back. They go around back to the alley, climb over fences and break into the houses.(Papa did say, check 'em out, right?") Most of the furniture is still in the places, but they obviously haven't been lived in for years.

The boys are narrowing their choices down to two homes, "WOOLD-STRAAT 35 and 37. WOOLDSTRAAT 35 has a black marble plaque at the front door that reads, "Dr. A. GLASS. (he spells it with two SS's, the German way!"

"CHIROPRACTIC and MASSAGE."

No. 37 has a small brass plate for a mailslot bearing the inscription;

"A.L. & M.L. BUISMANS." Those must be the old ladies that own the HATSTORE across from the church.

The old ladies' home is considerably roomier, but the pipes must have frozen inside the house, because the upstairs toilet is overflowing and the raw sewage is running out of the bathroom door, down the stairs, underneath the front door, down the steps and into the gutter. Even though the sewage is frozen solid, inside as well as outside the house, the whole house stinks

Wooldstraat 37 - February, 1945

like a sewer. The smell is so bad, it makes them want to vomit.

They leave the front door unlocked and open some rear windows, so the place can air out some. To their surprise, all the windows in back are intact, not even a crack. The front windows are all cardboard.

They report back and after some hot milk, they head out again, this time with Mama in tow. Paultje and Mama are walking hand in hand, while Frits paddles his sled.

First, they check out Dr. Glass' residence. As they're climbing the stairs, Mama asks, "How do you guys get into these places?"

"Oh Ma, that's easy. This one, I got onto the flat roof of the backroom by standing on their fence and then I climbed onto the windowsill and walked along that sill back there, over to the far window. You see? That one over there?" "Well, the handle wasn't down, so I got my knife in there and PFFFT, it was open."

"Don't you ever fall off? Here we are on the second floor and the sill is snowy and icy, aren't you afraid you'll fall and break your neck?"

"Mam, you worry too much. Then from here, I got into the gutter through the top floor window and I moved next door to 37 through the gutter. And you know, Mam? People hardly ever secure their attic windows, because they don't expect anybody to break in on third floor, so I climb in, go downstairs and open the door for the BOER."

"My God, what I have been raising, a couple of criminals?"

"No, Mam, just think of us as "ROBIN HOOD." We steal from the rich GERMANS and give to the poor; US!"

Mama can't help but laugh in spite of the tragic circumstances.

After they complete the inspection of "35," they move on to "37" and Mama approves of this one, in spite of the smell.

"Look no further, boys. Get a roaring, raging fire going in the hearth in the living room, the fireplace in the parlor and the stove in the kitchen. Close all windows and leave all inside doors open.

This place needs to thaw out! Forget about the smell, don't make faces like that. I know, I know, it's a waste of good wood, I know, but we've got to warm it up."

"Is the downstairs toilet working?"

She pulls the chain...Nothing..it's empty.

"Either the water's turned off or it's frozen. I'll send your father."

"Let's get going!"

It's getting dark as Pappa, Joop and Clasien arrive. They're the clean-up detail. The house is warming up and Pappa wonders where they can get another stove for the upstairs. The blacksmith across the street may have something.

He's got the water going, the boys are just returning with more logs on their sleds and Joop and Clasien are making progress with the hot water.

Unfortunately, the more the sewage melts, the more it stinks. "Make sure, you get back inside before eight o'clock, you hear! You don't wanna be arrested. Take my word for it!"

Pappa's off, the boys stack the wood in the back, top off the stoves and leave. Joop and Clasien follow a little while later.

They have no keys to lock the door with, but who's gonna come out and steal anything or what?"

There is not a soul in sight.

Back at the Hof Van Holland, a lot of hushed activity is taking place, as the cellar is being emptied out. All the glassware, all the liquor, the canned food, the liquid soap, limonade concentrate and bottled beer disappear through the side door of the "SLIJTERIJ," into the "VAN DUREN'S" cellar, next door.

Unbreakable stuff, potatoes, tobacco leaves, mildewed gray bread, goes into the shed out back. It's a smooth, quiet operation, mostly executed by kids, thirteen years and younger.

Mama has packed a lot of stuff already and has managed to get the

225

"GOOD" silver out of the kitchen, without getting caught.

It's stashed under the bed and every one is in KAMER VII, exhausted but exhilarated.

"Isn't it terrible that you have to steal your own junk in your own house, in order to hold onto it?" Mam sighs. "It's a little late, but "HAPPY BIRTHDAY PAULTJE!

Here are some presents, "Happy Birthday!" Next year, we'll have a real birthday party, we'll make it up to you. "Happy birthday, " "Happy Birthday!" hugs and hugs and more hugs. They may have problems, but they have something most precious, they have each other!"

Winter is not letting up and as they move furniture and bedding from the Hof Van Holland to WOOLDSTRAAT 37, the snow flakes fall softly over the entire North West of Europe. They are working with a flat handcart, borrowed from their neighbor, the wagon, inherited from the STEINS and the sleds built by Pappa.

The handcart has two large 5 foot wheels, that prove helpful in the snow, rather than small wheels that might get stuck.

A drawback is that the wheels stick out above the flatbed and you can only store stuff between them, but when the load shifts, the wheels rub up against it and cause damage. They load it to capacity, Frits and Paul line up inside the front bar, like oxen, leaning down on the bar, so the backrest comes off the ground. Mama and Pappa grab a hold of the spokes and get the whole contraption moving.

Once it's rolling, it's not so bad. It's just a matter of maintaining momentum. In a matter of ten minutes, they're in front of #37. With the snow coming down softly, it isn't as cold anymore and with their KLOMPEN and gloves on, they even work up a sweat. Joop, Clasien, and Hedwig, small as she is, clean room by room and once the furniture is in, they go about setting it up.

Pappa, Mama, Frits and Paul go back to the old house and start the whole process all over again.

The cook fixes food for them to take out to the cleaning kids and otherwise co-operates in any way possible. He has worked with the "FORRERS" now for more than four months and he's come to like these people. He hates to see what's happening to them and he whispers to Mama, "That miserable "SCHWEINHUND," that Hauptmann, he'll get his one day, you'll see. Before it's over, he'll wake up with a bayonet in his throat. Count on it!"

The "FORRERS" are virtually moved out on the second day, but Pappa insists on sleeping in the old house, one last night, even though the bedframes are all set up in the "new" house. It gives them a full third day, that they're entitled to,, and one more chance to smuggle things out of the house.

Paintings, silver plates, candle holders, pewter measuring cups and that sort of valuables. An appointed AUCTIONEER takes inventory with Mama of all that's left behind and Herr Hauptmann signs the triplicate forms, that show, that the "THIRD REICH, DEUTSCHLAND," now owes them a little over "Sixty-Three thousand REICHS MARKS"

Herr Hauptmann smirks as if he's thinking, "Now try to collect it."

"Sixty-three thousand Mark?" "Mam, we're rich!"

"No, we're not, if we would ever get the money, most of it would go to the brewery, because they own most of the bar inventory. Besides that, we'll never collect a cent!"

Jopie says "GRACE." They're having their first meal in their new lodgings and again by the light of the carbide lamp.

Nobody argues as the word comes, "Girls, use the downstairs bathroom, brush your teeth, we'll be up to tuck you in. Boys, you get going, when the girls are done, don't use the upstairs bathroom yet!"

Everyone is physically and mentally exhausted and once upstairs, they're in their "Jammies" in a second and under the sheets, shivering away until they warm up. It's below freezing in their third floor bedrooms.

It's February 7th 1945, and all over Europe, the snow continues to fall.

The duties of the day are neatly laid out, playtime is not considered.

"Joop, you will saw wood and chop, or chop wood and saw, as the case may be. Boys, you just keep bringing it. It looks like Herr Hauptmann does not object to us taking our wood, but maybe he doesn't know.

Boer and Frits, you take care of the milk. I don't care how you do it, together in shifts, by bike, cart or sled, as long as the milk is here before noon everyday! Frits, we need more carbide and can you get me a radio, somehow? Ya, a radio!"

Pappa's lost without his news, not knowing what's going on.

"Mama will contact farmers and stores about food, but you boys have to look for other sources too. We'll be going hungry within the week with our present supply!

It's not funny, but just about all the people in occupied Europe are in the same boat, but at least, we're in the country. We're lucky.

Frits, what are the chances of getting some coal? Anthracite, preferably, but coke if need be for the hearth here. This thing needs coal in order to throw off any heat. Can we get our hands on some at the old house?"

"We'll try, but I also know where the coal is being distributed, so I'll see what gives there. Do we have any JUTE sacks left over?"

With sacks tied to their "PRIKSLEES," like cushions, they're on their way. Now it's not fun and games anymore. Now it's survival.

They're on the prowl. The "coal-supply" place turns out to be a good idea. As trucks and horse wagons are loaded, a certain amount of coal is spilled below the platform and no one objects to them picking it out of the snow.

Frits climbs the platform and asks the soldier on duty if they need any help, but he laughingly tells him that the coal comes down in a chute and requires no shoveling, but he lets them sweep the floor and the platform and somehow, a lot of coal ends up in the snow that way.

Paultje is sent home with a fair load, considering their first attempt. "I'll be home in 45 minutes in time for dinner, so wait for me there."

He discovers two things of interest. First, there are several "BROTAUS-GABEN" in different parts of town, where they warehouse and distribute their loaves of sour bread. It is transported by men, forming a line. The first man picks up two loaves from a mountain of bread, pitches it to another man, some six feet away from him. That man swivels his body a half turn, his feet firmly planted, and pitches them to the next man, swivels back and catches two more and so on.

The last man stacks them neatly on the cart or truck until the UNTER-OFFIZIER with the clipboard says, "Halt."

The pony-cart or truck pulls out with their allotment and another vehicle backs into the space for loading.

One eighth grader, "Van Litt," whom Frits recognizes, is working in the line and when there's a break in the action, he comes out and explains that, indeed, loaders are needed and the pay is, one loaf for every vehicle loaded. But this is "HIS" BROTAUSGAGBE, he has a large family and would Frits be so kind as to find his own, and go somewhere else?"

"Where else?"

Well, it turns out that there's one in the same factory, where Frits "FOUND" his beautiful pistol, that first day of the war.

"Really? That's right in back of my new house!"

"Good, have a good trip!"

"Drop dead!"

Frits continues his tour, "prikking" his way toward the tracks and as he gets closer, he's amazed at the damage to the warehouses and silo's.

Those bombs have created a lot of devastation.

The new silo, that used to be gleaming white before the war, is all smudgy and scarred up and sports a bright yellow ribbon around it, some twenty feet away from the building. He asks a soldier, sitting on a fender, eating a sandwich, "What's with the ribbon?"

The soldier mumbles something with his mouth full,

"A what? A blindganger?" "A time bomb?"

"Probably. Those Tommies play some kind of games. We don't know when it will go off or IF. It hit on the other side, walk over to that building there and you'll be able to see a big gash in the side of the building. The bomb experts don't want to play with it; it may blow up in their faces, so it just lies there. One day it will go POOF and the building will come down."

Frits pulls his sled around the corner and sees a gash, like a scar, along-side the wall, where the bomb has penetrated at an angle.

He walks back to the truck. "How long has it been there?"

"I don't know, when was our last night attack? 7, 10 days ago? That's when it happened."

"What's in the building?"

The soldier bursts out laughing, "That's the bad part, buddy. It's loaded with Rum and ARAK GIN and I could use some of that right now! HA-HAHAH!" Must be funny.

"What's ARAK GIN? Pappa?"

"It's like JENEVER and I guess it comes from TURKEY, but I'm not sure. Why do you ask?"

"I may be able to get some. Can we use it?"

"Damn right. Liquor is like gold and we're fast running out of gold. By the way, thanks for the coal, what are our chances of getting a load like that everyday?"

"We can try, Pap. If nobody beats us to it, our chances are pretty good."

In the afternoon, they check out the WILLINKS factory out back. It seems strange that nearly 90% is out of operation. The bicycle racks are mostly empty and no smoke comes out of the tall chimney.

"Wanna climb that sometime?"

"Not me! Those metal rungs is all you can hold onto...BRRR, not me!"

"Chicken, I'm gonna try it sometime!"

They're walking around the entire factory, pulling their sleds and finally come upon the BROTAUSGABE. If they had started in the opposite direction, they would have hit upon it in the first minutes.

There is a lone pony wagon backed up to the open double doors and just two soldiers are loading their own brown bread.

"KÖNNEN WIR HELFEN?"

"NEIN, DANKE, WIR SIND GENAU FERTIG!" "No thanks, we're just finishing!"

The driver covers his cargo with a tarpaulin, takes off the brake and with a gentle tap of the reigns, sends his ponies scurrying away at a modest trot. The soldier inside is done for the day and when he picks up a broom,

Frits jumps in, "I'll do it? When do you need the most help?"

"In the mornings? Is that when most of the trucks and carts come in?"

He's sweeping away. The soldier smiles at his eagerness to please.

"On clear days, we start at three in the morning, but when it's cloudy and we know that the JABO's aren't coming, we start at six. And yes, we get busy and we pay with a loaf of bread!"

He takes the broom. "I'll do it, come here!"

He goes over to a table and collects a bunch of broken loaves that add up to, perhaps three whole ones. The boys tuck them in their windbreakers and with a "DANKE SCHÖN, GRÜSZ GOTT," they're off. He smiles after him, shaking his head and marveling at the way these young kids can pick up a language, just like that! He's been in different countries and it's the same anywhere.

It must be great to be a kid in these days, it beats being a solider. If only he can stay in this warehouse a couple more months, this whole mess will be over and he can go home and get married.

He sighs; "Handling bread is a lot better than having your butt shot off in some frozen SPLITTERGRABEN." He locks the doors.

After delivering the bread at home, Frits has Paultje follow him to the silo with the time bomb. He doesn't tell Paul about the time bomb. If he knew and made a slip of the tongue, Mama would have knipchens.

They circle the silo from a distance, never really indicating that the silo is their main interest. They cross the tracks at a regular railroad crossing, like good boys would do and then take in the scene from the far side of the track.

They're separated from the silo by the road, a ditch, a fence, that's mostly flattened, six pairs of tracks with some busted boxcars here and there, then a loading platform and a scarlike gash in the side of the silo.

A plan starts to form..."Wait here!" They've moved across the street between two buildings. As far as they eye can see, there's not a building in sight that does not have bomb or machine gun damage. He dashes across the street, through the snowfilled ditch, snow getting into his wooden shoes, across some tracks and into an open boxcar and out of sight

Paultje, who's used to his brother's antics by now, doesn't even worry. He has every confidence in his Frits, he's keeping a look out and is ready to whistle on his fingers at the first sign of danger.

Frits reappears, walking backwards, retracing his tracks, swinging his windbreaker back and forth across the snow, erasing any signs of wooden shoe imprints. Once back on the hardpacked snow on the road, he shakes out his jacket, puts it back on and shakes the snow out of his KLOMPEN, one by one. He has to tap 'em on the ground with the heels to get it all out

230

and slipping them back on he joins Paultje.

"No good! Let's look in these buildings!" They crawl into and out of a few decrepit buildings and after the third one, he says, "Let's go, we got it. Just walk back and forth!"

They stomp out path about 4 feet side to make it look like a lot of foot traffic has gone into the building, not just a single track through the fresh snow.

On the way back home, they walk side by side, while Frits explains his plan. Then they hop on their sleds and PRIK their way home.

Supper is enjoyed in the livingroom. The kitchen is just big enough to stand in. They linger in the warmth of the hearth and listen to Pappa telling them about his success with the upstairs toilet. The carbide lamps is their only light and candles don't get lit until it's time to go to bed or for the necessary bathroom trips.

Mama asks if there's a chance to slip back into the old house and OR-GANIZE some blankets, THE GIRLS DON'T HAVE ENOUGH COVER, with what the O.T. allowed them.

"We'll try Mam." "We'll be back!"

As they're pulling out of the yard into the alley, Paul states, "This is the wrong direction!"

"No, it isn't!"

The night is pitch dark with low hanging snow clouds right overhead and not a light insight. They have an hour and fifteen minutes till curfew, so it's "hurry-up!"

"Aren't we going for blankets?"

"Not tonight, we're not!"

Not another word is spoken until they're at the building on the far side of the tracks. The sleds are moved inside. Not a sound anywhere. Nobody lives here anymore. About a mile and a half away, at the station some trains are being moved and they can vaguely see some swinging lights and they spot a glow when cabdoors are opened and closed. Otherwise, NOTHING!"

"Follow me!" Again across the street, through the ditch, snow in their klompen, over the fence, that crunches so loud, they stop and hold their breath. Nothing..nobody stirs…they cross some tracks and stop between the cars, shaking snow out of their wooden shoes.

"Stay here!"

Frits proceeds across the remaining track and onto the platform. He stops, peeks around the corner and not seeing anything, slips toward the gash in the wall. Even though it's pitch dark, the white snow and the dirty white of the silo makes him feel as if he stands out like a flame.

There is no guard. They must feel that a time bomb is a great sentry in itself. He reaches the gash and gingerly steps in.

The soldier had said that the bomb was in the basement, so at least he won't explode it by stepping on it.

He can't see a thing. Holding on to the wall, he feels for a foot hold with his toe, but there's nothing, lower..nothing...This must be the hole in the floor that's been created by the bomb. "DAMN." Still holding onto the wall he reaches as far as possible to his right with his toe, but again...nothing.

Now to his left, he feels something...he puts some weight on it...it holds...His face to the wall, feet spread apart, holding on to the edge of the gash with one hand, feeling for something with the other. He feels a box, nothing to hold onto, he needs a flap or something.. He slides his hand up.. down...he's got a flap.

He's got his eyes closed. He can't see anything anyway and his imagination is more vivid with his eyes closed. His left foot is down solidly, a flap in his left hand, he yanks it and it stays. He's got a solid grip and the flap isn't tearing. Holding on for dear life, he pushes off his right foot, pulls on the flap and swings across the hole he can't see and finds himself embracing a box. He rests a second, "I'm IN!" He looks back and to his surprise, the gash is clearly visible. It must be all that snow, reflecting in spite of the darkness.

He moves his left foot further out...solid...he joins his right one.. solid! He stands inside unsupported.

He takes out his matches, cups his hands, puts his body between the gash and the flame and strikes it. He blows it out immediately. He's seen enough for the time being. He goes off to his right, climbs over a bunch of boxes, feels his way between a bunch of crates and lights another one. Now he takes more time. He locates the big doors that open up to the loading platform, feels for the big cross-bar, lifts it and opens one of the big doors about half an inch.

"Okay, Okay!" he can see snow. Leaving the door at a crack, he turns back inside and studies the supplies; Food, lots of food. "Schweinenfleisch," TUNA, ARAK GIN...there you go!!! He grabs one box, brings it to the door and goes for another one. This time he opens the door, slides the box through, then the other and carries them to the edge of the platform.

He neatly closes the big door and after jumping down, he grabs one of them and brings it to Paul, who's shivering,

"What took you so long?"

"Take this and bring it to the sled." He turns around, retrieves the other box and rushes back across the track, between the boxcars, over the croaking fence, through the ditch, across the street into the warehouse. "This is heavy and I'm cold!"

"Oh shut up and stay here." Back again across the street again, swishing his jacket back across the snow eliminating the tell-tale tracks.

Back in the building, they untie their JUTE sacks, cover their prize and pull out into the road, coil their ropes and get on to prik their way home. Not a soul in sight, just darkened houses, lining the street. No sign of life. As they round the corner into the alley the clock strikes eight.

With wet feet, but otherwise sweating, they walk in with their treasures. "TWO BOXES OF ARAK GIN!" 24 bottles total.

That's a lot of trading gold. After the family is through with their oohing and aahing, Frits wants to know, what's so precious about the stuff. Pappa opens one up and Mama produces little glasses.

In spite of being a bar owner, Pappa is not a drinker, but he'll have a little and Mama joins in too.

Well, Frits gets past the smell, takes a little sip and nearly chokes. It burns his guts out, tears well in his eyes and he races to the kitchen for some water. The family, meanwhile think it's hilarious.

Now Joop has to try it, he survives courageously, but the tears in his eyes give him away.

Pappa takes a sip, smacks his lips and says, "If it weren't for these damn ulcers, I could get in the habit of drinking this stuff!" Mama agrees, but the rest decline, so the bottle is put away, one drink short.

They'll save this one for medicinal purposes.

The little ones go up to bed, carrying their candles, with Mama in tow and now Pappa wants to know, "Where did you find that gold?"

Frits nearly tells him the truth, all but the time bomb, and then he tells them his plan.

"Tomorrow, we can hide our sleds, slip into the building unseen, I left the door unlocked, I select what we want, stash it by the door and that way we can make two runs a night, two boxes each! The questions is what do you want most or what do you need most? I didn't see any rum yet, but there was TUNA, SCHWEINEFLEISCH, VEGETABLES, and a lot more. It's loaded to the ceiling and on nights like this or especially if it snows, no one will see us and we should not have any problems getting two runs a night.

We can't take more than one case each, I don't think, it would be too obvious, we can't hide them, so.."

"Aren't you afraid to get caught?"

"Afraid?" "Ya, I guess, but what could they do? Take the stuff away? We don't have it to start with, so what did we loose?"

Joop shakes his wise head as if he's thinking, "These little foolish brothers of mine!"

233

"So, Pap, tell me what you need most or maybe after we've been in there tomorrow, I can give you a better inventory. Right now, I wanna go to bed, cause I'm working in the BROTAUSGABE at 6 in the morning! Believe me or not, I'm tired!"

Pappa laughs out loud, "I believe that, YA, I'll believe that!"

"Welterusten, Jongen!" Welterusten!"

He doesn't get to work at 6 that morning because he was not needed. He hangs around anyway, and during a break in the action, when there's nobody to serve, he enjoys a cheese sandwich with the troops.

By 8:30 he's working. Turn left with your upper torso, catch two loaves, swing the other way, pitch the loaves away towards the other man and turn fast enough to see two more loaves come flying at you. On and on, it's not hard. It's just without letup, until a vehicle is loaded. He can't loose his concentration for a second or the bread will be on the floor.

He does alright. One wagon loaded, one loaf earned. Short break, next wagon. Turn left, catch loaves.... on one of the his swings to the right, he catches something in the corner of his eye. No time to look...by God...he's right.. What he thought he saw, is really what he saw...it's TANTE MARIA, Mama's oldest sister. Swing left, catch two, swing right...she smiles at him...Tante Maria is one of the relatives, he's not supposed to talk to... swing right..she waves..."Hi Frits!" swing left....what the hell is she doin here?" swing left..swing right...pitch them away..she holds out her hands... like give me one...He's flabbergasted...he only gets a glance of her in church sometimes...swing right...she's the spinster in the family...she wanted to become a NUN, but according to Pappa, she went "RELIGION CRAZY"... swing right...and they kicked her out of the order...swing right...she must be hungry...swing right...on the spur of the moment he pitches one loaf to the next man and one that lands right in her chest. She didn't catch it, but it knocked her off balance and she fell right on her butt. Swing left...right... she's scrambling in the snow, gathering up the bread...left...she waves... smiles...right..I'll be darn...she's hobbles off..swing left..."WAIT TILL I TELL MAMA!.".WOW!"

With his jacket wide open, as if it's mid-summer, clenching three loaves of hard gray-brown bread, he arrives at the back door, smiling from ear to ear, sweating like a pig.

"You'll catch cold like that, dry yourself off!"

"Mama, Mama, listen..."

"You forgot your turn for the milkrun!"

"Oh, Jeez, I forgot, I'll go right now, but listen Mam..."

"Your sister went!"

"Clasien?" Really?" "What is the world coming to?" "Really?" "Hey

Mam…you got to listen a second! Guess who I saw?"

At the dinner table, the whole family gets to enjoy that story and it get many a belly laugh! "Tante Maria, no less!"

As they eat, the next question is, "What next?"

Wood and blankets from the old house?" "WOOD for sure, BLAN-KETS maybe."

Then we'll hit the silo afterwards.

The wood is no problem. Nobody at the old house has been anything but friendly.

Ingrid, the O.T. men, the P.O.W.s, everyone greets them with a smile as they enter the kitchen. They get a snack, some milk and make their way to the Café. They chat with the P.O.W.s and while Paul plays with "SPITZ," Frits slides into the hall very leisurely and then sprints up the stairs, two treads at the time. At the top of the stairs he turns left to the cupboard next to the MANGEL, opens the door, snatches out four blankets, closes the door, and races down the hall to the bathroom, locks the door and opens the little tilt window. He forces the blankets through, one by one, closes window, opens door, chases down the hall and the stairs and is petting SPITZ, all within two minutes.

"Say, GRÜSZ GOTT, Boer, we've gotta load some wood."

"Good bye!" "Auf wiedersehen" and they're out of there. They slip into their wooden shoes at the back door, load some wood on the sled and pull their wagons out of the backyard. They wave at Uncle Otto's kids as they round the corner and after passing the front of the Café, Frits ducks into the alley, and Paultje keeps right on walking with the sled.

Under the bathroom window, he shakes the snow off the blankets, rolls them in his jacket and rushes to catch up to Paul.

"Nothing to it!" "Life's so simple, if you don't complicate it!"

Paultje just nods… It's too much wisdom for him, but he'll buy it!

"Who needs blankets? Who needs wood?"

"Thanks Mam, Yes, I know I'm a genius, but thanks just the same!"

"But I'd rather have some cocoa!" "What? Just milk?" "Okay" "No more cocoa?"

"Just a little? Okay, I'll take a little. What's tomorrow? Why save it for tomorrow?"

"The 11th, Joop's birthday! Your brother will be fifteen!"

"Hurrah for Joop, now he can join the ARMY and we'll be rid of him. I'll have the cocoa now!"

"Frits, don't say things like that!"

"Now that he's fifteen, will he develop a brain?"

"Get out of here, drink your milk and get!"

"Frits, Wait!" Pappa comes in the kitchen. "Frits, how can we get a radio?"

"I don't know, Pap, I don't know where to start looking! Besides that, you don't have electricity and you don't have batteries."

"I'll figure something, but first I need a radio. Where did they store those, remember when everybody had to turn them in?"

"Ya, I remember, I also remember where they stored them, but I believe they hauled them off. We'll check it out! See you later!"

That poor man, nothing to do all day and no paper and no radio! He's going bonkers, not knowing where the war is being fought now!

"We've got to think, Boer, let's go on one sled."

Tandem, prikking along in rhythm, they have reliable transportation.

"Where to?"

"Silo!"

They cross the tracks again and now approach the Silo from the south end, to see it from a different angle. Still looking good, guarded by a yellow ribbon!

They hide their sled and they make the same trek.

Across the street, through the ditch, over the fence and the tracks and between the boxcars.

"Hold it, hold it, let's look!"

Frits lowers himself, edges forward, looks left and right and orders, "Back. A train coming or just switching!"

A few cars over a door is open.

"Let's move over there, lead the way!!"

"Where are you going?"

"Would you move, I'm erasing the tracks!" He's swishing his jacket across the snow behind them as they move and finding the boxcar empty, they crawl in.

Just in time, the train wasn't switching, the train keeps coming, it's leaving town. Frits wishes he'd done a better job with their footprints, in the fresh snow, they may still be obvious.

While they're cleaning the snow out of their wooden shoes and socks, they listen to the train picking up speed as it passes them.

"Can you imagine sitting in here and 8 JABO's coming out of the clouds and dropping bombs on our heads? It's a good thing it's so cloudy, we haven't seen or heard an airplane for weeks. Pappa's going crazy..he needs a radio. Do you know what we're gonna do? We're gonna go to the big VILLA's where all the officers are quartered and check those out. They must have radios. Or at least papers!"

"Pappa can't read German!"

"True, but Mama can. That would really tickle him. Have somebody read to him as if he were a little baby!"

"Well, at least he would know what's going on!"

"True, let's try it when we're done over here!"

"Boy, this is a long train, Frits!"

"Listen, there's another locomotive. I bet you he's pushing…that must be the end of it! Right…let's wait another minute! Okay, looks like we're clear! Let's go, easy like!"

They slide out and return to their spot between the boxcars and again peer left and right…Clear! "Let's walk slowly, as if we belong!"

They cross the last few tracks and to their left they can see the train disappear. They jump on the platform, after Frits gives his little brother a helping hand. Paul is about as tall as the platform is high!

The door is still unlocked and they disappear slowly into the building, closing the door carefully behind them.

Frits wonders what Paultje's reaction would be if he told him, there was a time bomb under their feet. "He'd shit," Frits laughs to himself.

"What's so funny?"

"shsshsh"

With the light coming in through the high windows and the gash in the wall, they can see fairly well, at least all they need to see.

They spot the RUM and carry two cases to the door. "TWO TUNA," "What's TUNA?"

"Fish, I guess!" SALMON, two of each, SCHWEINENFLEISCH, POWDERED EGGS, POWDERED MILK?"

"EGGS, YA, MILK, NO"

"That's enough!"

Peeping through a crack in the door, Frits signals, "Let's go!" and they reverse the whole trip, erasing their tracks as they go.

They visit several of the large villas and find to their surprise, other kids, their own age, working in the kitchens. Some of them are from their own schools. This leaves them no jobs, although in one of the villas it lands them a good bowl of pea soup with pig-knuckles.

"They have an awful lot of officers in their Army, don't they Frits?"

"They sure do. Let's concentrate on radios. Let's go by the GYM, remember, that's where they were turned in!"

They must have looked comical; A sled, two boys on it, wearing wooden shoes, the little one in front, propelling themselves with short sticks in perfect unison.

The GYM is now a LAGER. A hundred mattresses along the walls, tables in the middle and about a dozen soldiers hanging around.

Just one radio, with a group of soldiers sitting around it, so the boys wave "Hello" and join them. The Germans are still winning the war, especially at sea, but the Americans are now fighting in the SCHWARZ WALD, in southern Germany, but there's no news about Holland.

With an apple in hand, the boys leave for home. They have a big night in store.

After supper, they're off again as planned and just as if it were part of the planning, it's started to snow again.

"What do you mean? You asked for snow?"

First run, RUM and SALMON, second run, RUM and TUNA!

Good show!!! They beat the curfew by ten minutes.

This turns out to be a good way to celebrate Jopie's birthday!

Hot chocolate, brown bread with SALMON, what a treat! It's one of the most delicious snacks they've ever tasted.

TUNA isn't bad either, but SALMON, boy, that's something.

"Turn the clock back to twelve o'clock. We may as well keep celebrating. Bring on more SALMON from NOVA SEMBLA!"

"Where's NOVA SEMBLA?"

"Easy, boys, it may still be a long winter!"

"What does RUM taste like?"

"Here we go again, Mama, hand me a little glass!"

"OOOH, this is not bad Pap, but OOOH, does it warm your guts!"

"Yes, sir, it will warm you up!"

"Yes, that it will!"

CHAPTER XII
February 11, 1945

"HAPPY BIRTHDAY, JOOP! FIFTEEN AND SHAVING!!!"

"You'd better not stick your nose outside that door or you may be digging coal."

"IM RUHRTAL! Now tell us what will you be when you grow up?"

"Frits, cut that out!"

"Here comes the last of the cocoa, "Happy Birthday!" Mama is doing her OFF-KEY rendition of the birthday song. "Sorry, Joop, we have only one present, here unwrap it, and the only reason why we have a present at all is because I bought it a year and a half ago. I hope it still fits."

"AAH!! It's beautiful!!!" It is indeed a beautiful sweater, BAVARIAN type, really heavy wool.

"Thank, thank you, Mam, Pap, everybody! Thanks!"

"Well, at least you can fatten up some more before it's too small!"

"Boer, do you know why they have all these deer embroidered on the sweater?"

"Because they're cute??"

"So you'll know where to shoot him!"

"FRITS, THAT'S ENOUGH! Don't you guys have something to do before dinner?"

Frits is already back from the BROTAUSGABE with two loaves and Paul already made the MILKRUN. It's 10 in the morning.

"Ya, Boer, let's go get some coal."

They bum out with the coal this morning, because two old ladies with paper bags in their arms are just leaving as the boys arrive. They picked the area clean. They hang around for a while, but no other vehicles show up, so they decide to recoup some logs from the old house. They explore the possibility of digging into the O.T.'s coal supply, but the guard out back makes that impossible.

239

"Damn, then just wood." The stack is shrinking fast.

"Ya, I think so!"

They're right! It is the coldest winter on record.

During dinner, Frits gives Joop a beautiful S.A. knife, similar to the HAJOT (Hitler Jugend) knife that he still carries.

It's the same length, a 4$^1/_2$ inch blade, a leather over metal sheath, a brown handle with a red diamond holding the letters, "S.A."

Pappa explains what "S.A." stands for, but the main thing that registers with them is that those were the original BROWN SHIRTS, Hitler's early party honchos.

The important thing is, that it's beautiful and Joop is touched by the generosity of his brothers.

It's a great birthday, if only there were some girls, or even just ONE!

The primary objective has become, RADIO, RADIO, RADIO!

Pappa's going mad! He's met the neighbor across the street, one of the few people still living on the block, but he knows nothing either.

He's a Pharmacist, (Apotheker), and he has no way of finding out anything either. Pappa couldn't possibly go back to the Hof Van Holland to listen to his own radio! He might get shot.

He considers walking to the market square and buying a cup of coffee at STAD MUNSTER Café and to listen to the radio over there, but Mama is adamant.

"You stay right here! The war will manage just fine without your help and we're not taking a chance at having you picked up or getting into an argument with another German officer. That gets to be too expensive, thank you!"

"O.K. boys, a radio or bust!"

On one sled, they catch a ride with a slow moving truck and then off to the richer part of town.

Catching a ride with a ponycart is already a challenge, but catching a truck that's moving a little faster is even more interesting.

Because of the snow, their wood-gas driven engines and the narrow streets, the trucks move at about 20-25 MPH.

The boys sprint after it, drop their sled-rope through a hook, bumper or chain, then, holding on to the rope, they gallop along their sled and jump on. (they hope.) Once one's on, the other jumps behind him and they hold on until destination "doth them part!"

If the truck turns the wrong way or goes too fast, all they do is drop the rope and they're on their own. Nothing to it.

If the truck suddenly stops…that's different..that's dangerous. The momentum is liable to slam their faces right into the back of the truck.

BRAKING with their klompen and steering by digging in one more than the other, they hope to avoid disaster. So far they have. Each trip is an interesting challenge and they LOVE it.

As they're cruising by the "WILLINK-MANSION," with all of its lush gardens covered with snow, Frits tells Paul that Mama told him about the WILLINKS.

Mama's youngest sister, TANTE NEL, used to work for them as the UPSTAIRS MAID, so she knows all this stuff first hand.

"The "WILLINKS" and a lot of other rich people in town are "FREE-MASONS" (Vrij Metselaars)."

"What's that?"

"According to Tante Nel, they make a plot with the DEVIL. On earth, they get a lot of wealth, but it's in trade for their souls. So when they die, they go to HELL, because the DEVIL owns their souls."

"Really? Is that true?"

"That's true, ask Mama, she'll tell you!"

"I'd rather be poor on earth and go to heaven!"

"Boer, me too!"

Their next visit is pleasant, but fruitless. They meet two Generals. One kinda young, the other one old, older than Pappa. They wear the shiniest riding boots and magnificent leather coats. Boy, do they look impressive.

Their chauffeurs open their door, click their heels and salute smartly!

"Jawohl, Herr General! Nein, Herr General!" "Natürlich, Herr General!"

The boys wonder if they're famous and if Pappa would know of them? They get some snacks and drinks, but no clear shot at a radio.

They utter their frustration at the supper table, but Pappa said, "Don't fret it. I know you're out there trying!" He sounds sooo benign!

"Mama, Mama, tell us about FREE-MASONS!"

What mama tells 'em is essentially the same as what Frits had said, but Mam also talks about secret meetings, secret handshakes and SATANISM. (Another new word for them). The boys are in awe.

"How many people are FREE-MASONS? Mam?"

"Millions, all rich people, all over the world!"

"Millions, WOW! That devil is really powerful!!!" They shiver, involuntarily.

After supper, the boys prepare for two more runs to the Silo.

"Please, be careful boys!"

"Mothers!" They are so sentimental. They should stay out of a men's world, like theirs."

All goes as planned and even though there's no snow falling tonight, it's a dark night out. "Darn-it, Boer, I forgot to order snow!"

Pautlje gets shoved on the platform and Frits follows. No one in sight. They pull the door..OOPS! It stuck. Pull harder..It's locked! "What happened?"

"Get down off the platform, hide between the cars and wait for me!"

He figures, he'll have to go through that whole stupid routine again, crawling through the slash, working his way over the hole! He's muttering to himself a he slides silently around the corner. "What's this?" "What the hell?"

The gash is boarded up. Solid! "Damn!" The ribbon is gone too. "Damn"

Back to Paultje. "Let's go, the Hell with the tracks!"

Back on their sleds, prikking away, thoroughly disappointed, he starts analyzing, "Maybe after a certain number of days, they consider a time-bomb harmless! Who knows!"

"Time-bomb? What time-bomb?"

"Oh shit!" "I'm just thinking out loud!" "Let's go looking for a radio. It's 7 o'clock, we've got an hour!"

They make their way to the residential section and aren't doing much of anything until they hit the third house.

With their sleds parked in the driveway, they're having "ERZATZ" coffee with some UNTEROFFIZIEREN, as a leather coated Major barges in.

"Who's sleds are those in the drive way?"

"Oh, sorry, I'll move them. Are you trying to get out?"

"ICH HAB KEIN AUTO!"

Ah, he's not trying to get out, he's trying to recruit their services!

"COME HERE!" The boys follow him outside.

"Do you know, where the "BAHNHOF" is?"

Sure, they know the railroad station!

"SCHÖN! Here's five MARK each and two cigars for Pappa! Take these suitcases, just a minute...one more coming..to the BAHNHOF. Wait here for us, we're coming by bike!"

"YA, SICHER, HERR MAJOR!"

They tie the suitcases down, sling the rope over their shoulder and start out of the driveway, pulling their sleds. They make it down the quiet street, onto the main drag and ten minutes later, on cue, not a word said between them, they duck into the alley on their left. They race down the alley and stop at the end, check out the street, left and right, cross over and into another alley between the houses. In and out of another alley, and another one,,, and into their backyard.

"Look what we got!" Three suitcases, 2 big ones and one small one.

"Uniforms, such fine materials. I can make pants from these and shorts and skirts too!" Mama's all excited!

"Socks, look at all these socks! And "LONG-JOHNS," Pappa, look, your size, the guy must have been in Russia!" "Hey Pappa, TARAH!! All for you, riding boots, TARAH!"

Beautiful black riding boots, just about a perfect fit. Room enough for extra socks. Beautiful. He struts around the room like a peacock.

"Mama, real soap...and look here...tooth brushes, real toothbrushes, real pigshair brushes, Mama. I get this one!"

"Handkerchiefs.. linen, I think, or is this cotton' MAM?"

This is better than CHRISTMAS!!! It's like SAINT NICOLAAS' EVE in the small diningroom. "What a haul!"

"What happened to the food?"

"Food?" "Oh, ja. I don't think that's available anymore!"

"Well this is better anyway, where'd you get it?"

"Oh that reminds me, here are two cigars. One for Joop. Happy birthday!"

"Are you really gonna make it?"

"YA! Then I want some rum, I think we've earned it." "PROOST!" Many more years!"

THE WINTER IS NOT LETTING UP.

The old Dutch saying, "BEGINNEN DE DAGEN TE LENGEN, BEGINT DE WINTER TE STRENGEN (when the days grow longer, the winter becomes more severe.) is certainly true this year.

More frost, more snow! It feels like the winter has put the brakes on everything.

No air raids, no news, no new round-ups, just routine things everyday, day after day!

"GET MILK!!! DON'T FIGHT!!! THROW BREAD!! DON'T FIGHT!! NO RADIO??

"NO RADIO!!! "NO COAL???" "GET COAL!!! DON'T FIGHT!!!"

God, it's cold everywhere! It is bitter, bitter cold.

"How's the food??" "I can't believe how much this family eats!"

"We're at the end of the bacon!" "How's the ham holding out??"

"One week, ten days maybe!"

"Christ, where are the Americans?" "What's keeping them?? Why can't I get a damn radio??"

"Easy, Herman!!! Have a glass of milk, don't let your ulcer start acting up! We'll be alright. I'm going to 'tWOOLD. Today. I'm taking some booze, some frying pans and that copper pot. I'll scrounge up some food!"

She did. Two days later, as the first rain of 1945 is falling, turning the roads to slush, the boys are on their way to 'tWOOLD. It's a suburb, so small, that you don't see it, when you pass through. Just one little corner store and lots of farms that make up this agricultural community.

They're pulling the wagon, the HANS STEIN wagon, a rope attached to each side, slung over their shoulders and one hand each on the handle bar. An empty wagon is easy to pull, no sweat.

Mama has done all the negotiating and Mama has done real well and delivered the barter stuff. All the boys have to do is pick up the merchandise, 50 pounds of flour and 100 pounds of potatoes.

Mama has already brought home a side of bacon and a ham.

The going is miserable from the beginning. The slush is deep enough, that it runs into their wooden shoes and they suffer from cold feet, right from the start. Normally, wooden shoes are warm, but not with ice-water in them.

The rain is just about two degrees above freezing and the wind tries to drive it into every crevice of their clothing in order to get to their skin. Their faces feel frozen and marching into the wind, doesn't help any.

"Why couldn't we wait for dry weather, one or two days would not make a whole lot of difference!"

"We're out of potatoes, that's why! Let's jog a while, that'll warm us up!"

An occasional truck passes by, making them scurry into the deeper snow off the shoulder of the road and then the truck tires seem to take pleasure in throwing rivers of slush at them

"We should have left early!" They're trotting now. "Clasien could have gone on the milk run and you didn't have to throw bread this morning. This mess wouldn't have been so slushy either. It would have been a lot easier. We would have been home by now!"

"Tell me something, Boer, what have you just accomplished by all that bitching? Is it raining less? Has it warmed up some? Is the distance shorter? If not, if you didn't improve anything with all your damn negatives, then SHUT UP!" He's shouting now. "So if you can't say anything constructive, JUST SHUT UP! We have a mission. Granted. A miserable mission, but we're going to complete it. You and I are the only ones that can help this family survive. We've done it so far, we're doing it today and we'll keep doing it, you hear! So SHUT UP!"

Nothing is said for about five minutes.

"Can we slow down?"

100 paces fast, 100 paces slow. Like the great "WINETOU," the famous Indian leader and the hunter. It warms them up, although the cold rain beats on them relentlessly.

"We turn here. See the sign? "DEURNE 12 kilometers?" Now two k's till we see a little house with a thatched roof, then right."

One hundred fast, one hundred slow…In the books of KARL MAY, WINETOU and his white sidekick "OLD SHATTERHAND" would have traveled this way, but WINETOU would have done it bare-chested.

"It does work!" Frits is thinking. Counting as they jog numbs the brain.

"Boer, as you count, you can't think of anything else. You block out the environment, you block out the cold, you block out pain. That's how people must do it when they're tortured. Let's practice it!"

"HUH?" Paul doesn't know what he's been thinking. "HUH?"

"Let's practice something…wait…we turn here!"

Now they're on the dirt road. One and a half kilometers to go.

"O.K. listen. Winetou would do this, "What part of your body hurts you the most?"

"All of it!"

"NO, NO, CUT THAT OUT! Select one, your feet, your nose, your eyes, pick one!"

"My hands!"

"YOUR HANDS?"

"Yes, they're soaked and freezing!"

"O.K., O.K., Now concentrate on another part of your body. I'm thinking of every movement my knees make; Bend, Straight, Pressure, Bend, Straight, Concentrate."

It's a good thing they're concentrating on something, because the path is murder. The two right wheels are in the rut caused by the horse-drawn wagons, and the left wheels bounce up and down on the tracks and holes of a thousand hooves, while the slush tugs at the wheels, trying to hold them back. They really have to pull the ropes taut, their inside hands gripping the handles.

"ARE YOU CONCENTRATING? What hurts now? What are you feeling now?"

"EVERYTHING!"

"Drop dead, suffer, see if I care!"

There's the farm. They pull into the "DEHLE," as the big doors are being opened and closed behind them by a very comely young lady of about 19.

"HI, how are you boys? You look soaked. Here, put hay in your klompen, hang them here, upside down, good! They'll dry better that way. Come on in, here, take a towel, dry yourselves!"

They are brought into a big kitchen, with about twelve people scattered around. It's big and warm and hot milk does wonders. They thaw out fast.

They're introduced all around and it turns out that besides the farmer and his family, two more families live on the farm, one of which they know from church and school. The two girls are in Paul's school, (until last August Frits' school too), so it's a bit like ol' homecoming.

The boys are hustled out of their socks and dry ones put on. Their shirts, sweaters and gloves are hung by the stove and cups of soup shoved in their hands. They are given the chairs closest to the stove, warming up rapidly.

Mama has already clued in the farmer's family about the O.T. and their expulsion, but another hundred questions are thrown at them, about what's happening in town.

Along with the warmth, they're getting wound up too and excitedly tell of some of the things that have occurred lately and as he's talking, Frits keeps wondering if the farmer's daughter is the one that all the jokes are about. Boy, she's a beauty.

The suitcase story has them howling with laughter and after that they have to get cracking, if they want to make it home before dark. The farmer has wrapped the flour in the tarpaulin and tied both sacks securely to the wagon with another tarpaulin covering it all.

After they put their gloves on, warm and dry, the farmer wraps their hands with some thin rubber and ties it securely at the wrists with string.

He then pulls their sleeves down over it all and with a lot of "TJU's, STAY DRY! and "THANK YOU" they're back in the weather.

"THESE FIRST 1½ K's ARE GOING TO BE THE HARDEST, SO LET'S GRIT OUR TEETH AND DO IT!"

He isn't just kidding, the additional 150 pound load makes it harder than ever and as somewhere behind those low clouds the sun is sinking, so is the temperature.

The rain is getting interspersed with ice pellets that drive relentlessly into their faces. Their heads bent low, they pull hard at the wagon as it bounces behind them. At least their hands are warm and dry, but their legs are starting to ache.

"Let's rest a second!" Paultje is slacking up.

"Like hell, we will. Not here! We may never get out. Wait till we get on the road!" He's shouting, partially because of the wind and partially because he's annoyed.

"I'm tired and I can't go anymore!"

"THEN DROP DEAD AND I'LL DO IT ALONE!"

That is not what Paul expected, so he grits his teeth, puts his shoulder into the rope and goes on, trying to think of WINETOU and long marches over the frozen plains.

Once on the road, he collapses on top of sacks, completely out of breath, heaving and coughing.

"My legs hurt, Frits!"

"I know, I knooow! The worst is behind us. The wind will be at our back, mostly. It'll be easier!"

"We're going to go one hundred fast and one hundred slow again and just concentrate on counting. Let's count in German, it'll take your mind of your problems.

Two kilometers down the road at the little store, we'll rest Okay? Not till then, Okay! Let's trade places! You Okay?" "Alright, double time!" EINZ, ZWEI, DREI!"

They're jogging along, the wooden shoes making sloshing sounds in the slush while the wagon rolls noiselessly behind them, just groaning every so often.

After "EIN HUNDERT," they pick up a fast march tempo. The wind and icy rain is mostly from behind now and by turning their heads a little, they manage to keep their faces away from the rain.

There is not a soul or a light in sight anywhere, not a sound either. Just themselves and the wind.

Frits starts to sing! "KAMERADEN, WIR HABEN DIE WELT GE-SEHN, SAN DIEGO, DAS HEILIGE LOCH. *(Comrades, we have seen the world. San Diego, that Holy hole.)* Inadvertently, they're putting a little spring in their step, and Paultje joins in.

"WIR HABEN DIE SEHLE IN'S MEHR GEKOTSCHT, BEI AUS-TRALIEN DA LIEGEN SIE NOG! *(We threw up our souls in the sea, they're still floating near Australia)* The little wagon seems to roll more easily and they're not thinking about the icy slosh in their klompen or the ache in their thighs. They've got the spirit now.

"KAMERADEN, DIE WELT, YA, DIE WELT IST SO SCHÖN, WAS GIBT ES FOR UNS NOCH ZU SEHN? *(Comrades, the world, yes the world is so beautiful, what else is there for us to see?)*

They turn west at the store and don't even consider stopping.

BEI HAMBURG AN DIE ELBE, WEIT HINTEN DEN OZEAN! *(Near Hamburg on the Elbe, far from the ocean,)*

One, two, three, four, leaning into their ropes, their heads turned a little toward the other side, as the wind now hits them from a different angle. They continue a stiff pace.

WIE EIN MÄDEL VON SAN PAULI, EIN MÄDEL VON DIE RE-PELBAHN. *(Like a girl from San Pauli, a girl from the Repelbahn.)* Their pace is great. The temperature is dropping below freezing and about three quarters of the way home, they stop exhausted.

They sit on their haunches, heads bowed, breathing deeply. The rain has turned to snow and somehow, that makes it feel less cold. At least not as biting as the freezing rain. It's getting dark rapidly and they could easily have gone to sleep like that, with not a sound to be heard. The silence of the snow-covered landscape gives them a strange sense of power; they are the only living things around!

Inside their clothes, it's warm and snug, their body warmth greatly enhanced by the exercise. It's easy to doze off and Paultje actually does and wakes up with a start when he topples over.

"I fell asleep!" he says sheepishly.

"OH NO! We can't have that. That's what happens to people who freeze to death, they're nice and cozy and warm and then they fall asleep and wake up dead."

"How can they wake up if they're dead?"

"True, let's go, it's not far anymore and my feet are getting cold!"

Maybe it's not far anymore, but the weariness is inescapable.

They can't get that spring back in their step anymore and forget about the 100 and 100. Every muscle in their legs, arms and shoulders hurts and the ropes are cutting deeper into their collarbones with every step.

Every move becomes a chore. They're grateful, that the steady snow has taken the chilly, biting edge of the wind, but it stiffens the sludge along with the freezing temperature and it feels like a thousand little hands try to hold down the wheels of the wagon.

The slush sucks at their wooden shoes and doesn't want to relinquish them. Each step becomes more of a struggle than the last.

Time drags, the fields crawl by and just as they get into town, Paultje collapses. Nothing works this time. He's sprawled in the snow and cursing, cajoling and pleading have no effect at all this time. He's down and out.

Frits can't even pick him up. The strength just escapes him. He brushes the snow off the tarpaulin and with Paul's assistance, finally gets him on his feet and drapes him over the sacks on the wagon.

"Hold on, don't fall off!" He wraps both ropes around his shoulders, grabs both handles with two hands and leans into the ropes.

Slowly, very slowly, the wagon starts rolling again and straining against the ropes, pulling with all his might, every muscle screaming with pain, he drags on home. Step after dragging step.

He doesn't even attempt to go around back. He knocks on the front door and as it opens, he walks up the stairs without a word and collapses on the bed, wet clothes and all.

"Frits, don't you want to eat something?"

He doesn't even hear! He's out. On his sister's bed. He missed his own bed by one flight.

Until early March, there's snow. Then the Dutch weather sets in, cold misty, dreary, miserable rain. Rain, rain, rain, no let-up, day or night.

The beautiful white world of the last few months turns gray and dirty. The formerly packed snow, turns the streets into a maze of slush. The ground has been frozen for so long and remains frozen solid, therefore not providing any run-off whatsoever. The result: overflowing ditches and sewers, swollen creeks and flooded pastures.

The war? What war? If it weren't for occupation forces, they wouldn't even know there was a war. Except of course, that schools and stores are closed, the town is empty and the 8 o'clock curfew. And of course, no electricity.

They haven't heard an airplane in weeks, the weather the way it is. The nearby BROTAUSGABE has been vacated, costing Frits his jobs and two to three loaves of bread a day.

With seven mouths to feed, that's unacceptable.

They're walking. No more sleds and no wagon, too slushy. The whole world seems like one big slushy puddle.

There's little activity in town. Most of the troops have been sent further south, where the allied breech into Germany is widening and most schools and Villas deserted. Most places are easy to get into, but food and radios are nowhere to be found.

At the AMBACHTSCHOOL, the tech school, now converted into a Hospital, a nice military Doctor gives them some sausage and nearly a whole loaf of bread, but that's not enough. He does encourage them to come back and look for work in the kitchen, for some of his people are being called away.

They arrive at the BROTAUSGABE near their school and sure as the dickens "Van Litt" is in there, pitching bread, loading a little pony-wagon.

They're told that they're not needed and Van Litt says NO to their request, "Pitch us one!" It's disheartening.

On a side street, a little while later, they spot the little pony wagon, heading out through the slush. Van Litt sits up front with the driver.

"Stay here!"

They've stopped into the little hallway of the Photographer's shop and stay out of sight until the wagon passes.

Frits slips out, tiptoes up to the rear of the wagon, lifts the tarp, takes out a loaf and tiptoes back to Paultje, who slips it into his windbreaker.

Again Frits takes off after it, but this time, just as he has a loaf in his hand, Van Litt spots him, signals the driver, who stops the cart and hollers,

"Halt! Halt! Oder ich schiese!"

"Like hell!" Frits takes off running, bread in hand, the soldier jumps down and starts his pursuit, still hollering, "Halt, oder ich schiese!"

Frits is pretty fast, but as he looks over his shoulder, he sees the soldier pulling out his pistol.

Frits may be crazy, but not THAT CRAZY. He drops the loaf and loses a wooden shoe at the same time.

He keeps running, zig-zaggin as best as he can and as he turns sharply into the first alley he comes to, he sees the soldier pick up the loaf and the KLOMP. Totally out of breath, but with a grin on his face, the "DEUTSCHER" wanders back to his cart and drives off, wooden shoe and all.

Peeking around the corner at the disappearing wagon, Frits shakes his fist at Van Litt as they vanish from sight.

"THAT BASTARD!" Paultje comes out of hiding and as he approaches he points to the shoeless foot, "Pappa is going to have a fit. You know, you can't get KLOMPEN anymore!"

"Oh, shit, that bastard, I know where he lives, we're gonna get him, we'll teach him!"

"He has a lot of older brothers!" Joop tells them later on.

"Here we are, a loaf and a half, one klomp, far from home, what is Pappa gonna say?"

"I don't know and I don't think I wanna know!"

"Well, let's go home!"

As they pass the church, they check with the RECTORY, but no, they don't have any wooden shoes, no, not even old ones.

Just before hitting the WOOLDSTRAAT, they come upon the back of RUPERT's toystore, that doesn't have toys anymore. They do have kids in the same school though, one girl in Frits' class.

A knock on the back door gets them in and after some hearty laughs they go through some worn-out shoes in the shed and find one that fits. It's worn, but it fits. More laughs, embarrassing. It's a lady's klomp. Tops are cut back further with a leather strap for the lady's tender feet. More laughter, Frits feels like an ass, especially as Mr. Rupert says, "I must say, "It's becoming, FOKKIE FLINK."

Well at least he can face Pappa.

Pappa laughs louder than the rest. The only time he turns serious is when he hears about the pistol being pulled.

"Do you think he might have shot you over a lousy loaf of bread?"

"I don't know, but I wasn't taking any chances!" More laughter!

"Didn't you shit in your pants, Fritsie?"

"No Jopie, I know you would have, but I didn't."
"Cut it out, boys!"

As the days warm up, there's more outdoor activity and now that the ground starts to thaw out, they decide to bury their silverware. They may have to flee someday.

Joop and Frits have a new game now. With their, sizewise identical knives, they stalk one another. The idea is to take the other one's knife away. They can only hurt one another's hands, nothing else, so they circle each other, knife in their right hand, the left one poised to grab.

Sloughed over, they move from left to right, making quick stabs at the hand with the knife, while trying to grab that right wrist with the left hand. Once one of them has a hold of the others wrist, a stab in the hand usually makes the looser drop the knife and leaves the other the unqualified victor.

Mama has told them twelve times to quit that stupid game, she's out of bandages and they're impossible to get.

One morning, Frits' left hand flashes out to grab Joops right wrist but Joop reacts and his knife enters Frits' hand at the palm and in one hundredth of a second has slashed his skin halfway up his lower arm. It missed his pulse artery by a half inch.

That's it. No more knife fights. Pappa takes both their knives away.

"Half an inch to the left and you would have killed him!"

"O.K.!"

"O.K,?" WHAP, Joop may have been as tall as his Dad, but that "WHAP" was real. It sends Joop flying.

"In the house, I'll talk to you later! Now you, you get your Mam to wrap you up!"

"NO MORE KNIFE, BOER, WHAT A BUMMER!"

That night there's an air-raid. They light the hearth, put a mattress on the floor, so the kids can try to sleep.

Pappa and the older boys walk out back, but there's nothing unusual. The cloud base is fairly high, but it's still overcast. Not a star in sight. The temperature is not spring-like yet, but ten, maybe twelve degrees above freezing. Maybe winter is finally over. The upstairs windows are open at a crack, to let some fresh air in and in case of close bombing, to avoid breaking by concussion.

There's not much noise, one sole airplane. It sounds like a twin engine, maybe a spotter. It's not a fighter that's for sure. It's too slow. The sound fades away in the distance, but returns again.

"Pappa says, "Let's go to bed, nothings happening!" and turns to the

251

door. Just as he pulls it open, broad daylight appears, a flare.

"UNDER THE STAIRS, UNDER THE STAIRS!"

Everyone hustles under the stairs, Mama sitting on the toilet lid, everyone packed in around her. Pap just squeezes in and there it is.

"YEEEEEEEEYEEE, KABOOM, KABOOM!" the girls scream. YEEEEYEEEYEEEE, KABOOM, KABOOM!" The house rocks so bad, that paintings fall off the walls and dishes shatter on the kitchen floor.

They know, they've been hit. They're being hit...they wait for next impact, it doesn't come! Just four bombs?

Pap opens the door, dust just rains down from cracks in the plaster overhead, while the drone of the plane is becoming faint in the distance and the flare goes out.

"SCREAMS, LOUD, HYSTERICAL SCREAMS.."

"STAY HERE! EVERYBODY, STAY HERE!"

Pappa runs out back, Frits on his heels.

The screams are coming from next door, out front.

Back into and through the house, out the front door, and into the street. There's a cloud right in the middle of the intersection and a fountain spewing water high into the air.

"No, it's not next door. Next door is empty and so is the next house. It's the Timmers bakery."

The store is four doors down. They race over. There's a huge hole in the middle of the street and the fountain is smack in the middle. The windows of the bakery have shattered backwards into the empty display cases and its gable is dangerously dangling down. Across the street, on the opposite corner, all the windows are blasted out, but no one seems to live there.

The screams come from inside the bakery and Herman, Frits right behind him, jumps into the display window on top of all the crunching glass fragments and runs to the rear, where by candle light, two women are restraining a third one, who's screaming at the top of her lungs.

"What's going on?"

"IT'S JAN, OUT BACK!"

Out the back door, where two men are feverishly digging in the rubble and pitching chunks of brick and mortar aside. Pap and Frits pitch in.

"Who is it?"

"JAN! He's under here!"

Five more minutes, there's JAN, 18 years old. DEAD.

"No thank you, there's nothing else you can do, thank you, thank you very much."

Through the showroom, out the display window, they stop and look at the hole and holding hands, they walk home.

252

Jan Timmer died here - February, 1945

Sirens are coming their way, but there's nothing that they can do.

At the dining room table, the little ones asleep on the mattress, they sit and reflect, "WHY, WHY, WHY?" "It doesn't make any kind of sense. Four lousy bombs! Have you ever heard of such a thing?" Never. Four bombs, one hundred meters from here, maybe just eighty. There is nothing of strategic value within a kilometer from here and that would be the railroad. It doesn't make any kind of sense!"

"What about JAN? Joop, did you know JAN?"

"He was a few years ahead of me in school, nice guy, good student, wanted to become a doctor!"

"But how did he die?"

"Oh, he had gone out to check things out, like we do and the concussion of the bomb blast pushed the brick wall around their yard into their kitchen wall and he was caught between them. Somehow, he got hit wrong, probably a broken neck."

"He should have stayed inside!" Mama feels.

"Pappa, the toilet won't flush, no water!"

OH BOY!

The next day, part of the mystery is solved.

In the next street over, parallel to their street is a very large house, with a very tall antenna. It's the Radio Control Center for the whole military region. The bombs missed it by 50 meters.

The bombs did knock out the water mains and from now on they have to go for water around the corner, buckets at the time. At six in the morning they line up and walk back and forth until the bathtub is filled up for the day. If they run out...tough!

The control center must be very important, right underneath their noses. The moment the sun comes out, the JABO's are back and the springlike weather must be right up their alley.

The fighters can be seen or heard or both, from early morning till sundown. At ten, one morning, the boys are in the backyard, about to disappear into the alley in spite of the AIRRAID alarm.

Just as they reach the back gate, four of them come screaming down, engines howling, and RATTATATTAT, guns spitting fire.

"DOWN!" They fall flat on their faces against the neighbor's garden wall.

"THEY'RE SHOOTING AT US!! THEY'RE SHOOTING AT OUR HOUSE!"

"KABOOM!" "Damn, that's close!" their ears are ringing from the concussion.

Here comes the next one, RATATATATATA...

"THEY'VE HIT OUR HOUSE! FRITS...OUR HOUSE IS BOMBED!"

"KEEP YOUR FACE DOWN AND YOUR HEAD COVERED!"

"KABOOM"

"RATATATATAT....KABOOM!"

After the fourth pass, they race to the house. The women are screaming and crying, but everyone seems O.K.

"Oh God, are you boys alright? Oh Thank God!"

Bomb and powder smoke, mixed with plaster dust fills the whole house.

"I THINK WE'VE BEEN HIT, BUT WHERE? EVERYTHING LOOKS ALRIGHT!"

Out the front door they charge, all the menfolk. Smoke pours out of every window of the APOTHEEK across the street, a mere 30 feet away. The street is covered with broken glass, but no damage shows to their own façade.

All four of them race into the front door of the pharmacy and "Oh My God, what a mess." The place is a shambles. The whole store is littered with broken bottles and glass.

As they charge through the living room door, they stop in amazement, There's no rear wall! Nothing. They're looking straight into the backyard. The whole Pharmacist family is there, looking up at the house.

"Are you Okay?" They're huddled together and crying. They just nod

P-51 Coming right at us!

and keep looking up and as the Forrers follow their glances, all they can do is stare in sheer amazement.

"THIS IS UNBELIEVABLE!" there is no more rear wall. The whole back wall is gone, making it look like a three-story dollhouse, with furniture neatly in place in every room. Smoke pours out of the rooms, but that's from the bomb blast, there's no fire. Weird, very weird. Nobody's hurt. They were in the cellar and got shook up badly, but that's all.

This time, the JABO's got the big house with the antenna, 50 meters from the back of the Pharmacy.

As they're eating dinner, "They were shooting right at our house and the bombs were aimed at our house, I could see it!"

"Paultje, you're right! Thank God, they overshot us by a hundred feet!"

NOT QUITE! When Joop gets upstairs to his rear third floor bedroom, he finds the mirror on his dresser shattered in a thousand pieces and a neat round hole in the wooden frame.

His screams got everyone upstairs in a flash and the "EXPERTS" determine that a "LONE POINT 50" came in through the open window and hit the mirror.

"If you move the dresser, I'll get it out of the wall for you!"

"NO, NO, NO! It may explode!"

"Point 50's don't explode, they're solid!"

"How do you know that it's a something 50, or whatever you're saying?"

"The fighters were Americans and they fire point 50's and besides that, a 20 millimeter round would make a much bigger hole and would have exploded."

"GOOD GOD. THIS WAR IS COMING TOO CLOSE!"

CHAPTER XIII
March 30, 1945, The Final Day

THE WAR IS COMING AWFULLY CLOSE.

They can feel it, they sense it. The fighters are overhead, just unopposed. A few of the new GERMAN JET-FIGHTERS have been seen, chasing SPITFIRES and MUSTANGS across the skies, but they haven't been seen or heard in weeks. These DÜSZEN JÄGER make an awful racket after they've passed over and Joop has drawn them sketches of the RAM-JET principals and the advanced techniques of the Germans. SCARY!

Yet they're not flying much anymore, thank God.

The nervous activity of the German troops is getting more nervous and feverish as tanks and cannons appear in town on a regular basis.

They can't come through their street, because of the gaping holes at the corner, so they detour through the WILLINKSTRAAT.

Crews are busy working on the sewage and water lines, but the constant harassment of the air raid alarms, sends the workers scurrying for cover all the time.

Something weird is happening. The war is coming from the wrong direction, the liberation is coming from the EAST, from Germany.

All the bunkers, all the defense works, so diligently built by all the Dutch slave workers, are facing the wrong way!!! They're facing WEST! Some joke, some CRUDE JOKE. On the Germans that is.

Frits is off early to the farm on Mama's old bicycle. Regular tires haven't been available for years and everyone has been riding on "SOLIDS." "SOLIDS" are actually strips of old automobile tires that are attached by huge staples. The result is, that with every revolution of the wheel, you hear a "THUD" as the staples hit the road. So it creates a kind of "CLICKETY-CLACK" like the "clickety-clack" of a train as the staples hit at irregular intervals.

It's a nice morning and at 7:30, he's already on the way back, his two-liter can of fresh milk swinging from the handlebars.

Spitfires

There's an awful lot of activity on the roads. German soldiers on foot, on bikes, on horse wagons, on trucks and motorcycles are clogging the roads, going in the opposite direction, away from the front. They're actually fleeing. A lot of them have no weapons on them, most of them have cut off all insignia's and rank indications. They're carrying minimal baggage and keep filing past him, out of town.

Frits is nearly back in town, right on the outskirts, as he's stopped by three Germans. They block his path.

"WIR BRAUCHEN DAS FAHRRAD!" "We need the bike!"

"I NEED THE BIKE TOO, I HAVE TO BRING HOME THE MILK!"

"HAVE YOUR MILK, WE JUST WANT THE BIKE!"

Two pairs of hands grab him and he's removed from the bike, held by the third one. They hand him the milk, but he's not giving in that easily.

"NO, NO, NO, MY FATHER WILL KILL ME. IT'S MY MOTHER'S BIKE!"

One German gets on the bike and starts pedaling. The others turn him loose and jump on a man's bike, one pedaling, and one riding on the back.

Frits sprints after his bike and jumps on back in two seconds, holding on to the soldier and his milkcan.

"I'm going with you, I'm not leaving my Mam's bike."

They stop. The one with Mama's bike holds the other one by the handle-

258

bars, the other two, rip Frits' arms loose from the man's waist, but Frits holds on to the bike with his legs. He gets kicked in the shins by a steel-heeled boot, but they manage to tear him loose and send him sprawling, spilling his milk. One holds him pinned down on the ground while the two others take off on the bikes, then, with a vicious kick in the ribs, releases him and runs after the disappearing deserters and jumps on.

Frits gathers his can, half empty, picks up his klompen that got lost in the struggle, and sits down by the roadside crying his heart out.

He's not crying for pain, he's not crying about his bike, he's crying out of frustration, sheer frustration!

"THE LOUSY BASTARDS, THOSE STINKING COWARDS, THREE GROWN MEN AGAINST ONE KID!" he's sooo mad, he's liable to kill someone. Still crying from frustration, he picks himself up and starts the trek home.

The road becomes even more jammed with fleeing Krauts and at one point a lone MUSTANG dives down the length of the road, TATATATAT, sending people diving for the ditches. One horse wagon rolls over into the ditch, pulling the tumbling horses right with it.

Some twenty soldiers right the wagon and after untangling the horses, string them back in and continue.

Some of the Germans fire their rifles at the MUSTANG, but the plane is the obvious winner in this battle.

It creates chaos and stagnation, which must have been its purpose. Frits stands behind a fat oak tree, taking in the scene, knowing that a POINT 50 can not travel through 20 inches of solid oak.

He finally makes it home, two hours later and meets Pappa in the backyard.

"What happened to you? And where is the "FIETS"?

Frits tells him the story and the tears of frustration start flowing again. They haven't seen him crying in years.

"Why didn't you fight them?"

"Why didn't I fight them? WHY DIDN'T I FIGHT THEM?" he's screaming now. He hands the can to Joop, pulls up his shirt and shows them the black and blue marks on his chest and his shins.

"I fought them, but there were three of them and if you hadn't taken away my knife, I would have killed them or if those damn cowards had been wearing bayonets, I could have pulled one and I would have killed the lousy bastards!"

"Calm down, calm down. Come in here, let's look at that chest! Herman, you're terrible!"

Mama feeds him some milk, cleans the marks with iodine, but the skin is not damaged badly and the ribs are just bruised. She pulls his head to her chest.

"Never mind your Pappa, in my book, you're a hero!"

Ten minutes later, he's checking out some news that Paultje related. "Remember the "BROTAUSGABE" at the back of the factory? Well' the next building is a warehouse and they're raiding it!"

Within minutes Frits is there. He's watching all types of vehicles being loaded with all sorts of merchandise, by all sorts of Military human beings. Soldiers and Officers from every branch of the services seem to be loading merchandise, regardless of rank.

As he's trying to figure out, how to get in on the action, he's tapped on the shoulder by a "LUFTWAFFE HAUPTMANN," with beautiful brown boots.

"Hey, boy, here's a guilder. Hold my bike, I'll be back in ten minutes!"

"Oh Ya? Oh Ya?" "He's got to be kidding!!!"

He can't quite reach the pedals from the saddle, but with his butt on the crossbar, he pedals home as fast as his skinny legs can get him there.

"PAPPA, PAPPA!" he's shouting as he comes down the path through the yard.

"Pappa, look what I've got! I've got a new bike!"

It is a beauty indeed, virtually new. Real chrome rims, real inflated tires, yellow tires no less. Chrome front and rear handbrakes. WOW!

"WOW! HURRAH, let's give him a hand! How'd you get it?"

"There's a very mad AIR FORCE CAPTAIN out there somewhere, who's cursing some Dutch kid and maybe now he can appreciate the feelings of the man that he stole it from."

More laughter and cheers, "GOOD SHOW!"

Pappa rides his new bike in a small circle and shouts out, "Best bike I've ever owned." More laughter!!

Around the dinner table, they discuss their options about the warehouse, the retreating Krauts and the advancing Allies.

Planes keep buzzing overhead and the "ALL-CLEAR" simply doesn't sound anymore. The siege is upon them. In the distance, there's the sound of heavy artillery and constant bombing.

The liberation is approaching with all its frightening possibilities. The town may be heavily defended and consequently, heavily shelled and bombed. That means that the town could be obliterated, especially if it gets down to house-to-house combat.

They've seen newsreels in the movies about STALINGRAD and NORMANDY.

WINTERSWIJK may be next.

The center room, the dining room will be their shelter. The table goes out. The French doors on both sides, leading to the parlor in front and to the porch in the rear, are blocked with mattresses, put on end.

Mattresses will be put on the floor, knapsacks packed with survival gear. Canteens washed and ready, they have to be prepared to move out on foot. The wagon will be packed with blankets and essentials ready to pull out, but also ready to be deserted. A blanket is rolled and tied to each knapsack. Thank God for warmer weather.

Everyone will wash, though it isn't Saturday, and don clean underwear with the most practical upper garments.

Now; the immediate situation at hand, the warehouse and its possibilities.

Frits takes over, "I don't know exactly what's left over in there, but most of what was carried out was food in sacks, bags and boxes. Now this is what we can do: Joop and Paul, oh, don't worry Joop, nobody's interested in you today, everybody's interested in saving their ass. Now you two go in back of the building underneath the high windows. That's only a couple of hundred paces from our backyard. The windows are up high, but Joop, by standing in the wagon you should be able to reach them.

I go inside, stack something underneath the window, table, boxes, anything, I waste the window and hand things down. Whatever is the best I can find is what I'll grab, you guys load up the cart, carry what you can, race home and come back for more. We do it until stuff runs out or until we get chased, whatever comes first. Make sense?"

"LET'S DO IT!"

Things go pretty much as planned.

Nobody pays attention to a skinny 13 year-old on wooden shoes, who doesn't look a day over ten.

"HAUPTMANN DER LUFTWAFFE" is nowhere in sight and Frits says to himself, "He's probably out stealing bicycles!"

As he locates the window, that they've designated for "FOOD TRANS-PORT," he finds it inaccessible, because of giant weaving machinery in front of the windows. A few windows over, he builds himself a staircase, by stacking boxes in a staggered form, while literally dozens of Germans of all sizes and in all different types of uniforms, rush around, lugging their treasures.

He doesn't have to "waste" the window, it opens on top hinges, couldn't be easier! "Over here, boys! Get me a two foot stick to hold this open!"

He decided on "SCHWEINENFLEISH" first, grabs a box, walks up on his new staircase, pushes the window out again, accepts a piece of branch from Joop, shores up the window and hands over box one.

The process is repeated four more times and they're off.

Now Frits has time to browse. A roll of beautiful curtain lace is stashed behind the machine near his window. A roll of tweed garberdine, British style, is added, but no salmon anywhere in sight. Lots of vegetables, the selection is getting slimmer. But there's butter, powdered eggs and milk.

Paul's whistle tells him that they're back, so up he goes again, rolls first, four more boxes and they're off again, each clutching a roll of cloth.

The rumble of the war is getting closer and as Frits returns to his window with a roll of flowered material, someone is taking down his steps. Everything is getting more frantic. He pitches his roll of cotton out of the window and just as he drops a box to the ground, his steps disappear from under him. With his platform gone, he picks up a box of "ZWEIBACK" (rusk) under each arm and makes it out of the front door.

Dozens of disheveled soldiers rush out of the door with him, but everyone is busy with his own survival. He joins his brothers out back, who have already gathered up the busted box and flowered cloth and now loaded with the boxes of RUSK, (ZWEIBACK), he sends them home.

"I'm going to look for another "FIETS"

History repeats itself. Nearly five years ago, MAY 10, 1940, at this same complex, at the main entrance, he "ORGANIZED" his first pistol.

Now on the prowl around the same factory, he spots a MERCEDES convertible, the chauffeur casually leaning against the fender, smoking a cigarette.

He walks to the wall and sits down, taking in the action of all those soldiers, carrying their loot.

Frits sneaks up to the car, carefully keeping the car between the chauffeur and himself. The chauffeur is either tired or engrossed in the goings on, cause he doesn't notice a little head above the passenger door and a hand reaching in. In the glove box, his hand comes out with a TEN-PACK of JANTJES cigarettes and a FIVE-PACK of CIGARILLOS. They disappear inside his shirt and the hand slides back in the glove box. This time it comes out with a pistol, so small, it nearly fits in his hand. WOW. A white shawl from the backseat and he's gone.

Halfway home, he sits down in the alley and admires his new gun. As he slides it from the holster, he removes the clip, moves back the slide and out jumps a round. He picks it up and cleans it. He empties out the clip, nine rounds total. One by one he puts them back, inserts the clip, releases the catch, the slide hammers forward, she's ready to fire.

He looks for something to shoot at and decides on a knot in a wooden gate. He takes aim, squeezes the trigger and PEW, the knot explodes outward. He grins, it hardly sounded like a shot, it was more of a "PING" and it didn't buck at all. He pockets the empty shell that had flown about six feet to his right and goes over to examine the hole. He grins again, this little bullet left a one-inch wide hole because of the knot. He puts the safety on, slides it back into the tiny holster and puts it in his left back pocket.

He feels powerful as he walks into the house, the white scarf carelessly slung around his neck, movie star style. Supplies are being stashed and fortification built.

He grins as Clasien comments, "What a beautiful shawl!"

"When is your birthday, kid?"

"AUGUST 30"

"HAPPY BIRTHDAY," "HERE" Boy, he's feeling good today!!!

They have their first SCHWEINEFLEISH supper that night and it's different, than what anyone expected.

It's ground cooked pork and even with a lot of specks of bacon and fat throughout, it's very tasty. It can be eaten, right out of the can, spread on bread or mashed in with the potatoes. It's great stuff. Mama has fried some as patties that comes out great too. They have at least a month and half supply of that stuff alone.

At the supper table, it's decided that any further exploring could be dangerous for more than one reason.

German troops, returning from the front or retreating may be very short tempered when it comes to food and tempers may flare more as fighting intensifies. Besides, the fighter planes are shooting at anything that moves and most anything must have been raided by now anyway.

The explosions are getting closer by the hour and Pappa is convinced that the Allies have crossed the German border and by now are into Holland, just about 10 kilometers away.

"Why can't I get a radio from somewhere? Damnit!"

"Only the German resistance will determine if the Allies will be here tonight, tomorrow or next week! From here on in, we're prepared!

How the hell I wish I had some damn radio!"

A check from the top of the roof shows distant fires and Frits shouts down his estimates.

"There are four fires, and from here I would say, they're all in't WOOLD, about where we got that merchandise last month."

Near the good-looking farmer's daughter, he thinks. Funny, how he doesn't hate girls anymore like he used to. As a matter of fact, he can't remember hating a girl for more than a year. "Strange!" "Well, maybe the war has improved them!"

Other than subdued BOOMS and the pretty steady return of the JABO's, there is not much to be observed.

"Interesting note," he says to himself, "More TOMMIES up there than YANKS today. The SPITFIRES have a very special look about them and he can see them diving in on a target way out on the horizon.

"They wouldn't just attack a farm house, would they?"

That would be ironic; fleeing town, moving to a farm to escape bombardment and then get clobbered way out in the country.

"One day I would like to tell that girl all of my "Farmers-daughter" jokes. Wonder if she would laugh? Probably! She laughed so loud about the "suit-case" affair that time. Hope she's alright!"

He slides down the gutter, next to the dormer of Joop's bedroom and swings inside. "Wonder if they have something to snack?"

They sit out on the porch, the doors wide open. It's nearly a Spring-evening. The atmosphere is strangely "exhilarating" because of the impending liberation after five years of occupation and the thought that pretty soon all the hardship and grief will be behind them.

On the other hand, the recollection of newsreels' of images of towns in France, Italy, Belgium, and Russia, totally obliterated, gives them the shivers. They shudder at the thought of all the horror that may lay ahead within just hours.

They're all set. Mattresses are standing by to block the doors behind them. They can be away from this table and blocked in, in two minutes.

It has been the case very often, they have seen it themselves, that a house may be in total ruin, but in the center room of the house, the occupants survived with very little damage.

The parlor doors are blocked with mattresses. Jackets, coats and their "GOOD" shoes are lined up along the walls, ready to be slipped on. They're hoping they won't need them, but they're ready.

As the sun sinks in the West, Frits resumes his observation post again and reports most fires gone, but an increase in flashes from cannons and rockets being fired. The activity has shifted to the north, toward GROENLO. There appears to be little or no advance in the direction of town, the firing remains at a distance of 8 to 10 kilometers.

The white backdrop of the RED CROSS on top of the hospital is glowing bright orange in the light of the setting sun, as if there's a light burning from inside. The neat row of houses in front of the hospital makes him think of the KAMPHUISES and he wonders how they're coping right now. Ever since the take-over of the O.T. they have hardly seen one another as if their worlds have drifted apart.

With the falling darkness, glowing bullets can be seen. They race across the sky in an arc, travelling about 15 kilometers before impacting with a bright yellow glow.

As the tracers across the sky intensify and come closer, more overhead, Herman calls Frits down, "Leave the windows half open!"

For a while they watch the tracers streaking overhead, but as spectacular as the fireworks may be, the increasing frequency and noise makes Pappa move everyone inside.

Canteens are filled, "GOOD" clothes and shoes put on and laced and all they can do now is wait and pray.

"Let's pray the ROSARY!"

The lamp on the floor throws grotesque shadows on the walls as Joop leads them in prayer and they follow, "GEEF ONS HEDEN ONS DAGE-LIJKS BROOD" and "HIELIGE MARIA, MOEDER VAN GOD, BID VOOR ONS ZONDAARS, NU EN IN HET UUR VAN ONZE DOOD, AMEN." It never held as much significance in their hearts as it does now.

When through praying, they lay down, trying to get some sleep. "Get as much sleep as you can, we may not get to sleep again for a long time!"

Good thinking, but it doesn't work, they can't sleep. So, as artillery shells keep screaming overhead, Joop, Clasien and Frits take turns reading a book, while the others rest.

It's one of Mama's favorite writers, Pearl Buck. And finally, the tale of Love and Intrigue in faraway China, puts them all to sleep.

When he wakes up, light spills in over the mattresses and the silence is eerie. Frits slips out of the room, up the stairs, onto his bed and onto the windowsill, so he can see out of the dormer window.

He sticks his head out at a world that is already aglow with the rising sun's light, but deadly quiet. Except, he hears voices. He leans out further, to spot who's talking and directly below him, there they are. Five TOM-MIES, walking in line, their funny helmets askew, cigarettes dangling from their mouth, rifle slung over the shoulder, hand in their pocket, just strolling along. They're talking and grinning, one behind the other like ducks, apparently without a care in the world.

He races downstairs, "Mama, Pappa, the TOMMIES are here! The TOMMIES are in the street. Come on!"

An hour later, the town is covered with ORANGE BANNERS, RED WHITE AND BLUE flags and thousands of cheering people.

It's MARCH 31, 1945 and for them the war is over, really over.

When they're finally sitting down for breakfast, at about nine, the questions start pouring in, "What will happen now Pap?"

"Are we going back to HOF VAN HOLLAND today Pap?"

"What are the TOMMIES like?"

"What will happen?"

"What will happen is that slowly the town will be rebuilt, people will return from labor camps, factories will fire up again and life will return to normal!"

"Will schools open again?"

"Schools will open again!"

"No more air raids, sleep all night? Back to school?"

"Behave all day? Oh no!" "That's PEACE?"

"How boring!"

At least "WAR IS FUN!"

Part II
Peace and Quiet

Quiet?
What quiet?

CHAPTER XIV
Peace Is Fun Too
March 31, 1945

The "TOMMIES," strolling leisurely down the WOOLDSTRAAT, WINTERSWIJK, NEDERLAND, signaled the start of the liberation of the eastern part of Holland.

The south has been in Allied hands for more than six months and these folks have been spared the hard realities of a miserable winter without food, electricity or coal. Besides that, they have been spared German persecution and execution as well as relentless bombing by the Allies, day and night. NOT THIS TOWN!

This town is deadly quiet, at least from Frits' point of view, the 3rd floor window of Wooldstraat 37. One reason; the gaping hole in the middle of the intersection of the WOOLDSTRAAT and the SPOORSTRAAT, just a hundred yards to his left.

The hole is diverting British Military traffic around the edges of town.

The other reason; fighting that started due east of Winterswijk, proceeded in a northwesterly direction, bypassing the town. If the fighting had continued "due west," it might have obliterated the town in house-to-house combat.

As yet, the sun is just up, not a soul is in sight besides the TOMMIES. Nobody is cheering yet, until Joop and Frits run out of the front door, to shake hands with the Britishers. Eighty percent of the homes are deserted, but the other twenty percent awaken one by one to the sound of "SILENCE" and show their enthusiasm by sticking flags out of every window that's not boarded up.

In a matter of minutes, people start to appear from anywhere.

The repair crew that has been working on water and sewer lines in the bomb-crater for weeks, now finishes the job in a half-hour and with the

"Tommies" in Winterswijk. March 31, 1945

help of many volunteers, fill the hole and pave it as best as possible. By eight o'clock, trucks and jeeps roll through the street again, but this time, they're British.

Heaven knows where all the people come from! By nine, the town stands on its head! Beer starts to flow out of every bar and restaurant. Music blares out of open doors and windows. (These folks are not supposed to have any radios!) Soldiers get hugged and kissed. Beers and tea are pressed in their hands and it becomes impossible for them to move on. People that have moved out to the farms for safety's sake are streaming back into town in droves. Tears flow freely as people encounter friends and relatives they haven't seen for years and whose fate was completely unknown to them. In some cases, people, who were feared dead or interned in German concentration camps, simply appear in the street in the best of health.

As small groups of German prisoners are marched through the streets or ride through on open trucks, they're spit upon, kicked and pelted. The British guards have their hands full, keeping the Krauts from being lynched on the spot.

Five years of pent-up emotion and hatred is hard to contain and many a man or woman would gladly have choked a Kraut to death with their bare hands. Especially when a handful of young, under 20 maybe, "SS" ers in their black uniforms are hustled by, the population goes nuts. The open defiance on the faces of the Germans probably triggered it, cause in seconds they're swarmed by punching, kicking and screaming people. They were lucky to escape with their lives. Additional British troops and B.S.ers (Orange Banders) had to jump in the fray and liberate the Germans. Two Tommies, guarding five Germans simply doesn't work in newly liberated Holland.

It's impossible to blame anybody for their feelings. Many Dutch citizens have lost immediate family and friends during this miserable war and it'll be a long time before they "forgive and forget!"

MAINLY, THEY CELEBRATE! And boy, oh boy... DO THEY CEL-EBRATE!

There are still obvious concerns about relatives in the still occupied part of Holland, but the fact that they're FREE, FINALLY FREE, gives cause to sing and dance and celebrate!

New Proclamations appear. This time in DUTCH and ENGLISH.

A "MILITARY MAYOR" is in charge, assisted by the V.D. (Vrijheids Dienst, The men in the blue overalls and the Orange Armbands, armed with pistols and rifles)

No LOOTING or REPRISALS will be allowed.

Everyone is ordered to cooperate in the orderly arrest of NAZI sympathizers and all violence is to be avoided.

Anybody can handle that. Generally speaking, celebrating is more important than anything and as the day goes by, the town fills up with civilians and soldiers alike, dancing, drinking, singing and embracing. Girls, that haven't had a date for years or maybe never, throw themselves at the Tommies and they valiantly do battle with bras, skirts and panties.

Can't blame the girls. Eligible Dutch boys haven't been around for years. Some are still in labor and concentration camps, some are somewhere in the underground and some may never return. Poor Tommies! The girls are holding up the war! What WAR?

Ten a.m. and all seems under control. No German bombers, no counter attack, no air-raid alarms... Nothing! It's really over!

The boys decide to check out their home; HOF VAN HOLLAND. They haven't been in the place for a month. What a disaster! Tanks, parked halfway on the sidewalk have busted most of the pavers. The tanks in the backyard have wrecked the lawn, the path and the flowerbeds. The heavy tracks have just about plowed the whole yard. Besides the tanks, there's a ROVER staff-car, some small trucks and a jeep. Through the open French doors of the EETZAAL, they can see Officers bent over maps on the table and the floor.

In the pantry (BIJKEUKEN), the floor-tiles have been ripped up and a foot deep trench has been dug, the entire length of the floor, some 15 feet. Grills, holding pots, pans and kettles of all sorts, cover the trench. At the far end of the trench, a flame-thrower spews its roaring flame underneath all the pots and steam rises all the way to the ceiling.

The kitchen itself is a disaster area. It looks as if someone with a giant hacksaw has been turned loose in here. All the wall paneling has been ripped off, the cabinets are gone and there are no more doors or door-trim on either end. The same with the window trim; GONE!. Under the stairs; doors, benches, paneling, trim...GONE! In the parlor... same scene....All wood...GONE! In the restaurant; even the wooden floor is GONE! The bar, the phone-booth... GONE! COMPLETELY GONE! In the dirt, where the floor used to be, bonfire circles and ashes bear obvious witness to the fact that this is where all the wood ended up. The POW's must have burned it all to keep from freezing. In the cellar and the SLIJTERIJ, the racks and benches are no more. The entire beautiful dark paneling, the handsomely carved wainscoating and the crown moldings along the ceiling; all BURNED. The banisters, the doors upstairs, everything that was wood is gone, GONE! BURNED! Everything, except "THE WOODEN TOILETSEATS."

The porcelain toilets must have been too cold to sit on.

What happened? Did the OT just pull out and leave the POW's? That doesn't make sense! Did the POW's just have to fend for themselves, trying to survive while waiting for the liberators?

Did the ORGANIZATION TODT run out of coal and wood as well?

"Oh God, Oh God!" The boys are sitting on the remains of the stairs. "How do we tell Mamma and Pappa?"

In the kitchen, they have some tea with milk (yech) and WHITE bread. (wow). They get to understand that the British will only remain for a few days and that they grabbed this building, because it was SIZABLE and DESERTED. For a few days, a "fortnight" maybe, they'll feed the troops, passing through and then they'll move on.

Frits has only one month of English lessons under his belt, but he understands enough to carry the message home. To Paul, it might as well be Greek.

Two dejected boys, 10 and13, walk home. "How do we tell Mam and Pap?"

As they tell their gruesome story, tears run freely down their cheeks. There's not a dry eye in the house.

"What are we going to do, Pappa? We can't stay here and we can't go back to the old house. What are we gonna do?"

"I don't know! I just don't know! The ladies that own this house may be back any time. Maybe even today! I don't know!"

"They can't just put us in the street!"

"Pappa, the proclamation says that the English Mayors office has to be contacted about food, housing, relatives and all that stuff, so we might check that out!"

"Ya, ya' Joop, You speak English. Go find out what our options are and then go by the owner of the Hof van Holland, tell'em where we are and see if we can get together and go by the place. You know where his store is, don't you?"

"Sure do!"

"Okay, take my bike and take a lock.. Hurry as best as you can!"

"What do you mean, Pap? Owner? Don't we own it? It's our place, isn't it?"

"No, no! Remember when it was auctioned off in early '41?"

"It isn't ours anymore?"

"No, it hasn't been for years.!"

"Oh, no! What's gonna happen now?"

"It seemed all so simple. We get liberated, we move back in, open up for business and live happily ever after!"

"Oh God, help us!"

The day of liberation, the day they've waited for all those years, the day that should ring in the end of misery and suffering, the day that should be one of celebration, is turning into one of the darkest days of their lives.

Huddled in the dining-room, now cleared of all backpacks and protective mattresses, they sit around the table, one of the few belongings they still own, and pray, tears flowing freely.

It's twelve noon, March 30, 1945. The factory whistle blows. For the first time in years

The whistle blows the noon hour. The lone bell of the new Saint Jacobus rings the ANGELUS. It hasn't rung for years either. It was too small for the German raiders to bother with when they were stealing all the bells of Europe and the Priests were afraid to wake up sleeping dogs. Now, the ringing of the bell and the sound of the whistle are like music in their ears, chiming in a new era, an era of freedom, an era of opportunity and somehow, it shakes the little family out of their reverie and back to reality.

"Let's eat! Clasien, set the table. Boys, don't go anywhere, we're going to eat in a minute! Hey, do you know something? We've survived a lot of things together and we'll survive this one too! Let's quit looking so gloomy. Joop will be home soon and will probably have some good news! SO, let's get back into the spirit of things, Okay?"

"Okay!"

As the bell keeps ringing and the whistle keeps blowing, it seems to be the first official announcement that it's all over.

When planes roar over they still tend to jump, but after a while they settle down in the knowledge that there will be no more air-raids! Never! NEVER ANYMORE!

While eating, their spirits rise again and with that, questions start rolling in again as well.

"Are any stores open yet?"

"Is the baker baking again? Did you see if Wiggers had any veggies? Did the Proclamation say anything about food or stamps? Bread is the only thing we're going to need soon. No signs yet?"

"Well Ida, it's only been a few hours and everything has to be cranked up again!"

"Are we getting new money again?"

"Oh, good point! They must have some sort of new, free money printed up, Right?"

"Joop may have some answers, when he gets back!"

Joop does! "We stay here for the moment. We're registered with them now, but we must inform them immediately when the Ladies Buisman reappear. I found the owner. He'll be over in a little bit. He was shocked when I told him about the condition of the house."

"Money? No, I didn't ask about money. I did ask about food. Tomorrow, temporary stamps will be issued. Come to City Hall in alphabetical order. "A to D"; 8 till 9. "E to G"; 9 to 10. That's us. Some bread may be distributed this afternoon. Watch for proclamations. It sounds like we're still occupied."

"We are! By the British!"

"Something else. All the furnishings from the places that were occupied by the Germans will be brought to "Het Vereenigings Gebouw" (Community Center). They'll be tagged and in a few days we can go and seek out our own stuff and upon positive identification, it can be claimed. We may get some of our stuff back that way. Who knows? Maybe your radio never left town, Pap!"

"Ya, let's hope so. It has been miserable without it."

"They didn't say anything about money at all?" Mama wants to know.

"Remember "Radio Orange" telling people to honor "Occupation Money" of the Allies, but that was last year during the summer. I'm sure, though, that they're going to pay with money, other than what we now have and I'm sure that they won't be paying in REICHSMARKS." General laughter. "Good point, Mam!"

"Ya, these Tommies just pulled in here from Germany and they didn't have time to change their money at the border.!" More laughter.

274

"Well, I didn't think of it and by the way, I didn't have to speak English, everyone at City Hall is Dutch and they have it all under control!"

"A lot of underground planning must have gone into all this. Can you imagine? Every town that gets liberated has to keep right on functioning. Water, Electricity, housing, sewage, stamps, police, banks, food distribution, everything has to work and they must have organized all of it right under those German noses. By the way, we have water again!"

"Alright! No more buckets in the morning and toilets that flush! How 'bout that?"

"There's the doorbell. I'll get it!"

Mama's up and returns with Mr. Blauvelt, the owner of the Hof Van Holland.

"So this is where you live? Not bad, not bad!" He waves at everyone and shakes hands with Pappa. "You people have some experiences behind you, don't you? We worried about you, but we didn't dare to stick our nose outside the door and believe it or not, not even gossip reached us! The only thing we heard was that the OT had taken over!"

"Ya," Frits butts in, "and now the Tommies have it, you should see the place!"

"So I heard. Joop told me something about that. Why don't we walk over? The streets are getting to be unbelievable. Can I bring my bike around the back?"

"Joop, bring Mr. Blauvelts bike to the back yard!"

"Thanks. Trucks, cars, foot soldiers, V.D.'s, civilians going in both directions! What a madhouse out there! I walked my bike most of the way. Well, I'm glad it's over with. I'm sure you are too.. It's been one hell of a long winter. Herman, tell me how you survived while we're walking. Are you ready? Ida, do you wanna come too?"

"No, I don't think so, not after what I have heard. I'll have the coffee ready when you get back, Okay?"

"We'll see you in a little while then!"

They're off. Herman and Mr. Blauvelt with the boys trailing behind, stopping and gaping at everything that's new and exciting. The bomb crater that was filled up in a hurry this morning is being tended to again. The traffic had compacted the dirt to such an extent that it has become a dangerous dip in the road, an oversized pothole.

They wave at people, shake hands, stop to talk and generally have a great time encountering people that they haven't seen since September, the last day of school, the first day of GARDEN-MARKET.

The boys have lost sight of the grownups in front of them, but they weren't really needed anyway.

When they finally do walk into the EETZAAL (dining room) of the old HOF VAN HOLLAND, they're in for a shock. Pappa is being tended to on the floor. Someone is holding up his head as two other people are trying to get tea and rum into him.

"Mr. Blauvelt, what happened"

Mr. Blauvelt brings in a wet washcloth that he lays on Pappa's forehead

"Your Daddy just passed out. He probably had not imagined the extent of the devastation. He simply said; "Oh my God, Oh, my God a few times, got real pale and would have fallen flat on his face if I hadn't caught him!"

"He's alright, though. He'll be all right! He's had some terrible experiences lately and this was just too much for him. The rum will bring him on back around. The Leftenant already told me, he'd have him taken home in a car, so don't worry. I'm staying with him; we have a lot to talk about anyway, so you guys go and play. It's time for you guys to celebrate, let us old folks do the worrying, so scoot, go! Get going! Your Dad's Okay!" GO!"

In the backyard, their worries about their Dad are soon forgotten as they get to climb on top of a tank. My gosh, they're big! They're hard to get onto when you're little. Frits has to come down to give Paul a boost and just then a TOMMIE calls from the kitchen to come down off the tank.

This is a good time to play stupid as if they don't understand what the TOMMIE is saying, so Frits waves at him, turns his back to him and continues to climb. Here he comes! He's in an imposing black coverall with a lot of zippers and he seems annoyed. The boys stay as friendly as they can be. (Paultje does not smile too much, though!) The man in black hollers for them to come down, but Frits answers him in Dutch; "I live here, that's my house!" as he points at the house and in turn at his chest. It's as if he's trying to say; " If your tank is in MY yard, I should have free access to it!" The TOMMIE can't help but smile, guessing the meaning of it all and says;" WAIT!' don't move!"

He disappears inside and comes back with a younger man in black with a thousand zippers, who says; " So you chaps want the grand tour, hay? Just a moment, I'll show you around"

The boys don't understand a word he's saying and even if they could speak English, they probably would not have understood his COCKNEY accent.

Somehow they understand, though! The soldier climbs aboard, signals them aside and climbs in the top of the tank. With his upper torso protruding from the turret he waves them over and as he lowers himself, the boys follow him one by one, as he guides their feet onto the little metal rungs that are mounted on the inside of the turret.

There is not much room in the crowded belly of the tank. Two seats out front, one for the driver and one for the machine gunner "Go a'ead, sit down!" The tanker pulls down the little metal gates in front of the seats and asks; "Now 'ow can you see?" He makes them sit on their knees on the seats and points at something that looks like a pocket mirror. With their noses right up to it, they can see out front. "WOW, dit is een periskoop!" "That's raight, some sort of a periscope, 'ats 'ow we see out!"

"WOW, look at those big bullets!" All around the tank the walls are lined with ammo.

"105's?" He doesn't understand. "Point 50's?" Frits points at the smaller rounds.

"Yes!"

"105's?" Now pointing at the big ones.

"NO!" Now he understands. "No, no, these are 84 millimeter"

"Beautiful!"

"Yeah, beautiful is raight! Come on chaps, come on. End of tour!"

He helps them out of and down the tank and with a soft pat on the butt he shoves them away; "Off with you now, TATA!"

"TATA, TATA!?" That's funny. "TATA!"

"Lets go see Jan and Henkie."

It's as if they're having a day off. Not hunting for food, coal or wood. It's been a while since they did not have some assignment or another.

Through the EELINKSTRAAT, past OPA's house, (no more chickens, wonder if he ate them all?), past the old hazeltree lady (it's getting big) and the hospital.

Lots of activity again, this time British trucks with Red Crosses.

Everywhere, flags are out. The Red, White and Blue, with their Orange banners dress the streets in a colorful holiday costume.

Jan and Henkie aren't home but Mrs. Kamphuis and the baby are there and she wants to hear what's been happening to them.

She's sorry, she has no cocoa or milk, but when Mr. Kamphuis comes home. He'll have some.

Meanwhile, she says ;"OH MY, OH MY !" a hundred times as the boys relate the experiences of the last few months.

Just as they're saying;"Goodbye," the Kamphuis boys show up. Handshakes, "ORANJE BOVEN" shouts, and a lot of laughter indicates a happy reunion.

Frits and Paul tell'em about their "tank" experience in glowing terms and Jan in turn relays that according to his father, nine British tanks are lying along the roadside in't WOOLD, disabled or burned out or both.

Of course they should check it out!

Today's too late already, but tomorrow?

"Why not? We don't have to work tomorrow, right? We're liberated now, right?"

"Good!" Meanwhile let's go downtown, the whole town is standing on its head. People are going crazy!"

"Let's check it out!"

"Bye Mother, Bye Mrs. Kamphuis!"

She starts to say; " Be careful, boys!" but she catches herself. The war is over. What's there to be careful about? YEAH, WHAT??? If only she knew.

"HOOMPA, HOOMPA, HOOMPA, HOOMPAPA!" The music is not great, but it's loud and that's what counts. The marketplace is full of people, singing, dancing, hugging, drinking. It hasn't stopped! The stars provide about the only light after dark, because there's still no electricity. The British have provided a generator to the MARKET RESTAURANT and it provides light inside and some outside through the large picture windows where all the activity seems to be. The boys are still out there and haven't gone home for supper.

They encounter Joop, arm in arm with girls and guys from school and he acts like he's the only one who has been liberated. In his mind that's true. Other than the February move, he hasn't been out of the house since September and he hasn't seen a girl in all that time and he's ready to break loose and he does!

Heaven knows where all these people have come from. The marketplace and the nearby streets are packed with people, body to body. Herman and Ida are staying at home. They can't get in the mood. The boys don't mind, nobody to watch them, that's all.

About 8 o'clock the little ones get tired and want to go home. First it's decided that it's perfectly safe for them to go home by themselves, but Jan has seconds thoughts and feels responsible, so he walks both of them home. "TJU!" Till tomorrow!"

Frits swipes a beer in the MARKET RESTAURANT and looks disgustedly at all the people, hugging and kissing! In the restaurant, in the market square, in the streets, in the alleys, everywhere! "SICK, SICK, SICK!" "Grownups are sick, kinda!" There are some cute girls amongst them, but he wouldn't know what to say to them, so he meanders home, singing; ORANJE BOVEN, ORANJE BOVEN!"

The home is like a morgue. He was afraid they'd jump all over him for being late, but they didn't seem to have missed him.

"Have you been crying Mama?"

No answers but tears are flowing again.

"What happened, Pappa? What's going on? "Mama? What's going on?

Will somebody tell me, please? What's going on?"

Clasien has put the little ones to bed and comes down to join them. She's been crying too!

" Somebody! anybody!, What's going on?"

"Frits, did you eat anything? You smell like a brewery! Have you been drinking beer?"

"Ya, I drank beer, ya, I'm hungry, but why are you crying?"

"The sandwiches are in the kitchen. Go get 'em and we'll talk"

He's back in two minutes with sandwiches and milk, sits down and sighs; "Okay!"

"Frits, we have some bad news!"

"On liberation day?"

"Yes, on liberation day! We won't get HOF VAN HOLLAND back."

"We won't? Why not? It's our place, isn't it? They can't just take it away from us, just like that! It's been in the family a thousand years!"

Pappa has to smile, in spite of himself. "A long time, yes, but not quite a thousand years though. The damn ORGANIZATION TODD made ONE payment, ONE lousy monthly rental payment, ONE, only ONE!, Just ONE!"

"So?"

"That makes them the last tenant, not us!"

"So what?"

"Listen, just LISTEN !, Okay?" He's starting to shout.

"The owner has no obligations towards us whatsoever, legally that is, because we are NOT the tenant of record. He does not have to rent it to us anymore if he doesn't want to. Rebuilding into a Hotel-Café-Restaurant would be too costly. We don't have the money, he doesn't either or he doesn't want to spend it for that purpose!"

"How about that 63,000 guilders that the Germans owe us?"

"Come on, Frits, be reasonable. We'll never see that money, forget about that. Besides, Mr. Blauvelt wants to turn it into a furniture store because the location is much better than where he is at now and there's nothing we can do to stop him. If the O.T. was still here, he couldn't get them out, but they're not here obviously."

"Oh boy, oh boy, oh boy! What are we gonna do?"

"We don't know! That damn grandfather of yours!"

"Oh, Herman!"

"It's true! And the damn OT! They've done us in! I'm too old, nearly fifty, to hope to land a decent job. Not now, with all the young guys coming back from labor camps, concentration camps, the underground and God knows, maybe even from England and Indie. Who's going to hire an ulcer ridden 50-year-old man? DAMN, DAMN DAMN!"

279

"Herman!"

"Ya, DAMN, DAMN!"

"Herman!" Mama's yelling at him now! "Cut that out! That won't help at all!"

"Pap, I'm going to be 14 this year and Joop is already 15, so we can go to work and...."

""Frits, that's fine, but we have other problems. Where are we going to live? We can't stay here, it's not ours. We don't know what the government can provide, if any. There are tens of thousands that are homeless. What can the government do?"

"Ida, would you stop crying! That won't help either. Clasien, you too! Girls, please, please! Thanks, that's better. Clasien, go make some tea and then we'll talk about something positive!""

"Something positive? Is there anything positive left?"

"Sure is! Hurry, put the water on and come back. You look prettier when you smile. That's good!"

"Now for the positive; WE OWN THE LIQUOR LICENSE!"

"So?"

"The liquor license does not go with the building, it's in MY name.!"

"SO?"

"There are only so many liquor licenses in this town and you can't get new ones!"

"So?"

"So, a liquor license is worth a lot of money!"

"HA! HURRAY! NOW YOU'RE TALKING! How much money?"

"I don't know! No, really, I don't know, seriously. Don't look like that. Let me explain!"

"HOTEL STAD MUNSTER, right? If they only had a beer and wine license, how much would a FULL liquor license be worth to them? LOTS! Right? Okay. Now think of the AMSTEL place in Meddo, where you guys got all the ice-cream, remember?"

"Oh, ya, after our aircraft raid!"

"Right, now how much would it improve their business if they had a FULL license? The same as HOTEL STAD MUNSTER?"

"No way!"

"So it depends on the location. So with our "CLASS "A"" license, we have something to sell and maybe we can start up something else. It may not be easy, it won't happen overnight, but we have something that we can build a future on again!"

"Oh, Herman, you're such a dreamer!"

"Ya, ya, but that's why you married me in the first place, Right?"

"Well, I wouldn't say that!"

"No? Because I'm so good-looking maybe?"

"Well, at least you were!"

The ice is broken, everyone laughs and even the kettle in the kitchen joins in by whistling that the water is ready for the tea.

"We'll make it, Pap, we'll make it!"

"Yes, we will, son. Yes, we will!"

It was not to be tomorrow!

The boys are gone after breakfast and it's good to be on the road again with the KAMPHUIS brothers.

There is so much to talk about, so much catching up to do, it's just great!

Not a care in the world. April one and sunny. No school, no jobs, no chores! What a way to go!

They walk and talk, wave at passing troops and stop to chat with TOM-MIES of parked vehicles. Their English vocabulary consists of; "CIGA-RETTES FOR PAPPA? CHOCOLAT FOR MY SISTER?," but it works most any time.

They relax in the grassy slopes along the road and smoke their REAL cigarettes. Boy, they're strong!

But they make them feel real grownup and manly.

As they proceed, it becomes obvious that they're approaching a battle-field. First a cracked up Jeep. Upside down. They carefully inspect it. Nothing of value. Next a small truck, partially burned.

The gastank must not have exploded, for the damage is mostly up front. In the glove compartment is a "TOMMY KNIFE," the handle burned or melted. Must have been rubber or plastic.

"I can make handles for it!" It's Henkie's, he found it, It has a good size blade and on the other side a "PRIEM," a round, $1/4$ inch pin, big enough to kill somebody. Happy find!

They come upon a group of soldiers, eating in the grass along the road and they happily join them.

"What's this?"

"Corned beef!"

"Huh? Never heard of it." But boy, is it good on a slice of white bread.

"Great! Thanks, TATA!" Laughter all around.

"Hey, wait boys! Wait! Do not go off the roads and do NOT go in the fields, do you understand? Here! On the road! " He points to the road. "Here, Yes!"

"There," he points to the field; "NO!" "NOT Okay! Landmines, Okay?" He looks each one in the eye; "Do you understand? LANDMINES? Boom?"

"Do you get it? We're putting up ribbons around the minefields, but'll be days before we'll be done with it, do you understand? NO? Okay! STAY ON THE ROAD, NOT OVER THERE! Okay? You understand? Okay! TATA!"

"Okay! TATA!"

From a distance they can see a shot-up farmhouse and a burned down barn behind it.

"Look at BOER WESTERVELDS place! That's what our house could have looked like if the fighting had continued into town."

The roof is nearly all gone, kinda collapsed into the attic and the front of the house is in shambles. Probably the master bedroom and the parlor. As the road curves to the right towards WESTERVELDS place, they see them; THREE, FOUR, FIVE tanks off the road. It looks like other tanks, trying to make room for passing have shoved them off the road. Each tank is in a different phase of destruction. Some have gaping holes in them, but their tracks are in good shape. Others have no tracks at all or just on one side. Another one has no turret. As they climb on the first one, the smell of burned flesh and rubber greets them with such an overwhelming stench that they jump right off again.

"Did you smell that? Those guys must have burned alive! What a hell of a way to die!"

"Hey, look here!" Henkie's behind the tank. There are three rifles stuck in the ground with their bayonets and their helmets resting on the riffle butts.

"These must be the tank crew!"

" I didn't know they had rifles in the tanks!"

"They don't. And they don't wear those funny helmets either!"

"Then who are they? "

"Beats me! You see the rifles aren't burned, right? Right! They're just using them as markers for the graves, I guess. "

"Beats me too!"

The next tank virtually has its turret blown off and sports only one rifle with a helmet. This one did not burn, but shrapnel has pretty much shot up the inside of the tank. The ammo is still in very good shape and they each collect a few as souvenirs. The little mirror-like periscopes come out easily with a knife, but unscrewing the folding seats takes a lot more effort. They're nice seats. Foam rubber with plastic covering, the boys can think of many good uses for them. Loaded down with all their treasures, they check out the third one. This one is in fine shape. Just the tracks and wheels shot to smithereens and no rifles this time. All the ammo has been taken off, probably because it was all in mint condition. The seats and the periscopes are of great value though. They take turns at the machine gun, going "TATATATATAT," but the turret wont budge. Maybe jumped off the track. As they're having the

Het Woold, 30 March 1945

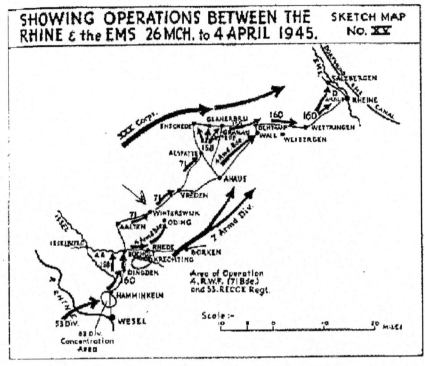

Winterswijk, liberated from the "wrong" direction

Shot up farm and British tank

time of their lives; "Look guys, playing cards!" They also have the start of
their lives. Everything is quiet all around them except for their own voices,
when suddenly; "DOOMDOOMDOOMDOOOM!" the engine turns over.
Frits jumps and busts his head against the turret wall, Jan nearly breaks his
neck, flying out of the turret and Paul screams bloody murder, deserts his
machine gun and he's right on Jan's heels.

"VERDOMME!" my head!"

Only Henkie is reasonably calm. He's the one who found and pushed
the starter button. After just a mild start, he laughs himself silly and when
his grinning head appears out of the turret, the others don't know whether
to laugh with him or kill him.

After that experience, they decide; "That's enough for one day, let's
check out WESTERVELDS place.

The Westervelds are busy moving broken lumber and busted walls
out of the way in order to clear the way for some repair of the front of the
farmhouse. The boys put their treasures aside and pitch in. Some of the
furniture is salvageable and taken around back and the clumps of brick are
stacked to one side, lumber on the other. They lucked out that the farmhouse
didn't burn like the barn did, cause that would have been the end of it. They
couldn't have gotten a fire truck to come out during battle and they could
not possibly have contained the fire by themselves. During a break over
soup and milk they get to hear what happened here two nights ago. It was
still daylight on March 30th when tanks appeared from the east, Westerveld
tells them. His farm is exactly two kilometers from the German border; you
can nearly see it from here. According to the farmer, there was no fighting
or shooting, just tanks approaching on the roadway with infantrymen on
top and behind them. His family was in the kitchen, which faces the other
way and he was in back of the house, taking in the scene, ready to duck at
a moment's notice. It was quiet all around, he could not hear the tanks yet
and he just started to wonder why they were coming in on the open road
instead of spread out through the fields, when "PFFFFFFFFT," a bullet of
sorts went flying and hit the lead tank. The tank behind it opened fire and
hit the barn. Westerveld said, he dropped right where he was when another
shell hit the house and then "PFFFFFFFFFFT," the second tank was hit.
He got up to run to the house and another "PFFFFFFFFT" and then he saw
where it came from, a foxhole near the front of his house. When he got into
the house, his family was hysterical, but Okay, so he hustled them under
the stairs to the loft and grabbed a spade. When he got outside again, he
saw that a fourth tank was burning, so he ran across his yard to the hedge,
crawled alongside till he came upon the foxhole with a single soldier in it.

He had some sort of a stovepipe (Panzerfaust or bazooka, Frits explains)

Het Woold, 30 March 1945, heavy losses

Het Woold, 30 March 1945

and he was so busy lining it up for another shot, that he didn't even duck when another shell hit the house. Just as he lifted his head a little to fire again, Westerveld swung and hit him as hard as he could, right under his left ear. He nearly took his head off. The problem now was, the tanks kept shooting at him. He dove behind the house again and since he only had a red handkerchief, he took of his jacket, shirt and wrapped his white undershirt around the bloody part of the spade. He made it to the back of the house and standing between his house and the burning barn and frantically waved his shirt. The tanks stopped firing and while some drove by, two of them drove right up on his lawn. At first the British treated him roughly, thinking that he was the German who had fired on them, but when he showed them the corpse in the foxhole, they started to believe him and when they found no other Germans in or around the house, they started to treat him like a hero.

It took them a while to realize that just one solitary German had shot up 5 British tanks and had held up the whole advance. The Brits became very apologetic, but he was stuck with a partially demolished house.

After the soup, everyone has to go and see the grave that once was a foxhole, now just a mound of dirt with a German rifle and helmet on top.

"You've earned a medal!" says Frits, "maybe the RIDDER VAN ORANJE" medal

Mr. Westerveld laughs; " I need no medal, just a little help rebuilding my house. I'm just glad that my family didn't get hurt."

Over milk again, Frits explains the difference between the PANZER-SCHRECK and the PANZERFAUST.

"They're both self propelled (Joops explanations are still ingrained in his brain), like the VEE ONE, remember? They're both anti-tank weapons. The PANZERSCHRECK uses a tube, a barrel or a "stovepipe" as you called it and a grenade like a mortar grenade, but it's a little rocket. The soldier slides the grenade in, puts the pipe over his shoulder, lines up the sight, pulls the trigger and "PFFFFFFT," the rocket shoots out of the front and the flame out of the back."

"Right, right, I saw the flame coming out of the back."

"That's why it's called a recoilless weapon, there's no recoil or kick like a rifle or a cannon. Now the PANZERFAUST is different. It is self-contained. It has a much bigger, more explosive head with a smaller tube attached. You hold it under your arm, fire the front part, the grenade and throw away the tube."

"How do you know all that stuff?"

" I have an older brother who keeps up with all that junk and his know-how comes in handy on occasion"

"Well, fellas, we're going to work some more and see if we can at least get it boarded up today. You fellas gonna stay and help?" Westerveld's getting up.

"Of course," Jan chimes in. "We can't just eat and run now, can we?"

With a smile on their faces they pitch in again and when some neigh-bors come to help the boys get excused and with a "TJU" and "THANKS," they're on their way with all their treasures.

Today, Mrs. Kamphuis has milk, no cocoa, but at least she's got milk.

Paul and Frits are in the best of moods as they come strolling into the back yard and they're babbling away like a couple of schoolgirls. Then, like a thunderclap, they're hit between the eyes with the news:

"PAPPA'S BEEN ARRESTED.!!!!!!"

Clasien, tears streaming down her cheeks, runs out to them the moment they come into view; "They've picked up Pappa and..."

"Who?" Frits is screaming. "WHO AND WHAT FOR?"

Clasien tries to explain, but he's not listening. He runs through the kitchen into the diningroom where Mama is sobbing at the table, her head on her arms and her whole body shaking with the sobs.

"Mama, Mama, what's happening? Mama, don't cry!"

He's holding her and he tries lifting her head while begging; "Mama, Mamie, don't cry, don't cry! God, oh God, what now? Can't anybody just leave that man alone? Who picked him up? Where's Joop? Did they get him too?'

Clasien shakes; "NO!" tears running down her cheeks. She's sitting down with Hedwig in her lap and that little one is just sobbing; " I want my Pappie, I want my Pappie!" The little body is wracked with sadness.

"What a lousy damn situation!" Frits never cursed like his Dad before! "Can somebody stop their damn whimpering and tell me what the hell is going on?"

Mama bolts upright and hollers back ; "DON'T YOU TALK TO ME LIKE THAT AND DON'T YOU SWEAR LIKE THAT EITHER!"

"OH NO? THEN TELL ME WHAT'S GOING ON SO WE CAN DO SOMETHING AND MAYBE KILL SOME PEOPLE IF NECESSARY!"

"No, you don't!" Mama is regaining control. Looks for a handkerchief and loudly blows her nose. She's still shaking, but she catches her breath. "Your right! Clasien, stop crying!" She lowers her voice. "Hedwig, please come here." Lovingly, "Please come sit with Mama and stop crying, Okay?"

"Where's Joop?"

"We don't know. Out somewhere, like you guys. OUT! We don't know and he doesn't know either, otherwise he'd be home too, I'm sure."

"Now can you tell us what happened, Mam?" His tone is more subdued too.

"See this mess?" She waves her arm around the room, "Four men from the V.D. rang the bell, they had rifles and pistols and the pushed Pappa up against the wall and...and...and...." She starts sobbing again.

"Do we have tea or something, Clasien? Glass of milk? Get your Mama something to drink! Now take it easy Mam. Remember Willem of Orange when he said in 1672; "ALLES SAL RECH KOM?," everything will be alright?" Mam, we've gone through soooo much lately, we'll get through this as well!"

"Boer, run and get Oom Gerrit and Tante Gerda! Go ahead! RUN!"

Somehow he feels that Mama needs some adult support and he likes his uncle Gerrit better than his uncle Otto. Oom Gerrit has more heart.

Tea is produced and the story unfolds.

Apparently, Pappa has been labeled as a "COLLABORATOR" with the German occupation forces and was marked for arrest and internment, to be sentenced in due time.

They didn't know where to look for him until Joop registered them at City Hall and Mam confirmed it by showing up for foodstamps this morning. An hour or so later, four men appeared, two took Pappa away and the other two searched the house. They confiscated just about all the food, the rum and the ARAK gin. According to them, that was solid proof that the Germans favored them and secondly, there were still plenty of families with little or nothing to eat, who were going to benefit from this. The beautiful black riding boots that the boys had "ORGANIZED" from the German officers were seen as further proof of collaboration with the enemy and they took them too!

Mam has gotten calmer as she's talking and as OOM Gerrit arrives, she hugs him warmly and thanks him for coming. She kinda repeats the whole story, but she's now under control.

Oom Gerrit has a calming effect on the situation.

"Herman has not committed any crimes against this country, he may have sympathized somewhat with the NAZIS for a while, but his arrest in February and the loss of HOF VAN HOLLAND will prove to anybody that he was NOT a danger to society and NOT a collaborator!

I'll go and find out where they took him. I know those guys. I'll find out what they're planning, but I do know that they're picking up a lot of people and they'll set up some sort of court and they'll punish some and they'll release others. They're not going to hurt him or anything, so don't worry.

Okay, give me a hug!

Hey kids, you're great! Take good care of your Mam, she's a good woman. I'll tell Gerda to fix some food for you guys too and we'll all eat at my house tonight. I'll be back!" Gone, like a whirlwind, but an uplifting one. Everything seems sooo much brighter, all of a sudden. Mama's back together.

" Let's straighten up this house! Let's go! Frits, would you have any idea where to look for Joop?"

"Not really, but don't worry about him, he's having fun and I don't blame him. He's been cooped up for 7 months, so let him run awhile. He can suffer long enough when he finds out!"

Mama sighs and thinks; "Good grief, these kids are starting to talk like little adults, although I wish he wouldn't curse like his Father. That's frightening"

Frits is happy he didn't summon Oom Otto instead of Oom Gerrit. He knows just what Oom Otto would have said, things like; "I told him so, he's so stupid and Herman is so stubborn! He's always right, right?"

Otto would have tried to lay a guilt trip on them; especially Mama and that would only have made matters worse instead of better.

Oom Gerrit is all right, though. He's a few years younger than Mama and he has a great sense of humor and so does his wife, Tante Gerda. They're going to be some solid support for Mama in these difficult days coming up.

Mama meanwhile explains the food and money situation. For the time being they'll receive weekly food stamps, enough to survive on. The milk runs will have to resume, but most food will become available again in regular stores. Everything is rationed and clothes and clothes stamps won't be available for at least a few more weeks.

Electricity should come back on in the next day or two. Repair crews are working feverishly, but until all the forced laborers come back, help is very scarce.

All their money has to be turned in to the bank and accounted for.

"No, they're not going to take our money away!"

There's very little to take anyway! Every week' they'll receive ten guilders per person, seventy guilders a week to survive on.

"Yes, yes, you can see the new money!"

"As soon as the war is over, new Dutch money will be printed and issued, but right now all we're using is temporary "occupation" money!"

"For how long?"

"We'll get 70 guilders a week until we have another source of income, but remember, this present government is just a haphazard bunch of people thrown together, so we'll have to see if it will really all work out that way! Bear in mind that all these assurances were given before Pappa was arrested and it may all change again. I hope to God that we won't have to go back to stealing food in order to survive!"

"You mean "ORGANIZE," don't you Mam?"

She chuckles; "Same thing, actually! I feel good about Gerrit getting into the action. He knows everyone in this town and after all I was raised here and our family has been here for hundreds of years, so I don't think the local society is going to let us starve to death. Pretty soon the English will be gone and everything will be back to normal. There should be plenty of work for a long time to come, just rebuilding this country.

It may take ten years to rebuild all the roads, bridges and houses, railroads and stations. The place is a mess. Maybe even more than ten years before all the scars from this war are healed. There's going to be enough work for everyone. I said that before, didn't I? Anyway, you know what I mean. The economy of Holland should be much stronger than before the war and we should flourish right along with it. Oh, my God, I'm starting to sound just like Papa, don't I?" She actually has to laugh at herself.

"Ya, you sound just like Pappa, but you might as well, you're going to play a dual role here for a while, both Mama and Pappa, so you might as well act it!"

"Mama, what did they say about this house and about furniture?"

."Oh, ya. For the time being, nobody can or will throw us out. When the spinsters "Buisman" re-appear, they and we will have to go to the "housing board" and they'll work something out. They don't know what or how, but they're working day and night on the problem. There are so many homeless people and so many demolished houses, it's frightful. We can't expect glass for the windows for at least a month, so the front rooms will stay as dark as they are for the time being and about the furniture? As early as tomorrow, we go to the "VEREENIGINGS GEBOUW" and identify our furniture, if any. What I plan to do, I'll take Joop and maybe Clasien and we'll go and inspect the place and tag our things as we find them. Let's just hope we do. The rumor is that our furniture ended up in an expensive "VILLA" on the other side of town, so if we get it back, Pappa my have his precious radio again. Oh, Pappa? I wonder where he is?"

Her lip starts to quiver again.

"Why don't Paultje and I go and find out what...!"

"No, no, you stay right here. Oom Gerrit is taking care of that and as soon as he comes back, we'll go over to his house and if Joop isn't back by then, we'll just have to leave him a note. I wish that boy would show up!"

"Mam, don't worry about him. He's fifteen, looks like he's eighteen and has the mind of a four year old, so he's alright!"

"Frits, I wish you'd quit picking on your older brother. he's alright!"

"Oh yeah? He's hanging out with a bunch of girls, I'm sure and I call that sick, sick, sick."

"Wait till you're fifteen!"

"Me and girls? Never, never!"

"I'll remind you some day. It won't be long!"

Oom Gerrit gets back, kinda out of breath.

"You guys ready? Let's go to my house, we can talk there."

"But what about Herman?"

"He's alright. He won't be back tonight but he's alright."

"But, where is he?"

"He's in KAMP VOSSEVELD" and .....!"

"KAMP VOSSEVELD? We know that place and..."

"Shut up, Frits. He's with the "non-criminals" so he'll eat and sleep well, so he's Okay for today. So quit worrying and let's go!"

"Wait, let me leave a note for Joop! We have to leave the back door open. Isn't that funny? We have been here for two months and we can't lock our doors from the outside yet! Clasien, there are thumbtacks in the back drawer in the kitchen!"

"I know, I know!"

"Frits, latch the door behind us and then run out back and join us!"

"Okay! Boer, go with Mama!"

The little procession marches a block east to the SLAGERIJ KWAK and for the first time in 4 years they're back in the butcher-shop and are hugging Tante Gerda and the kids. Some tears are shed, but mostly warmth and joviality spreads amongst them. It's a good feeling that now that war is over, the hostility within the family can stop too.

The kids are out back admiring Oom Gerrits pigeons, all the ones that the Germans did not get.

The grownups are in the parlor with a drink. Mama, in all her forty years, has not had a drink as early as five in the afternoon, but the shot of OUWE KLARE (Dutch gin) is doing her good, just as Gerrit had assured her. He's explaining the situation as he sees it.

" Herman and a lot of other people have been listed for a long time as "SYMPATHISERS." Others are listed as "WAR CRIMINALS," some "SEVERE" and some "MINIMAL" and everybody on those lists is being arrested. These lists do not find anybody "guilty" or "innocent," that will be determined by a "tribunal" in due time."

"But how can they say that, when the Germans nearly shot him and had him arrested and put him out of his own place and...!"

"Hold it! This is not the TRIBUNAL! All I'm doing now is relating to you what's going on. I'm not sitting here in judgement, so don't jump all over me. Let me fill up your glass. Here you go, now sit and relax and listen. And don't start sniffling again! Have a sip. This is still some of the good old stuff from SCHIEDAM, so enjoy!

As I was saying,,,,,what the hell was I saying?"

He fills his own glass again but Tante Gerda covers hers with her hand. "I still have to cook!"

"Oh come on. One more! You know; a drunk woman is an angel in bed."

Ida has to laugh in spite of everything and it does feel good to be back amongst her relatives, from whom she's been banned so long, too long!

Gerrit picks up the thread of his thoughts and continues on'

"What you're saying is right! Everything should be taken in consideration and it will be, but bear in mind that these lists were made up a long time ago. Let's say when your place was loaded with singing, dancing, money spending KRAUTS, while your radio was blaring and no one else was allowed to own one,"

"But...!"

"Hold it, I'm not finished. When you paraded down the aisle in church in your fancy fur coat.....HOLD IT, HOLD IT!.....I'm telling you...and don't make a face like that and don't start crying again, I'm telling you the facts, so shut up and hear me out!"

He may be younger, but right now he's the man in charge.

"So at one point, NO-ONE can deny, not even YOU, that on the surface you certainly deserved the label "COLLABORATOR." That's what the list says. Not "CRIMINAL" or "WAR-CRIMINAL." Herman did not report any Jews or...HOLD IT!" He raises his hand again, stopping Ida from saying anything, "or UNDERGROUND people. So as I understand it and as I see it, there will be some preliminary selections made and remember, this is just my opinion, all right? In a few days, Herman"...WOULD YOU SHUT UP?, in a few days, no, not tomorrow, but maybe a few weeks at the most, Herman will be released and a hearing will be set for a future date. At that time, all arguments, including the ones that are trying to jump out of your mouth, will be heard and he may go free or he may be sentenced to something. That's the way I see it. In the next day or two, don't pin me down now, I'll arrange for a visit for you to KAMP VOSSEVELD if he's not released yet, so you can see for yourself that's he's Okay.

Right now, HIS biggest worry is YOU and the KIDS. I assure you, he's NOT worried about himself, so the best thing YOU can do is make sure that you and kids are alright, physically and mentally, so when you see him you can assure him of that. Do you understand me?"

"Oh, God! " Gerda breaks in, "I'm so sorry!" Ida is sobbing uncontrollably again.

"Let her cry, Gerda, she needs to. She's been through soo much lately, let her cry!"

Gerrit is right. After a good hearty cry, Ida washes up, has another drink, "THREE BEFORE DINNER? I'm getting to be like some of my customers, I may be an alcoholic before all of this is over!"

" I wouldn't worry about it if I were you, Ida. You won' t get enough money to buy booze! Hahahahaha!"

In spite of everything, everybody laughs. It breaks the mood and when the kids pile in, "I'm hungry!" "When do we eat?" The morbid spell is broken and the atmosphere becomes one of warmth and laughter.

Tante Gerda is making "BALKENBREI," an old country favorite and the smell fills the house. As a matter of fact, the smell makes them more hungry. BALKENBREI is made from the juices left over from the sausages that Oom Gerrit makes himself. Into the juices, chopped bacon and flour is stirred in and it sits overnight until it jells. Then it's sliced into the size of square hamburger and pan fried to a golden brown crust. It's delicious and when they've finally have said their last "AMEN," they dig in as if they haven't eaten for weeks.

"Wonder what's keeping Joop?" Ida frowns.

"Don't worry, Ida, he's getting laid somewhere!"

"GERRIT!" Both women shout at him in indignation, but Oom Gerrit says; "I hope he is!"

"GERRIT!" "There are children at this table, Gerrit!"

"What's getting laid?" Little Gerard wants to know.

"See what you started?"

"Just eat Gerard, Just eat!" Gerrit has a big malicious grin on his face. Gerda is smirking too, but Ida's looking shocked and worried. "He's only 15 years old, just 15 last month. Would they really???"

"He's 15 years old and I've never considered that! Good God, these kids are getting sooo big sooo fast!"

A little after eight, after dark, no curfew, they meander home. Filled up solidly, pretty much at peace with the world, still worried, but at peace. For now!

Frits runs ahead in order to go through they alley to the back yard in order to get in and unlatch the front door. Still no Joop.

The kids go to bed. Frits doesn't consider himself one of the kids anymore. He'll be 14 this year. Still a long way off, but still…THIS year!

Joop shows a little after nine .

"Where's Pappa?"

"Oh, NO!" Here we go again.

Less emotional this time. They're getting seasoned.

CHAPTER XV
Peace In Winterswijk

APRIL 2, 1945. Liberated for two whole days. Or is it two months? It certainly seems a lot longer than two days... So much has happened. It's hard to imagine there ever was an occupation. It seems so remote! The streets remain crowded. The milk wagons are stuck in traffic for as much as two hours and are detoured in order to free the roads for the British convoys, but they get jammed up too. The tanks are not particularly helpful, they tear up the roads. At the intersection of the WOOLDSTRAAT and the WINKELSTRAAT, the tanks turn right towards "GROLLE" and churn up big chunks of pavement with their tracks as they pivot on the spot. Their right tracks stop; the left ones spin faster and dig up the roadway, throwing asphalt projectiles at the storefronts.

The front door of the ALBERT HEIN store and the upstairs windows have survived 5 years of war and many bombardments and are now shattered to smithereens.. Poor people, now that the war is over, they're sustaining more damage than when the war was on. It's a good thing they haven't been able to replace the big display window, cause it wouldn't have survived one hour of "tank attack."

Tanks and jeeps are everywhere. Unofficially, the advance is stopped at the rivers; the RHINE and the IJSEL. ARNHEM, on the north bank of the RHINE, is still in German hands.

Ida wonders how her sisters Paula, Hetty and Nel are holding up. This is the third time in five years that they're under siege. First in '40, when the Germans were stalled at the same place the British are stalled now, then in September of '44 when the British jumped north of the rivers and the towns of ARNHEM and VELP were practically wiped off the map.

Good God, what did they do to deserve this?

Most of Arnhem is in complete shambles and Ida has no idea if her sisters are dead or alive.

Compared to her sisters, maybe Ida is well off.

Now, she's going through rows and rows of furniture and she's being told that much more will be coming in. "Just have patience, Lady!"

The only thing she has definitely identified is her electric stove. It sticks out like a sore thumb, because hardly anybody in Holland has ever seen a modern appliance like that. When she shows her disappointment at the fact that hardly any of her furniture is there, she's assured that a lot of furniture that was moved to German quarters is now being used by the British, but it'll show up in due time. Just wait for the British to leave.

Well, at least it's something! She loads Clasien up on the old bike, (her better bike somehow disappeared three days ago) and pedals to City Hall. She knows most of the people there and when she addresses the guard on duty as "WIMPY," she's corrected; "IT'S "WIM," Mrs. Kwak." . Good grief, he's the son of an old classmate of hers.

"The last time I saw you was in 1940, in a boy-scout uniform. You were skinny then and you're still skinny, but you look good. How's your Mam?"

"Mam's fine and you're right Mrs. Kwak, I've been gone since' 40."

"Were you in a labor camp?"

"No, I joined the resistance, first in Belgium, then in France and after the D-day, back to Belgium and then right on the heels of the British, back into Holland."

"My, you must have some stories to tell! By the way, I haven't been a Kwak now for sixteen years; do you know my husband Herman Forrer? He was arrested yesterday and he's in KAMP VOSSEVELD. Who can I talk to about seeing him?"

"I'm sorry, I still think of all of you as "KWAK," but the man that you need to see is not here and you should wait one more day anyway. Everyone is being assigned to barracks and bunks and things are still in a shamble and they might not even know where to look for him. By tomorrow, they'll be let out for air and they'll have a bed number assigned and they'll be able to locate him. It's just a detention camp. It's not a jail. They'll be fed Okay, so give it another day, Okay?

I'm sure he's all right. Fellow WINTERSWIJKERS, neighbors and acquaintances and friends are guarding him. He'll be all right. It's not like being in a German concentration camp and he won't get shot at.

So go home for today. Tomorrow, pedal out there and you'll probably see him, Okay?"

"Alright, thanks. Say "Hello" to your Mam for me!"

"Sure will, Miss Kwak. Have a nice day!"

The boys are home when Mama gets back.

"Mama, do you know what we need? We need eggs. With eggs you can buy anything from the TOMMIES, so how can we get lots of eggs?"

"Slow down, you guys. Let me sit a minute. Do you have tea ready? Good guys! Sorry Joop! You made it? Good boy! By the way, you never told me what you did all day?"

"Ya, Joop, did you get laid?"

"FRITS!" Mama snaps. "I DON'T WANT THAT KIND OF TALK IN THIS HOUSE, YOU HEAR?"

Out of all things, Joop is blushing like they've never seen him blush before.

"I was hanging out with kids from school, mostly Nico. Remember Nico?"

"Oh, are they back too?"

"Yes, their house is in shambles, but they're Okay. His Dad is back at the factory already and we kinda went around looking up kids from our class that we hadn't seen all this time and we kinda celebrated the "liberation." That's all! Everyone is celebrating!"

"Any girls?"

"FRITS! Last warning! You leave Joop alone! Anyone hungry? And what were you saying about eggs?"

"Oh ya, Mama. We asked the TOMMIES what they wanted for cigarettes, corned beef, white bread, beefstew and all that stuff and they said; " fresh eggs." And they said; we have NYLONS. What are NYLONS?'

"Since when do you guys speak English? Since today?"

"Yes, professor Joop. I started two days ago and in another week Boer and I will speak better than you can. Wanna hear : CHOCOLATE FOR MAMA? CIGARETTES FOR PAPPA? HOW ARE WE DOING?"

"Hahahahaha! That's good, real good!"

"Anyway, Mam, they don't need Rum and Arak gin, they can use it, but they really want eggs. The question is; "what do we need and how do we get eggs? And by the way," he hands her a little can, "for Pappa, will you bring it to him or shall we take it?"

"What's this? A CAN of cigarettes?"

"It's called "a TIN," it's got 50 cigarettes and Mam, they say that these "PLAYERS" are really good."

" I don't know if I can give him anything, but I won't be going till tomorrow anyway. I'll try though!

How did you get these by the way?"

"Oh, we got a lot of things from shot up tanks and trucks, some of them were burned pretty badly, but some still have a lot of good stuff, like these cigarettes."

"It sure still looks good, as a matter of fact they look like they came right off a grocery store shelf. You didn't steal them, did you?"

"Mam, we might "ORGANIZE" something, but STEAL? Perish the thought! We just asked for eggs, so we can get some more. See what you can do, Mam. Meanwhile Pa is dying without his cigarettes, I'm sure, so do you want us to go by there and see...?"

"No, No! I was asked to wait till tomorrow, so we'll wait. Let me talk to WIGGERS and Oom Gerrit about eggs and see what we can do. Oh, good, Clasien! You have dinner ready? Boys, clear the table! Clasien, go ahead, set the table. Joop you pray! Remember Pappies favorite song; "BRENG ONZE PAPPIE GAUW WEEROM!" (Bring Pappie back soon!)"

"IN THE NAME OF THE FATHER, THE SON......"

After the boys catch up with the KAMPHUIS boys, they decide to check out the market place. Jeeps are lined all around the area, while the TOMMIES enjoy their food and beer. The whole scene is reminiscent of May 10, 1940, except that the uniforms and the language are different. Just like in 1940, the soldiers don't seem concerned about an upcoming battle at all, the possible loss of life or limb, death or destruction, the loss of their buddies, no, they seem relaxed and happy. They show no mental scars from all the fighting and death that they have experienced over the years, no, they act like they're on a family picnic.

The attitude is one of open friendliness and enthusiasm and the town folks join right in. Most of the celebrating and dancing is over, but the attitude is still very upbeat. The market place looks real festive with all the flags and banners hanging out of windows and music blasting out of every door.

The boys already know some of the new songs; 'LAY THAT PISTOL DOWN, BABE, LAY THAT PISTOL DOWN. PISTOL PACKIN' MAMA, LAY THAT PISTOL DOWN!" They're singing along with the ANDREW SISTERS at the top of their lungs.

The Dutch version is funnier, though. "LEENTJE, WAAR IS MAMMIE? MAMMIE LIGT IN BED. MET EEN CANADEESE VOOR EEN CIGARETTE. NEGEN MAANDEN LATER STOND ER IN DE KRANT, CANADEES GEBOREN, CHOCLAT IN ZIJN HAND."

(Leentje, where is Mammie? Mammie is in bed with a Canadian for a cigarette. Nine months later, the newspaper announces; CANADIAN BORN, CHOCOLATE IN HAND!" "Nine months later, darling, the paper's gonna say; CANADIAN KID WAS BORN HERE, HIS FIRST WORD WAS ; "Okay!")

By hanging around jeeps for two days already, Frits thinks he know all about them and right now he's showing off his skills to the other boys. On the far side of the old SAINT JACOB church, the "quiet" side, away from the bustle of the market place, Jeeps are parked between the buttresses of the church structure and here's where the old Master Driver Frits will show off his skills. He has watched many TOMMIES' start their vehicles, but he hasn't really seen what their feet were doing with clutches, brakes and gas pedals. He also has no clue about "shifting gears," so as all four of them are sitting in a jeep for their first lesson, he turns the starter switch and the jeep jerks forward, TJUCK, TJUCK, TJUCK, BOOM! He clobbers into the wall, five feet in front of him. Paul hits his head against the dash, Jan and Henkie fly forward into the front seat, head first and Frits hits the steering wheel with his chin. Other than crunching the bumper a little bit, the jeep's Okay, but the bang was so loud, that the boys scramble out of the jeep and flee in four different directions. No military men are chasing them and the civilians, who witnessed the event, just shake their heads, so the boys regroup and go see what other action there might be.

Oh, there's action all right! As they check out some of the big, expensive homes where the German staff used to hang out, they now find TOMMIES. They bum some cigarettes and there they are; ages 10 through 13, cigarettes dangling from their lips, making conversation, chewing TJOKLAT and drinking orange juice. This is the life! No worries about curfews, bombings, bringing home bread, being shot at, no, this is neat! Their English improves by a hundred words a day. Along with some officers, who are shaving for the first time in days, they're singing; " SISTER WHATCHA CALLING', WHATCHA DOIN' TONIGHT? HOPE YOU'LL BE IN THE MOOD, CAUSE I'M FEELIN' ALL RIGHT. HOW ABOUT A CORNER WITH A TABLE FOR TWO, WHERE THE MUSIC'S MELLOW IN A GAY RENDEZ-VOUS?"

They may not have the foggiest idea what they're singing, but that doesn't matter at all!

"IN THE MOOD, TARARARA, IN THE MOOD!" They can handle that! What a blast! Lots of laughs and good cheer. "GOOD BYE! BYE, BYE! TATA AND ALL THAT GOOD ROT!" The British soldiers enjoy themselves immensely; "What a gang!"

When the "gang" is out of sight, they congregate in a little roadside park and ask; "What have you got?"

Well, one's got some cigarettes, another's got a lighter, (very valuable), some candy and......TARAAH!!!

"A WHAT?????" A beautiful, black, shiny COLT REVOLVER!

"How'd you get that?" Where'd you get that?" "Can I see it?" "Can I hold it?"

"Wait, wait, wait you guys! Let me see how it works before we kill one of us. "

"All the other TOMMIES have pistols, so who had a revolver? I thought only Americans carried revolvers? "

"I don't know. It was there and now it's here and that's what counts. I can't figure out how to get the bullets out. No, no, keep your hands off it, before you shoot yourself in the back!"

"In my back? How could I shoot myself in the back?"

"You have to be real stupid, that's how! Wait a minute, I got it! You move this little pal and the whole cylinder swings out. I still can't get to the bullets, oh, yeah, wait, there they come. Just push this pin in the middle of the cylinder, six of 'em. That's why ZANE GREY calls 'em SIX SHOOTERS, right?"

"Okay, hold the bullets, now I can try it." He aims the empty weapon at the ground, pulls at the trigger with all his might, but it won't budge. His left hand comes to help and now the hammer comes back as he pulls on the trigger and then; "CLICK," the hammer falls on the empty chamber.

"My God, this is terrible compared to my pistol!"

"What pistol?"

"Oh, I have a little pistol, but with the rifles at the STEENGROEVE and my Russian machinegun, all we had to do is touch the trigger and "BLAM!" Right? This thing is murder.

"Let me try! Let me try!"

Everybody gets to try it and everyone agrees that "COLT" revolvers may be great in Cowboy books and movies, but as toys, they stink.

Half an hour later, they pass the VEREENIGINGS GEBOUW where all the furniture is being stored and distributed and even though they're not allowed to enter and "browse," they find enough activity outside.

The British have set up a bivouac. Tents are lined up in perfect orderly rows and latrines are dug in the back of the property.

They're just trenches in the ground with two horizontal bare pinetree poles in front of each trench.

One to sit on, the other, a little higher and to the front, to hold on to. On top of the "hold-on" bar, nails stick up every few feet with toilet rolls on top of them. Clever, real clever! Real toilet paper too. On real rolls! They haven't seen those for years and they each need at least one! Their windbreakers are starting to bulge.

Something else, that's new. White bread with "marmalade." And real butter. Pappa's ulcers would appreciate that!

Cars, half-tracks and jeeps are all over the place. Weapons, stand, lie or hang all over the place. Every conceivable variety and make. A boys paradise! To them it's like a living museum.

They run into their old classmate Gerrit, who's gone on to trade school. He wants to become a carpenter instead of a farmer, like his Dad. A lot of backslapping and reminiscing about the first few days of the war when the same type of action attracted them with one difference; these are friends, not enemies. When the subject "Pyramid of Riffles" comes up again, they laugh themselves silly about their childish ignorance of those days. How they had worried about a platoon of German soldiers being on their heels, ready to shoot them. What a riot!

When talking about present "achievements," Gerrit produces a comb. A REAL COMB! Brown plastic with streaks of yellow in it. Fine teeth on one side, bigger ones on the other. What a beauty! Wow, they haven't had anything but wooden ones as long as they can remember.

"Wanna trade?"

"For what?"

"I've got a COLT revolver!"

"Really? Lemme see! Oh, wow!"

"Deal?"

"Deal!" Merchandise is slipped from one windbreaker to another and the happy traders part ways.

"What a sucker! Let him try to pull that trigger! I've got a real comb. Wait till Joop sees it!"

Frits had that part right. Joop would kill someone for a real comb. Frits is holding off. He wants something of real value in return or else; he'd just as soon keep it.

When they tell Joop how they "organized" the comb, Joops reaction is degrading!

"You dumb asses! You gave away a valuable revolver for a comb?"

"We couldn't shoot it anyway! That trigger doesn't budge. We needed two hands to even fire it AND THAT IS TOO HARD. Give me a pistol anytime!"

"You didn't cock it, did you?"

"We did what?"

"You should read your cowboy books with more comprehension!"

"What's comprehension?" Paul wants to know.

"That means understanding what you read!"

"Oh, Ya? Wise guy! What didn't I understand?"

"You cock a revolver by bringing back the hammer, the same way you slide back the action on a pistol, that cocks the pistol. With a revolver, you do that with your thumb and then the trigger-pull is as light as a feather."

"How would you know?"

"I went through a hundred cowboy books before you could read!"

"You mean to say that in order to fire a revolver, you first bring back the hammer and then you pull the trigger? How could you be the fastest gun in the west if you had to go though all of that?"

"Haven't you noticed how the cowboys kinda "slap" their left hand across the back of the revolver in their right hand? That's how they cock it!" Joop demonstrates, acting as if he's making a "quick-draw" with his right hand and when it's nearly in firing position, he quickly slaps across it with his left hand and hollers; "POW!"

Frits hates to admit that he may have been stupid, so he covers up by saying; "Okay, Okay, Max Brand, I'll get another revolver and you demonstrate!"

"You're on and I'm sure I'll outshoot you!"

"Let's go Boer, before we're too impressed with this gunslinger from DODGE!"

"Don't go too far! We're eating in a few minutes!" Mama hollers after them.

"Okay, Mam!" They waltz out the door and on their way to the alley, they encounter a neighbor, moving in next door. A youngish looking gentleman with ashblond hair and rimless glasses is pulling a handcart.

"You must be Dr. Glass?"

"I sure am! How'd you figure that?"

"Your name plate out front. Let's give you a hand."

They grab hold of the spokes of the cart, but when they get to the back gate of the Doctors yard, the gate proves too narrow for the Doctors cart.

"What do you wanna do, Doc? Take the post out or carry the stuff?"

"Let's take the post out!"

While they're shaking the pole back and forth in order to loosen it, Frits introduces his brother and himself.

"Paul is also known as "BOER" and we nearly came to live in your house!"

"Really?" The Doctor finds that amusing and with a final shove, he breaks off the pole.

"Oh, well, I guess we needed a new pole anyway, didn't we? Okay! Now we can get through!"

Back at the wheels again, pushing the wooden spokes, they get the cart to the back of the house.

There they get to meet Mrs. Glass, who has ashblond hair and rimless glasses. The two children, 3 and 5, have ashblond hair, but no glasses.

Sitting down with some "limonade," they bring the Glass family up to date in about ten minutes, until Mama's voice interrupts from across the wall; "Jongens, kom eten!"

They're gone in a flash! Wooden shoes come off, one is up and over the fence, wooden shoes get pitched over the fence and the next one is up and gone!

Mrs. Glass laughs; "I used to think that two meter fences would keep people out, but to them, it's not even an obstacle."

At the supper table, Mama gets to hear all about the Glass family and says; "After supper, I'll go over and meet them. See if they need any help."

"I'm going out, Mam!" Joop is not interested in neighbors.

"Don't be late, Joop!"

"And don't get l..., you know!"

"Frits! Stay out of this! Why don't you boys stay here and help Dr. Glass move his stuff in."

"He seems like a nice man, so that's Okay!" Frits is agreeable.

"But Mam, the boys are waiting for me!" Joop's not! He sounds urgent.

"Let him go, Mam. He would probably break things anyway!"

The evening with Dr. Glass is interesting, to say the least. While they're unpacking, Dr. Glass tells them HIS story about the war.

The Germans had wanted him to work in Germany in a rehabilitation center for wounded soldiers, but he felt that that would be supporting the German war effort and THAT he couldn't do. So he packed up his young family and disappeared into the farm country, right along the border. He learned to sow, harvest, milk cows, dig potatoes and beets and generally became a farmer. The important thing was that he and his family survived, but now he can't wait to get back to his practice.

"My name?"

"GLASS" with 2 SS's, spelled the German way?"

"Well, I'm from Groningen, close to the German border too and somewhere in the past, way back when, I may have been related to some "GLASS'S" on the other side of the border in "OST FRIESLAND, GERMANY."

"Or," Mrs. Glass interjects, "the name may have survived the changes in the Dutch language over the years, because in the Middle Ages the Dutch also spelled names like ours with double "S" or "SCH." Anyway, he's proud of his name and he'll stick with it."

His wife, "DIERKE," is also from up there and talks funny like he does. "YA, I know it's funny, but we do look alike, don't we? and NO! we're not otherwise related. NOT cousins or anything, just husband and wife."

"Well, maybe she's my first cousin and I just don't know it! Hahahaha!"

"Well, nice to have you as neighbors and call on us anytime you need something."

"Good night!"

"Goodnight!"

The weather remains fair and after the long hard winter it is certainly a pleasure to be out and about.

Full of spring fever, the boys arrive at the KAMPHUIS residence, but instead of going out, they're called inside where they receive a stern lecture. Mr. Kamphuis is receiving newspapers again and he shows one of the leading articles. Three stupid kids have received injuries and have received treatment across the street at the hospital. According to the report, one boy blew part of his hand off by hitting a bullet with a hammer. It seems he found a 20-millimeter "live round" and decided to explode it.

"Stupid, MOST stupid!" Everyone agrees. "You treat ammo like a woman, tenderly and never hit it!'

The second guy that got hurt burned away part of his hand and face, but the article is not very clear as to how it happened.

"This writer used to do COOKING ARTICLES and should stay away from things, she doesn't understand!" Mr. Kamphuis sounds convincing.

Frits helps out; "It sounds like the guy fired a PANZERFAUST and instead of holding the weapon under his arm when he pulled the trigger, he held it in front of him and the blast hit him right in the face and hands."

"Like I said, that woman shouldn't write WAR ARTICLES without consulting you boys first!"

"Ya, the guy just didn't know what to expect. He must have just stood there and aimed it like a rifle, the dumb ass! Dumb, dumb, dumb!"

"These kids have probably not been out of the house during the entire war and now suddenly are exposed to all sorts of war material, that's laying all around them!"

"The stuff must be very unfamiliar to them, listen to this strange one; BOY LOSES EYE AND PART OF HIS FACE BECAUSE OF A "JERRY-CAN" EXPLOSION! How do you explode a JERRY-CAN?"

"That's different. Empty JERRY-CANS are strewn all over the place and some still have some gas in them.

And when they're near empty and you leave them lying in the sun, the gasoline evaporates inside the can and becomes a very explosive gas. If you then open it and light a match even near it, it will probably spew a flame like a flame-thrower."

"I bet ya, thats what happened to this guy!"

"I'm sure it was. If you leave the can open, even with gasoline in it, then you can drop a lighted match in it and it'll just burn without that explosion kind of reaction. So I bet you these kids were having fun setting discarded JERRY CANS on fire and one of them torched him right in the face! Moral of this whole story is DON'T DO ANYTHING STUPID LIKE THAT! DO YOU HEAR? ALL OF YOU, DO YOU HEAR?"

"Ya, Father!"

"Ya, mijnheer Kamphuis!"

"By the way, Frits, how's your Dad?"

"You know he's in KAMP VOSSEVELD, don't you?"

"Yes I know. Have you seen him, heard from him?"

"No, my Mam is going for the first time today, but my Oom Gerrit says; they're Okay and they're keeping him for just a few days."

"Oh, that's good. Any news about HOF VAN HOLLAND? When are you moving back or do you have to wait till the Brits leave?"

"We're never going to move back in, we lost it!"

"YOU WHAT?" Mr. Kamphuis shouts. "YOU WHAT?" Mrs. Kamphuis chimes in.

Frits tells the long sad story and since the Kamphuises didn't live in town when the auction took place, they naturally assumed that the Forrers owned the place, not leased it.

After a lot of; "WHAT ARE YOU GOING TO DO?" and;"WE'RE SO SORRY!" the boys finally hit the street. Their mood is depressed, but adventure comes their way in many shapes and forms and it's easy for them to forget their worries about the future.

"Where do you suppose these guys found the JERRY-CANS?"

That's funny! All four of them were thinking the same thing!

"Wherever the British camped out!"

"Let's go!"

They come upon their goal more easily then they had imagined. Just a 20 minute stroll along the Kottenseweg they reach the intersection to 't WOOLD and DEURNE and there, right in front of them, are the remains of a giant bivouac. Trucks and tanks must have simply run across the barbed wire fences and kinda plowed up half of the huge pasture. The tell-tale cooking trenches with their flame blackened walls are laid out in 4 neat rows. The British way of cooking seems a lot less cumbersome than the big German kettles with their KARTOFFELENSUPPE. All the equipment needed for a British field kitchen could probably fit in the back of a pick-up truck and be set up in ten minutes.

Garbage is everywhere and the latrines are only partially filled in and stink to high heaven.

Amongst the discarded boxes and cans are many unopened ones. "PEACHES IN THEIR NATURAL JUICES" from GEORGIA!, "CORNED BEEF" from Frothinham, "TEA TOASTIES" from LONDON!

Half packs and tins of "PLAYERS." The place is a little goldmine. It was hard to say if the camp had been abandoned, One, Two or Three days ago, but it was obvious that no one had scavenged it so far.

And......there are.... The JERRY-CANS!

After the stern lecture from Father Kamphuis, they decide to play it cool with the JERRY-CANS and instead, with the help of Henkies Tommie-knife, they devour can after can of GEORGIA peaches.

"Wherever GEORGIA is in ENGLAND, they must have great weather."

If they had read the label more closely, they would have figured out that GEORGIA was somewhere in the USA, but at that point it doesn't matter much.

After some conferring they decide to approach the JERRY-CANS with great caution. Inasmuch as all of them have burning cigarettes dangling from their mouths, they'll use cigarette butts instead of matches.

"Who's first?" "Chickens!"

"Remember what Father said; the open cans are the safest!"

Most of the cans are open anyhow, cause who would bother to close an empty can??

"Okay, number one!"

A JERRY-CAN is put upright and with the cigarette butt between the tips of his fingers, Frits leans toward the can, arms outstretched. Just as he's about to drop the butt, "WHOOOOSH!" a five-foot flame spouts into the air with such a sudden explosion that Frits jumps back like a Jack-in-the box.

"DAMNIT!' He's shook up, but the others just roar with laughter!

"You should have seen yourself, I didn't know you could jump that high! Hahahahahah!"

It's so hilarious that Frits cant help but join in once his heart has started again.

"Did you see that? I didn't even have the glow of the butt over the opening yet and WHOOPS! there it blew already! Less then a hundredth of a second! I'm lucky I didn't burn my fingers. Now how about you people trying one!"

A new technique is decided upon. A burning strip of cardboard gives an extra foot of safety margin and indeed the art of JERRY-CAN torching is immediately refined. There's no fear of them blowing up, but the heat melts and peels the green paint and gives the cans that thoroughly burned look. The rubber seal inside the lid also burns away, leaving the cans totally worthless.

"Question! Do these cans have any value? Could your Father use them or some farmers, maybe?"

"Let's hide the rest in the woods and cover'em up. We can come back for'em later; we may have something here that we can negotiate with."

It takes many trips back and forth into the strip of woods that separates the pastures, but they stash a considerable treasure for future use.

It's decided to go further into KOTTEN and see if anything is happening in that direction.

The truck shelters that line the roads have lost their usefulness because there are no more air attacks on any military convoys. Result: the neat little pine posts that make up the overhead structure can now be used for something more creative, like their log cabin and the raft they want to build. All they have to do is dump the poles in the creek up the road and the creek will deliver them right to their door or sandbar if you prefer. All they have to do is wait at the sandbar and fish them out.

NOT today, though. Too much action going on! (What they don't know is that their guardian angel is looking out after them. They should stay away from their spot right now!)

Just 15 minutes further down the road, just past the little grocery store, is some activity. A burned out half-track, a shot up truck, a group of jeeps and LORRIES and a few dozen soldiers. Where there are soldiers, there's always excitement. After the usual; "Cigarettes?" they get involved in the activity at hand. The troops are tying ribbons around mine fields, making slow progress moving west away from Germany.

A few soldiers have mine detectors, broomsticks with a frying pan on the bottom and earphones on their heads. They move slowly along the roadside and into the fields and when they "hear" mines, they signal and other troops string yellow ribbons around trees and fence post, thereby marking off the minefield.

The burned half-track and the damaged truck didn't run over landmines, they were shot up. Land mines are usually off the road, forcing the advancing columns to stay on the road, where they can easily be picked off.

The boys are intrigued by the goings-on and slowly meander with the troops in the direction of town.

"HOLY MARIA!" Jan comes running back.

"WHAT? WHAT?"

"Do you know, if we'd gone back to our log cabin spot we might be dead by now?"

"This whole area is mined, the Major says, all the way past our two bridges!"

"Thank you Saint Michael!"

"What did you say?"

"I was thanking my guardian angel, Saint Michael, for steering...."

"BOOOM!" A SCREAM!!!!!! MORE SCREAMS and a lot of yelling and a truck racing to a spot a hundred yards ahead of them.

"STAY BACK, YOU KIDS!!! STAY BACK, DAMNIT!!"

"What happened? What happened?"

Nobody knows yet, except that one of the mine searchers has stepped on a mine!

"No, come on! That doesn't sound right! How could he step on a mine? He can hear them before he gets to them!"

Two rescuers, led by two other mine detectors, inch their way to the wounded soldier and carefully pick him up and drag him back to the shoulder of the road.

"How could that happen?"

"Is he alive?" "Is he hurt bad?"

"Yes, yes and yes, I think, but don't ask so many questions!

Actually in English their questions come across like; "WHA HAPPEN? HE LIFE?, HE BAD?"

Finally, things sort out and he's taken away. He died! One leg and half his guts were torn out, so he couldn't have lived anyway. Too bad!

That blows their spirit. The boys are shushed away by the soldiers; "Go home!" and as they're walking, the older boys explain what they think they've overheard.

Apparently, the mine searcher stepped up to the next field to which he was assigned and when he put his earphones on he immediately "heard" a mine and instinctively stepped back. He must have stepped over the mine and when he took half a step backwards, he stepped right on it and BOOOOOM, up he went, blowing him to bits.

WOW, somehow, death seams soooo unfair and unacceptable. They walk on, but their mood is low, until Henkie says; "Wanna see what I got?"

"What? What?"

"Wait a minute, let's get off the road!"

"NO, NO, LET'S NOT GET OFF THE ROAD! TOO MANY LAND-MINES!"

"Okay."

"Let's see what you got, Henkie!"

Henkie unbuckles his "PLUS-FOUR," his KNICKERBOCKERS, and up he pulls a "STENGUN!"

" A brand new, shiny, goodlookin' STENGUN!"

"What do you mean; goodlookin'? Compared to the German ones, these are UGLY! Look at the welding spots! Not very professional, are they? Is

"Tommie" tea break, April 1945

it empty? WAIT! Point it over there! Pull the action back! Yep, it's empty!
Did you get a clip?"

"Huh?"

"Did you get a clip, a magazine? Bullets?"

"No, I didn't."

"Where are you gonna hide it?"

"I'm taking it home!"

"NO, YOU'RE NOT! Your Father will kill you!" Jan is adamant!

"I'll hide it in the shed. I'm not gonna leave it in the woods to rust.
Look at Frits' Russian gun, we haven't seen it for six months, it's probably
rusted solid. I'm taking mine home even if I have to give it to my Father!"

"It's your neck!"

"Hey guys, how do we get ammo for that thing!" Frits is interested
in shooting the gun, he's not interested in storing it. "We better check out

British tanks, shot to hell, 30 March 1945

some vehicles that carry ammo. Their clips look just as simple and cheap looking as the STENGUN itself, but they throw out 30 rounds pretty fast!"

"How do you know?"

"Remember we saw that in the newsreels once? Anyway, they use a very standard caliber, so we shouldn't have much of a problem getting ammo for it, the question still is; "what's you gonna do with it?"

"I'm gonna hide it in the shack and tell my Father when he's in a good mood!"

"Like I said; it's your neck!" Jan is giving in, reluctantly.

Well, Mr. Kamphuis is asleep, so no one tells anybody anything, certainly not about the landmine affair. Mrs. Kamphuis would never let her kids out of the yard any more.

As the boys get home with their cans of food, Mama is back from her visit to KAMP VOSSEVELD. She seems all right, although it's obvious that she's been crying.

"How's Pappa? What'd he say? Could he have cigarettes? Are his ulcers bothering him? How'd he look?

Is he scared? Did you tell him about Oom Gerrit or did you think that would make him mad? Are they getting enough blankets? That place is pretty drafty, you know?"

"Just a minute, JUST A MINUTE! I'm nearly done in here and this kitchen is too small for so many people, so put the cans on the counter and go inside. I'll be right there!"

Joop takes a look at the harvest the boys brought in and gives a dissertation as to the origin and benefits of CORNED BEEF, ("Who cares?") Georgia peaches puzzle him. Georgia is part of southern Russia. There was some heavy fighting there, not too long ago. In Georgia, the Caucasus, Kiev, Stalingrad, the Ukraine and Odessa, he remembers all those German victories and later the defeats in those areas, but he didn't expect peaches to grow in that part of the world and besides, how did the British get a hold of them?

He shrugs, "How do you know, nowadays? Yesterday, they had oranges from Haifa, Palestine. It's getting to be a small world."

Mama joins them in the dining room with her first cup of REAL COFFEE in many months. Complete with hot milk, she sits down to savor THIS treat, just great! Too bad Herman is going to miss this! Tears are welling up in her eyes again, but she fights them back. She's got to be strong in front of these kids!

"O.K.,Okay.Okay.,Okay., your Pappa is Okay! A little shook up, but Okay. Everything is pretty much like Oom Gerrit told us. They're just interned in that kamp."

"What's interned?"

"Locked up, Boer. Locked up, stupid!"

"Joop!' Easy now! They have not talked to him personally and.."

"Interrogated!"

"Joop, stay out of this, let me talk! Oh, by the way, I could not give him his cigarettes personally, but one of the guards put his name on it and said he would see to it that Pappa would get them."

"Oh, ya? How many are they gonna steal for themselves first? But I don't care, we'll get more! You tell'em, we'll get zillions more, right Boer? Tell 'em not to worry, we'll get him cigarettes.. Those stinking guards! You shouldn't have given 'em to them, you know Pappa may never get any and, and.."

"Hold it, hold it! Can you hold it, please?" Mama has a hard time getting a word in edgewise. "I thought I was talking!"

"Ya, man, stay out of it!"

"You shut up!"

"Joop, Frits, HUSH! Let me enjoy my coffee and talk. Pappa is worried about US, Not himself! He feels so helpless having left us all on our own."

"He can't help that, he didn't just walk away, you know!"

"Yes, yes, I know that, but that's the way he feels. From what he has heard, the "V.D." wants every Nazi sympathizer....HOLD IT, HOLD IT! I know, I know. Those were HIS words, they feel that everyone who dealt with the KRAUTS and benefited from it," She raises her hands before a flood of words is about to interrupt her again. "should be punished. Thank God, they are not the tribunal. Now suppose the tribunal finds him guilty of some infraction and sentences him to 30 days in jail, Okay? Each day he spends now will be deducted from his jail term, so it doesn't matter to him whether he spends time now or later, as long as WE are Okay.. He wants to be here with us now, to help us relocate, find our stuff, start a new business and so on. He feels his time with us is crucial and YES, he's dying for a cigarette."

"Did you get to see where he sleeps?"

"Oh, no! I nearly forgot. Today we met in a little room with a mesh screen between us and a guard looking in, but in the future they'll let me in the camp and we'll be able to walk and sit in a restricted area. But today, all I could do was touch his fingers through the screen."

The tears well up again when she thinks about how she could only kiss his fingertips and he kissed hers. Bravely, she fights back her tears.

"Anyway, boys, is there any news about ARNHEM or VELP? Are they still not liberated out there?"

"No, Mam. The word is that the liberation troops are still stuck on this side of the rivers, but the Americans are pushing very fast into lower Germany, so they'll meet up with the Russians and then squeeze Berlin into giving up. Here in Holland the rivers, all the way to the coast are holding everything up. If they get just one bridgehead on the other side, it'll be over soon. Half of Holland is now free, but the west and northwest are still bottled up. Maybe they'll surrender soon. They can't get out. They can't get back to Germany!"

Frits isn't listening to Professor Joop, he's got his mind made up.

"Boer, give me your cigarettes, how many do you have? Good, now go in the house and get Joops too!"

"What are you gonna do?'

"Don't say anything! I'm gonna supply Pappa. Go and steal Joops, he's too young to smoke anyway!"

The broad smile on Paul's face as he goes in, is replaced by a frown as he comes out.

"He's got them in his shirt pocket! I can't get to them!"

"Alright, don't worry. Stay here!"

"I wanna come!"

"No, this is going to be a "BLITZ" operation, mostly "checking out." I'll be back soon. Tomorrow we go together, Okay?"

Paul's lower lip doesn't spell approval, but Frits grabs Hans Steins scooter, the AUTOPED, and is off.

A minor delay deters him, nearly strands him at the far end of town, near where the retreating Germans took his bicycle four days ago, is a giant British encampment.

"FOUR DAYS AGO?" He mutters to himself, "ONLY FOUR DAYS AGO? IT SEEMS LIKE A YEAR!"

HARMONIE DANCE HALL, the gas station, the tennis courts and the soccer field have all been converted into a huge encampment. The place literally crawls with soldiers and he pauses briefly, determined to come back and really check the place out. He's just starting to pedal again when his attention is caught by an unusual scene. BRAM ZOETHOUT, one of his classmates, is sitting under the flap of a tent, being tattooed! He's bare-chested and a neat little eagle is appearing on his upper arm, the same little eagle that the troops have on the shoulders of their tunics. Underneath the eagle, in small print it says; A.B.Z.

"Hi, Frits!" He hollers, "want a tattoo?"

"No, thanks!"

"Come on!"

The British chime in; "Yeah, mate, have a tattoo!" About six of them

British camp

are hanging around, with or without tattoos. "Come on, lad, it's fun! It doesn't hurt!"

"No, No, no tattoos! What's A.B.Z.?"

"My name!"

"Your name?

"Ya, Abraham Bernardus Zoethout! Hahahaha!"

"Have fun! I'm on an important mission!"

"I'm nearly done. What mission, I'll go with you!"

"WOULD YOU TALK BLOODY ENGLISH, PLEASE?" The tattooer is getting annoyed.

"We try, we try!"

"Yes you try, my bloody arse you try! When you want something, you bloody well speak English!"

"Yes, we try, we try! " The British don't think this is very humorous.

Bram, with his brand new eagle on his arm, gets out of his chair and comes over; "Isn't this neat? It doesn't hurt at all!"

"Ya, but it never comes off, right?"

"No, that's the whole idea. I'll be an honorary member of this battalion the rest of my life!"

"Good, enjoy it! Not for me! This is quite a camp! How big is it?"

"I don't know, but it's huge, all the way from the dance hall to the MANÈGE over there."

"Are there still horses in the MANÈGE?"

"No, No, No! It's an ammo dump now, but I think it's a German ammo dump, because it's guarded by the "V.D," not by the British!"

"Really? How interesting! Gotta check that out sometime. Now I'm on a mission!"

"Okay. Man, come by here again, I'm always here! I practically live here!"

"Okay! Tju!"

"Tju!"

Frits turns right at the sign to MEDDO and in a matter of fifteen minutes the camp comes in sight. He knows it well. He spent many a day here when he "helped" train Hitler's VOLKSSTURM. He wonders how many of the kids and old men of that "RAG-TAG" army are still alive? "Shame!"

He slows to a crawl, now keeping his mind on his target; "the camp!" He stares intently at the men walking about the camp or sitting on barracks steps and benches. NO Pappa! Most men are wearing overcoats, it's about 50-55 degrees out and he wonders if Pappa is warm enough. No sign of Pappa anywhere though. Time for a different approach. He parks his scooter, walks to the entrance, ignores the guard until; "Halt, halt! Hold it, you there! Little one, hold it, HALT!"

"WHO? Me?"

"Ya, you! Where do think you're going?"

"I'm gonna see the COMMANDANT!" He turns again, walking towards the guardhouse.

"WAIT!" That stupid guard again, "You can't just walk in there!"

"I can't? Okay, then I'll take my AUTOPED!"

"No, NO! You can't take that either! Put that thing away! Over there!" He points to the bicycle rack.

Frits puts up his little scooter in the designated rack and walks toward the sign that says; "WACHTCOMMANDANT!" while saying over his shoulder; "I'll talk to him!"

The guard is more flabbergasted than anything else. Fighting the Germans in the resistance was easier than dealing with these civilians that he has been facing for the last few days.

Inside the guardhouse, Frits says to the ORANGE BANDER behind the desk; "You the WACHTCOMMANDANT?"

The man grins; "No, he's in there!!" and points to a door that says; *H.v.d.Hoeve*, but when Frits turns towards the door, he hollers; "Hey, wait a minute! You can't go in there!" He jumps up from behind his desk, but he's too late.

Frits looks at the surprised old man behind the desk and asks; "Which barracks is Herman Forrer in?"

"Who are you?" He seems amused and waves the ORANGEBANDER out of the room and turns his hands up to the lady he was talking to as if to say; "Excuse me, what can I do?"

He again signals to the outside desk man to leave the room and turns to Frits;

"Can I ask; who are you and why do want to know this?"

"He's my Dad and I'm Frits and I gotta talk to him!"

"I see. Well, visiting hours are over, but you can come back tomorrow and see him. Promise!"

"No, I want to see him now! He's not a well man and his ulcers will kill him, so I've gotta see him now!""

"Well, Frits," he smiles at the woman, " you cannot see him now, we're having a headcount in the barracks and then they'll line up outside for dinner, so you can probably see him from the roadside. He'll be coming from the rear, he's way in back, but he has to walk to the kitchen for his food, so you'll be able to see him, but you can't visit with him today! Let me assure you, though, he's fine and.."

"Ya, but maybe he's cold and then his ulcers flare up and..."

"He can ask for more blankets. This is NOT a Nazi concentration camp, so stop worrying. We'll see you tomorrow, Frits Okay?" Have a safe trip back! Be careful!"

Without another word, Frits is gone. MAD, but PLEASED, if that's possible. MAD, because he wasn't able to bluff his way in, PLEASED that he knows about where to find his Dad.

He innocently seems to pedal his way to MEDDO, but once out of sight of the watchtowers he turns right onto a dirt road. After about half a mile, he passes a row of trees that divide the pastures and that's where he hides his scooter in the brush. He keeps the trees between him and the camp and moves on until he feels he's directly in line with the camp. He crawls through the line of trees and peers out. The watchtower on the nearest corner could easily spot him, but it isn't manned.

"What's this? Don't they expect people to escape? Maybe not. Escape to where?" He's talking to himself; "That's right! Where could they possibly go? Germany?

The war will be over soon and there'll be no place to hide anywhere! Anyway, that makes life easy!"

He hits the ditch that crosses the field to the corner of the camp and on his toes and elbows he slithers through the ditch like a snake at high speed.

The only way anyone could have spotted him would be if there was someone in the tower looking down and since there isn't anyone up there, he's sure that he's unobserved. The barbed wire around the compound is so tightly woven, that it would be impossible to get in without cutters. In the ditch though, the lower strands of wire are secured with tent-rods and with a little shaking back and forth, they come loose and two of the rods come up, giving him enough room to slip underneath. And.... He's IN THE CAMP!

Thank God it hasn't rained for a week, cause the ditch would have been full of water and this approach wouldn't have worked.

Flat on his belly, he crawls underneath the building closest to him. In between supports and pipes, he makes his way to the front of the building from where he can see the parade grounds. Peering through the front door steps, he ponders; "Without a back door, these places are a death trap in case of fire or attacks! Well, that's not my problem, right now." His problem is; "There are four buildings back here, which one is Pappa's?"

He's sure there are no kids in the camp, so he would stick out like a sore thumb if he got up and was spotted. "So how do I figure this one out?"

"When the men walk to the kitchen, they have to walk between the mall with the flagpole, RED, WHITE and BLUE this time, and the building, two over. Okay, that's it!"

Underneath the building, he crawls to the edge nearest the flagpole, makes sure that he's clear, left and right and bellies through the grass to the next building. He repeats that procedure once more and when he's underneath his target building, he's in place.

"Let 'em come, I'm ready!"

He digs out his cigarettes, four half empty packs. He fills one pack to the brim, probably 24-25 cigarettes squashed together, "Well, beggars can't be choosers! That'll do!" He has two cigarettes left for himself. "That's enough! I can get more1"

Now all he can do is wait. He has no idea what time it is. His stomach is his only clock and that clock is way off. The peaches have been digested, but he doesn't quite feel that it's suppertime yet.

So; patience, patience, patience! That's one virtue he doesn't have, but he's in luck. The farthest door opens and carrying British mess tins, the men file out talking in low tones. About twenty of them pass him in ones or two's. There's not a guard in sight, so why this hushed conversation? It puzzles him.

Pappa is not amongst them.

The second door opens, NO PAPPA! The third one, THERE HE IS! Suit and vest, no collar, no tie. Maybe he's cold. Mama's got to bring his coat!

He's talking with another man and as they come close to his hiding place, Frits whistles through his teeth; "SWEETSWEET!" "PAPPA!" Herman stops, looks…, nothing!!

"Shshshshssssh! Sit on the steps! Keep moving, you guys!" This last order for three other men that also came to a stop. "Tie your shoelace, Pap!" Herman sits down at the end of the steps, going through the motions of tying shoelaces and Frits is over there in two seconds flat. Between the steps, he slips the cigarettes into Pappa's hands and with a "TOT KIJK!" He's gone.

Pappa' whispering things like; "You shouldn't be doing this and…." But Frits doesn't hear, he slips from underneath one building, through the grass, another building, the third one, into the ditch, restakes the rods and he's off!" Mission accomplished!

After crawling the length of the ditch, he retraces his steps along the trees, retrieves his scooter and starts to pedal his way back home. In front of the camp, he slows down in order to catch a glimpse of his Dad, but there is no sign of him anywhere!

For the first time, anger, excitement and frustration make way for profound sadness. A sadness for his Pappa and his predicament. Sadness, coupled with a feeling of helplessness and a deep love for that man, make him sit down by the roadside and burst into tears. The little skinny body is wracked with sobs, as he feels like LITTLE LINDA; "IF ONLY I COULD BRING MY PAPPIE HOME!"

For a while he just pedals along slowly, shifting feet from pedaling to standing and back to pedaling with the other foot in order to keep from any one leg to get too tired. He's talking courage into himself again, assuring himself that Pappa will be alright; "JUST A FEW DAYS, THAT'S ALL!"

He's back at the intersection and ponders his options; "Go home to eat?" , "Go and find Bram at the bivouac?" "Check out the MANÉGE? (THE HORSESTABLE?) "Let's check out the manége!"

The decision was easy because that was the most "unknown" of his options, so consequently, that appealed the most. He glides by the building in the direction of GROLLE, the same way the fleeing Germans had gone after they stole his Mothers bicycle. He grins to himself when he thinks of the beautiful bike he got for his Pappa, just a few hours later. The MANÈGE is a long, long, red brick building with high narrow windows all along the top, just under the overhang. It is set in the open, about 50 yards off the road. Pastures surround it on all sides, no trees, no bushes, no vehicles, and no places to hide.

The grass hasn't been cut for years and there haven't been any horses to eat it either. He pedals past the building for about a kilometer and then slowly works his way back. He times the lone guard. The "VD"er, in blue overalls and an orange band, rifle slung over his shoulder takes 55 seconds to march one way along the front of the building. He halts at the end, looks around, turns and within 8 seconds he heads back toward the other end of the building. Same 55 seconds. Well, that should be a cinch!

Frits stops about 50 yards past the dirt road that leads to the barn and hides behind a huge oak. He gets ready, waits till the guard is at the near end of the building, turns and starts his trek away from Frits. He takes off full speed! The man in blue is one-third down his stretch as Frits shoots up the path and by the time the guard is two-thirds toward the end, Frits is next to the building, flat in the grass.

If the guard caught a flash out of the corner of his eye or notices the tire track in the grass next to the building, he'd be standing over Frits within two minutes, rifle at ready. He'll find a little boy, about eleven, with his coveralls down his ankles, peacefully taking a crap.

The guard doesn't show. A clump of grass serves as toilet paper and he's ready for business. He proceeds to the back of the building.

Some of the high windows are not completely pulled shut, so he parks his scooter under a window and climbs onto the handlebars. The window he's tackling won't budge easily. The long bottom latch is stuck in "ajar" position and trying to push it up isn't working. He considers breaking the window, but he's afraid of the noise. No choice! He jumps down and moves to another "ajar" window and this time his knife does the trick, it lifts the latch and now the window comes open. He has to lean backward in order to move the window upwards past his head. Hanging on to the sill with one hand, he lifts the window with the other and nearly screams as the scooter slips from under feet, the window hits him in the head and he dangles from the window sill. He tries desperately to hang on with one hand and lift the window with the other, but he has no choice and drops to the ground. Up goes the scooter again; up goes the skinny kid, but this time he does it differently. He holds the long latch with the many holes up with his knife as he opens the window a little at a time. The pin on the sill slips into one hole after the other as he moves the window further up and out. When the latch is in the fifth notch, he can pull himself up and wiggle through the opening. He's halfway in and now he can pick up the latch and put it against the outside of the sill and the window stays full open. Now it's a cinch, he swings his leg up and over, sits astride the sill, half in, half out and catches his breath. He listens patiently, but there's no sound inside or out.

Right under the window are some boxes and after testing their strength, he lets his whole body down, reaches out for the latch-arm and closes the window behind him. Now he wishes he had kicked over the scooter again, cause that would have hidden it somewhat in the high grass, but it's too late to worry about that now.

He takes inventory. The warehouse is stacked with boxes, but mostly with things he doesn't need. Boxes and boxes of ammo, but none that would fit his little pistol. His pistol takes a 25 caliber or. 5.76mm and there's nothing like that here. Neither is there any ammo for the Russian sub-machinegun or Henkies stengun. Plenty of cannon shells and he wonders if the British can use any of these for their artillery? The sand floor helps him move about noiselessly as he inspects one stall after the other. Finally, in one of the stalls he finds a crate with bayonets. With his knife he gets under one of the boards, pulls it up and nearly chokes! The board comes off with a loud CRACK! His heart in his throat, he stands still for about a full minute, but nothing happens. All stays quiet. He lets out a sigh of relief and takes out four brand-new, shiny, oil-paper wrapped bayonets. They disappear under his windbreaker and on he moves to the next stall.

What have we here? Flares! A flare pistol! "ALARM PISTOLE!" it says. "Oh, oh, oh, how neat!"

A double-barreled flare pistol with barrels so big, you could slide an egg in it! Yea! This is what he always needed! "Just one?" He checks all around and yes, there's just one!

"Now ammo!" Flares with parachutes! Beautiful, but wrong gauge! Okay, here we go! A box with seemingly the right size, labeled: DIFFER-ENT COLORS! He opens the box and tries one for size. "YEP!" he's talking to himself, "Twenty four in a box. I'll take two boxes and I'm outta here!"

He carries his load to the entry window and puts his new-found treasures on top of the boxes. Once on top of the boxes, he opens the window at a little crack and peeks left, right and underneath the window. All's clear, so he sets the latch arm to wide open and pitches the bayonets, one by one, as far as he can throw them into the high brown grass. Next the boxes with the cartridges and then he stashes the pistol carefully on the windowsill against the far side of the opening and hoists himself up, one leg at a time. Once upon the sill, he lets his legs down and feels with his feet for the handlebars of his scooter. His right foot finds them, but by trying to position himself, he kicks over the scooter and he simply drops down in the grass.

Okay! Up goes the scooter again, back on the handlebars and now he can pack the pistol under his jacket. He carefully moves the latch back into the building and the window closes softly into its original position.

The boxes cracked open a little when he dropped them, but the rounds seem undamaged. He buries three of the bayonets and one and a half boxes of shells in the dirt against the building and the other twelve rounds are div-vied up between his coverall pockets and his windbreaker. He looks a little like a pregnant goose, but that can't be helped. With scooter in hand he eases back to the corner of the building, where the scooter gets dropped and he falls to his belly and inches forward to the edge of the building. Hidden by the high grass, he peeks around the corner; "NOTHING! GOOD SHOW!"

He retrieves the scooter and moves along the side of the building and at the next corner he repeats the whole procedure, but this time he listens a while before peeking. His eyes are barely off the ground and because of the grass he sees nothing until he raises his head a bit and..."THERE HE IS!" The man in blue is about to reach the far end of the building! "NOW COUNT! " He halts and looks...."TWENTY-ONE, TWENTY-TWO,,,," Frits inches back carefully, flat against the building wall and keeps counting..."THIRTY-TWO, THIRTY-THREE....." He must be nearly halfway! He can hear him now! "SEVENTY-FIVE, SEVENTY-SIX..."

Good God, he's close! "EIGHTY-THREE, EIGHTY-FOUR..." he should be stopping soon! Frits' heart is pounding so loudly, he's afraid the guard will hear him. He's holding his breath.."NINETY-ONE, NINETY-TWO...".......NINETY-NINE..." he stops! He should be going the other way by now! It seems like an eternity! .....There he goes!

Frits jumps up, grabs his scooter and noiselessly gets moving on the hard packed dirt path, away from the building. Once on the road he turns right and moves across the road onto the bicycle path and waits for the guard to make his stop and turns and just as the guard turns, Frits is turned in the same direction, pedaling towards town. All the guard can see is some little innocent kid pushing his scooter leisurely down the path, showing no interest in his MANÈGE whatsoever!

Once out of sight, Frits picks up speed and fights the temptation to show his treasures to Sam and really brag a little, but he continues home instead.

In the back yard he hides his catch under the big pine tree for the time being and when Mama looks at his dirty clothes, she says; "WHERE HAVE YOU BEEN? We've already eaten, WHERE HAVE YOU BEEN?"

"OH, I BROUGHT PAPPA SOME CIGARETTES!'

CHAPTER XVI
British Occupation

"LAY THAT PISTOL DOWN, BABE, LAY THAT PISTOL DOWN!"
"PISTOL PACKIN' MAMA, LAY THAT PISTOL DOWN!"
"Tararararara," making like a trumpet, "Tararararararara" "OH, LAY THAT PISTOL DOWN!"

The happy foursome is in a good mood! They're trudging along, on their way to check out a rumor.

"LEENTJE, WAAR IS MAMIE? MAMIE LIGT IN BED" "Tararararara"

They're on their way to the swimming pool. The weather is far from warm yet, but rumor has it that the British are camping and swimming there, in the ....NUDE!

And....there are girls..... Now, the boys may hate girls, but the whole scene sounds intriguing, certainly worth checking out!

"Tararararara!" "SISTER WHATCHA CALLING, WHATCHA DOIN' TONIGHT?"

"Tararara" IN THE MOOD!" Tararara!" IN THE MOOD!" The ANDREWS SISTERS would have been jealous!

They have spent some two hours in Frits' and Paul's bedroom, admiring his new flare pistol. It's really neat! It has a lever on the back, that, when moved to the left, fires the left barrel and when moved to the right, fires the right barrel. When left in the middle, it fires both! The weapon cocks itself when the barrels are snapped open and the hammer and springs are all internal, unlike a revolver. Just the little firing pins pop out briefly when fired. Very simple, very high gloss, very beautiful! Now it's back in its hiding place.

The boys have a neat set of hiding places. When arriving in the attic and turning right, you'd face the door to Joop's room, turning left you'd walk into the boys' room facing the street. The roof structure is that of a Dutch colonial with a fairly flat top and steep roof flanks down to the top of the second story walls. The front and back bedrooms are built into the attic and with the bedroom walls being vertical, a narrow triangular space was created, about 3 feet on the bottom and 2 inches on top. The triangular space runs the length of the bedroom of course, but because of the trusses and rafters that block the openings, they cannot be used as storage space. Stored boxes and odds and ends block access to whatever little opening there might be, so the only access is from the top. By crawling on top of their bedroom, the boys can lower "stuff" into the narrow space and by tying ropes and strings to nails on top, they can pull it up and retrieve it anytime they want it. Anything that is "harmless" is displayed on top of the bedroom in full view. Helmets, flags, banners and shields decorate the front bedroom top. Anything that's NOT for public viewing is dangling from strings, looped around nails in the top boards of the bedroom walls. On the right side of the front bedroom, the opening is not as restricted, so by crawling under two chairs and a coffee table loaded with boxes, they arrive in a "cave" created by the slanting roof and the vertical bedroom wall.

Frits is working on electricity for their cave, but so far candlelight provides their only illumination. In the hole ('t holletje), their treasures are safe and secret meetings can be held. It's a kid's paradise. The only thing undecided this morning is: when and where to fire the flares? The consensus is: "Let's clear this one with Father Kamphuis!"

Now though, with another sunny April day upon them, they're out of the attic and off to the swimming pool.

"Tararararara!" "PARDON ME BOY? IS THIS THE CHATTANOOGA CHOO-CHOO?" "Tararararara!" Where did all these people get all these radios from? Electricity is back on, windows are wide open, spring-cleaning is in full swing and music blares out of the windows.

"The ANDREW SISTERS are the top singers in free Holland. The MODERNAIRES are great too! An outside observer would probably not believe how much English these kids have picked up in just a few days. Adults marvel at the easy with which they switch from "HOLLANDS" that the Kamphuisers speak, to "PLAT," the local dialect, to "GERMAN" and to "ENGLISH" without hesitation.

As they approach the swimming pool, with it's parking lot swarmed with military vehicles, they're stopped, friendly, but firmly; "Military personnel only!"

"But we have season passes!"

"Come back when the season starts! By the by, you forgot to bring towels! OFF YOU GO! TATA!"

Acting disappointed, they back away. So far, everything is going as expected. They casually continue down the road, but the minute they pass the perimeter fence, they turn right, skirting the ZWEMBAD across a freshly plowed field to the creek, DE SLINGE.

Once they reach the creek, it's simply a matter of climbing the fence and they're on swimming pool property. The backside of the pool is landscaped in a park-like fashion and is usually lush with green, bordering the creek on one side and the lake on the other. With spring barely arriving, the bushes and trees are still pretty bare and this keeps the boys from getting very close to the action. A couple of small evergreens provide some camouflage and from there they can scan the area. There are not many people in view.

Only one guy is on the diving board and a dozen maybe scattered on the beach. There are only two girls, both wearing bathing suits, one guy in uniform and all the rest are in swimming trunks. Nobody's naked!

The temperature is about 60 and out of the wind and in the brilliant sunshine, it's probably very comfortable. It's an odd scene, kinda calm with nothing obscene going on.

Soldiers and girls appear and disappear in and out of the buildings and with their limited knowledge of sex, the boys speculate about what's going on inside. Their imagination runs rampant. Outside, the whole scene looks like a quiet Sunday afternoon picnic. No naked girls at all, darn it!

Bored with the whole setup, they continue along the rear of the lake that makes up the swimming pool and what normally would be very scenic is rather dull in it's winter browns and greys. After all, it has been a very harsh winter and nature is just starting to add a few green touches here and there. After clearing the fence at the far side of the pool, they're on the property of the factory "DYE" yard. Pretty soon, rolls and rolls of fabric will be spread again between the rectangular ponds, drying after they've been dyed a multitude of colors. In the ponds are beautiful yellow "ZEELT" and huge mussels that they love to fish for. Right now, nothing is happening. The factories are just now starting to crank up again and production is still negligible.

They follow the creek to the BEKKENDELLE restaurant and recreation area, the area where pretty soon canoes and rowboats will reappear.

The waterfall, the watermill, the pond and the weeping willows will soon be the most romantic spot in town again. In a month or two, the thousands of rhododendrons will be blooming again and the area will be a feast to behold. Just beyond the waterfall do the falling waters form their favorite fishing hole, "DE KOLK," a little lake, where they fished with hand grenades when they were young.

After clearing another fence on the way to BEKKENDELLE, they're adjacent to the "SLOT," a little castle complete with moat and all. The castle was hit by incendiary bombs and is partially burned, but she still looks majestic.

"HEY! LOOK AT THAT!"

"WHAT? WHERE?"

"OVER TO THE RIGHT!"

"WHAT IS THAT?"

Behind some huge, bare rhododendron bushes they can see the outline of an aircraft auxiliary tank, maybe two! Fighters have dropped many of those tanks all over the countryside. After draining them or when getting into dogfights with German fighters, the American fighters simply dropped them and Germans on the ground scooped them up as soon as they could find them. It's hard to make out exactly what has been done with them, but it looks vaguely like they've been cut in half and then attached somehow. The longer they discuss it, the more they become convinced that some sort of a float or boat is hiding out behind the bushes. By repositioning themselves, they get a better look and indeed, the two torpedo like halves are attached with boards, resembling a Hawaiian catamaran or pontoon boat. What a neat boat! If only, they could ever own a boat like that! Or if they could find a gastank like that! They could make their own! Wow! That would be living! What a way to cruise the creek!

They look at one another, back at the boat, at the castle, at one another again and then;

"HOW?"

The question is not; "DO WE LIBERATE THAT BOAT?" No, the question is; "HOW?"

Across the bridge, the only access to the grounds? OUT OF THE QUESTION! There's no way anyone can get onto that property unseen.

"A big tree with branches reaching all the way over the moat?" Not a one in sight!

"Through the moat?" That moat has been stagnant for 500 years and full of weeds, lilies and plants. It probably has 15 feet of soft mud on the bottom. You can't swim it and probably not wade it.

The boys discuss their various options and it's interesting; not getting the boat is NOT one of their options!

Finally, Frits will try to swim it, weeds and all. He strips and sticks his toes in the water.

"THAT TOMMY ON THE DIVEBOARD NEVER DID DIVE IN, DID HE? IT'S FREEZING!"

The other boys test the water with their hands and readily agree; "MAN, IT'S COLD!"

The thought of giving up is finally considered! Considered? "YOU

P-51 drop tank (potential boat)

GOTTA BE KIDDING!"

Frits hits the water as flat and as hard as he can and in flying freestyle, he's across in seconds. His arms and legs move so rapidly, he couldn't have frozen if he wanted to.

Crawling up the bank, his skinny legs race to the catamaran, he turns it over onto its gastank pontoons and pulls it across the grass to the waiting boys.

The boat is in the water in seconds, Frits jumps aboard and is stuck in the weeds immediately. There's a rope attached to the "bow" and he tosses it across and within minutes he's towed ashore and hauled out. The whole operation took about 90 seconds.

He's so filthy, he crosses the narrow path and dives in the creek, turning as he hits the water and he's out again, shivering! He runs about 50 yards and back, trying to shed the water like a dog.

Back in his clothes and feeling warmer, he grabs one end as they carry "their boat" to the creek and launch it with a splash.

"No oars, No paddles?"

"Nope! Hands, I guess.!"

There go the young pirates, paddling their newly conquered ship upstream. It's indeed a beauty! The gastank halves are about 8 feet long and 18 to 20 inches wide. Planks have been attached to the open sides of the halves, giving them about a 5 by 5 foot platform to sit on with the ends of the tanks protruding from the front and back. Pardon me, the BOW and the STERN.

This is the neatest toy they've ever owned. All that's lacking is oars.

The thing is so light, it nearly glides on top of the water and they're a sight to behold; four boys, flat on their bellies, hands barely reaching the water, rowing with such vigor that the speed makes a little wake at each bow, creating a soft murmur at each stern. Fabulous!

"VAREN, VAREN, OVER DE BAREN. VAREN, VAREN OVER DE ZEE!"

They're singing away and laughing themselves silly, because their hand co-ordination stinks. They turn and twist, bang into the banks, turn in circles and generally put on a lousy rowing performance. If the hands on one side pull harder than the hands on the other, the light little craft turns on a dime.. They need rhythm and co-ordination. The two "leadmen" will steer. When the craft wants to move to the right, the right leadman paddles faster, while the left leadman lets up and vice versa.

"VAREN, VAREN, OVER DE BAREN!"

"Okay, now we have the rhythm!"

They've already passed the DYE farm,the swimming pool and after they cross underneath the Railroad Bridge, they beach in the next bend for a breather.

A shocking thought was presented;

"We can't bring it to our secret place!"

"Why not?"

"Landmines, remember?"

"Oh, wow!"

"So where can we keep it? In't BEUKENBOS?"

"Who says there are no landmines there?"

"Oh, God, there maybe landmines everywhere, including where we were today!"

Some of them turn very pale, all of them swallow hard.

"Well, that takes the fun out of most of this, doesn't it?"

A moment ago, they were having the time of their lives and now they may be in a dire predicament. There may be landmines where they're sitting or on top of the bridge, or along the railroad tracks, anywhere! Jeez, what a mess!

"Wait a minute, wait a minute! Trains have been running on these tracks, right? In the last few days, right?"

"I don't know, have they?"

"I don't know, either!"

"Have the British run any trains? Have the Dutch any reason to run in and out of Germany?"

"What for?"

"Oh, boy! We can't give up our ship. We have to build a mast, a rudder, get sails, get oars, but we can't give it up! Besides, what are we gonna name it?"

"Name it? How about the AMSTERDAM?"

"Oh come on, this is a pirate ship!"

"The MIRABELLA?"

"What's a MIRABELLA?"

"I don't know, but during the "EIGHTY YEAR WAR" with SPAIN, one of their ships was called the MIRABELLA and I love that name."

"Nah, something real pirate like, like the DEMON or the DEVIL IN THE NIGHT!"

"How about the FLYING DUTCHMAN?"

"Boer, you're a genius! With aircraft gastanks we can really make this baby fly over the waters! I remember something about that ship; THE VLIEGENDE HOLLANDER! Do you remember anything, Jan?"

"Yea, I remember something about the FLYING DUTCHMAN attacking Spanish and English galleons, but I don't remember the whole story and ..."

"We'll ask Joop tonight, he'll know! Do we agree on the name FLYING DUTCHMAN?"

"Ya, ya, ya, ya!"

"Next time, we'll bring a bottle of beer and we'll baptize it!"

"Beer? You need champagne for that!"

"Okay! You bring the champagne!"

"How am I supposed to come up with champagne?"

"Hahahaha, that's why I said beer, cause beer is something we can come up with. Or maybe rum? Pirates drink rum, right?"

"Sounds good to me!"

"I don't like beer!"

"For you we'll bring milk, Boer! Okay?" Hahahahaha!

"Hey, guys, how about it near the swimming pool? We already know there are no landmines because we wouldn't be here if there were, right?"

"Right!"

"We'll hide it in the bushes alongside the pool. Nobody is going to work on the pool or the park until at least May and by then, the landmines should all have been cleared or marked off. Then we'll move it all the way up to our secret place, if at all possible and if everything has been cleared!"

"Meanwhile, let's think about constructing a collapsible mast and rudder, something we can build at home in the mean time until we come back to it!"

"Well, we'll need a long stick!" Frits starts up the bank.

"Don't go up there! Mines, remember!"

"Oh shit! I forgot! Okay, I'll take this!"

He grabs a dead branch. "Gentlemen, shall we? The sun is over the mast arm, it's time for grog!"

They're enjoying this scene. After shoving off, Frits announces; "Just sit back gentlemen, I've got the rudder!" and indeed, drifting with the current and the branch trailing in the water, he keeps it pretty well midstream except when they reach the point where they want to dock. The current wont let them hit the bank and they end up back on their bellies, rowing like hell.

Henkie jumps ashore, rope in hand and pulls them in. Paultje jumps, looses a klomp, but Jan snatches it out of the water before it can take off down stream. The bank is considerably steeper than where they launched the craft so they have to struggle to get the FLYING DUTCHMAN up on the bank. Fifty yards further down, there's a nice cluster of evergreens and brush and that's where the boat gets hidden, covered with branches and leaves. There are no trails or paths nearby, so discovery is highly unlikely, yet they're not taking chances, they cover it thoroughly. Most of the trees and bushes are still fairly bare and evergreen branches are about the only good camouflage available.

One more week of this kinda weather and the frost will be out of the ground and the world will turn green again.

"You guys, you wanna take one more look at the girls?"

"Sure!"

They crawl to the lake and being that they're on the side of the lake this time, they have a better view of the beach area.

"Why don't you take your clothes off and join 'em?"

"Are you nuts?"

"No we're NOT! I'm not! You can go if you want to, but I'm not!"

The sun is high and warm by now and there are many more people on the beach now. The girls are still wearing bathing suits or have their dresses hiked way up their thighs.

"No BOOBIE show today!"

"Too bad!"

"Let's get outta here before they catch us and make us swim!"

"Oh you clowns, lets go make a mast!"

"I'm hungry! Let's eat first!"

"Okay, Let's go and eat!"

"IT'S A LONG WAY TO TIPPERARY, IT'S A LONG WAY TO GO!"

They're marching along again, not a care in the world. Besides; how many kids have their own little pirate ship?

"TO THE SWEETEST GIRL I GO!"

Frits remembers that one from before the war when they had dances on Sunday nights and apparently the song is still popular. They don't know half of the words that they're singing, but that doesn't dampen their enthusiasm at all.

People passing on their bikes can't help but smile at the happy innocent little angels, just singing away. Little do they know!

"TJU, TJU!" The Kamphuises turn toward home as the noon whistle blows. It's time for dinner.

Spirits are high at home. Everyone is smiling and even though the boys are a little late and cause dinner to be cold, nobody's mad.

"What's the good news? C'mon, somebody talk!"

"ONZE PAPPIE KOMT GAUW WEEROM!" Clasien is singing his favorite tune.

"Really? Pappa? He's coming home? Already?"

"Well, maybe!" Mama chimes in. "I was there this morning and the WACHTCOMMANDANT, by the way, he was expecting YOU, not ME!"

"Oh ya, I forgot!"

"Anyway, he said registration is all done. Those who are not criminals and have a family to go to will be released, pending the hearing. That includes Pappa. I have to call this afternoon and see when we can go and get him.

After we eat, run to Oom Gerrit and see if his phone is hooked up yet. I'd like to call from there, otherwise I'll have to go to the market and call from there."

"Does Doctor Glass have his phone yet?"

"Oh I don't know. I didn't think of that! Alright, we'll ask him first."

"When will we get a phone again Mam?"

"Not until we have a business again. We aren't on any priority list as a common household. It may take years!"

"How about the APOTHEEK across the street?"

"Not as of this morning. All he had was water. No electricity either, they're rewiring his whole house!"

Joop seems to be well informed.

"Oh, Joop, that reminds me. Who was the FLYING DUTCHMAN?"

"Now hold it!" Mamma interjects, "I was talking about Pappa! Anyway, at one o'clock they'll have a release schedule ready and we'll know when to get him. So Frits, run to Oom Gerrit, see if his phone is working and come right back!"

"Okay, MAM!"

He picks up his wooden shoes at the backdoor and scoots out of the frontdoor like a bullet.

"ALS EEN SCHEET IN DE WOESTIJN DIE VERVLOEKT IS!" his Dad would say.

He grins as he's running. His Dad has all these crazy expressions, like this one; HE DISAPPEARED LIKE A CONDEMNED FART IN THE DESERT!!" It'll be good to have him home again!

"Oh, shoot! I was going to check with Dr. Glass first, I forgot all about that! Well, hell, I'm halfway there anyway!"

"Hi, Oom Gerrit! Is your phone working?"

"Sure is! Who do you wanna call, CHURCHILL, HITLER? End this whole thing?"

"No!" He stops a minute. He forgot for the moment there was still a war on. "NO, Mama needs it! Bye!"

"Wait, wait a minute! What's going on? Who does your Mamma need to call and can I help?"

"No, you can't help! Mam has to call KAMP VOSSEVELT and find out when Pappa can be picked up!"

"Well, young man," he hands Frits a slice of homemade Bologna, " I can do that!"

"Is it one o'clock yet?"

"Yes it is. Do you know the number?"

"The number? No, I don't know the number!"

"Then how can I call them?" He loves to tease Frits.

"Mama's got the number, so I'll go get her and she can call! Goodbye!"

"No, come back! I have the number! Just teasing!"

Frits watches him dial. Then; "Hello, this Gerrit Kwak. That you, Bert? Good, and you? Good! Say hello!"

Frits wants to kick him. "Hurry up, Oom Gerrit!"

"Oh, ya Bert, do you know about releases or who should I ask for? I'll wait!" To Frits; "He's getting the list!"

"Ya, ya, FORRER, right! HERMAN. IDA'S HUSBAND? Right, right, right! Thanks! TJU!"

"What'd he say?

"Go get him boy! He'll be ready by two, go boy! Do you want another slice....?

The kid is gone already, wooden shoes klep-klep-kleping down the street. Panting for breath, he leaves the frontdoor wide open and runs into the diningroom, klompen and all,(capital sin) hollering; "LET'S GO, LET'S GET HIM!"

"Wait, slow down! I have to call first!"

"Oom Gerrit did! Let's go!"

"Hold it, hold! I know you're excited, but hold it! What did they say?"

He repeats the events and now Mama gets enthused too!

"You ride Pappa's bike, you can ride back with him and I'll take Hedwig. He missed his baby the most. You guys wait here!"

"Aw, Mam?"

"We can't go with the whole family!"

"Why not?"

"We don't have enough bikes, for one. Besides that, the streets are crowded and we'll make better time this way!"

"You got any cigarettes, Joop, to give your Pap?"

"Don't you have any yourself?"

"No, I don't. How many you got? Okay, I'll take five. He can take the rest from you when he gets here! Are you ready, Mam? Let's move out! ROMMEL would say!'

"You better learn some slogans of British and American Generals, you may get arrested yourself!"

"Hahahaha, fat chance. TJU!"

His legs are too short to sit on the saddle and reach the pedals, so he sits with his butt riding on the crossbar and cruises alongside his Mother. In his opinion, she's too slow, so he babbles with Hedwig, who's going on eight years old. She's at her prettiest. A head full of blonde curls, topped by a big pink bow and a matching pink and white dress and pink little socks with white shoes. Too much! Her new teeth have all come in front and when she smiles, her blue eyes light up her whole face! She's a doll. HIS doll, he loves that little sister. She probably missed her Daddie more than anyone, the little dear.

It's been a rough time for her and the rest of the bunch, but now it's over, at least for the time being.

As they drive up, they can't see him, but when they park their bikes they spot him in the guardhouse, waiting for them.

Frits holds the door for them and a voice on his left says; "So, Mister Forrer, you did come back after all?"

"SURE DID!" Frits is smiling from ear to ear and saying to himself; "If only you knew what I did last night, you wouldn't be so friendly!" Instead he says; "I wouldn't forget!"

"Well, Mr. Forrer, Mrs. Forrer, take good care of him. Keep him out of trouble. Bye, you too, pretty thing!"

After all the appropriate hugs and some tears, they're off, Frits on the back of Pappa's bike.

"Cigarette, Pappa?"

"Ya, thanks. I gave the rest to the men staying behind. Do you have a light?"

"Of course!"

As they're riding, Pappa relates what he already told Mama twice. The whole affair, arrest included, was not too bad. They were treated decently, some hardliners had cursed and shoved a little, but all in all the worst part was the uncertainty and not knowing what would become of his little family.

"Now, for the time being, it's all over. Let's enjoy it while we can!"

Once home, Joop tells them; "The Kamphuises were here and they'll be in touch later!"

"Oh, shoot! Thanks! I forgot all about them, but they'll understand, I'm sure!"

The rest of the day is spent catching up on all that's happened in these first few days of the liberation, both from Pappa's viewpoint as well as from the rest of them.

Oom Gerrit comes by, shakes Pappa's hand and after looking one another in the eye for a long, long moment, they embrace and cry!.

"It's a terrible war that can tear families apart like ours was. Four long years, Herman, four long years! NEVER, NEVER NO MORE! You're coming to my house to eat, LET'S GO! EVERYBODY!"

For the first time since the liberation the whole family is going to celebrate the liberation. FINALLY! RIGHT NOW!

And celebrate they do! Herman can't drink because of his ulcers, but has one anyway! Ida is BOOZING again, in her own words.

Gerrit eggs her on; "Two drinks isn't boozing yet, wait till we really start boozing. I'll have to take you home in a wheelbarrow!"

Joop and Frits are drinking GROLSCH beer, it's nice to be considered one of the grownups.

Paul and Frits demonstrate their new repertoire; "PISTOL PACKIN' MAMA," "LEENTJE WAAR IS MAMA?""

Everybody has a belly laugh about the Canadian baby and Tante Gerda wants to know? "Who dreams those dirty songs, so fast?"

Professor Joop informs her that Canadians have occupied the southern part of Holland for seven months already and that dirty songs travel as fast as bad news.

For dinner they're having "BIEFSTUK" and "VARKENSLAPJES," (filet and porkchops) and the Forrers have not eaten that much meat in ten years and they do the chef justice! The filets are browned to perfection and the porkchops are thick and tender. Obviously, they're eating in the house of a good butcher; Oom Gerrit!

A cold, bone-chilling drizzle has started as they walk home, but as far as the Forrers are concerned, everything is warm and bright and lovely. It's good to be alive and together!

The days go swiftly. Pappa's radio is located in the VEREENIGINGS GEBOUW and recovered. It took two days to get clearance to take it out, but when Pappa and the boys show up with Hans Steins wagon and a blanket, it's like going Christmas shopping.

It takes Pappa a few frustrating hours to get it going again, but now the news is blasting all over the house and the back yard.

The Dutch stations; HILVERSUM I and II, are still under German control, but Brussels is free and doles out accurate information about the war. Pappa is ecstatic! He's back in the groove!

The piano has been discovered and identified, but they can't move it home yet because of the anticipated arrival of the Ladies Buisman, the owners of the house. One hitch develops. Mama's expensive electric stove has also been claimed by a Jewish lady, who has been hiding out all these years and is now trying to retrieve her belongings.

Mama isn't mad, but determined. She reappears with receipts and serial numbers dating back to 1937, eight years ago! She's the obvious owner. This woman is meticulous! She probably still has the pattern for the first sweater she ever knitted in 1913!

Mama offers the stove for sale, because she has no place to put it or use it and Mr. Blauvelt, the "owner" of Hof Van Holland makes the best offer and gets it.

The news about the fronts is encouraging. ARNHEM is on the brink of being liberated, nearly all of eastern Holland and all of southern Holland is now in allied hands. The Germans can now only escape to the sea, they're completely cut off from the VATERLAND by land and they could save a lot of lives if they simply gave up. Word is that Hitler wants to fight to the last man and he's hurting his own people the worst. The vapor trails of the B-17's are overhead every day, bombing the living hell out of the German cities. Patton's 3rd Army is already in Austria, if the reports are true, and the Russians have liberated all the Balkan states. The Russians are in eastern Germany, pushing toward Berlin and thousands of lives could be saved if this Godawful slaughter just stopped. But... the Germans keep resisting!

It's agonizing, not knowing how other family members are doing. Oom Paul and Tante Mientje with three children are somewhere in SUMATRA. Dead? Alive? Hurt? In prison camps? Who knows?

Tante Paula, Tante Hetty and their families and Tante Nel are somewhere in or about ARNHEM. Dead? Alive? Hurt?

Pappa's brothers, Nol, Piet, Joop, Gerard and sister Engelien are somewhere in occupied Holland, but no one knows their fate.

Oom Karel, Mama's youngest brother was in a labor camp in KIEL, Germany and that area is being hit just about every day by the American high altitude bombers. Is he still alive? What a mess!

It does take some of the fun out of "celebrating" the liberation, yet it should be just a matter of days before it's all over! For real! ALL OVER!

In the pacific, America is making great strides against the Japanese and everyone is confident that the NIPPON Empire will soon collapse as well. Let's hope so!

One evening, a warm spring evening, the boys arrive at home and find two TOMMIE OFFICERS at their dinner table, eating heartily. It's two hours after the family supper hour, the veranda doors, both the inner and outer doors, are wide open and the smell of spring is heavy in the air. As they're being introduced, the officers politely rise and shake hands. One is a LEFTENANT, the other a CAPTAIN. They explain they've been quartered with the family for the time being. Joop wasn't home either when they arrived, so they've communicated with hand signals so far and they've done well. That's interesting since neither Mama nor Pappa can even understand "YES" or "NO!"

Paultje is shoved off to bed, "AW, do I have to?" "Yes, good night, Paul, welterusten!" No arguing with Pappa's authority.

Now the conversation shifts to who they are, where they come from, etc.

An atlas is produced and JOE, The LEFTENANT points out that he's from a town called "BATH."

"BATH? That's a name of a town?"

"Named after the Roman baths, I'll tell you more about it!"

The CAPTAIN, IAN is from CRIEFF in Scotland, he's SCOTCH, he announces proudly.

Joe is only 21 and has been in the service for 4 years already! That's uncanny. He hopes to be a captain soon. WOW! He's young!

The captain from Crieff has the bluest blue eyes they've ever seen with very contrasting pitch-black hair. He's married and has a little girl, 2 years old. Last time he saw her was last June. He's dying to go home and see them.

Frits' vocabulary is maybe 200 words in English, but all through the evening, they chatter along as if a language barrier is non-existent.

The men had brought some tea and Mama prepares it for them, but she can't stomach it with their heavy cream, so the British drink it their way and the Dutch drink it with just a bit of sugar.

When the subject changes to WAR and ARNHEM, Joe goes to the car that's parked half on the sidewalk and half in the street and retrieves some maps. He explains that what he's going to show them is "classified" and would Frits kindly explain that to his parents? Frits huddles with his parents!

"Do they understand? Do you understand?" "Yes!" He doesn't have the foggiest idea what he's talking about, but "yes" seems like a better answer than "no!"

The maps are confusing. The towns are not circles, like in school, but odd shaped yellow blotches. Swamps and marshes are striped areas and hills are contour lines with elevations in feet.

The things that are very clear on the maps, "charts," Joe calls them, are roads and waterways. Waterways, plenty of waterways! Rivers, canals, creeks! Holland is crisscrossed in waterways. The important thing is that the main waterways will be crossed shortly and occupied Holland will be open to the liberation forces. It's like a litany they've heard before, in 1940, 1944 and now again in 1945. The IJSEL, the LOWER RHINE, the MAAS-WAAL CANAL, the WAAL, HOLLANDS DIEP, the NIEUWE WATERWEG, just a matter of days!, Again, just a matter of days, but this time they believe it!

Questions pop up; "How long before phone lines will be restored?" "A WEEK!" "Transportation?" "FORGET THAT! Two years or maybe more. Bridges will have to be built, railroad stations; built from scratch, railroads restored. No, forget rail transportation for years. We can build BAILEY bridges and PONTOON bridges in days, so bus traffic maybe? But regular bridges will take years! You cannot imagine the damage that has been done and it's not over yet. Those crazy Krauts may still blow every bridge in Holland, some three thousand plus and I wouldn't put it past them.!"

Time for bed. The TOMMIES are going to sleep in the girl's room on the second floor, the girls are in Joop's room and Joop will stay with the boys!

"NO, NOT JOOP!"

"Yes, Joop! Now say goodnight, ask them is everything satisfactory? Towels, Soap?" "Fine?" "Oh ya? Fine?"

Mama's first word in English; "FINE!" They'll get along well!

Joop arrives a little while later and Frits forgets all about being nasty, cause Joop is in high spirits and needs to know all about the TOMMIES. He also starts confiding in Frits about some of his experiences out there with his school gang. Most of the kids in his school are upper middle class or upper class and besides money they have one interest; "SEX!" At this stage in life, Frits has no way of knowing that money and sex are fairly irrelative, that the age bracket and sex are the overriding factor. It seems at Joop's age that SEX is all they talk about, pursue and believe in. They live in a different world from Paultje, Frits and the Kamphuis boys, but Frits is fascinated just the same.

He tells Joop about the scene at the ZWEMBAD. Joop finds that hard to believe. "How many guys and how many girls?"

"First there were two girls in bathing suits and maybe ten guys and only one of them wore a bathing suit. Later, a couple of hours later, there were 4 girls in bathing suits and two in dresses and there were about 20 men, most of them naked.!"

"No naked girls?"

"No, not outside. Of course we couldn't see inside the buildings or the cars...."

"Hey Frits," Joop interrupts, "did you hear about the "GERMAN WHORES" as they're called? They were rounded up and shaven bald and one of them was in my class, Ria van der Meer, remember? Remember when she and I were in sixth grade and Ria got a "permanent"? Mama couldn't get over the thought that a girl that young would already have a "PERM." Remember? Well anyhow, she apparently screwed around with the KRAUTS and now she's bald, hahahahahaha! How about that?"

CHAPTER XVII
Peace, But No Quiet

Life with the BRITS is interesting. The Forrers learn NOT to call them ENGLISH, because the Captain is not, "I REPEAT, NOT ENGLISH!" but SCOTCH or SCOTS. Not SCOTTISCH either. He's a SCOTSMAN! Leftenant Joe is ENGLISH, and they're both BRITISH! Yes (laughter here), they're also both TOMMIES. On the third day of their stay, they provide a truck and a few soldiers and the whole gang ends up at the VEREENIGINGS GEBOUW, where they load up the piano and some furniture. Main reason? The Captain plays piano and he has missed it terribly! Now everybody can sing;

"IT'S A LONG WAY TO TIPPERARY!" "WHITE CLIFFS OF DOVER." LILY MARLENE."

(The Tommies sing it in English, the boys in German)

There's peace in the Forrer living room, if not on earth!

A radio broadcast later that evening has some good news and some bad news; "ARNHEM IS IN BRITISH HANDS! TWO-THIRDS OF THE CITY IS LEVELED!" It's April 14, 1945. FINALLY, FINALLY, FINALLY!

Ida is anxious to hear about her family, but the British can't do anything about tracking down civilians. Besides that, they are well rested by now and will probably relieve the lads at the front. They themselves had a hard "GO" for a while. They had been at the front for twenty-two days straight and at one point did not shave, shower or sleep in a bed for nine days. Now they've been in Winterswijk for six days and are ready to take over and "MOP-UP." This might be their last day with them.

"OH... that's too bad!" Mama and Pappa have really enjoyed their company and have learned much about England and Scotland and have an open invitation to "look them up" and visit any time.

After the Brits have gone to bed, the radio talks of the bridge at DEVENTER, in Allied hands, unscratched, the Railroad Bridge at ZUTPHEN in one piece and on and on. Things are happening out there!

"We still haven't heard a word from the old Ladies, I wonder where they're hiding out?"

"Maybe they're dead!"

"Frits, don't say that!"

"Why not? It would certainly simplify things a lot, wouldn't it?"

"Frits, don't even think terrible things like that!"

"Okay! They'll be here in the morning!"

"No, that's terrible too! Now off to bed, you guys. Welterusten!"

"Welterusten Mama, Pappa! Slaap ze!"

The next day the Tommies pull out. The entire encampments at the VEREENIGINGS GEBOUW and the Dance Hall, there must have been two thousand of them. As souvenirs, Mama has plenty of tea and Frits has a Paratroopers helmet to add to his collection.

"We're never going to jump in war situations again!" were Joe's parting words.

"Jolly good trip!"

"Thank you, thank you very much indeed. It was lovely, indeed!" and they're gone. A little slice of their hearts remains behind.

Within two days, the empty bivouacs are filled up again with soldiers returning from the front. It's hard to imagine these soldiers have been fighting within an hours drive from Winterswijk. They get to shower and shave. They receive new uniforms, underwear, weapons and....time off in town. There's dancing every night at the Market Square and every evening the place jumps into the early hours. If you do have to fight a war, this has got to be the way to do it. The Tommies are having a blast. The Dutch population goes overboard to make their liberators feel at home and the soldiers obviously love every minute of it.

The boys are having a fair trade going, eggs for everything else. Because Oom Gerrit, being a butcher, knows every farmer within a ten-mile radius he can arrange for eggs. Born and raised in Winterswijk, he has done the "fall-butchering" for half the farmers around town and has made many a trip on his bike and before the war, on his motorbike, to slaughter a cow or a calf that got hurt or hung up in the barbed wire.

If he can get to a fallen animal within a half hour of the accident and "bleed" (blood-let) it, the animal is considered "eatable" and keeps the farmer from losing a lot of money. Past 30 minutes, the farmer may as well throw it away. Consequently, everyone knows his name. Comes in handy.

The hottest items that the boys trade for are: cigarettes and nylons. Where these soldiers get nylons from is beyond comprehension, but they've got them and that's what counts.

Tommies coming through

Between all the trading and the food stamps, the family's eating well. Nothing elaborate, but well!

Somewhere along the line, Frits comes up with the neatest toy: an AIR PISTOL! Its outer barrel is an air pump and it shoots pellets and feathered darts. They finally have a sport that they can enjoy in their back yard. Pappa takes time out from building a chicken coop and a rabbit run to build a target with a huge plywood back drop so the darts wont fly away when they miss the target. The pistol, about the size of a Colt 45 automatic, is accurate as can be and Pappa gets a kick out of competing with his boys.

This is something they can enjoy together for hours.

One afternoon, about three days after the Brits have left, Oom Gerrit interrupts the activity with good news.

All the families in Arnhem are all right! Tante Paula and Oom Henk with their three children are back in their old house on the AMSTERDAMSE WEG 93. No windows, some shrapnel damage, collapsed ceilings, but otherwise all right. Henk's parents house, nearer the railroad is in worse shape, but salvageable. Tante Hetty and Oom Gerard don't have a house any more. It just doesn't exist. All rubble! They're comfortable, though. They're sharing a house with some other family. Tante Nel's employers house is gone, totally gone and although she has a place to rest her head, she has no job and may come to Winterswijk when transportation becomes available again."

"That's good news, mostly!"

"Is everybody healthy"

"Everybody is happy and healthy and relieved that it's finally all over and everyone is optimistic about the future."

"Who called?"

"Oh, ya. Hetty and Paula were both on the phone from a Red Cross command post in Velp and they could only talk a few minutes, because very few phone lines are open so far and a lot of people are trying do a lot of calling. So... we can't call'em back yet, a few more weeks maybe. Hey, can I shoot that thing too? I spent six months in the Army in 1930, so let me try!"

"Pap, you better instruct him, so he won't shoot himself in the foot. Hahaha!"

"I'll show you guys!"

Well, he shoots all right, but at this point he wouldn't be family champ, that's for sure!

"Come back to practice any time, Oom Gerrit!"

"I'll show you little wise asses one day!"

"Any time, any time! You're welcome any time!"

CHAPTER XVIII
May 5, 1945

FINALLY.....MAY 5TH. Early morning news.........
ARMISTICE FOR NORTHWESTERN EUROPE WILL BE SIGNED TODAY!!!!!!
WAR IS OVER IN HOLLAND! ALL OF HOLLAND!!!

Everyone goes crazy! The most shy, the most conservative, the most hurt, it doesn't matter. Everyone is out in the streets. Flags, banners and orange ribbons are everywhere. Every house, every building, every church is decorated. Every person wears orange and everyone is out and about! More so than "Dolle Dinsdag," more so than March 31st, Winterswijk's liberation, everyone is out on the town. Traffic is impossible. Arm in arm, in arm, in arm, in arm, people march and dance in the streets! "ORANJE BOVEN, ORANJE BOVEN, LEVE DE KONINGIN!" "ORANGE ABOVE ALL, ORANGE ABOVE ALL, LONG LIVE THE QUEEN!" It is being sung, shouted and screamed, time and time again.

The town is nuts. It's safe to assume that all the countries in Western Europe are absolutely and totally nuts. Soldiers shoot round after round into the air and the factory whistle doesn't stop. The lone church bell rings incessantly and the sirens blast their "ALL CLEAR" all through the day.

Every door in town is wide open and total strangers, as well as family and friends are invited in, fed and toasted; "ORANJE BOVEN

IT'S OVER, IT'S OVER! AFTER FIVE AGONIZING YEARS....IT'S OVER! Heaven only knows, how much grief, hardship, human suffering and death has been bestowed on this world since the start of World War II, but for this part of the world, it's temporarily forgotten. People just shake hands, hug, laugh and cry with unabashed relief and pleasure. Today is finally "V"-day!

A loudspeaker in the market place blares the news all over town and when at about 11 O'clock, the emotional announcer broadcasts the actual signing of the "UNCONDITIONAL SURRENDER," a roar goes up, so loud that the walls seem to shake! The noise is incredible. Human beings have never been known to create such volume of unadulterated enthusiasm and it doesn't want to cease. Hitler would have shook in his bunker if he were still alive to hear it

Certainly, the heavens appreciate it, because the sun shines brightly upon the festivities as in full agreement with the goings-on on earth. It just couldn't be better.

Herman, Ida and the girls are in there somewhere and Herman, hanging on to them for dear life, has to shout at the top of his lungs to be heard; "HOW DO YOU LIKE THE PARTY I FIXED FOR YOUR BIRTHDAY?" She smiles from ear to ear while tears are running freely down her cheeks at the same time. It's her fortieth birthday!

"HAPPY BIRTHDAY, VROUWTJE!" He kisses some of the tears away. Hedwig, on his shoulders, has both ears covered with her hands and her eyes are wide with a mixture of fright and awe. It's some sight!

Literally, thousands of heads are bopping up and down in front of her, like a restless sea. IT IS FANTASTIC!

The chant; "ORANJE BOVEN, LEVE DE KONINGIN" just rolls and rolls over the waves of singing people and travels down the crowded side streets to the extremities of the town.

They've heard of similar massive outburst in other cities, primarily in EINDHOVEN when General HORROX's tanks rolled into town last September. The masses held up the tank advance for three hours, climbing on top of the tanks, hugging and kissing the British while singing ORANJE BOVEN!

Well, here in Winterswijk, a tank column could not have gotten through in 12 hours and thank God, no one is trying to. Any traffic at all is detoured around town and if anyone does get caught in this jubilant mess, the best advice would be; "Desert the vehicle and join the party! Try your vehicle in about 20 hours."

By then, everybody should be drunk and bedded down. The beer and booze just flows out of the hotels, bars and restaurants around the market place. Heaven knows what will happen when they run out? The GROLSCH brewery is only 9 miles up the road in GROLLE (GROENLO), but at this point they would need a tank escort just to get a beer truck into town, Or maybe, the party-goers would respect the need for a beer truck enough to let it through.

The former "FORMER" Mayor, the one that was replaced by the Nazi Mayor in '41, is trying to make a speech! Forget it. Before he can get more than one word out, he's interrupted by "ORANJE BOVEN."

May 5, 1945. The crowd listens to the armistice announcement

The British Military Mayor doesn't even try. They're standing on top of the cab of a military truck and all they have to do is raise their hands and the people holler; "HIEP, HIEP, HIEP, HOERA! (heep, heep, heep, hoorah) ORANJE BOVEN, ORANJE BOVEN" there's no point in trying to speak. Everyone knows that the Mayor is going to applaud the British Army for liberating Holland; "HIEP, HIEP, HIEP, HOERA!" and that he's going to compliment the Dutch resistance: "HIEP,HIEP, HIEP,HOERA!" and the determination of the people of Winterswijk; "HIEP, HIEP, HIEP, HOERA!" The folks can't hear a words that's spoken, but every time arms are raised on top of the truck, they holler in unison; "HIEP, HIEP, HIEP, HOERA! It is just an unbelievable madhouse!

Our boys are in the church tower looking down on it. From up here, where giant bells once sounded, they have a panoramic view of the activities below and the whole little town, bathed in sunshine. The whistles of the factories and the voices of the people give the whole scene a dramatic effect. It's overpowering!

As they were trying to make their way through the throngs of people, they found themselves stuck in front of the old Saint Jacob church. They planned to use the church as a shortcut, but once inside it seemed logical that they check out the church tower. They had never been in a protestant church before, which is one more reason to want to explore.

Way up there, they have a front row seat to all the activity below. The town is all red and green and the sun makes the reds of the roofs sparkle and the green glimmer with a beautiful sheen.

It's always good weather on Mama's birthday and this morning they surprised her with a beautiful, homemade poem and a painting of red poppies in a multicolored vase. It's called :"KLAPROZEN" and the boys believe Vincent van Gogh painted it. They may be right, they may be wrong, but it's the thought that counts.

"Hey, guys, we have to be home for Mama's birthday dinner, but we may never be able to get through this crowd in time!"

"What time is it?"

"I don't know. Normally the whistle would tell me, but that thing's been blowing for hours, so who knows?"

Henkie butts in; "There are four clocks right here"

"Oh, ya, let's check it out!"

Up one more flight and there it is. A huge mechanism, that turns the hands on all four sides of the tower. It's a magnificent contraption of levers, cogwheels, springs and rods, but the actual time is shown on the OUTSIDE of the building so they're no wiser than before.

"Boer," Frits orders his younger brother, "climb on the arm outside and tell us what time it is!"

"Are you crazy? Do it yourself!"

"Wasn't there a movie about a guy getting caught out there on the arms of the clock?"

"Yeah, Charley Chaplin or somebody like that. Want to try it, Frits?"

"No Jan, YOU try it!"

"Let's look!"

"No, let's NOT!"

"Shall we screw up the works and stop the clock?"

"I'm getting out of here, There's no escape. If somebody wants to catch us, all they have to do is wait at the bottom of the stairs! I don't like these odds. Let's go celebrate"

"ORANJE BOVEN!" One hundred and eighty-one spiral steps later they're down and fall all over themselves. They're absolutely topsy-turvy from turning and turning and turning so they just fall into one big laughing heap until their heads are unspun.

Back into the maelstrom of people, arm in arm, in arm, in arm, four happy young people; " LAY THAT PISTOL DOWN, BABE, LAY THAT PISTOL DOWN! PISTOL PACKIN' MAMA, LAY THAT PISTOL DOWN."

Dinner doesn't happen on Mama's 40th birthday. Nobody even comes close to the house. The boys dance with the soldiers and the girls. The floor is so crowded, that no one seems to know or care with whom he or she is dancing. The boys run out of money in the first hour, but there's still plenty to drink for everybody.

Henkie and Frits are still drinking beer, but the other two have quit after one. No problem, drink what you want! "IN THE MOOD, tatatatata, IN THE MOOD!" The place is jumping!

Folks drift in and out, hug and kiss, laugh and cry, drink and dance and on to the next pub or the next person for more of the same.

At one point, Frits is dancing with an "old" lady, at least as old as his mother, and she crushes his head between her boobs while Frits and the soldiers sing;

"I'M IN THE MOOD FOR LOVE, SIMPLY BECAUSE YOU'RE NEAR ME, FUNNY BUT WHEN YOU'RE NEAR ME, I'M IN THE MOOD FOR LOVE!" What a way to live!

Somewhere during the afternoon, they do make it home and arrange to meet at the Kamphuis home tonight. Frits will bring his flare-gun and ammo, so when the announced fireworks go off, they can have some of their own.

"Will Mijnheer Kamphuis go along with this?"

"Of course, why not?"

"How about Pappa?"

"Oh, NO! Somebody will say he got the gun from the Germans and they'll lock'em up again. No, No!, we're too glad to have him home again! See ya tonight at your house!"

"Tju!"

"Tju!"

The birthday supper turns out to be a delightful dinner party and the boys find out for the first time that they are not the only ones who didn't make it home for dinner, NOBODY did. Well, that makes it more fun. After "LANG ZAL ZE LEVEN!" (LONG SHALL SHE LIVE!) and a few; "HIEP, HIEP, HIEP,HOERA's!" many more years and other good wishes, a gourmet meal is attacked and enjoyed.

Mama thinks that 40 is ancient and Frits agrees, ducking just in time to miss his Dad's left hand. Pappa says; "She's as beautiful as ever!" and everyone chimes in.

After dinner, (normally supper) everybody heads out to see the fireworks. After rounding the corner, the boys double back in order to retrieve their pistol and flares. Now, all the stuff well hidden under their windbreakers, they're really on their way.

Mr. Kamphuis is duly in awe. He has never seen a double-barreled flare pistol before and he patiently verifies Frits' instructions. He breaks the action, dry fires, first the left, then the right cylinder and then both. He seems satisfied with the overall operation of the gun and they get ready for the action. They'll fire from the field, directly in back of the house. That way they can check whatever debris may fall back down to earth. If it does, it will fall in a freshly plowed wheat-field, adjacent to their yard.

The boys are anxious to get going, but Mr. Kamphuis says; "We're waiting for the real fireworks to start, so we won't be too conspicuous.:"

It does test their patience, but darkness starts to settle quickly over the little town and "YEAEAEAEAEA!"

"There they go!" The fireworks are a little far from where they're standing, but still plenty exciting.

"Are you ready, Mr. Kamphuis?"

"Darn tootin'! Give me a round!"

"One red flare coming up!"

Mr. Kamphuis carefully injects the flare into the left barrel, closes it, sets the selector to "left," aims into the sky, everybody covers their ears and....."click," NOTHING!

"TRY THE SAFETY! Hahahaha!"

"Okay, wise guys, Here goes" "BLAM" A beautiful red burning ball streaks into the sky, hesitates momentarily and slowly falls back to earth.

"WOW!, HOERA!, BEAUTIFUL, GREAT! HOW ABOUT A WHITE ONE NEXT?"

This time he puts it into the right barrel, sets the selector to "right," aims at the stars, pulls the trigger and..."click" .....NOTHING!

Apparently, after breaking open the action, the safety comes back on automatically. Good feature, excellent feature!

"Okay, here we go again!" "BLAM!" The white one lights up the whole landscape.

"Too bad that the ones with the parachutes were the wrong caliber. That would've been neat, we could've lit up the whole town. Mr. K, does it kick badly? Can I try it?"

"Go ahead. It has a good kick to it, but nothing you can't handle!"

"How about a green one?" Some neighbors have come out to join in the festivities from their back yards.

Someone says; "Isn't that a little loud, so close to the hospital?"

"That's what we're doing it for, so they won't miss out on some of the festivities!"

"They asked us!"

"That's nice!"

"Yeah, it is!"

BLAM.....Frits fires a green one!

"Wow! Not bad. It kicks alright, but not bad!"

Jan's turn. This is fun, another white one.

"Henkie, you wanna try?"

"Ya, of course!"

"Son, you might break your wrist!"

"Maybe I won't!"

"Me neither!"

"Okay, Boer. Mr. K. can you shoot two at once?"

Okay, I'll try, one blue, one white. That should be pretty!"

Down town the fireworks are blasting away and so is the gang in back of the Kamphuis home

BLAAAM! Two at a time! Blue and white fireballs racing one another to the sky!

"Oh," "Ah," "Oh," "AH!" They've gathered a good size audience by now. This is May 5th, liberation day and they're loving it.

"Now let me try something!"

They've noticed that the selection lever automatically slides back from the "left" and "right" to the center or "both" position.

Frits feels that he can fire two, rapid fire. First fire "left," the lever moves to the "both," fire again and the right one should go off. This way he could go BLAM, BLAM, one right after the other. He loads two rounds, sets the selector to "left," takes off the safety and BLAAAM! "DAMNIT!" Both of them soar into the sky and Frits is holding his wrist. "DAMNIT!" he says again. "SNOTVERDOMME!" "What happened? How come they both went off at the same time? And I had the selector on "left." "

"How bad is your wrist, Frits?"

"Oh, it hurts, it'll swell a little, maybe!"

"MAMMIE!" Mr. Kamphuis calls his wife, "Bring a roll of gauze, please!"

Mr. Kamphuis is letting one of the neighbors fire too. "BLAM!' Why not? They have twenty-four of them.

Mr. Kamphuis is now trying Frits' trick, but from the "right" position. "BLAAAM!" both of them fire again.

"There's something wrong with this mechanism. If we want to fire one, we just load one and if we want to fire two, we load two, Okay?"

"No problem!" "BLAM!" "Oh!" "Ah," "Oh!" "AH!" "BLAM!" HOLLAND IS FREE AGAIN!!!

The rounds are exhausted and it was fun. The Kamphuis boys are not allowed back to the festivities. "It's past 9.30!" " AW?" So with a "Goodnight" and "TJUS," the bobsy twins are off.

From their backyard at the Wooldstraat, they can tell that the folks are home already, so not taking chances, they hide the pistol in a tree and continue on to the market. If they had shown their faces inside, they might not have been allowed out anymore and on "SURRENDER DAY" that would have been tragic.

The festive crowd hasn't let up very much, the main differences are the darkness, which allows more couples to neck in alleys and doorways and the crowd is decidedly more drunk.

"ORANJE BOVEN" has been replaced by; "WIE GAOT NOG NEET NAOR HUUS, NOG LANGE NEET, NOG LANGE NEET!" "WE'RE NOT GOING HOME, NOT FOR A LONG TIME YET!" and many other standard drinking songs. The spirit is the same though! Just a lot more "spirit" in the "spirited people."

"EN VAN JE HELA, HOLA, HOUDT ER DE MOED MAAR IN! HOUDT ER DE MOED MAAR IN!"

The boys are marching arm in arm with a bunch of totally unknowns, but they are happy and most of them are also happily loaded, so who cares? Music still blares out of every open door around the market place and nobody cares that they're hearing three different tunes in three different languages at the same time.

In the MARKET RESTAURANT, they encounter Joop, who is swooning away with a redhead who couldn't be any older than Frits, but is made up as if she's twenty. "PARLEZ-MOI D'AMOUR," the record player coos and Joop dances as if he's in a trance. When the darling brothers tug his sleeve, he snarls; "Go home you pests. Get lost!"

"He's a lousy lover!" Frits shouts at the redhead, but she just grins and hauls Joop back in.

"Wanna beer, Boer?"

"No, I don't like beer and I have no more money!"

"Me neither. What do you want?"

"Sinas or Cola or something!"

"Stay here!" Frits brings him a bottle of"SINAS," (orange drink) 3/4 full and he himself tosses back some beer from a half-empty bottle.

"WIE GAOT NOG NEET NAOR HUUS, NOG LANGE NEET!" out the door again, onto the square and into another bar. "EN VAN JE HELA, HOLA!" and another beer. "PISTOL PACKIN' MAMA, LAY THAT PISTOL DOWN!" and back into the throngs that don't know how to quit.

Well, the crowd is not quitting, but the kids are getting exhausted and especially Paultje, he's about to fall asleep standing up!

They head for home and Paultje just barely makes it up the stairs, while

Frits joins the family that includes Dr. and Mrs. Glass, Oom Gerrit and Tante
Gerda, the pharmacist from across the street, the one with the dollhouse,
with his wife and two daughters. Quite a crowd.

Well, who's tired now? Not Fritsie!

"Yes, thank you, I'll have a beer! No thank you, I don't like that stuff!
Rum is all right, with some cola? Okay!" What a party! "WIE GAOT NOG
NEET NAOR HUUS!" The old folks are in the best of moods too. Frits has
to perform the English and the dirty Dutch version of "PISTOL PACKIN'
MAMA!" and everyone applauds, including the girls from across the street.
They're only 9 and 11, but they're kinda cute and as the old folks are busy
singing, laughing and telling jokes, Frits entertains the girls in the parlor
with their recently recovered furniture.

"Ya, I'll have another rum and coke. You girls want one? Wanna zip of
mine?" His tongue is so thick, he's talking double.

In spite of all the fun and all the folks, he falls asleep behind the couch.
Nobody misses him! Until 2 AM.

Joop has joined the happy revelers at about 12.30 and when he makes
it upstairs at 2 o'clock, he notices Frits' and Paul's door wide open. A little
loaded, he turns left into the room he shared when the British Officers
stayed over, turns on the light and sees Paultje sleeping like a baby. His
beer-soaked brain signals him to make a U-turn to his own room inasmuch
as there are no more Britishers in the house.

Once inside his room, it hits him! "Paultje was alone in bed!" Another
U-turn. He switches on the light again and sure as the dickens; ""NO
FRITS!" "FRISH, FRISH!" as loud as he can holler. "FRISH!"

He's slurring badly. He looks out the third floor window to check if
that crazy clown is somewhere in the gutter or on the roof. "FRISH!" Not
a sign of him! Down the stairs he goes, still hollering; "FRISH!, FRISH!"
into the kitchen, where he bumps into Mama, apron in place, dishtowel in
hand, running out to check out the commotion. "Where's Frits?"

"I dunno!" his tongue is as thick as a steak. "Heez not inis bed!"

Mama runs up the stairs anyway and finds Joop to be right, he's not IN
his bed, not UNDER the bed, he's NOWHERE! She shakes Paultje, it's
like trying to revive him! "WHERE'S FRITS?"

"HUH?"

"WHERE'S FRITS?"

"I DUNNO!" and he's asleep again. The windows are wide open and not
realizing that Joop opened them that wide, she goes; "OH, NO!" Standing
on the bed, she leans out of the window, looking at the street below. Thank
God, no Frits there!

"FRITS!" as loud as she can holler. "Would that crazy kid really climb the roof in the dark? Oh, God, I hope not! That boy is going to be the death of me yet!"

A thought hits her: maybe he's crawled into his secret place next to the room, underneath the chairs and the coffee table that block the entrance.

"PAULTJE, WORDT WAKKER!" She shakes him vigorously, "WAKE UP, WAKE UP! You got to get into your secret room and see if Frits is in there!"

"HUH?"

She bangs on the wall! "Frits!" Bang, bang, bang! Frits, are you in there?"

Joop and Herman join her. "I can't get Paultje up. Joop can you get back there? We may have to pull some stuff out?"

"I zink I can!" He's so sleepy, he can barely stand up.

"Did you look downstairs Ida?"

"No, I came straight up here. Joop, let me get you a flashlight. Just a sec!"

She's back in twenty seconds and hands Joop the flashlight.

Pappa runs down the stairs, races around the rooms, hollers into the backyard; "FRITS, FRITS! Damn!" and back up the stairs. He's panting; "I'm getting to old for this! Anything Joop?"

"No! He's not in there!" Joop slurs, "lot's a junk tho!"

"Not in your room, Joop? How 'bout ours? Remember when he passed out in the girls room on that miserable day?"

Down one flight of stairs.....NOTHING! Joop wants to sleep, but he's sure they won't let him, so he sits down on the couch in the parlor, topples over and is sound asleep. Mama runs out the front door though she doesn't know why and Pappa checks out the veranda again and the shed out back. He swings his flashlight around the lawn and under bushes, NO FRITS! He meets Ida as she's coming back in and he can read the panic on her face. He hugs her and turns into the dining room where most of the partying took place and for some reason, he doesn't know why, he looks under the table. NOTHING!, but it gives him an idea. He turns to the parlor and see-ing Joop stretched out on the couch, he bends over Joop and the backrest and there is Frits.

"IDA, IDA, I FOUND HIM!"

"Oh, my God, what made you look there? We might not have found him for a day, called the police and everything!"

"Remember the story I've heard so often about your brother Karel when he was just a toddler and somebody gave him some GENEVER GIN at a party and he crawled underneath the cupboard? Well, that's what animals do when they want to sleep. They find a hiding space. That's what our little animal did!"

"I say the hell with the dishes and the glasses, let's lock up and get our little animals to bed! It's been a long day!"

"And an exiting one! For most of the world the war is finally over. Finally! FINALLY! HAPPY BIRTHDAY!"

May 8th, 1945 The final armistice with Germany is signed. Now the war is over for ALL OF EUROPE!

Holland celebrates again, but in Winterswijk more modestly, compared to May 5th. After all, May 5th is Holland's liberation day! It does spark some excitement, though. Loved ones, long lost behind German lines in labor camps and concentration camps, will soon be returning home. But how many? In what condition? How? Nobody knows, but a special bureau is set up for repatriation and everyone is encouraged to register any and all relatives that are missing with as much detail as possible about their last known whereabouts. It's going to be a chore to sort all that out and then get proper medical care arranged for the many who need it. Winterswijk and many other cities in Europe now face the Herculean task of rebuilding their towns. Winterswijk has only 20% NON-DAMAGED houses. A lot of it is just glass damage, easily spotted by all the boarded up windows. The bridges have suffered tremendously. First the allied fighter bombers knocked out as many as they could to keep the Germans from re-supplying their fronts and then the Germans blew up most of the rest of them to slow down the Allied advance. It'll take years and years. The road and railway system will take months. The work is cut out for everybody.

The transition from "Nazi-administration" to "Freedom-service" under British Military supervision is already rocky. Lots of former functionaries, who have hidden out for years, and lots of "Freedom people" who have fought in the resistance, are already clashing over power in government

"COMMUNISM" is suddenly very active. Their newspaper "de WAARHEID" (the TRUTH) is on display everywhere and it's free! The communists expect to take over the country. In due time, elections will be held, but right now "Queen Wilhelmina" is back in the saddle. Her "exile government" that she brought over from England is not as popular as they would have liked to believe.

The sentiment is: "YOU COWARDS, WHO LIVED IN LONDON IN COMFORT, ARE NOT GOING TO TELL US "RESISTANCE HEROES" WHO SUFFERED AND DIED, HOW TO RUN OUR COUNTRY!" "IT'S OUR COUNTRY, SO JUST BUTT OUT AND "WE'LL" RUN IT!"

In spite of all that, things get done. Supplies are starting to show up, trains start running, phone lines are being fixed and roads are being uncluttered from war remnants. Some elaborate transportation schemes start to develop. A trip to MAASTRICHT from Winterswijk, 100 miles as the crow flies, will go as follows; A train to ZEVENAAR, transfer to a bus that will cross the IJSEL over a pontoon bridge, switch busses in ARMHEM, cross a pontoon bridge over the LOWER RHINE, across the WAAL bridge to the NIJMEGEN railstation, take a train to 'sHERTOGENBOSCH, change trains to BEST. In BEST another change to busses, this time to the EIND-HOVEN railstation, a train to WEERT, a bus across a pontoon bridge to ROERMOND and from there another train to MAASTRICHT. Trip time; ONE AND A HALF DAYS! Worst part; this can NOT be confirmed yet! Best advice; "STAY HOME!"

May 9, 1945

It's raining out! It's a good day to work at home. The boys have finally gotten electricity in their "Cave" and even though it's just a bare bulb that burns their fingers when they have to unscrew it, it's a bright addition to their "treasure hut." Frits is deeply puzzled. Sitting on British Airplane foam rubber seats, leaning against foam padded British tank backrests, he's been working on his German flare pistol with Dutch tools. Finding the problem was not hard. A small spring had come loose on one side and that kinda left a little lever dangling inside the pistol grip. Hooking up the spring and tightening the loop with a pair of needlepoint pliers seemed to solve the problem. When set to the "left" position, only the left hammer strikes and by moving it to the "right" position, the right hammer strikes the firing pin. Centering the lever makes both hammers hit. GREAT! That was simple enough! But that is not his problem! Two long, tough springs that sit on a little notch in the bottom of the grip and end up around the bot-tom of a ball-headed gadget, are giving him fits. All the parts have to end up inside the framework, no exposed hammers on this one. Compressing a spring, putting it's rounded attachment in its socket and the bottom end on the notch is nothing. He just tells Paul; "Hold your finger on it!" then he does number two. Nothing to it!

"Now I slide the back plate of the grip on top of it and that will hold everything in place, right? WRONG!"

The moment they move the fingers that hold the springs in place, the springs just bend out in the middle and jump right out.

"VERDOMMETJE!"

They can't get the plates on with their fingers inside the grip, because it makes like a JACK-IN-THE-BOX,. PHFFFT,,,,,OUT! They've done it ten times now, their fingers are sore and their patience is shot.

"VERDOMMETJE, VERDOMMETJE! LET ME THINK! A little tube that the springs can ride up and down in without friction?"

"Where do find that?"

"No idea! Tape? Tape maybe? Do we have any tape up here?"

"Not a piece."

"Go down and ask Pappa for some electrical tape, I need some for the wiring anyway."

"Okay!"

While Paul is gone, Frits analyzes the possibilities. The tape could get stuck in between the spring. It could disintegrate in time and gum up the works. Too much tape might keep it from closing properly. "VERDOM-METJE!" How do they do this at the factory? They take a very thin knife to hold the springs in place and they pull it out at the very last second. Worth a try! A knife is thinner than a finger, that's for sure. Or a thin wire that we pull out before tightening? That's what we need to do. I sent the Boer down too fast. Or something inside the spring? Like a nail? Let me check my nails....this'n will fit! It's half the length of the spring and if I get it in the middle of it, it'll hold it straight long enough to give me a chance to close it up. The nail is thin enough to allow the spring to compress and relax; it's just thin enough. Okay, just twist it down, down, down so the head is a quarter of its length from the top. Good show, she slides in and stays. Now the other side. Okay, compress the spring, put it's head in the socket, release....it stays!! Screw on the back plate....READY!!! done!!! Testing; "left," "ping," "right," "ping," "center," "ping." Perfect. That's resolved.

"OH, here comes Paultje, Forgot all about him and the tape."

"Frits, Frits! Come out, come here!" He's hollering from the end of their tunnel. "Come out quick!"

He forgot all about the tape too! "What's up?"

"They're here! The Ladies, they're here!"

Frits doesn't have to ask; "WHAT LADIES?" He knows! It's been on their minds for three months. He scoots out of the hole on his belly and races Paul down the stairs. There they are! He knows them from church. They're sipping tea in the parlor. "Their parlor, our furniture!" he thinks. The atmosphere is tense. Their awkward hats remind him of the business the ladies were in. "Are in!" he corrects himself. Their store is still there, across the street from the church. They nod politely as Mama introduces her boys and the boys, equally polite, say; "Dames!"

"Go and play, boys," says Pappa, "We'll see you later!"

"But Pappa, are they gonna take the house away from us?"

"Go outside or upstairs, but GO!,,, NOW! NOW! We'll talk later. NOW!"

They slowly make their way upstairs again, but sit down at the first landing, so they can listen in.

They learn that the Ladies have spent the last 10 months on the VE-LUWE near APELDOORN to escape the daily bombing, but nearly got caught in the middle of some intense combat. They didn't actually get liberated, but the armistice on May 5th simply ended it all for them and now they're anxious to get back to work and to move back into their house. "WOULD THE FORRERS JUST BE KIND ENOUGH TO LEAVE? NOW, IF POSSIBLE!"

Pappa walks out of the room. The boys know what that means! He's about to explode and his ulcer tells him; "DON'T DO IT!"

He pours himself some milk in the kitchen. That usually settles his stomach.

Mama explains, a little more diplomatically than Pappa would have done, that the housing administration will handle this and to please contact THEM!

The charming, devout Catholic Ladies demand immediate expulsion of the homeless family and five children, but Mama assures them that God and the Law are on her side.

The charming, fuming Ladies assure her that they'll be back in fifteen minutes with the Police and bristling with indignity they slam the door behind them. After all, it's their door!

Mama is not even uptight. "I've had worse crises than this lately!" And so she has!

During dinner it's decided that Mam will go to "housing" anyway to make sure that everything goes according to schedule. Joop will go with her.

"Why Joop?"

"Because they know, I'll stay awake!"

Nasty dig! Frits has to grin anyway, just thinking about it! He doesn't remember the first thing about falling asleep behind the couch, but he does remember the splitting headache the next morning. His first KATER (hangover), Herman told him and Frits resolved he would never drink anymore. The headache wasn't worth it! Besides, his Father told him that alcohol would stunt his growth and as small as he is right now, he needs some stimulant to help him GROW, so NO MORE BOOZE! NEVER!

When Mama and Joop return, soaking wet, they bring relatively good news.

The Ladies cannot throw them out, but tomorrow, inspectors are going to check out their store and this house and see if additional living quarters can be built, one way or the other.

The inspection team, consisting of two men with measuring tapes and scratch pads are very efficient, but commit themselves to nothing.

"What are they thinking of, Pap?"

"They're trying to figure out if a "two-family home" can be made out of this "one-family home!"

"Oh, boy! Have those witches live here with us? That won't work!"

"Maybe it will and maybe it won't! Right now, we're simply negotiating. The Ladies have to live somewhere too and they have their rights too. The "housing" people are also checking out what can be done with their store. See, the second floor of their store is an apartment and has been rented out for a long time, so they can't throw these people out either. The third story is just an attic full of junk and downstairs, in back of their shop, is office and storage space, so that may have possibilities too! We'll see! We'll make it!"

"MAKING IT!" is quite a statement. Until this day they haven't paid rent to anybody at WOOLDSTRAAT 37, but now they'll have to, whether they occupy the whole house or half.

Out of 70 guilders a week, ten per person, that might take a good chunk and that wouldn't leave much money for necessities. Clothing is going to be a big factor. Everybody has grown so much and everybody is going to need new school clothes, but where is the money going to come from?

The "egg-trade" with the Tommies is good business, but they'll be going home to England pretty soon.

Pappa's been looking for work, but other than physical labor, he hasn't been offered much and physical labor is out. Ulcers over the last thirty years have left his body weak and wracked. Negotiating for another business may be their only hope, but until the country's economy is back to normal, that's going to be difficult.

THEN IT HAPPENS! THE INEVITABLE, THE UNBELIEVABLE, THE UNTHINKABLE!

The one thing the boys have feared more than anything has happened! SCHOOL! "SCHOOL" as in: sitting at a desk! As in: studying! As in: homework! As in: behaving! ATROCIOUS! How could anyone be so cruel? Well, those bureaucrats are just that CRUEL!

Of course, THEY have a different way of putting it; "IF WE CAN GET CLASSES GOING AT A NORMAL TO ACCELERATED PACE, WE CAN STILL LEGALLY CONSIDER THIS A "SCHOOL YEAR" AND WONT HAVE TO WRITE OFF THE ENTIRE YEAR!"

That's easy for them to say!

To make it worse, Frits will be the first one to get started. Of all the rotten luck!

Since all schools are still warehouses or military bivouacs, a devout parishioner with 3 kids in Catholic school has volunteered his place of business as a "school-location!" Damn him!

School benches, books and blackboards are hauled out of storage and put out in the enclosed areas of his lumberyard. The classrooms will be rather drafty! The weather is warming up, so maybe it will work.

The school asked for volunteers to move furniture and supplies to the new school facility, but in spite of Mama's urging, Frits refuses to participate in something that goes against his conscience.

"That's like being asked to build your own guillotine before being beheaded! NO WAY!"

It doesn't alter the fact that one bright morning he walks off to school, at 7AM, while the rest of the creeps wave him "Goodbye!" He hates them.. Joop is grinning from ear to ear because his school hasn't even attempted to start anything. Clasien, Paul and Hedwig are still in grammar school and their education is not a "priority."

"BULLSHIT!, MINE IS NOT EITHER! I'M NOT GOING IF THEY'RE NOT GOING!"

He's been throwing tantrums. He might as well have been howling at the moon. HE'S GOING AND THAT'S IT!

Dressed up, socks, klompen, shorts, white shirt and tie, the works!

"My, you're cute!" Clasien's remarks make it worse, but, here he goes, sticking his tongue out at the waving "creeps."

School isn't bad though. Lots to talk about, lots of old buddies he hasn't seen for months and with Jan Kamphuis next to him, it doesn't seem all that oppressive.

The schedule isn't too bad either. Starting at 7.30, 45-minute classes with10 minute breaks and at 12.30, it's all over. So here they go!

I AM, YOU ARE, HE IS, WE ARE, YOU ARE, THEY ARE. JE SUIS, TU ES, IL EST, NOUS SOMMES, VOUS ÊTES, ILS SONT. ICH BIN, DU BIST, ER IST, WIR SIND, SIE SIND, SIE SIND, etc.

Algebra, geometry, chemistry, Dutch grammar, history, literature, religion and geography, it's all kinda interesting and he loves to learn. That little brain of his is like a sponge, it just soaks things up and his pride is a great stimulant. No way will a teacher ever call on him and catch him, not knowing the answer!

No, Sir! He has this inflated ego. If he's not the best one in his class in any given subject, you bet he's working on it! He's fortunate, that due to the circumstances, languages just roll off his tongue and he feels, if they had taught ten languages instead of four, he would have learned ten just as easily. By associating the different words, it seems as easy to learn four meanings of a word as it is to learn just one. So when he's taught the meaning of the word "fiets" in German, "fahrrad," it takes just a minute to look up the word in English, "bicycle" and in French, "velo." When "deur" in French proves to be "porte," then "tür" in German and "door" in English are immediately made part of his vocabulary.

Math is his favorite. Chemistry and geography are interesting subjects and all in all, going to school again is not at all the pain in the neck that he believed it to be.

When the other schools crank up again and the rest of the kids have to go to school as well, it doesn't even seem like a chore anymore. Another consolation is that Joop really has to study a lot at night and somehow that makes things more acceptable.

From the lumberyard, the M.U.L.O. is moved to the library and his schedule becomes the same as the other's, 9 to 12 and 1:30 till 4. In a way that's too bad, because the long afternoons had left them a lot of time for other activities. Now, life is nearly normal again. NEARLY!!!! NOT QUITE!!!

Construction is taking place at the house. Dividing walls are erected and a complete kitchen is being installed upstairs. The old "DAMES" will get the parlor and the entire second floor. The Forrers get the rest. That's not much! Pappa and Mama will sleep in the veranda. Thank God for warmer weather. They'll just LIVE in the dining room. The girls will have the rear attic bedroom and all three boys will share the top front bedroom. It will be tight, but dry! That's more than some people have! It's a little messy during construction and there is not much privacy for studying. Sometimes Joop and Frits sit on the floor and use their beds as desks. When it comes to just reading a subject, Frits can sit in the third floor window and read.

Being cooped up like that, Joop starts to confide in Frits more and more, but the topic is always the same; "SEX!" Joop seems to have nothing else on his mind. Unfortunately, Joop's thoughts about sex are frequently interrupted by school and homework, otherwise sex would be his only interest.

Something that's helping that along is a new event in town. SCHOOL "C," the public school in back of their yard has not yet been converted from warehouse and bivouac back to school. Now, suddenly, it's a QUARANTINE! Dozens of former camp inmates are being repatriated and are first put into quarantine near the border. They are medically checked, de-liced, fed, sometimes operated on and generally well cared for. SCHOOL "C" gets its allotment and under some security, the repatriates are housed in the school.

ALL WOMEN! Well, women and children, but NO MEN! About 40 women and 60 children are trucked in, registered and cleaned. The women vary in ages and sizes, but the have one thing in common! NO SEX! MAYBE FOR YEARS! Now they're back in Holland and they can't get out!

Another phenomena; THOUSANDS OF BRITISH TROOPS! Only hundreds of available Dutch girls, thousands of available men and all that adds up to an explosive situation. What a time bomb! What to do?

This age-old urge between the sexes has always found some sort of compromise and this situation in Winterswijk is no exception! The women speak NO English; the Tommies speak NO Dutch, so a new trade, really a new form of an old trade, is created. Joop and some of his cronies have established a "sex-for-cigarettes" business. During the noon break and after four o'clock, the guys negotiate with the soldiers that hang around the school fence. The women hang out in front of the classroom windows and establish contact with a Tommie out front, across the schoolyard. He waves, she waves! CONTACT! The Tommie points out the woman of his choice, three packs of cigarettes change hands and the "interpreter" dashes across the yard when the security guard rounds the corner and out of sight. The "interpreter" locates the appropriate woman, establishes a time, place and name of the soldier, pays her ONE pack down and races back across the yard to confirm time, place and name of the "LAY" with the soldier. Each one of those transactions earns them two packs of weeds. Five, six deals a day like that pays rather well.

At night, after dark, the "LADY" climbs out of the window, races across the yard, finds her man and earns two more packs of cigarettes. Nice deal!

One night, Joop and Frits hide out in the trees behind the bandstand. There are no lights and the grass is soft. Frits is about to get his first lesson in "sex-education!!

"THAT'S WHAT GROWNUPS DO?" "WOW!" He comes home bewildered. Sexuality about himself, that he never knew or cared about, is starting to change his life. He starts to regard girls differently in school and on the streets. He becomes aware of their build, their clothes, and their hair! He's too shy to say or do anything out of the ordinary, anything he wouldn't have done last year or even last month, but the girls have sure caught his attention!

Corner of Winkel, Wooldse en Meddose Streets
Old St. Jacob in the background

CHAPTER XIX
Bomb Blast

Summer is NOT official until the swimming pool opens! It doesn't matter if it's only 45 degrees out! It doesn't matter if it's chilly and rainy, nor does it matter that it's only June 1. When "HET ZWEMBAD" opens... it's SUMMER!!!

Money for season passes is a problem. Two and a half guilders has become a lot of money, but with "earnings" from eggs and cigarettes, the boys get their passes. On a misty, dreary day, they're off to the pool. A lot of young die-hards are already there and though the temperature is not expected to reach 55 degrees, there's a good crowd on that first Saturday of June. The polo-team, mostly 16 and 17 year olds, are having free-style drills and it's good to be back in the water and practice along with them. While racing across the pool or practicing "treading-water" with both hands in the air, the cold is soon forgotten.

In the cafeteria, "warming" up with an ice-cream cone, they get into a bragging session with two skinny "emigrants" from SCHEVENINGEN. Their homes are now bunkers along the beach and they'll live in Winterswijk for awhile until they can get "re-patriated." The two are known as "WAT EN HALFWAT," which literally means; "SOMETHING AND HALF OF SOMETHING," But in English would be more like "MUTT AND JEFF." Being Catholic, they ended up in the same schools and now they're sounding off about their big adventures in little boats, battling the waves of the North Sea. According to them, going out on HERRING boats was just a routine matter for them and "YOU HICKS" out here in the East have never seen excitement yet!"

The decision is made fast.

"WE'LL SHOW THESE "BIG-MOUTHS" SOME EXITEMENT!"

The weather is typical for the time of year. Whether in London, Brussels, Copenhagen, Amsterdam or Winterswijk, it's all the same. When the sun is out, it's fine. When clouds drift over, the temperature drops by 10 degrees and the icy, misty rain drenches everything.. Best never go out without a raincoat and an umbrella.

The real fishermen of SCHEVENINGEN are known to wear wooden shoes on their boats, but "WAT and HALF-WAT" have never owned any. They wear nice, dressy, Sunday kind of shoes and they're likely to ruin them before the afternoon is over. When the boys point this out to them, they're assured; "My Mam doesn't care!"

"How about your DAD?"

"We don't have a Dad, we don't know where he is!"

"You don't know where he is?"

"No, he left in '42 on a boat with the resistance and we haven't heard from him since!"

"Not from the Dutch Government when they got back from England either?"

"No, my mother is checking everything out, but we don't know anything yet. They have no record of him arriving in England. He got a notice to go to work in Germany and he went to the "labor-office" in The Hague and tried to prove that his work here was essential, but they turned that down. So he told Mam, that he wouldn't work for the Germans that he'd rather go to England and fight. Four of them left in a little boat one night and we've never heard from any of them. They may never have reached England. They're checking all Army and Navy records and even the RAF, to see if they turned up anywhere at all."

"Wow, you haven't seen your Daddy for three years?"

"Two and a half, actually, he wasn't there for SINTERKLAAS in '42, so he probably left sometime in November, I think!"

"Yes," HALF-WAT interrupts, "I remember. We had a lousy SINTER-KLAAS that year."

"Yeah, so it's going on three years."

"That's a long time without a Father!" Paultje musses. He knows from experience what that means.

"You're not kidding!" WAT is doing all the talking it seems, "and my Dad is a really neat guy. A lot of fun to be with, so we keep hoping!"

It's interesting that he doesn't refer to his Dad in the past tense. He has not written him off!

Not having heard their story before, Frits has a guilt cloud hover over his head. They could have been nicer to those guys; they could have involved them in some of their activities. It would have helped them some, he's sure. POOR MOTHER!

Must tell Mama about her. That lady may be very lonely in a strange town without a husband! And she's Catholic too! Imagine three years without Pappa! Oh, boy!! What a thought.!"

When they reach the edge of the ZWEMBAD property, the boys from the West prove to be rather clumsy when it comes to climbing fences. They get hooked, caught and scratched, trying to get over or between the strands of barbed wire. They'll learn! If they're going to hang out with this gang, they'll learn! Either learn or get left behind.

The FLYING DUTCHMAN is as they left it, although it's a good thing they showed up when they did!

The camouflage is wearing off! All the leaves have fallen off and even the evergreen branches have turned brown and don't provide much cover anymore. It only takes seconds to uncover it and after tilting it on it's side, they cart it off. It surprises them again how light it is. One man could nearly carry it, if it weren't so big.

They launch the craft, admire its beauty and climb aboard. It easily holds six because of the length of the gastanks. Now they have six hands to propel the boat and with all the experience they have gained, it's working rather well. The skinny kids are positioned in the center, one facing forward, the other toward the stern. The older boys are up front on either side and the little ones behind them, paddling like hell. By having the skinny guys in the middle, they can't goof up the steering, but they do add to the propulsion.

After just a few involuntary turns, they get the rhythm going perfectly and there they go!!! "VAREN, VAREN, OVER DE BAREN! VAREN, VAREN OVER DE ZEE!" Just a-gliding along!

In one of the many turns, they beach the craft, to rest their arms and confer. They switch positions, so now the other arm gets a workout and they sail along until the next break. It's pee-break time anyway! Nature has provided neat little beaches in each turn and that's where the planning session is taking place.

"Shall we go all the way to our secret place?"

"What about landmines?" The Kamphuis brothers have good questions.

"Have you been in that direction lately, Jan?"

"No, the last time was when we were there with you and they were just starting to tape the mined areas, but I hear from my Father, that they have roped off all the mined areas and that they've been busy removing them!"

"Yeah," Henkie adds, "they're using German P.O.W.'s to round up the mines, so if they screw up, they get blown up by their own evil, isn't that neat?"

"Yeah, that's better than what happened to that Tommie, remember?"

"So, let's row all the way to the Kottense Weg Bridge. If we see ribbons from there, we go no further. If we don't see ribbons, we can go ashore and scout the area and check if it's all clear all the way to our secret place! Okay?"

"Okay!" "Alright, let's row!"

The creek is beautiful this time of year. The tall trees provide a solid roof overhead, moss and fern line the banks and rhododendrons display their white and purple beauty, while birds perform a concert, devoted to the splendor of it all!!!!! Another beautiful part of the scenario is; "NO HUMAN BEINGS!"

When the weather gets warmer, young families will be coming out and young lovers will be strolling the paths, but right now, the only sounds are Mother Nature's and the soft splashing of hands in the water.

When they reach the bridge, they can't really see anything because of the high banks. So they have no way of knowing if yellow ribbons line the road from tree to tree or not. "WAT" wants to jump off and take a look, but he's held down quickly.

"YOU DON'T WANNA WALK INTO A MINEFIELD TO SEE IF IT'S REALLY A MINEFIELD! Take our word for it!"

"You two guys paddle and keep us under the bridge. "WAT" and Jan, give me a boost!"

WAT and Jan face each other and lock their hands together. Frits steps on their hands, steadying himself by holding on to their heads, then on to their shoulders and... he's got the bridge. The boys below are shoving him upward by his feet and he disappears from sight.

He's back in a few minutes and signals them to the shore.

"I ran a hundred yards in both directions and there's no sign of a ribbon anywhere! A little closer, please? Thank you!" He jumps aboard.

"FULL STEAM AHEAD!"

"That means;" he continues, "that there were no mines here to begin with or they have cleared them away by now!"

It doesn't take them very long to get to their final destination; THEIR OWN, PRIVATE, SECRET BEACH with its beautiful high bank.

They pull the FLYING DUTCHMAN ashore and give "WAT" and "HALF-WAT" a tour of their KINGDOM. Frits wonders if he should clue them in on the secret of the Russian sub-machinegun, but decides against it. It proves to be well hidden, because there is no obvious sign of it. He's afraid that the two strangers might babble too much and as yet, he doesn't know them that well. It can wait.

They are truly in the most beautiful part of the forest, undisturbed and serene. Not a path or human footprint anywhere. As they cross the woods to where the pastures lie, they have a sudden start! A GRAVE! A low mound with a German helmet and a riffle, bayonet fixed, lying across it. The riffle was probably stuck in the ground to mark the grave, but toppled over in the wind. The rifle is badly rusted and a tag is attached to it with a little chain. "RUDOLPH AREND KOCHER" it reads. "5-12-26"

"My God, just 19 years old!"

"I wonder if anyone knows the grave is here?"

"Hey, leave that rifle alone. We don't take anything from here! Let's mark it better. Stick that bayonet back into the ground. NO, NO! Not in the middle of that mound! That body may not be in too deep, you ass. Here, at the end. Okay! Helmet on top! NOW they can see it! Who wants to run to the road and pace off the distance? Count both ways, coming and going, just to be sure.!"

Jan and WAT jog in the direction of the road while the sun peeps out for the first time that day.. The other boys scout the edge of the field in the other direction and find another grave.

"I DIDN'T REALIZE THAT THERE HAD BEEN ANY FIGHTING ALONG HERE, THIS CLOSE TO TOWN!" says HALF-WAT.

"Man, you should see near't WOOLD! Tanks and trucks shot to hell all over the place, only twenty minutes from here!"

"Could we go and see?"

"Ya, maybe, but let's check something first! Let's pace the distance to the other grave!"

"125"

Jan is back, puffing like mad, "491 paces to the road!, but there are no recognizable markers anywhere nearby!"

"Well, did you mark the spot on the road?"

"No, I don't have anything to mark with, but it's the first open field east of the bridge, so that should be easy to report, right?"

"True! Okay, let's hide the ship. I'm hungry! Do we go home or what do we do?"

"No, No, let's NOT go home!" It's unanimous.

"Then let's hide the boat! C'mon! "

Before pulling away from their hideout, they check and make sure their PIRATE SHIP is well hidden. They also take inventory of their logs and try to figure out how many more they're going to need to build their log cabin

"A lot! Hundreds! An awful lot!"

Yep, that's what'll take. Thank God they have no deadlines.

As they cross a railroad track on their way to 'tWOOLD, they stop, look at one another and "YEP!" instead of crossing the tracks, they start following them in an easterly direction, towards DEUTSCHLAND!

"Where are we going?" WAT and HALF-WAT don't understand, "I thought we were going to 't WOOLD to look at tanks and ruins.?"

"We will, we will! Patience! Are you guys ready for WINETOU time?"

"What's WINETOU time?"

"Don't you guys read?" The gang breaks into a trot, which is actually easier then walking on the tracks.

The ties are too close together for a normal walking pace and too far apart for skipping one with each step. Jogging is perfect. Skipping one tie is just right for their short legs. The only problem is, the ZUID HOLLAND-ERS are not in durable condition and they have to slow down regularly to give them a chance to catch up. As they come to the crossing they've been aiming for, they turn north.

"You're going the wrong way!"

"Don't worry! We know what we're doing!"

After another 100 paces, they turn right onto a dirt road and thirty more steps, left into the woods.

The "WAT" boys don't notice the markings on the trees, but the "four-some does" and ignoring questions like; "What are we doing here?" And "Where are we going now?," they stop at a low pine tree and start digging.

"How many?"

"Let's take two!"

"What are you talking about?" "WOW!, What are these?" "How many do you have?"

"Cover it up, boys! These are "105 HOWITZERS!"

"What are Howitzers?"

"Some sort of a fishing boat! Hahahaha!" The foursome is enjoying this, just showing off! When they find the tree with the elevated roots, Jan gets to do his thing, provoking more questions.

"What's he doing?"

"Is he crazy? Won't it explode? Can I do that? Can we have one of them?"

Jan is getting results and the bullet is coming looser with each drop.

Jan explains; "The weight of the bullet makes the brass give a little each time I drop it and eventually, it's loose enough where we can pull it out."

"What are you gonna do with it after you get it out?"

"Throw it away!"

"Why?"

"Because we have no tanks to shoot at, hahahahahaha!"

"Ah, come on, man. Really, what are you gonna do with them?"

"Play soccer with them, hahahahaha!" Boy, they're on a roll!

"Let's try it!" Jan holds the shell, Frits twists the bullet and it gives a little, but not enough.

"A little more, Jan!" Next try; results.

"Here, you want it?" Frits hands WAT the bullet, but he drops it like a hot potato! More laughter!

"Stupid! Holding it is not half as dangerous as dropping it, you dope! If it had exploded, it might have killed all of us!"

Jan starts on number two, while the others start at the solidly packed "macaroni." The first one is always the hardest. Each piece is about the length of their lower arm and once one piece is out, the rest follows fairly easily. Finally, the center pack shakes into Henkies waiting hands and here come the questions again.

"What is that stuff and what are you gonna do with it?"

"It's macaroni and after we find some tomatoes, we're going to make an Italian dinner, right guys? Hahahahahaha!" They're having a ball picking on the "WAT" guys.

"Seriously, don't be so impatient! How's it coming, Jan?"

"I'm ready to try!"

The procedure is repeated again and....with a few twists, ..."She's coming!" ... "That's it!"

"What are you guys doing with those shells?"

Jan and Frits look at one another, nod, and Henkie hands his shell to "WAT." "Give it to your Mam, but don't let her put flowers in it!!"

"Gee, thanks! But why no flowers?"

"Don't you guys ever quit with the questions?"

Paultje gets the second shell and he's all smiles. He's going to shine it up and he'll... He dreams right on! Jan, Henk and Frits stuff the "macaroni" under their windbreakers and under a barrage of questions, they resume their trek to 't WOOLD.

As soon as they hit a hard surface road, they pull out some macaroni and here comes the first shot!

Jan lights a piece, puts it down and steps on it with his "klomp," extinguishing the flame and there it goes......... "SHEESHEESHEESHEESH!" It shoots down the road like a mad snake, doing a hundred miles an hour.

"Can I do it? Can I try? What makes it do that?"

"VAU EINZ!" Frits answers.

"Huh?"

"VAU EINZ!" The fun is unending. These skinny kids from the westcoast are such "schmoes," he could kid 'em all day long!

Of course everyone wants to try and shoot a "macaroni rocker" and everybody gets their chance.

The "WAT" boys are burning up their shoe soles, but that's all in the game and well worth it.

"We'll do more of it when we get home! Let's attack some tanks!"

"I'm hungry!"

"Henkie, you're the fattest of the bunch and you're always the first one to get hungry! How come?"

"Ya, but I'm hungry too!"

"Like I said; the fattest ones are always the first ones to get hungry, and BOER, you're obviously the second fattest one!"

"Frits, do you know if there are any cherries in this area?"

"Nothing is ripe yet. Most trees were just in bloom recently!"

Jan answers; "I know where there are some apple and pear orchards around here. But like you said, they've just blossomed.!"

"How about WESTERVELD?"

"Boer, you're brilliant! Ya, let's stop by WESTERVELD, they may break out some goodies.!"

"What's a WESTERVELD?"

No, not WHAT's a WESTERVELD, it's WHO's WESTERVELD? He's the man who we're nominating for "the ORDER of ORANJE NASSAU!"

"What's that?"

"May I ask you ZUID-HOLLANDSE gentlemen something? Where have you been all your lives? Lived with your head up your ass or in the sand?" This is too funny! The foursome is hysterical!

The "WATS" just laugh along too! They don't know what else to do.

WESTERVELD proudly shows them around all the construction that's going on. The front of the house is already repaired. By chiseling the mortar off the old bricks and re-using them, he has rebuilt the front of the house without creating that "new addition" look. All that's left to be done on the inside is the wallpaper. He has painted it temporarily until such time that wallpaper will come back on the market.

The barn in back is all framed out. It's going to be twice as big as it was before.

The boys are all in awe of what's going on, but not as much as they're in awe of Mrs. WESTERVELD's suggestion; "Would any of you like some soup and rolls?"

"You bet!"

They're brought up to date on what's been happening, while they're happily munching away.

Busted tanks, jeeps and trucks have all been removed and "yes," they've heard about Hof van Holland and "no," they weren't aware of KAMP VOSSEVELD and the "DAMES."

"By the way, what do you kids have under your blouses?"

After exchanging some glances, the boys decide to show them. "No, thanks!" The WESTERVELDS do not need a demonstration of "green macaroni rocket," but Mrs. WESTERVELD'S eyes light up when she sees the "105 shells." She "oohs" and "aaahs" so much, that Paultje hands her his; "You can have it!"

All protests are rejected and she hugs "the biggest brass shell, I've ever seen!"

Paultje assures her, that he can get another one, might his mother want one and Mrs. WESTERVELD wonders how one could establish a market value for something like that.

"When you find out, let us know. We might establish a little business! Thanks for the goodies, Mrs. WESTERVELD."

"Thanks for the beautiful vase!'

"VASE????? GOOD GOD, NOT AGAIN!"

On Sunday, they decide to entertain the re-patriated LADIES and children at "School C."

After the Sunday dinner, they get back into their work-clothes; blue coveralls and klompen.

On the large school playground, they're joined by the "WATS" and with an audience of women and children in the school and soldiers at the fence, they start to shoot their "squeezies."

The directional control of the green macaronis is unpredictable. Some shoot straight out, some wiggle like snakes, others go in circles and some come back at the shooters like a boomerang. All of them are entertaining and most of them get applause and laughter.

Everybody is enjoying the show, except the security guard. He comes out explaining that they're not supposed to be on school property and that what they're doing is dangerous. The Tommies boo him, 'tho they can't understand him and the women and children in the open windows root them on; "GO! GO! GO!"

The old guard is told off and retreats, hollering; "I'M GONNA CALL THE POLICE!"

He gets a cheer from the audience and the boys continue their entertainment….until…."POLICE!…. "POLICE!"

"Paul, take the stuff and ease out! We'll wait!"

Paultje, the smallest of the bunch, meanders away with the macaroni under his shirt and slips over the fence between some onlookers.

The Policeman, all of 19 years old, swings his leg over his saddle and marches, military like, over to the remaining three boys while balancing his bike by the handlebars.

The Tommies at the fence holler encouragement; such as; "Go get'em,tiger! Atta boy, arrest the criminals!" and are having a ball at the young policeman's expense. That probably does not improve matters. The now irate policeman walks right up to them, bike in hand; "WHAT WERE YOU SHOOTING?"

"MACARONI!"

"MACARONI? I HAVE A REPORT ABOUT A DANGEROUS SUB-STANCE," he's shouting! "LET ME HAVE IT!"

'WE DON'T HAVE ANYMORE!" The "WAT" boys are backing up slowly.

"WHAT IS IT AND WERE DID YOU GET IT?"

"It's macaroni!" Frits starts to lower his voice, "and we got it from the soldiers." He forgot to say "GERMAN SOLDIERS."

"For the last time; WHAT IS IT AND HAND IT OVER!" By now, the "WAT" boys are five paces back.

The soldiers are shouting; "They're real baby criminals, they should be hung!"

"Why don't you pick on a guy your own size!"

The young cop is getting flustered and if he'd only said; "You're tres-passing, leave the school-ground!" it would have settled the whole affair. Instead he says; "I'LL HAVE TO TAKE YOU IN!" Dumb move!

"RUN!" Frits shouts as he runs to his right toward the school building, thus giving the "WAT" boys a chance to get to the fence and disappear. They take the hint and are gone over the fence in no time flat as the cop chases Frits into the school-house after leaning his bike against the old ELM. Frits runs into the first door to his right, through a throng of cheering women and children to the window and out. The Tommies cheer as he sails out the window and races toward the tree. With the help of the bike, he's, one, two, three up in the tree. Crawling along the biggest branch, he's over the school roof in seconds and simply drops down to the roof.

By now the policeman, slightly delayed by the women inside, also ap-pears at the window and jumps. Scouting the yard for the elusive Frits, he's about to take his bike and give up, when someone shouts; "He's on the roof!"

Backing away from the building and the green luster of the elm tree, he spots Frits and Frits spots him at the same time. Frits races to the top of the roof, while the cop orders him :"COME HERE!, COME DOWN !" Frits disappears over the top, the Cop races to the other side of the building to intercept him and immediately Frits reappears, races down, grabs the tree limb, slides down, crosses the schoolyard, hops the fence and is gone.

The cheers on this side of the school must be telling the Cop on the other side that he's been had and that some little punk made a public ass of him.

When he retrieves his bike, the indignity is enhanced by the cheering he gets from inside and outside the building. He's boiling!

After Sunday supper, while the whole family sits around the radio, listening to Holland's #1 variety show, the doorbell rings.

"I'll get it!" Clasien jumps up. It rang once. That means, it's for downstairs.

She rushes back in the room; "PAPPA, TWO POLICEMEN!"

"Oh, my God! Not again! Herman, I'll go!"

"No, No, sit down, Mam. I'll go!"

Ten seconds later, he's back. Snapping his fingers, he points at Frits; "GET YOUR KLOMPEN!" That's all.

In the setting dusk, a scrawny, skinny kid is marched to the station between two big policemen, bicycles in hand.

"LOUSY COWARD!" is all Frits can think of, "Not fair! He lost! He couldn't catch me! He should take it like a man! Admit; "I LOST!" Coming to somebody's door at night, that stinks!" THE LOUSY COWARD!"

He's back by ten. He has little to say. Joop has already told Mama and Pappa about their show. He had heard it from somebody, who had heard it from somebody and the whole thing got very exaggerated something fierce. At the supper table, Frits and Paul had a chance to downplay it and it had kinda blown over,,,, until the policemen came.

"They gave me a lecture about listening to authority and not running away from policemen and I'm tired! Welterusten!"

"Welterusten! Goodnight!"

Upstairs, it's a different story. Thank God, Joop is still downstairs and Paultje is still awake.

"What happened? What did they say to you?"

""THE LOUSY, DAMN COWARDS! First they got tough with me. "WHO DO THINK YOU ARE, MAKING A FOOL OF A POLICE OF-FICER? You'll rot in jail for disobeying an order from an official!

WE WANT TO KNOW, RIGHT NOW, WHAT YOU WERE SHOOT-ING, WHERE YOU GOT IT and on and on"

"What did you say? Did you tell 'em where we got it?"

"No, of course not! I told them the truth! We don't know what it is! It looks like long green macaroni and it goes; 'SHEESHEESHEESH!" when you light it and stomp out the flame. Do you know something, Boer? They don't have the foggiest either. They have no idea what we have!"

"Did you tell'em how we got it?"

"Yes. I told'em we got it from the military and somebody taught us how to shoot it!"

"That's true! The train was certainly military and the somebody who taught us how to shoot it was Joop!"

" Hahahahahaha," Paultje is nearly hysterical!

"But wait, wait! It's not finished! They became real nice, they gave me cocoa and cookies and asked me what happened at the schoolyard. Well, I told'em and when I was telling about running through the classroom and what the soldiers were saying, they started laughing and when I told'em how I went up the roof and back down, they laughed even harder and then the asked me again; "WHAT IS IT AND WHERE DID YOU GET IT?," so I laughed right along with'em and told'em the exact same thing and that's when the shit hit the fan! All of a sudden, it was like all three of them exploded. They must rehearse that crap. They hollered and shouted and threatened and when I answered the same way, they grabbed me by the collar and threw me in a cell! Well, at first I was little rattled to say the least, but I remembered what WINETOU and OLD SHATTERHAND would have done and I didn't think about it anymore. I started reading all the messages on the wall. All the walls are yellow brick and guys must have scratched in them with forks or knives or something, I guess. There were initials, dates, poems, hearts with arrows, all sortsastuff! Then I started counting the bricks in the walls, but they came and got me before I could finish 'em all. They asked me the same questions again, put me on the back of a bike and took me home! THOSE LOUSY COWARDS! THREE BIG GUYS AGAINST ONE LITTLE KID!"

"COWARDS?" Paultje thinks it's funny as hell until a sobering thought hits him; "Are they gonna come and get me too?"

"I don't think so. They asked me once, who was with me and I said; Some evacuees! And they didn't ask anymore. THE COWARDS! We better get some sleep, I didn't finish all my homework yet, I was planning on doing it tonight but now I'll have to do it early in the morning. THOSE LOUSY COWARDS!"

"Good night!"

"Those cowards!"

The nice thing about their life is; THEY NEVER HAVE TO LOOK FOR TROUBLE. IT FINDS THEM!

Especially Frits is good at that.

Walking back from the library classrooms for dinner, "WAT" catches up with Frits and Jan. "WAT" is a classmate of theirs, while "HALF-WAT" is still in sixth grade.

"Hey guys! Wait up for me!

He's slightly out of breath.

"Hi, guys! Hey, Jan, you missed a fun afternoon Sunday!"

"So I've heard, so I've heard!"

"You should have been there. The stupid cop chasing Frits into the school, outta the window, up on the roof like a squirrel and everybody cheering him on! It was hilarious!"

"Something less hilarious for the moment!" Frits cuts in, "Who in the hell called out; "HE'S ON THE ROOF!?""

"I don't know. Maybe one of the soldiers!"

"Don't give me that crap! The soldiers don't know how to say "ON THE ROOF " in Dutch!"

"Oh, that's right. It was in Dutch. I thought it was funny, though, because the whole comedy routine continued that way! It was funny and you're so quick! You should have seen yourself! Hup, onto the bike, stood on the saddle, grabbed a branch, swung your legs up and GONE! Just like TARZAN! If you blinked your eyes you would have missed it!"

"I must admit, I was enjoying it, because I knew the bastard couldn't catch me, the COWARD!"

"By the way, I wanted to tell you guys something else; WE FOUND A BOMB!"

"You found a BOMB?" They stop dead in their tracks. "What kind of a bomb?"

"I don't know, a bomb is a bomb!"

"No, but that's alright. Where is it?"

"At the "HOUTLADING!""

"The lumberyard at the tracks?"

"Yes and it just lies there!'

"And nobody from BOMB-REMOVAL has found it yet?"

"Guess not! It's in the middle of a stack of lumber. You know how they have all those piles of wood? Well, it's in the middle of one of them!"

"How'd you find it?"

"Well, my brother and I go over there to gather kindling wood from the scraps sometimes and we were jumping from one stack to the next, just playing, when "ANDREUS" saw it!"

"ANDREUS?"

"Yea, that's my brother..."

"ANDREUS? Well, that's a good name for him! Would you be able to find it again?"

"Oh sure! Wanna see it?"

"Of course we should report the location of the bomb, but let's first look at it! That reminds me! With all the commotion, I forgot to give the location of the graves to GRAVE REGISTRATION!"

"I took care of that!" Jan interrupts, "We marked them on my Fathers map and he reported them on Monday morning."

"Oh, good! You guys are on the ball. Back to the bomb. Let's look at it 4 o'clock!"

"Frits, we have a lot of homework and we oughtta ...."

"Just fifteen minutes, Frits cuts him off, "just look at it! Just evaluate the situation!" He mimics Jan's high Dutch.

"Okay, evaluate after school, just 15 minutes!"

Looking out of place in their good shoes, white shirts and ties, they cross the many tracks as if it were their day off. There are huge piles of 2 by 2's, 4 by 4's, 2 by 4's, 2 by 6's and 2 by 8's. Jan stays down with their school gear while "WAT" and Frits climb on top of the stacks, jumping from one to the other until they come upon a little valley amongst the mountains of wood.

"There it is!" Indeed! In the bottom of the little valley lies a bomb.

"500 pounder," says Frits, "American!"

"How do you know?"

"See the markings below the fins? American. And the size! It's about the smallest bomb made and it's carried by American fighters. That's also probably the reason why it didn't explode. More than likely, it came down at a low angle and hit something soft or something that gave way, like a stack of wood and then it skipped, like a stone on water, till it came to rest. The detonator is in the nose and it probably didn't hit anything solid hard enough to make it go off, so it just lies there!"

"Couldn't it be a time bomb?"

"No! Time bombs are set to go off between one and ten days, max. This one has been there for at least two months!"

"How do know so much about this stuff?"

"Hahahaha! If you'd lived through five years of war and 4 years of bombing, you're bound to have picked up something! Go relieve Jan by the books and tell him to come up here for a moment!"

"WAT" leaves and Frits starts to trace the possible path of the bomb. When Jan comes up, he points to the horizon and says; "Picture the fighter coming in! He's coming out of his dive and is nearly level. He hits the bomb switch just as he starts his pull-up and the bomb shoots forward like a bullet, instead of dropping down like a bomb. Now the bomb hits something flat, like the top of a boxcar, skips over it, looses a lot of its momentum, hits the top of a woodpile that collapses and the bomb slides to a stop without ever hitting anything solid! Possible?"

"Possible!"

"Look at its path, it skipped nearly fifty yards through and between these stacks and there it is!"

"Ya! That's what must have happened! 500 pounds, I would say!"

"That's what I think!"

"Let's go back and see what we're going to do about it!"

Again, the thought of reporting it to the authorities doesn't even enter their minds. During 5 years of German occupation they have learned that anybody in a position of authority is an "enemy," some "force that you work against, not with!" Having been liberated has so far not changed their minds at all! Authorities are people you distrust and in their young minds, that's entirely logical.

After picking up their schoolbooks, they talk about the possibilities.

"Let's face it, there's nothing we can do with a bomb! The bomb weighs more than the six of us together, so transporting it some place is impossible and besides that, that might be dangerous! A drop on its nose might send all six of us to heaven! Well,,,, at least four of us!"

"What do mean, FOUR of us?"

"Well… you "WAT" guys will probably go to hell for being nasty to your mother!" Jan chokes on that one!

"Whadaya mean, you never even met my Mother!"

"We don't make the decisions about Heaven or Hell. The One who does, knows how you treat your Mother!" By now, Jan can't walk anymore from laughing so hard and with "WAT's" face showing genuine concern about the prospect of HELL, Frits can't control himself any longer and doubles up with laughter. "WAT" can't see the humor, though! "I wish you wouldn't say things like that! It isn't fair!"

"Okay, Okay, Okay!, We hit a touchy cord, I guess. Let's talk about the bomb. Let's give it a name!"

"A name?"

"Yea! A name! We can't go around talking about a bomb when there's someone else around, so we got to give it a name, like MARY, CATHERINE, YOLANDA or something, so no one else will know what we're talking about, right?"

"Right! How about MIRABELLA?"

"MIRABELLA? What's with MIRABELLA? That's what you wanted to call our ship, right?"

"No, that was Henkie's idea, but I like the name."

"What's a MIRABELLA?" WAT wants to know.

"Oh, it's a long story, but that name is as good as any, so MIRABELLA IT IS!"

"It may prove to be an explosive name! Hahahaha! Now, what can we do with it? I'm not going to take it apart!"

"Why not, Jan? You should be able to defuse it! You know that kinda stuff!"

"Ya! And have the thing blow up in my face!"

"That's Okay! We'll be hiding in a safe place, so don't worry about us!"

"Don't flatter yourself. I wasn't thinking about you guys, I was worried about scarring my own pretty face!"

"Tut, tut, tut! Nothing but selfish thoughts! Shame on you!"

"Okay, shame on me, but seriously, could we make it blow? How much damage will it do?" They're at Frits' doorstep now. "Let's think about it. Right now, we have a pile of homework, so I'll see you in church tomorrow!"

"Tju!" "Tju!"

As the days go by, MIRABELLA is a major topic of conversation. It's also a secret topic!

"No-one but us six is to be let in on this, agreed?"

"AGREED!"

"WAT and HALF-ANDREUS?"

"Just call me HALF-WAT, I don't like the name ANDREUS!"

"Okay! Top secret, Okay? Nobody, not NOBODY! Okay?"

"I said Okay! Didn't I?"

"Alright! Here's the problem. The way a bomb explodes, is as follows. When it impacts, a pin, that's held back by a spring, hits a primer. The primer is pretty much like the primer of a rifle bullet or your "105 Howitzer." When hit, it spews a flame that ignites the dynamite, or whatever is in that bomb, and KABOOM!, the bomb goes off! Jan, Boer, Henkie, do you remember what the Germans called that yellow stuff inside that bomb that was split open? That stuff that looked like sand?"

"NO!" "NO!" "I don't either, but it's not dynamite. Whatever it is, is not important! It burns slowly when it's loose, like gunpowder or "macaroni," but it gives one hell of a blast, when it's enclosed and compacted! Now that we know all that, what are we gonna do with it, short of hitting it with a sledge hammer?"

Jan speaks first. "Can we build a "RUBE GOLDBERG?"

"What's a "RUBE GOLDBERG?"

"I don't know why they call it that, but you've seen in cartoons, how a ball rolls, hits a plate that turns a knob that releases water, that fills a cup and tips a scale that makes contact with and on and on and on!

In other words, some contraption, that hits the detonator after we activate it from a safe distance!"

"That sounds great! Especially that part about "safe distance!" "WAT" is not the most courageous of men.

"Jan, you may have something there and it may not be as complicated as it sounds. Picture this; we put MIRABELLA on its end, supported by lumber, so she won't budge."

"MIRABELLA was a MAN, not a "SHE!" Henkie objects.

"Oh, shit! I insulted MIRABELLA! My apologies!! Sorry, Henk! Back to business! Above it we suspend…Excuse me!…above "HIM," we suspend a big piece of rock, concrete or metal, a long rope releases it and "KABOOM!" we got it!"

"Who's going to put that thing on it's end! NOT ME!"

"First say; "I'M SORRY!" That THING is not "IT," it's MIRABELLA! Now say you're sorry to Henkie!"

They're enjoying this. They're sitting in a circle in the grass of Dr. Glass' huge backyard. He has a beautifully sculptured lawn and nobody can come close enough to hear them, without being seen.

The June sun is nice and warm today and if it weren't for this important "business meeting," they'd all be at the swimming pool by now! Summers are short in Holland and they wouldn't want to miss a day of it, except for something important and THIS IS IMPORTANT!

"I'm sorry, Henk!"

"That's Okay! Just don't let me hear that anymore!" What a bunch of clowns!

"I'm not worried about putting that bo….sorry, MIRABELLA on end, but I'm wondering who's gonna put that rock on the trapdoor, hoping it will hold long enough to get away!" Jan has a point. A big sigh escapes from most chests.

"Is there any other way to explode it? Like fire?"

"Boer, sometimes I think you're brilliant, but it's "HE" or "HIM," not "IT!" Say "SORRY, HENKIE!"

"I'M SORRY, but remember that ammo train that was burning? The heat actually fired those bullets all around, 'member? The first time we saw it? "Member how far we stayed away because bullets were whizzing right over our heads?"

"Good point, good point! Question, though. Did the heat make the primers blow to explode the powder or did the HEAT explode the powder?"

"Huh?" "Huh?"

"What do you think, Jan?"

"I don't know. We've seen shells with the primers blown out, but whether that primer exploded before being ejected was impossible to tell!"

"Damn, another dead end!"

"Why don't we try one and find out?"

"Try what?"

"Try to heat a primer and see what happens."

"My God, Boer, you ARE brilliant! The question is; where do we try this and what burns hot enough to set it off? What do we have that burns real hot?"

"Our macaroni?"

"When that burns, it burns real fast and it doesn't burn real hot. Just a yellow flame!"

"Doesn't all fire have a yellow flame?" "WAT" wants to know.

"Hell, no! Just look at your gas stove. When it burns blue or white, stick your finger in it. It will be cooked in a fraction of a second. Stick that same finger in the flame of a match and nothing much happens unless you just hold it there! Boer, strike a match!"

Paul dutifully strikes a match, Frits wets his fingers and squashes the flame. Holding up his thumb and finger, he says; "You don't do that with a gas flame and certainly not with a welding torch! We have to find something that burns hot and slow and we have to find it soon! Jan, do you remember how that sand-like stuff burned out of that bomb?"

"It burned for a long time, I remember. That German soldier just lit it with a match and it burned and melted at the same time. Kinda brown, syrup like, like when you melt sugar to make caramel pudding, but the brown melted stuff also kept burning with a short hot flame."

"Would you be able to find that bomb again?"

"No sweat!"

"Alright, you clowns, we're going to run a test! We need an empty shell, primer intact. Got that, Boer?"

Paul nods; "Got it!"

"Need "BRIZANT." That's it, Jan, that's what they called it; "BREE-ZAND," "BRIEZANT," BRIZANT BOMB, right?"

"Yep, that's what they called it; The British were dropping "BREE-ZANT" bombs!"

"Okay, we need some BRISANT" and some macaroni and we're ready to test! Are you gentlemen ready?"

"When can we see the b...MIRABELLA?"

"All in due time! Boer, run in and get some shells, please?" Paul is up and gone!

"You keep a selection of that stuff in the house?" "WAT and "HALF-WAT" are astonished!

"Where would you keep it? In your pig-pen?" They laugh along with the guys, even though they're the brunt of the joke again. "HALF-WAT" continues; "I sometimes can't believe you guys! Like you live in a different world!"

"We do, pal, we do! We don't meet many kids our age in the world we move in!"

"I believe you! You guys are something!"

"Let me get some macaroni." Frits jogs off to the shed and reappears at the same time as Paul with his shells.

"Off to find a busted bomb!"

All has gone well, except the bomb has been moved! Not a trace! There's some discussion, that they may be at the wrong spot, but no matter how they re-analyze the position and re-trace their steps, the bomb is not to be found.

"HOT-DANG!" "Back to the drawing board!"

They stroll by the HOUTLADING and show off MIRABELLA to the young boys, who haven't seen HIM yet. They do some measuring and pacing and survey the whole general area. Standing on top of the highest woodpile, they're nearly level with the tops of the boxcars and have a perfect view of the surrounding. They agree, that when MIRABELLA blows, he'll just blast away some lumberstacks and all the shrapnel will probably be embedded in the lumber. A fair amount of lumber above the bomb will also keep shrapnel from flying way up and hurt somebody on the way down.

The feelings are mixed as they meander home. Their MIRABELLA project is as exciting a project as they've ever been involved with, but there's little hope they can blow it safely. "SAFELY" is the key word. Stories about people getting hurt are plentiful and appear in the paper nearly every day. Most of the country has been a battlefield, ammo and war materials are strewn everywhere and a lot of stupid people don't handle that stuff with caution and blow their limbs off or even kill themselves.

No decisions are reached and when they near their respective homes, they part with a "SEE YA IN CHURCH!" "TJU!"

Somewhere between "GLORIA TIBI DOMINUM" and "CREDO IN UNUM DEUM," it hits him!

Like a flash, Frits has the solution. He's been reading "SAINT EUSTACE" in church. The book about St. Eustace is about the same size as the average "MISSAL" and to his fellow churchgoers it might appear to be a French prayer book. He can't read all of it, but between seven years of Latin mass and his French classes in school, he can figure out a whole lot of it. On the cover of the book, it shows a big stag with a burning Cross between his antlers and the title; SAINT EUSTACE, is embossed on it in gold. It looks real religious, it's educational, it's interesting and it makes HIGH MASS go a lot faster. Even the sermons don't bother him anymore. He simply doesn't hear them.

So, as he's reading about the glowing cross between the antlers, it reminds him of one of the "BARON VON MÜNCHHAUSEN" stories, where the dapper Baron ran out of bullets and shot a stag with a cherry pit. Years later he came upon the same deer with a cherry tree growing out of his head! He chuckles as he thinks about the comparisons and the differences. Both stags, but one with a blooming tree and the other with a glowing cross! GLOWING? AGLOW? GLOWING AS IN FLARES? FLARES? THAT'S IT!

Like flares that glowed in the night on May 5th, Like 24 flares, still sitting in the attic!

He can't wait for Mass to end, but while he's sitting it out, he formulates the whole procedure in his mind.

All it will take is a test this afternoon and they'll be ready! SAINT EUSTACE! YOU'RE A GENIUS!

Forced to wait out the rest of the service he reflects on the changes since last year. Last year, when he was confirmed, he wanted to become a Priest, a Missionary, die for God in some forsaken wilderness while saving souls. Now he's sure that that is NOT his calling! Not since he discovered what girls are all about. No celibacy for him! Mercifully, church lets out! FINALLY!

Outside the church, while parishioners gather in their Sunday best, Frits reveals his ideas to his buddies, but although they're very enthused, none of them can make it that afternoon, because of other family commitments. As it turns out, the Forrers have family ideas too and along with the Glass', they head out to the swimming pool. Afterwards to BEKKENDELLE for ice cream and sodas as in the old days. They haven't done this for years as a family and it proves to be most enjoyable.

The water in "the SLINGE," the creek, looks pitch black, the rhododendrons on the castle grounds and along the creek are in full bloom and the little rowboats disappear under the long green arms of the weeping willows. The watermill turns slowly and the whole world seems at peace.

"DEGAS" could have sat there for days and painted hundreds of canvasses of beautiful scenery and happy people. Here it seems that the word PEACE finally has gotten some meaning. It's just like before the war, peaceful people enjoying themselves in a peaceful setting, knowing that "peace" is now really theirs. It's a great afternoon in Winterswijk!

On Wednesday afternoon, they face a new problem; How to get the "stuff" out of the flare round?

Any metal on metal contact might create a spark and that might set off the whole content of the shell. They remember the flash-fiery intensity of the flares as they shot them up on "Surrender day." They can just about imagine how hot it will burn.

A common corkscrew and some spit solve the problem. The shell is made of black painted aluminum, not brass. It does not have a bullet sticking out of the shell, like a rifle bullet, but the top rim is crimped like a shotgun shell. The crimped edges hold down an aluminum top plate, but they have no way of knowing, how thick or how thin it is. All the guys hide behind the trees, as Frits will perform the operation. He spits on the top plate in order to keep sparks from flying and inserts the corkscrew. A little pressure, a little turning, a little more spit and some more of the same. Henkies knife is the only one with a corkscrew and thank God, it's a good one! It's sharp! The point penetrates, Frits twists some more and up it comes. The thin aluminum top plate, a cardboard plate and some cotton. That was simple. Inside the shell is a brilliant white substance. Frits cleans the corkscrew, folds it away and unfolds the knife blade. He fishes out a pinch of the white stuff and carefully puts it on top of the aluminum top plate. He moves the shell behind a tree, out of the way, picks up a piece of "macaroni" and lays the end of it in the white stuff. He lights the macaroni and jumps back. The macaroni burns its neat white flame like a slow burning fuse and in twenty seconds it reaches the white little heap and immediately "PFFFFT," a brilliant white flash appears and dies. The white was intensely white with a brightness that nearly hurts his eyes.

"That'll work!" says Frits, "Now test number two!"

He clears some leaves, creating a small bare spot of dirt and shakes out about half the content of the flare's "stuff,"

"We need timing, everybody count! Timing for the macaroni and timing for the "stuff!"

None of them have watches, but all of them can count. He puts a stick of "macaroni" in the white "stuff," lights it and steps back, no need to jump this time. Result; the flame crawls along the macaroni, hits the "stuff" and a 4-inch intensely white flame shoots up creating considerable white smoke.

"Timing, please! Jan?"

"Twenty-one for the fuse, four minutes for the stuff!"

"Henkie?"

"Twenty-two for the macaroni, two hundred for the flare!"

"WAT"?

"I forgot to count! I started to and then I got so interested in…"

"HALF-WAT?" Frits interrupts.

"Twenty and then when the flame started, I closed my eyes and…."

"Boer?"

"Twenty and two hundred and four!"

"Good going! Did you see how it melts while it's burning, just like that "BRIZANT" or whatever that was!"

"What do think? Will it work?"

"I thinks so! I guess so!"

"Is 4 minutes long enough? It looks plenty hot!" All sorts of opinions are uttered, most of them positive.

"Good. Let's try one more thing."

With the "priem" of Henkie's knife, he creates a thin hole in the dirt and fills it with the remaining "Stuff," just showing a little white on top, so it will light

"Timing, gentlemen!" He lights a match, "GO!"

This time, when it ignites, it has a narrow flame that shoots up about 6 inches and dwindles to two inches before it's burned out.

"Time, gentlemen! Jan?"

"21 and 11 minutes, ten seconds!"

"Paul?"

"20 and six hundred and four!"

"Henk?"

"20 and six hundred and eleven!"

"Any others?"

"23 and five hundred ninety!" It's "WAT."

"I forget where I am or what I'm supposed to do!" HALF-WAT adds sheepishly.

"That's Okay!" Frits feels benevolent. "Conclusions, gentlemen! Jan?"

"If it's in a narrow, compacted area, it burns longer and higher, so you might have to dig a hole underneath the "slagpin!" But what if there's concrete or asphalt underneath it?"

"Other suggestions?"

"Could you just put the whole shell underneath it after you screw the top out and then light it somehow?"

"Do you think that 10 minutes is enough to heat it?"

"I think it will work!"

The opinions keep pouring in. The surface below the bomb remains a sore point. Nobody can state with any kind of certainty, how high the detonator is above the surface and what the surface consists of.

"Frits spreads his hands to imitate the circumference of the bomb and adds; "If this the size of MIRABELLA, then the detonator would be about 3 to 4 inches above the ground and the way the flame burns down to barely an inch, the heat might be insufficient!"

"Why don't we bring a can of dirt with the stuff in a hole in the middle and then we can adjust it to any height we want!"

They look at Paul in amazement.

"Boer, your Pap may call you; "STOMME BOER," but I swear, you have a touch of genius! Do you guys understand what he's saying?"

"It's so simple, it's sheer genius!"

"We take a coffee can, fill it with dirt, put the stuff, we gotta find a name for that "STUFF," in the middle, I make two holes under the rim to hold the macaroni in place and make sure it's covered by the stuff.

Then I tape five or six pieces of macaroni together and we're set. That will give me a minute and a half to run for shelter! BRILLIANT, BRIL-LIANT! We can put the top of the stuff just one inch under the pin, so we can expose the pin to the flame throughout the burn and it can't miss! Right?"

"BUT WE HAVEN'T TRIED YET IF THE HEAT WILL BLOW THE PRIMER!" Paultje chimes in.

"Damn, that's right! Damn, damn damn! Now you bring it up! Damn! I was so impressed with my own brilliance, I forgot all about that primer. We could have done it all at the same time, damnit!"

"We can still do it, can't we?" Jan makes a point.

"Waste another round?"

"Why not?"

"You're right! Why not? Henkie, your corkscrew again!" More spit! It works again!

This time he digs a nice round hole about the size of the flare, compacts the white substance, leaving about a thumbnails thickness above the ground. Two empty rifle shells and the empty flare shell are put on top of the little white heap, the primers over the center. Another macaroni is inserted, "HIDE YOURSELVES!... TIMING!..." He lights it and jumps behind a tree. After two minutes, one primer pops, throwing the shell a few feet from the flame, a few more seconds and there goes number two and twenty long, long seconds later, the flare shell pops! "Boy, I thought that flare was never gonna pop!"

They're coming out from behind the trees and shake hands all around. Success is all theirs!

The flame continues to burn above ground for a total of 14 minutes and a few more minutes inside the hole before it dies.

"We've got it, by Jove, we've got it! Or whatever Sherlock Holmes would have said at a time like this!"

"What time Saturday do we do it?"

"After work. After there are no more lumber or railroad people at work!"

"Makes sense, so Saturday after supper. Where shall we meet?"

Another successful business meeting concluded! Six in attendance, ages ten to fourteen!

Saturday night is becoming a typical weekend night in town. People have finished their 48-hour workweek, vendors are taking down their stalls and folks fill the lone movie house that has re-opened.

Sidewalk cafés are doing a crisp business and lovers are strolling arm in arm in the parks. Folks put their chairs in front of their houses and enjoy the warm evening weather. Swallows are sailing high in the sky, gliding and diving, adding to the summer scenery. It's a beautiful night in June. The air is heavy with the fragrance of thousands of flowers and at this latitude, about the same as LABRADOR in Canada, the sun sets very late this time of year. Life's routine is settling down to a pre-war kind of pace, full of happiness and contentment.

At the railroad yards, six pair of hands are busy as a bunch of bees. Boards of different sizes are placed above MIRABELLA, providing a protective roof of sorts. Frits has already put a pre-fabricated "gizmo" under the tip of the bomb and laid down a long, taped-together, string of macaronis, ending in an alley, formed by stacks of lumber.

The "gizmo" is a coffee can filled with dirt, showing a little white lump, the size of a sugar cube in the middle. A green tube, the size of a pencil, lays across the white heap coming out of and going into two little holes under the rim of the can. Taped to the green tube on the top are six more of them, forming a string of about 5 feet.

"Boards all in place? Scram!, No, No, Wait! I'll light it in five minutes. It'll take a minute and a half to ignite the stuff. The stuff will burn for fourteen minutes, so find a good spot to hide and don't move for twenty minutes, Okay? And don't come out for thirty minutes in case she...Sorry, "HE" won't blow! Okay? SCRAM!!.

Five of them take off as if the devil is chasing them.

Frits counts to three hundred, lights the fuse and is off like an arrow! Over lumber, across tracks, more tracks and stops in between two railroad cars, counting all the time 110 seconds gone! The "stuff" should be burning its brilliant hot white flame... Two minutes... Two and a half... nearly... KABOOM!

AN UNBELIEVABLE BLAST! WOOD FLIES EVERYWHERE! THE RAILROAD CAR ROCKS SO HARD THAT FRITS THINKS IT'S GONNA FALL OVER ON TOP OF HIM! HIS EARS ARE NUMB FROM THE CONCUSSION AND HE DIVES UNDERNEATH THE CAR BEHIND HIM IN ORDER NOT TO GET HIT BY FALLING LUMBER THAT'S RAINING DOWN ALL AROUND HIM.

In the distance he hears the tinkling of breaking glass. "WOW!" The deluge lasts only a few seconds and he dashes between two rows of cars to a warehouse along the tracks. His heart is going a hundred miles an hour. He sits in an alcove formed by three walls and is trying to catch his breath! "THAT WAS SOOOO LOUD!" He's never heard an explosion like that before, not that LOUD! "It was only a 500 pounder, I'm sure! I'M SURE!

Railroad yard with lumber

Was it a different type? Being above ground, in the open, would that cause more of a concussion? OH, GOD! He works his jaws to un-pop his ears. The buzzing won't stop! He holds his nose and blows up his cheeks as hard as he can! No good!

"I can't understand it, I've never seen or heard a bomb, that could rock a freightcar. Oh, God, I wonder how the boys are? Well, they had 5 minutes more than I did; they should be miles from here. They've got to be alright!"

He hears running footsteps, then voices, first some, then more.

"As expected!" he says to himself. After some of the people have passed him, he jumps from his hiding place and starts running in the same direction of the other runners, skipping across the tracks until he's on the cobblestone road with the other curiosity seekers, moving toward the blast. They're being halted. "No further!" The police are already on hand. "Danger of additional blasts! Go home!"

"No Lady!"

"Sir?"

"No Lady!" The cop has his hands full. "Make room for the truck!, BACK, BACK, LET 'EM THROUGH!" He's shouting at the top of his lungs.

An Army truck rolls through the crowd and a few minutes later; a military ambulance. Frits' heart stops.

"An ambulance? My boys hurt?"

"What happened?" Frits asks a gentleman, standing next to him in the crowd.

"A timebomb went off. It must have been a big one. it blew windows all the way in the SPOORSTRAAT. Damn shame. Some people had just gotten new windows. It must at least have been a 10,000 pound bomb. It was a big one. There may be more around yet."

It seems like a prophecy; Military police join in with the regular cops in moving back the crowd from the lumberyard and Frits reluctantly moves with them. About a hundred people keep milling around and considering that this is only one of the many accesses to the railroad yards, there may be as many as a thousand people around the blast area.

"Oh, God, Oh, God!" Frits keeps saying to himself, "I had no idea that it would give such a blast. Oh, God!"

Just then, two policemen in their sharp black uniforms appear from the direction of the blast, herding five boys between them! It's nearly comical! The five of them, the tallest one twice as tall as the shortest one and all of them looking young enough to be in bed by now!

AND HARMLESS! My, do they look harmless! Their HALOS a little askew, maybe, but soooo innocent looking. Their eyes downcast, you could just hug 'em!

Frits stands amongst the crowd, watching them with mixed emotions. Boy, talk about mixed emotions!

One part of him wants to run in there and shout; "LET'EM GO! I'M THE ONE THAT DID IT!" and the other part says; "DUMB SUCKERS, HOW DID YOU GET CAUGHT?"

Just as they pass, Paul looks straight up at Frits and Frits puts his fingers to his lips, as to say; "SHSHSHSHSH!" Paul nods imperceptibly and Frits even thinks that he smiled briefly. "THAT LITTLE DEVIL!"

The others are definitely NOT smiling! Henkie, maybe, but he has a laughing face anyway. Jan looks like LOUIS XVI on the way to the guillotine, HALF-WAT is actually crying and WAT looks like he may join him any minute.

"I know what went wrong," Frits says to himself, "they panicked, that's what! That BOOM was louder than they expected and it scared the crap out of them and they started running AWAY FROM THE SCENE! NO self-respecting streetbum runs AWAY from the action, they run TOWARD it! Of course it aroused the suspicion of some "on the ball" policeman, who grabbed them and said; "You'd better come to the stationhouse." The puzzling thing is; "How did they get to grab all five of them?"

"Jan, Henk and Paul would be smart enough to split, not run as a group? Can't figure that one."

"Of course, now they may implicate me and the cops may send their COWARDS to the front door to round me up." What to do? Frits figures; "I'd better go home and cover Paultje's butt, because heaven knows how long they're gonna keep them."

The music reaches his ears, before his feet reach the backyard. He stops, listens carefully with his pounding ears and realizes; "Darn, that's right. There's a concert in the park, right behind the house!

Better check it out.!" He climbs the garden wall and from the top, he can see the band as well as keep an eye on the alley, in case Paul comes home.

After a half-hour, it's getting dark and he's heard enough of the music to intelligently comment on it, in case the folks have any questions.

The moment he walks in, the first question is; "Where's Paultje?"

"Oh, he's not here yet?" This way he's not lying or denying anything, just answering a question with a question.

"There's a concert out back, that I've been listening to (Truth, no?), let's see if I can find him out there."

"All truths!" he thinks as he disappears again out of the backdoor, back to the music. He sits in the same spot on the wall, takes in the music and keeps an eye on the alley at the same time. Twenty minutes later, he's back in; "Boer here yet?"

"NO!"

"I didn't see him, but there are a lot of people out there." (All true)

The folks are listening to a comedy show and laughing heartily with the radio audience.

"I wouldn't worry about the Boer, he can take care of himself!" He assures them and settles down to enjoy the comedy as well.

At 10:30, Paul walks in. Before anyone can say a word, Frits says; "Hi, Boer, did you enjoy the concert?" With his back to Mam and Pap, he winks as he's talking.

"It's not really my kind of music, not really!" The kid is smart! "I'm tired, though. Goodnight Mama, Goodnight Pappa, Welterusten!"

"I'm going up too! Welterusten!"

The folks are so wrapped up in their show, they don't even get suspicious about their little darlings going to bed like good little lambs.

"What happened? What did they do to you? What did you tell 'em? What happened?" Frits has been on pins and needles so long, the questions are just exploding from his mouth!

Paultje tries to get a word in edgewise and finally just raises his hand and says; "You gotta be there in the morning!"

"What? I what? I have to be there in the morning? What time? What for? What did you tell 'em?"

Paul throws his eyes toward the heavens and being that he's already undressed, crawls in bed as if to say;

"Why don't you talk to yourself?"

Frits gets the hint. "I'll shut up. Go!"

Paul starts to tell the tale with few interruptions.

When the BOOM was much louder than anybody anticipated, when the debris was flying all over the place and the shockwaves were busting windows, they knew they had to get out. FAST! Jan, Henk and Paul were together behind a switching building and "WAT and HALF-WAT" were even further away at the railroad station. They couldn't see the "WATS" and didn't know what they were doing, until they were re-united by various policemen. What he did know was that the three of them split, Paul going one way and Jan and Henkie the other. Paul had to cross just six sets of tracks and he would have safely been at the loading platform of the station. He figured, he could mingle with some other people and get lost, but a railroad official spotted him running and caught him. "What happened out there, young man?"

Well, that was the end of Paultje, because the man literally collared him and told him; "I think you should tell your story to the police!" Paul had told him that he thought they were being bombed and that he was running for shelter! Likely story! By coincidence, the other two teams were caught about the same way, by police and security people. The "WATS" immediately spilled that they were guilty, what they had done and that "FRITS" really was the one, who did it. At the station, the police let Paultje do most of the talking and being that he was the smallest of the bunch, they believed him. The "WATS" were too eager to blame someone else, so the police assumed that they were the real ringleaders and ordered Paultje to deliver a message to Frits, to come in in the morning and make a statement. The cops had written down everything that was said on long sheets of paper, so they knew all the facts, including that the "WAT" guys found the bomb and showed it to us instead of reporting it to the police!

Frits bursts into uproarious laughter; "So the "WATS" are getting the blame and we are just innocent victims? That's funny! Hahahaha! What did Jan and Henkie say?"

"Oh, they just nodded and said; "That's right!" to whatever I was saying!"

"They're smart. They didn't say much, did they?"

"No, hardly anything!"

"Good for them. What did you tell 'em we blew it up with?"

"I told them with gun powder from the blown-up ammo train, remember? And they remembered and didn't ask much more about that."

"They didn't want any details how exactly we fused it and blew it?"

"No, they were much more interested in how they found the bomb, how it was laying there, why it hadn't exploded, what kind of bomb it was and stuff like that."

"What did you say?"

"I said nothing. The "WATS" started to do all the talking about all the things you had told them, like the size, it being American and why it didn't explode. They acted like it was their first-hand knowledge. I didn't mind, 'cause the more they were bragging, the more guilty they seemed and the less thought was given to you!"

"BROTHER BOER, I must tell you, sometimes you're the smartest kid on the block. Okay, it's late. Tomorrow morning, you repeat to me, best you can, everything that was said. Then, at 9 o'clock, I'll report to the police and confirm everything and maybe we'll get off shot-free! Those dumb "WAT" asses! Remind me not to hang out with them anymore. Ratting on me! Dumb asses!"

Let's get some sleep. Hey, by the way, THANKS BOER! Welterusten!"

At 9am sharp, in his gray confirmation suit, HALO included, shoes shined, white shirt and tie, our little Angel reports to the police station.

They ask questions, smile believingly when he says; "I didn't think that it was going to be that much of an explosion!"

"What did you think?"

"I heard thousand of bombs dropped by the "JABO'S," but they weren't that loud and this was supposed to be a small bomb from a fighter." (He didn't mention that HE was the one who had supposed that.)

"Well, maybe it was bigger than you thought. Maybe it was because it exploded ABOVE ground, rather than IN the ground, like most bombs do, but what does this tell you?"

"To report bombs and not fool with them, like we just reported two German graves that we found and we didn't touch the helmets or the rifles or nothing and we measured the distance from the road and from the bridge, gave it to Mr. Kamphuis and he reported it to the grave people. We didn't touch a thing."

The two cops exchange glances and continue; "That's exactly what we want everybody to do, you included, to report it to the proper authorities."

The other cop starts in; "Do you know, you could have gotten yourself killed?"

"KKKKKKILLEDD? YYYESS?"

"Do you know, you could have killed your friends and other people?"

"MMY FFRIENDS? MMMY BBBROTHER?"

"YES!"

"I'll report things for sure!" He seems close to tears.

"Promise?"

"PROMISE!"

"Go home! We'll hold you to that promise!"

"Tju!"

"Tju!"

Outside the station house, he sighs a sigh of relief; "Boy, did I luck out. These cops knew nothing about the school "C" incident. They think I'm a harmless little boy, who's scared shitless! That's good, that how they should think of me."

"One thing is for sure; NO MORE BOMB DETONATIONS! THAT WAS TOO BIG A "BOOM."

MUCH TOO BIG!!!

The newspapers have articles about a "HUGE" bomb blast, but other than hints at a "time bomb" and some damage reports, not many details were available at presstime. After HIGH MASS, the Forrer and Kamphuis boys wait till they're out of range of everybody's ears and eyes and shake hands.

"We've lucked out, so far and let's hope that nobody smartens up. We've got to find the "WATS" and tell 'em to shut up to anybody and everybody. They're liable to start bragging about their "heroics" and get our little asses in trouble."

"They weren't in early Mass either. Maybe they went at 8:30. Do you know, where they live?"

Jan answers; "Approximately, not exactly. I've never been to their house."

"Let's walk by there. We have time before dinner, maybe we'll find 'em."

As they're walking, they review last night's events and the more they reminisce, the more they laugh.

"You should have seen Henkie's face when he was halfway up the fence and that voice said; "HALT!"

He looked like he wet his pants!"

"You didn't look too heroic either, big Brother! You should have seen his face when we joined up with the other three. You see, as they marched us back across those damn tracks, we thought we were the only ones that got caught. Then, all of the sudden there is Boer, who looked like he dropped a load in his pants, one of the "WATS" crying crocodile tears and the other looking like he was gonna join him any minute. It was sooo comical, I thought Jan was gonna burst out laughing and I just bit my tongue and stared at my shoes, otherwise I would have roared all over the place! That was one of the stupidest sights I've ever seen."

"And I kept praying;" Jan follows Henkie, "Please, please, please, let's not see anyone we know. I would have died!"

"Is that why you looked so downcast?" Frits asks.

"You saw us?"

"Sure did. I stood with the spectators watching five arch-criminals being brought to justice! Hahahaha!

Paul winked at me, didn't you Boer?"

"Ya, and he went SHSHSHSH!" He demonstrates with his finger on his lips.

"You bastard! You lousy bastard! You actually stood there and laughed as we were marched by there like prisoners"

"Hahahahahahaha! I sure did! Now, it's funny. Last night it wasn't. Really!"

"Ya, I believe that. You probably thought it was hilarious!"

"No, no, really! See, I was hoping all along that you guys were Okay and that nobody caught you, because that would have been the simplest, right? Nobody would have known, right?"

"How come you didn't get caught?"

"Because I'm not as dumb as you clowns, hahahahaha!"

"NO, seriously?"

"I just ran a little way after the "BOOM." It scared the shit out of me at first. I thought it was going to drop a freight car on me. Anyway, I stopped, hid and waited for other people to run by me and then I ran with them to the scene of the crime!"

"Hahahahaha!" Now they all join in the laughter. "It's really funny, when you think of it!"

Just then, they spot the "WATS," loading an old truck. They're moving out! The boys walk up to the house and are about to ask something like' "What are you doing?" or ; "Where are you going?," when a good-looking blonde woman, very blonde woman with a lot of make-up and beautiful teeth, comes out of the house, takes one look at the foursome, puts down the chair she was carrying and screams; "YOU HAVE SOME DAMN NERVE COMING HERE AFTER WHAT YOU'VE DONE TO MY BOYS AND IF MY HUSBAND WAS HERE, HE WOULD BEAT THE LIVING CRAP OUTTA YOU RIGHT HERE! WE'RE BLOWING THIS CRUMMY

TOWN AND I DON'T EVER WANNA SEE IT ANYMORE! NEVER! I NEVER WANNA SEE YOU PEOPLE ANYMORE AND IF YOU DON'T SCRAM REAL FAST, I'LL HIT YOU RIGHT OVER THE HEAD WITH THIS CHAIR AND....AND..." she actually picks up the chair, but the boys are off! All the way down the street and around the corner.

"WOW!" "What possessed her?"

"What do you suppose those creeps told her?"

"And where did she get a truck?"

"Fellas, fellas, the important thing is; we don't care how much they talk in SCHEVENINGEN, at least they wont talk in WINTERSWIJK!"

"Let's go eat! We have steak, REAL STEAK!"

Things are getting back to normal, more and more. (Darn it) Classes continue every day and the "Old Schoolhouse" is being remodeled into an "Old Schoolhouse" again.

Pretty soon, everything will be back to normal. That could prove to be very boring. The British occupation forces are leaving, little by little and the homework starts piling up, more and more. Frits is humming to himself; *"My heart is sad and lonely. I long for you, for you dear only. Why haven't you seen it? I'm all for you, BODY AND SOUL!"* Lovely song, great singer...ELLA..somebody. It's lovely out and it's Wednesday, no school this afternoon. A French 300-word theme to write, a chapter of algebra, 100 German idioms, finish reading; EMIL, DER LAUSCHBUB, learn JOOST VAN DER VONDEL, just study, study, study!

Good God, he may not have time for anything else. He keeps on humming though; *"I spend my days in longing, it's for you, for you I'm longing, Lalalalalala"* All the homework in the world is not going to spoil his good mood. The Catholic School Board has decided to continue school through August and then consider that a WHOLE school year, although they've barely been on the benches for FOUR months.

AND.... They'll get a weeks break NOW! First classmen that is! And one more in September. They're going to stagger the weeks off, class by class. "Why?" He doesn't know and he couldn't care less.

Next week he's off and still, in September he'll become a second year man!

First things first! "Talk to Pappa!" As he saunters through the back door, he pecks at Mama's cheek, says "Hello" to Pappa, who's lost in his noon hour news and dumps his books on his third floor bed.

Don't ever disturb Pappa during the news. If he can't hear the news, he'll think that the world will come to an end.

Changed into his play clothes, he joins the rest at the dinner table and after "GRACE" said by Clasien, they dig in. Everyone is content and babbles away without interruptions from Pappa. He has mellowed a lot.

Just a year ago, nobody was allowed to say a word at the table, but maybe the lack of business pressures or the weight of the war being off his shoulders has slowly changed the atmosphere around the family table.

It has really gotten to be pleasant.

After the dishes are cleared, Frits is ready to hit his Dad with the big question. He times it right. Pappa is stretched out in his lazy chair, next to his bed in the veranda. He lights up a "cigarillo" and sighs a well-satisfied sigh.

"NOW!" "Pappa, I have a whole week off from school next week and.."

"You do?"

"Yes and one more in September, but that's our whole vacation for this year."

"Vacation? You just came off a whole years vacation...."

"But listen, Pap. I don't make the rules, I just obey them! The school says; "VACATION," I take vacation. I started to argue against it, but I'm learning to control my mouth, so I figured, I'll learn to live with it!"

"Hahahaha! Sure! I can just see you; "No, Sir, I'd rather come to school! Sure, I'll believe that any day! What are you leading up to?"

"You see, Pap, four of us, Jan Kamphuis, two other boys in my class and myself want to take a little trip next week and..."

"How little?" Pap interrupts.

"About eight days, 'cause that's all we got!"

"That's not what I mean, Frits and you know it. Whereto and how much will it cost?"

"To ROERMOND by bike and..."

"ROERMOND?"

"Pap, you never let me finish talking. Jan has an Uncle in ROERMOND. He hasn't seen him for years and he's his favorite Uncle and he's a POULIER and he wants to stay with him and I've never been in LIMBURG and the four of us can ride that in a day and..."

"And where are you going to get a bike?"

"Well, that's what I wanna talk with you about. You see, the bike that I gave you.."

"You want my new bike?" Herman is enjoying this. He loves to tease this boy!

"Well, that's what I need to talk with you about..."

"Where are you getting your legs stretched, so you can reach the pedals?"

"Aw, Pap, we can lower the saddle, that's no problem!" Now Frits is enjoying it. They're not arguing about the trip, just over the means of transportation. That means the trip is ON! "And we could put blocks on the pedals. Let's check it out!"

"Just one bloody minute!" Herman has picked up some English. "BLOODY" now spikes his sentences, "Let's hear from your Mama first!"

"Oh, Mam?" Frits is out of the room already and tackles his Mother in the kitchen, "Mama, next week, we're off from school and Jan and two others and me want to go to Limburg, to Roermond, to Jan's Uncle. I've never been there and it's Okay by Pappa, if it's Okay by you!"

"All the way to Roermond? Right after all the fighting out there? The roads are probably still very bad and with all those damaged vehicles and all the bombs and landmines? I don't know, I don't think it's a good idea."

"AW, Mama. We're not gonna throw bombs at one another and besides that, they've been liberated for a year already! There's probably not a sign of war anywhere any more!"

"Oh, I don't know, let's see what your Father says"

Father says; "I'm not worried about Frits, he can take care of himself. I'm worried about my bike!" He can't stop teasing. "Let's look at that bike!"

The saddle is lowered to its lowest point, blocks are put on the pedals and it's nearly perfect. Off for a test ride. His butt slides from left to right and back a little across the saddle, but all in all, it's not bad.

"He'll have blisters on his ass before he gets to DOETICHEM," Joop comments, "when are you ever gonna grow up?"

"I'm afraid, I'd be like you, so I'd rather stay short!" Frits snaps back.

Pappa soothes it all by saying; "When he gets to wear long pants, he'll shoot up. That's what happened to me!"

"Well," Joop again, looking at his Pa; " You're not too tall!" At 15, Joop is already taller than his Dad.

"Tall enough to beat your butt anytime I want to!"

"Oh, ya?" Joop jumps out of the way. "If you could only catch me!"

"What are you going to take with you?" Mama wants to know. "And what are you going to carry it in?"

"As little as possible and don't we have baggage bags for the bike somewhere?"

"Yes, but they're real old and nasty." Mama wants her son to look good.

"That's good enough for him!" Joop again. "That way he can't louse up much."

"You're just jealous, 'cause I'll be pedaling across the country side while you sit in your miserable classroom!"

"With my miserable girlfriends!"

"Whatever floats your boat!"

Papa cuts off the dialog between the two; "Come inside after you find those saddle bags, Frits"

"Ya Pappa!"

A few minutes later, Pap looks earnestly at his son; "My boy, I hope you realize, we have no money to send you on vacation and I cannot give you money or things, that I don't equally give to the others, you understand?"

"Ya, Pappa!"

"I just talked to your mother and I'm afraid that you're going to be the pauper amongst the four of you, because all the other boys will probably have a fair amount of money on them. The best we can do, is give you ten guilders for the whole trip and that's all! Do you still want to go?"

"Oh, Ya! I'm not worried. Jan's uncle is a POULIER and he should have plenty to eat at least!"

"Sure! You may have rabbit, chicken or duck all week, but that's not bad!"

"No, I can certainly live with that, but he also sells dove, partridge and pheasant! Have you thought of that?"

"True, true. You may live like a king. When were you guys thinking of leaving?"

"Right after school on Saturday, I would think, but I'll ask 'em tomorrow."

"And where will you sleep?"

"Sleep? At Jan's Uncle of course."

"Do you really believe, that if you leave here Saturday afternoon, you'll be there by Saturday night?"

"Why not?"

"Why not? Because of the distance, son. With the roads being as bad as they are, you won't average but 10 kilometers per hour and that means, you're going to run out of daylight!"

"Pap, we'll do better than twenty, I'm sure!"

"Yes, but you wont sit on your saddle for five hours straight. You'll eat, drink, pee, rest and walk around. You won't average twenty. No way!"

"We hadn't thought of that, but we can sleep at a farm, in a hayloft or something."

"Are you going to bring a blanket?"

"Oh, Pap!"

"Don't you "OH, Pap," me. Answer my questions and by the way, I'll bet you your ten guilders that the other fathers are asking the same questions!"

Pap's right! He's always right. It's aggravating! The other fathers had the same questions and objections.

An antiquated, six-year-old roadmap is dug up by someone and now they're confident, that they wont get lost, because most of those roads have been traveled for two thousand years.

The consensus is that indeed, they may have to sleep somewhere on the way down, or... leave early Sunday morning.

"NO WAY!" That's unanimous.

"You know what? We can stop for lunch in ARNHEM, at my Tante's place. Then we can get past NIJMEGEN before dark and we'll look to sleep somewhere before GRAVE or even in the tip of LIMBURG. The next day should be a snap. What do you say?"

"Sounds good!" all around. "Let's clear it with the old folks and we'll be all set!"

Talking Mama out of "taking good clothes" is harder than talking her into the trip, but finally on Saturday at one o'clock, they're off, two by two!

Clean clothes, shoes and socks, to Frits it's all too fancy, but it's thrilling to just be on the way!

The bicycle paths are generally pretty good, with just some bumpy patches where repairs have recently been made.

A lot of fighting, sometimes intense fighting has taken place along the roads that they're traveling and the repairmen, Russian and Polish P.O.W.'s, didn't have much engineering experience.

Chatting away, they quickly pass AALTEN and are heading for DOETICHEM. Frits is riding next to Bert, a nephew of the school principal, with whom he's staying while attending school. He's from THE HAGUE and in spite of his phony sounding accent, he's all right, Frits decides. As a matter of fact, he's a little shy and rather handsome. His hair is pitch black and his black eyes have a certain softness to them. If he were a girl, he would be pretty.

In front of them, Jan and Piet lead the way. Piet is a big, blondish guy, who lives on the far side of town and with whom Frits has been going to school since kindergarten. He's also kinda shy and studious. Very good reasons why Frits hasn't associated with him very much. He was also in the choir with him in the old days and Frits was very surprised when his name was mentioned as a traveling companion. He just never seemed to be the adventurous type.

It's strange how they suddenly got thrown together, when Jan said in geography class; "I have an Uncle there! It's a neat little town and we should get on a bike and go see him sometime!"

Well, sometime is NOW!. The weather is co-operating, nice and warm and hardly any wind.

This part of Holland is pretty farm country, flat as a board. Rich dark soil makes for rich green pastures and yellow grain fields. Just about all of the roads are tree lined and the boys pedal in the shade, most of the time, making the whole experience very pleasant.

Past DOETICHEM, the road gets worse. There's also considerable damage to the houses along the way. Some terrible fighting must have been going on around here and it gets worse as they approach ZEVENAAR. Here, hardly a house remained intact. The Boys stop for ice cream on the far side of town, (Frits has just water, "real thirsty," he says.) and they learn that during the "MARKET-GARDEN" maneuver, the Germans shipped dozens of tanks and trucks across the Rhine, near here at PANNERDAM on improvised ferries. Those were the tanks that prevented the Allied forces from joining up with the British in ARNHEM and in doing so, doomed the whole exercise. Had the MARKET-GARDEN plan worked, the war might have been over in '44 and a lot of lives and suffering could have been spared.

The fighter-bombers, the JABO's, had tried to stop the German efforts to move their Army across the river and in doing so, had clobbered the hell out of the town. Clean-up and construction crews are working even on Saturday afternoon, exposing many empty slabs, where houses used to be.

Half an hour further down the road, they come to a complete stop. They have to dismount and walk their bikes in a long line toward and across the pontoon bridge. Busses, long, long trailer-busses, trucks, cars, motorcycles and pedestrians cross the bridge at a snail's pace. Motor vehicle traffic moves in just one direction at a time.

Pedestrians, which includes handheld bikes, move on the narrow tracks on the side of the bridge. As they shuffle their way across, they can see the destroyed railroad and highway bridges. They're a mess. Spans dangle in the water, while float-born cranes work diligently to remove the wreckage. The surrounding areas look like a moonscape. Craters by the hundreds, all around them. They walk in silence, awed by the devastation they're watching. Apparently, part of the pontoon bridge can swing open for boat traffic and swings closed again for the road traffic. Fascinating! It takes them an hour to cross the bridge and now they begin the climb toward the VELUWE, the hilliest part of Holland. They really have to push the pedals now and they're working up a good sweat. The sign that points in the direction of AMSTERDAM gets them into heated arguments. They have to head SOUTH in order to get to ROERMOND, but Frits' aunt lives at the AMSTERDAMSE WEG 98 and that is in the opposite direction. They decide to let him lead the way and as they pass the beautiful park; SONS-BEEK, they detour long enough to pass underneath the beautiful waterfall, an experience the others never had. They arrive an hour behind schedule, but the BOLDERS are not surprised. They knew it would take a long time to get across the IJSEL on the pontoon bridge. Oom Gerrit had called the BOLDERS store, (private phones are still out) to let them know the foursome was coming and they had simply allowed an additional hour for their arrival. It works out all right. Oom Henk just walks in from work as the bikers pull up. He's a big, jovial, red-haired man, who smiles all the time. He and his Dad run a stove and hearth business, but Oom Henk has been working on the train station ever since the "liberation," taking down the wrecked structure with a welding torch. The first thing he does, produce chocolate bars and the first thing Tante Paula does, take away the chocolate bars from the boys and her own three children, till; "AFTER SUPPER!"

These are Frits' favorite relatives. They smile with their eyes at all times. The oldest girl, PAULINE, is about four years younger than the boys and looks just like her mother. Dimples in her cheeks from smiling so much. Jan, a year younger, looks just like his Dad, except he has blonde hair. Willy is a chubby little devil with a million white curls all over his head. During supper, their war experiences are exchanged and after hearing about the intense fighting and bombing that ARNHEM endured, WINTERSWIJK seems untouched in comparison!

Two hours behind schedule, they continue their trek to NIJMEGEN and now they get to see what real devastation means. House after house, store after store, building after building are nothing but ruins. Whole streets are nothing but debris. They pedal their way downhill into the center of town and when they arrive at the SINGEL, Frits lets out a gasp. That beautiful, wide, park-like avenue through town, where ROMANS, SAXONS, SPANISH and FRENCH troops once paraded, is one big disaster area. The MUSIS SACRUM, the beautiful concert hall is in shambles and the inner city simply DOES NOT EXIST ANYMORE! The heaps of bricks, concrete and wood along the road are as high as the houses used to be. The huge roof structure of the railroad station, where Oom Henk works, looks like dozens of giant matchsticks, crumbled by a huge, superhuman hand. In their wildest imagination, the boys had not been able to picture such an unbelievable scene. Totally bewildered, they cycle slowly through a town THAT WAS! It just isn't there anymore!

Close to the bridge that proved to be "A BRIDGE TOO FAR," they're lead to their right to the twin "BAILEY" bridges and from the bridge, they have a front line view of the once beautiful bridge, now in ruins. None of the boys seem to know, whether the Germans blew the bridge or whether the Allies bombed it. Just the same, the bridge is in smithereens. At the approaches to the once magnificent bridge, hardly a brick is still piled on top of the other and of the walls that are still standing in part, not a square inch is without pockmarks from bullets and shrapnel. Only newsreels of STALINGGRAD resemble the type of destruction the boys are witnessing here. The "one-way" flow on the BAILEY bridge would have allowed them to cycle across, but they're so in awe that they walk across in silence. They are having a first hand look at one of the most historic scenes of World War II. THREE times, this area has been under siege because of its strategic value. In May 1940, when the "BLITZKRIEG" was halted here, in September 1944, when the "war-ending," largest air-exercise the world had ever seen, MARKET-GARDEN, met it's doom here and again in April of '45, when the area was finally liberated from the "NAZI" monster.

It is indeed awesome!

Speechless and subdued, the boys climb on their bikes again and continue south on the dike that doubles as a highway. Just 8 miles from ARNHEM, they pass through he little town of ELST, where the German tanks throttled the Allied drive north. The little town, famous for it's jams and jellies, shows the heavy scars of that battle.

On this very dike, back in 1929, Pappa traveled back and forth from NIJMEGEN to ARNHEM, when he was courting Mama. It's the same dike, 16 miles long that kept the Allies from getting to that FINAL BRIDGE, back in '44. Holland and its dikes have been a source of agony for attacking forces through the ages. Napoleon lucked out. The winter was so cold, even the saltwater crossings were frozen, so he could march across. The dikes and the waters they help contain have always stymied other forces. Last, but not least, THE ALLIES!

In the distance, the boys can see the high span of the WAAL BRIDGE at NIJMEGEN, the one bridge that got spared. Involuntarily, they speed up a little and their spirits improve at the same time. There it is! THE ANCIENT CITY! NIJMEGEN!

NIJMEGEN, founded by the ROMANS in 100BC. The city gained its present prominence during the reign of CHARLEMAGNE in the latter part of the eighth century. The Emperor built his castle, "Het VALKENHOF" (FALCONCREST) on the southern banks of the river "WAAL." The "WAAL" bridge was gallantly fought over during the September '44 advance and fell into Allied hands without a scratch.

As the boys pass across the magnificent high structure, their spines tingle in awe of the 1200-year-old watchtower and the ruins of the old VALKENHOF chapel on the opposite bank. It looks as if the old structures are standing guard over the waters that flow all the way from Switzerland on their way to the North Sea.

After all they've heard and read about NIJMEGEN, they are still surprised at the magnificence of the view before them. Pappa used to live here when he was single, got married in nearby "BEEK" and Joop was born here, before Herman moved his young family to Belgium.

Many German, American, Canadian and British soldiers died here in their conquest for the bridge and here's where NAPOLEON stood, overlooking his latest addition to his Empire. The boys can nearly feel the presence of the historic figures that have passed and paused here!

They walk the paths of the park that was once the VALKENHOF and admire the heavy, thick walls and remaining arches of the old chapel. From their vantagepoint, they can see all the way to ELST and can nearly distinguish ARNHEM on the northern horizon. The view is magnificent and it's no wonder that so many people before them have stood there, admiring the same scene.

It's all so fascinating, that they forget all about time, until the park lights come on and darkness starts to creep up the hill. When they can't see the river below anymore, it finally sinks in; "It's dark and we haven't found a place to sleep yet!" Their plan was to be south of the town by dark and find a farm or a haystack to sleep in, but obviously, they ran out of time!

"We can sleep here somewhere!" Frits volunteers.

"Are we allowed?"

Frits thinks; "Damn novices!" but says; "Of course, we are allowed.! Did you see any signs; "NO SLEEPING!" "NO WALKING ON THE GRASS!" ? I didn't! Now if they had a sign; "NO DOGS ALLOWED!" we might have a problem if they found you sleeping with us, but WE"RE alright, 'cause there's no such sign!"

Bert smiles nervously, but the others laugh out loud and the question becomes; "What's the best spot?"

"Now already? Let's go into town and get some PATAT FRITES, (french fries), I'm hungry again!"

Jan's idea is well received and they cycle into town, admiring the sights and eating PATAT. Frits breaks his TEN.

By eleven, they're camped out in a little knoll, away from the lights. Their bikes are tied together and their bags are used as pillows. The night air is pretty cool, but the blankets prove to be sufficient and they sleep like babies. Nobody brushed their teeth.

The summer nights are short at this latitude and a little past four, dawn starts to dim the stars and the gang starts to stir. "Somebody stole our bikes!" gets everybody to jump up in panic. "Just kidding!, just kidding!" but it earns Frits a bunch of punches. Result; everyone is up and awake and that was his purpose!

It's still chilly. The grass is covered with dew and the early morning light gives it a silvery sheen. It's a good time of the day to make progress on a bike and within minutes, they're on the road again.

NIJMEGEN is a pretty city. Wide avenues, majestic trees and old, well-kept buildings. It's mostly down hill, and chomping on a chocolate bar, they're making good time.

Where General Gavin and the 82nd Air Born Division captured the bridge over the "MAAS-WAAL", canal, they have to stop a moment for a brief history lesson by Professor Frits. Having had a radio at home during the time of the aerial drop has it advantages.

The sun peeks over the horizon and lights up the miles and miles of apple orchards, for which the area is famous. Orchards as far as the eye can see! The land between the rivers is flat and rich from the flooding over thousands of years, before modern man built dikes and cultivated the land.

Contrary to what Frits told his Mam, there are signs of fighting all over. Every house shows scars and busted up tanks, half-tracks, trucks and jeeps are strewn all over the countryside. The immediate, tree-lined roadside is clear of all obstacles and the bicycle path is in excellent shape, probably because the bicycle is Holland's #1 means of transportation. In just about every little town or village they travel through, a tank or large gun adorns the marketplace as a monument to the days of the war. A monument to the gallant men who gave their lives to liberate this little nation. A monument to the suffering of the populace and the unselfish dedication of the resistance fighters.

By eight o'clock, they're deep into LIMBURG, Holland's southernmost province. The province that "dangles" underneath the NETHERLANDS like an appendix. The very southern tip of LIMBURG was liberated almost a year before the rest of Holland and has happily missed out on that last horrible "hunger winter" under Nazi occupation. They were lucky!

The boys take a break. It's Sunday morning, nothing is open, so they eat whatever they have left over and drink water from a fountain in the middle of an ancient marketplace. They're now in all Catholic country.

Statues, little chapels and crosses line the road. Little benches in front of the chapels invite passersby to kneel down and pray for a moment. St. Anthony, the Virgin Mary and Saint Joseph keep an eye on the boys from their perches in front yards and pedestals along the path.

The scenery inspires them; *"DOAR IS MIEN VADERLAND, LIMBURGS DIERBOAR OORD!"* is being sung at the top of their lungs and it seems to add to the serenity of the surroundings. At least, to them it does. It is LIMBURG's National Anthem, as far as they know and besides that; it's the only song they know about THIS PROVINCE.

Time and distances fly by and as the noon hour approaches, they roll into ROERMOND.

Like many other Dutch cities along the waterways, this town was also established by the ROMANS at about 100BC and there is no recorded history available prior to that date. Because of the many coal mines in the area, a lot of blue-collar labor is evident by the many little row houses that form the outskirts of the town.

A magnificent tenth century church, with its splendid high spheres dominates the center of the city. The houses toward the center become more majestic, the sidewalks become wider and the trees are just gigantic. The market-square is huge and as in any other medieval city, it surrounds the church and is dotted with numerous restaurants, bars and sidewalk cafés. It's a very pretty place.

Jan leads the way; he knows where to go. About half a block from the square, they stop in front of "BRUGGERS POULIER." The display window is empty, but the golden rabbits, ducks, and pheasants, painted on the window, tell an accurate story about the occupation of a POULIER. The shop is closed, it's Sunday, after all, so they make their way through the alley to the back door.

Uncle ROLF is a male duplicate of Jan's Mother. Roly-poly, with dark laughing eyes in a round face. He's a picture of laughter and contentment. Tante ANNA is just as roly-poly and red cheeked, but with blue eyes and brownish hair After a lot of hugging and handshaking, they're nestled around the large kitchen table with "ROBBIE," a spitting image of his Father and "LEEKE," who's just like his Mam, but thinner. "LEEKE" is really "LEO," but "LEEKE" is fine with the boys.

The food is great and they eat like wolves, urged on by Tante Anna; "Have some more of this!" and "Have some more of that!."

Much to their embarrassment, they must admit that they forgot all about going to MASS some place. They passed enough churches on the way, but they didn't even think about it. Shame, shame, shame!

After dinner, the bikes are stored in back and their luggage unloaded upstairs over the butchershop. Some rough bunks are set up and being that the attic is virtually bare, it feels like camping out!

After they wash up a little, all eight of them are off on a walking tour of the historic town. Down by the harbor, where the river ROER empties into the MAAS, they get to understand the origin of the name of the town. Simple, it's the "mouth (MOND) of the ROER." They make their way back up the banks and by the walls that the ROMANS built so many years ago and back into the old city that still looks as if "REMBRANDT" could round the corner any minute. Back at the market place, Uncle Rolf treats everyone to ice cream in the shadows of the thousand year old church with it's many statues and carvings that rise high above them. It's a great, leisurely afternoon.

After supper, a lot more catching up has to be done on all the events of the past few years, since Jan has seen his relatives. Apparently, here in the south, they had no real conception of the tremendous hardship that bitter cold winter of '44-'45 had caused the people in the occupied sector of the Netherlands. It proves to be a revelation.

When someone suggests; "bed," nobody argues. They're pooped and it will be an early day tomorrow.

"EARLY DAY?" The Uncle is not kidding! 4:30... "D'RUUT!" "OUT! LET'S GO!"

"What time is it?" None of the boys own a watch.

"It's time to get up, the chickens will be here any minute!"

"Chickens? What chickens?"

"Put on the oldest clothes you've got and come on down!"

MY God, their muscles and joints are sore and they feel like they could have slept another day.

They stagger down the steep ladder, where they're handed towels and orders; "Wash your hands and faces at the pump!"

One guy pumps while the others splash water on their faces and then on one another and before long, it erupts in a full-fledged water battle that leaves them drenched, but wide-awake.

Sandwiches and warm milk are waiting for them on the kitchen table and before they're even finished eating, they hear; "RAUSCH, the wagon is here." The LIMBURGER dialect is nearly perfect German, certainly the way they pronounce their "SCH's."

They hurry out back where a horse wagon with automobile wheels is backed up to the open barn doors.

The big Belgian horses have brought the wagon with a thousand cackling chickens right up the ramp, leading to the barn.

"UNLOAD!" They unload 30 crates with 12 chickens each and the wagon pulls out with the remaining crates. The racket that those 300 some odd chickens make is beyond comprehension. Human conversation consists of screaming at on another.

Rolf shouts; "TAKE TWO OF THEM, FOLLOW ME!"

They follow him out the other side of the barn and into the butcher shop.

"YOU'RE GOING TO LEARN TO KILL AND CLEAN CHICKENS! IT TAKES THREE MINUTES PER CHICKEN, SO PAY CLOSE AT-TENTION. WHEN YOU LEAVE HERE AT THE END OF THE WEEK, YOU'LL BE EXPERT CHICKEN PLUCKERS!"

The smirks on Robbies and Leekes faces should have told them something, but they didn't get the hint.

Uncle Rolf sticks his hand under the lid of one of the crates and says; "THREE MINUTES! WATCH!"

His hand digs in, comes out with a chicken, held by the neck, down on the butcher block, "chop" and the head's off. His big hands grab feathers by the handful and throw them in a barrel to this left. When the body of the chicken is naked, he dunks the wings in near boiling water behind him, jerks out the rest of the feathers and they land in a barrel on his right. He grabs a knife, sticks it the chicken's bottom and rips it right to the chest-bone, spilling out the intestines. He separates the heart, gizzard, liver and kidneys and they end up in a bucket in front of him, the rest of the guts in the trough on the floor.

"THREE MINUTES! WHEN YOU'RE DONE WITH THESE, GET THE OTHERS. THEN WE'RE GOING FOR DUCKS!" He and his sons walk out.

The boys are stumped.

"I'm not going to do this," says Bert immediately. "I don't mind pluck-ing it, but I don't wanna kill it!"

"Me neither!" Piet is turning a little green.

"I did this long ago!" Jan's not scared. "so I'll go first. Nothing to it!"

It becomes hilarious! The chicken won't co-operate. It screams, cackles, flaps its wings, picks at Jan's fingers and escapes. Thank God, Uncle Rolf closed the shop doors on both sides.

Maybe he knew something the boys didn't. At least, it can't get out. All four of them move in on the chicken, but when they have it cornered, it flies right at them, cackling to Kingdom come..

They duck just in time and the hunt now proceeds to the other side of the shop.

"Wait, wait!" Jan has a new strategy. " Stay back! I'll move up slowly, just close the gaps and I'll grab him."

He inches forward with the others close behind him, covering both sides of the butcher table, all hunched over, ready for the grab. Jan has the bird cornered. He lunges forward, the chicken escapes underneath his arms and Jan lands flat on his face. Jan brushes himself off as the others try not to cry from laughing so hard. Back to the other side again. This time Jan crouches lower and when the bird makes his dash, Jan pins it against the wall and with a little assistance, gets it under control. He's got one hand around its neck, the other around the legs. Back to the butcher block. Since Jan has only two hands and needs both of them to control the chicken, he will hold it and Frits will chop.

Sounds good! Doesn't work good! Frits chops and there's Jan, a chicken head in one hand and a chicken body dangling by it's legs in the other. The body jerks and jolts as if it's still alive, spraying blood in all directions, including all over the four of them, the ceiling and the walls. Jan finally has the sense to drop the head and steady the body. After the initial shock, they double up laughing. Jan, standing there with that stupid chicken, dotted with blood, is the most hilarious scene in memory. Jan can't help but go into hysterics as well.

"That took just 15 minutes, Jan. You're right on schedule!" Hahahaha!" More hysterics.

"Now pluck!"

Jan starts plucking, but they hadn't noticed that Uncle Rolf pulled the breast feathers against the grain, so Jan is having a hard time getting even the first handful out. Bert and Pete egg him on!

"You can do it, Jan. You've done it before! Show us, Jan!"

Just then Jan gets out his first handful and without hesitation sticks it in the nearest mouth. PIET's!

He spits and gags, feathers flying everywhere, sticking to every bloody surface, including Piet's clothes.

Now it's Jan's turn to go into hysterics! They're nearly rolling on the floor from laughing so much and as Bert doubles up over the butcher block, Jan swats him across the head with the chicken. They can't stop laughing!

Frits has hiccups and his side is hurting, while tears roll down his cheeks.

"OH, STOP, STOP, STOP! GUYS, STOP! THIS IS TOO MUCH! WE'RE SUPPOSED TO HAVE FINISHED A CRATEFUL ALREADY ! AT THIS RATE, ROERMOND WILL DIE OF STARVATION!"

Wrong result; more laughter!

They finally settle down and Jan resumes his plucking. It's not going well until someone suggest; "Dunk it in the hot water!" and that helps. It gets plucked. Not very neat, but plucked.

The procedure with the knife does not proceed with surgical precision either. Jan cuts the skin from the bottom to the chest-bone all right, but he cuts it too deep and slices half of the intestines and the whole smelly mess lands on the butcher block. It stinks to high Heaven, it looks like Hell, while Jan tries to separate the intestines from the naked chicken. He's cutting in the wrong places and when he's teased again, he throws a handful of manure at Bert, who ducks, but too late. Jan catches him behind the ear and the smelly stuff runs down his neck and behind his collar. The hysterics start all over again and at that point Uncle Rolf and the boys reappear. "YOU GUYS ALL FINISHED?"

The laughter is so infectious that the newcomers can't help but join in and when Uncle Rolf says;

"This is not as bad as I expected!" the laughter turns into real hysteria. Blood, feathers and chicken-shit all over the place and 7 guys having the time of their lives.

"You set us up, didn't you? You didn't have to go for ducks, did you?"

"No we didn't. We watched you through that window !" He points up at a window, high in the wall. That makes it even worse!

"Oh, my God, what a riot!"

Finally, finally, Uncle Rolf catches his breath again. "At least, now you're dressed for butchering, so let's go to work!"

They look at themselves and admit; "We couldn't get much filthier, so let's go do it!"

Uncle Rolf tells them that in due time, he expects them to be able to do it in three minutes, but right now, he'll do it slowly and explain.

This time, he tediously shows them just exactly how he grabs the chick, where he chops, how he pulls the feathers against the grain, how he slices the belly just under the skin and on and on and on! The boys are so engrossed by all the precision work he puts them through, that Bert and Piet forget all about their objections and practice right along with the rest of them.

There's still a lot of uncontrolled blood and gut spilling and every so often, a hand-full of feathers is thrown across the table, with the end result that when the dinner-bell rings and about half the chickens are done, the boys look like they've been tarred and feathered. Tante Anna thinks it's so funny, that she brings two of her customers out back to enjoy the scene as well.

The pump out back does wonders and the clothes end up in a tub for soaking. It was wonderful

At the dinnertable, Uncle Rolf announces, that he and his sons will finish the rest of the chickens and when the foursome protests, he adds; "We will move faster without you anyway, but besides, I want you to get on your bikes and visit our capitol, MAASTRICHT. And another thing, you don't have any more work-clothes until these are dry and that wont be till tomorrow. On other afternoons," he goes on," you should make a trip to our mushroom grottos, to the coalmines and to VALKENBURG and VAALS, the highest point in the NETHERLANDS. It's beautiful and it's rich in history. Mother," he turns to his wife" the boys have earned two guilders a piece this morning!" He raises his hands as the boys start to protest. " I run this business and this household and I'm in charge of your lives this week and that's the way it's gonna be! Case closed!"

With two guilders and instructions what to see and what to do, they head out to the southernmost tip of the NETHERLANDS. It's interesting that the people from this part of the country never refer to its name as HOLLAND, but always THE NETHERLANDS. (NEDERLAND.) They only refer to HOLLAND if they're talking about the two coastal provinces of NOORD and ZUID HOLLAND. They also refer to themselves as NEDERLAND-ERS, not HOLLANDERS.

One of the factors may be that LIMBURG and its neighboring province, NOORD BRABANT, are practically all Catholic, while the population "above the rivers" is mostly protestant. The "southerners" are known to be big hearted and hospitable, Tante Anna and Uncle Rolf definitely included.

Jan and Frits ride out front and rehash the mornings events and still grin about how Uncle Rolf had them set-up with those chickens. What a character! And his wife and sons were all in on it too, those stinkers.

What a sense of humor!

They're enjoying the contrasts of beauty and dirt. On their left, beautiful hills rise away from the MAAS (MEUSE) river on their right. The scenery along the river is not particularly pretty. Lots of coal loading machinery and belts, loading the flat riverboats, the RIJNAAKEN. River traffic is pretty busy and many of the flat boats are so overloaded, that it's a wonder they don't sink. At regular intervals, brick and roof-tile factories line the riverbanks, their tall chimneys spewing smoke into the perfectly blue skies. The industries are operating at full speed and this contrasts sharply with the peaceful scenery on their left. Yellow grain fields, gently sloping up the hillsides, beautiful green forest, nicely landscaped gardens with a multitude of flowers and pretty red brick homes with equally pretty red tiled roofs. It's a very pretty part of the world.

When the road bends slightly to the east, MAASTRICHT suddenly looms in the distance. The first town ever built in this country seems to beckon them with its high steeples rising above the green and red.

The main cathedral, the SINT SERVAAS, dominates the skyline. The official name is SINT SERVATIUS, but the locals know it lovingly as the SINT SERVAAS. Across the river is BELGIUM. Frits shivers in a moment of sentimental reverie about the country where he was born. The rest of the boys couldn't care less and the only comment he gets from them is; "We beat your RED DEVILS all the time anyway!" They're talking "soccer." The ORANGE LIONS and the RED DEVILS have a bitter, age-old rivalry going.

MAASTRICHT is a modern city. Five story high buildings, wide avenues and electric trams. Stores are well stocked and it's obvious, that their war has been over for nearly a year. No signs of war damage anywhere. Shops, restaurants, movie-houses and traffic function as if nothing ever happened. What a difference with ARNHEM and all it's devastation or WINTERSWIJK with its narrow little streets.

For Frits and Piet, this is the biggest city they've ever been in or at least remember. Jan and Bert of course have to say; " It's not as big as my city!" AMSTERDAM and THE HAGUE. "Wise guys!"

At the SAINT SERVAAS, they lock their bikes together and tour the magnificent middle-age structure, inside and out. When it comes to churches, statues, arches and stained glass windows, they have never seen the likes of it. They light a candle for the dead, adding their candle to the hundreds that are burning in front of a beautiful statue of the Virgin Mary with the Infant Jesus.

They kneel in silence and at first Frits can't think of a person to pray for until some scenes flash through his mind; A young German soldier, named HEINZ, crushed into a wall and a young British soldier, torn apart by a landmine. "Heilige Maria, take care of those guys, will you?" He's convinced St. Mary is listening and she will.

They tour the old walls, the fort, the "SINGEL" (the moat) and make like tourists sipping sodas on the sidewalk of an outdoor café. Coming to LIMBURG was a great idea. Getting up at 4.30 is starting to have its effect and by 4 PM, they head on home.

At the supper table, the entire morning's events are relived for the benefit of Tante Anna. Five different guys constantly interrupt one another with such gory details, that Tante Anna laughs till she cries.

When asked; "Are we getting up this early again?" The answers is "NO!" but "YES" they're going to work again in the morning. This time it'll be ducks. He explains that chickens are popular food, but he makes money with ducks, pheasant and quail. Most of his items are weekend dishes and he sells most of them on Friday and Saturday, so by Friday, all the butchering has to be completed. Saturday is a very busy day in the store and that's when they take in a week's money.

Rabbits used to be a big money maker before the war, but during the war, everybody started raising their own rabbits and chickens, so his business has become specialized. He doesn't mind. Less work and more profit. In season, dove, partridge, hare and venison are very popular, but there's no hunting right now, so it's ducks tomorrow and some rabbits.

"Do you do ducks also in three minutes?"

"Yep!"

"Wow! And rabbits?"

"In one!"

"In ONE? IN ONE MINUTE?"

The boys look at Tante Anna and her sons and they nod; "Yes, ONE minute!"

"I've got to learn that, so I can show my Pap!" says Frits, "he takes a half hour or more!"

"Most people do, but I'll show you!"

"Wow!"

After ice cream, they head for the loft, exhausted. They sleep like logs.

412

The ducks prove to be a surprise! "They're all WHITE?"

"What did you expect? PURPLE?"

Frits is flustered. "I don't know. I've seen white ducks and geese, but also a lot of brown and multi-colored ducks. But all white?"

"For human consumption, they breed this particular kind of duck, 'cause they're meaty without being too greasy. So, they're perfect for the dinner table! Are you gentlemen ready for work? Get your clothes from "MUTTI" and get ready!"

Yesterday's "tar and feathers" clothes are cleaned and dried and soon they're pitching in, in the butcher-shop. There are some distinct differences in procedures between yesterday's chickens and today's ducks. For one thing; the ducks get to keep their heads, another is the feathers. Yesterday, long and short feathers were separated, but today's feathers are even more carefully kept apart. The short feathers are real "down" and are really valuable, so they are very carefully kept clean and are moved from clean garbage cans to large clean bags. The "down" feels real light and now the boys learn to appreciate the softness of a "down pillow" and the tremendous amount of feathers that it takes to create just ONE!

After some instructions, the boys handle all the plucking and Uncle Rolf and his sons handle all the butchering. By noon, they're all done and the ducks move to the store, naked, while their former clothing moves to the barn in big bags.

After dinner and another two guilders apiece, it's agreed, not to bring out the bikes, but to walk down to the river and visit a "STEENFABRIEK." (a brick factory). It feels good to walk and not ride for a change.

Their butts can use some relief and so can some of the leg muscles. Considering that at home, he's lucky to get one ice cream cone a month, Frits is living like a king when they first walk by the market for a nice VENETIAN ICE CREAM CONE! Licking away, they follow the cobblestone road to the river. All over Europe, factories use the rich clay that has been dumped there by the rivers for millions of years. The factory that they have elected to see grows larger and larger as they come closer. The chimney seems to scratch the bottoms of the puffy clouds floating by. It has a base that's as wide as an average house.

Uncharacteristically, they ask permission to see the place. There are no tour guides of course, but in the hospitable ways of the south, they're told; "Help yourself, but don't get hurt!"

They're hit with a lot of surprises. They never knew that straw was an important ingredient in the making of bricks. Nor that "dye" makes the bricks either red or yellow. The amount of clay, that a giant crane scoops out of a pit in just ONE bucket, seems enough to build an entire house!

They've seen coal shoveled into a railroad steam engine, but they've never seen ovens like here at the factory.

Jan tells Frits; "Take a good look and remember it!"

"Why?"

"That's what hell will look like when you get there!"

"Thanks!"

In the days that follow, they clean pheasants and rabbits. The rabbits have Frits fascinated. He may never get the art down to one minute, but three or four? Yes!

Uncle Rolf's hands are like a surgeon's. He grabs the rabbit by the hind legs, pulls it up and at the same time hits it behind the ears with a stick. He hangs it on a sharp hook by the tendon of one of the hind legs, slashes around both hind legs with his knife, a few more slashes around the ears and the mouth and he pulls off the entire skin. The rabbit is stark naked in less than fifteen seconds. Demonstrating it more slowly, Frits copies every move on the rabbit next to him. He shows a circular cut just above the knee, then a slash to the crotch on each leg, a quick circle around the anus and then with both hands, he grabs the skin at the legs and pulls it down in one swift motion. A few cuts around the ears and mouth and the whole skin is dangling from his hands.

"My Dad pulls it down slowly, cutting the skin loose as he goes. It must take him fifteen minutes!"

"That's why he works in a bar and I work here. He may tap a better glass of beer than I can, who knows?"

"Why, like the ducks, do rabbits get to keep their heads on?"

"Why? So I can see their teeth!"

"Huh? Huh?"

"It's teeth?"

"Why it's teeth?"

"So you know it's not a cat! Cats have different kind of teeth.!"

"Ha!" The boys have heard about that! During the hunger years, cats were referred to as "DAKHAZEN" (roof-rabbits) because people would butcher them and sell them off as rabbits.

"Did you ever eat cats?"

"No, No," The boys concur on that one.

"They taste good, no problem there. Some foreign tribes eat dogs. I don't see why not!"

"Well, Uncle Rolf, we'll stick with rabbits, if you don't mind. Okay?"

"Okay!. As a matter of fact, Saturday, before you leave, we're gonna feed you HASENPFEPFER, as the Germans call it. The only thing is, we have no hares this time a year, so we will use rabbit instead and you'll just have to make believe that it has a gamy taste!"

The HASENPFEPFER is most interesting. In a big pot, they lay down rabbit parts, completely covering the bottom. On top of that goes a layer of bayleaves, cloves, spices, salt and pepper. A dark red wine is poured over it all, careful not to disturb the layer of spices. Next another layer of rabbit parts, more spices, more wine. The process is repeated a half dozen times.

"Now we let it sit and marinate for two days. Friday night, MUTTI will put on a slow simmer over night and by Saturday, you'll eat so much of it, we'll have to roll you home!"

"Sounds good!"

That afternoon, their target is VALKENBURG and VAALS, the highest point in the NETHERLANDS, nearly 1000 feet above sea level. Getting up there is a tough job. It's steep as hell and they have to stand on their pedals nearly all of the way up, but when they get there, it's all worth it. Because of it's height, it offers a beautiful view in all directions and they can see both Germany and Belgium from up here. Nearby VALKENBURG is a quaint little old town. The gorgeous buildings, the arched underpasses are all untouched by any war ravages and still stand there as they have for a thousand years. The old homes cling to the sides of the "mountain," the cobblestone streets call for careful treading and the ancient trees provide a protective umbrella over the sloping sidewalks. Beautiful! Just BEAUTIFUL!

They thoroughly enjoy this rustic town and reluctantly, they pedal back to ROERMOND, riding their brakes all the way.

The days go too fast! They're flying by! They had only one disappointment; the coal-mines. They were not allowed to "visit" one thousand feet down, but the above ground museum provided a pretty realistic picture of what life in the mines might be like. They tried to picture themselves down in the "guts" of the earth, but it was not the same! It did not give them that sense of danger that they had anticipated.

The mushroom caves were interesting and huge. Complete city blocks underneath the ground. The imitations of the CATACOMBS in ROME, gave them an additional education about the early Christians and their suffering. In one of the dark caves, surrounded by millions of mushrooms, Frits asked the gang;

"You now understand the meaning of the old saying; "THEY TREAT ME LIKE A MUSHROOM, right?"

No! The boys couldn't say they knew exactly what that meant.

Well, that means; "THEY KEEP YOU IN THE DARK AND FEED YOU SHIT!"

After Saturday dinner of plate after plate of HASENPFEPFER, they start for home. The farewells get to be a little sentimental.. The boys truly feel that they have never spent such a fabulous week in their lives and they tell'em so. The POULIER family hugs them tenderly and orders them to come back. SOON!

By noon on Sunday, Frits climbs off his Fathers bike at home and after telling most of the things they have encountered, he has to change clothes and do homework.

It's peacetime and things are back to normal.

In a quiet moment, he catches his Dad alone and gives him back his ten guilders.

"I didn't need it Pap, but," with a hug, "thanks! It was fun, all of it! Now it looks like I have to buckle down and do well in school, right?"

"That's the idea, son! If you want to become a pilot, you'd better. We still have a difficult road to hoe!"

"We'll make it Pap. We've come through some difficult times and we'll make it again!"

"You're right, Frits. We will! Now go do your homework!'

"I love you, Pap!"

"Give me a hug! Love you too!"

The end.

EPILOGUE

In the 1960's, Mrs. Ida Groot-Forrer-Kwak, widowed and remarried, moved out of her home in St. Pancras, Noord Holland.

She had to call the local police to remove an "ARSENAL" from an attic closet.

The police removed, amongst other things, NUMEROUS ROUNDS OF AMMO... RUBBER GAS-PROTECTIVE SUITS... BAYONETS... A DOUBLE BARRELED FLARE PISTOL AND A RUSTED, AIR-COOLED RUSSIAN SUB-MACHINE GUN.

COMPLIMENTS

FRITS

GLOSSARY

(D)		Dutch
(E)		English
(F)		French
(G)		German
(L)		Latin
(Y)		Yiddish

Aalten	(D)	City near Winterswijk.
Aardappel	(D)	Potato.
Abattoir	(F, D)	Slaughterhouse.
Achterhoek	(D)	Rear-corner. part of the Graafschap.
Angelus	(L)	Noon-hour prayer.
Arnhem	(D)	Major ancient City on the Rhine.
Bahnhof	(G)	Railroad station.
Balk	(D)	Beam (wood)
Beek	(D)	Creek.
Bekkendelle	(D)	Local park. (Beek-en-dal)
Beuk	(D)	Beech.
Beuken bos	(D)	Beech forest.
Biefstuk	(D)	Rare Tender Steak.
Bijkeuken	(D)	Large Pantry with stove and sink.
Bitte	(G)	Please.
Blitz-Krieg	(G)	Germany's Lightning-War.
Boche	(F)	Germans.
Bocholt	(G)	Small German border town.
Boer	(D)	Farmer.
Borkem	(G)	Small German border town.
Bouvier	(F)	Big, black, curly- haired dog.
Brandewijn	(D)	Tasty Dutch Gin.
Brot Ausgabe	(G)	Bread distribution center.
Burgemeester	(D)	Mayor.
Dag	(D)	Day or Good-Day.
Danke schön	(G).	Thank you very much.
Danke	(G)	Thank you
Dank U	(D)	Thank you.
Darf ich mal schiesen?	(G)	May I shoot once?

Das kann ja so nicht weiter gehn, Herr Dokter!	(G)	You can't go on like this, Doctor.
Dehle	(D)	Indoor barnyard.
Deutsch	(G)	German.
Deutschland über alles	(G)	German National Anthem.
Deventer	(D)	Ancient City, north of Zutfen.
Die Fahne Hogh	(G)	Horst Wessel Song. (S.A. song.)
Doar is mien Vaderland, Limburg's dierbaar oord	(D)	There is my homeland, Limburg's dear home.
Doch	(G)	Of course.
Doeltrappen	(D)	Goal kicking
Doetinchem	(D)	City, west of Winterswijk.
DOMINUS VOBISCUM	(L)	God be with you.
Drei bier bitte	(G)	Three beer, please.
Dutch	(D)	Netherlands (Hollands) language.
Eetzaal	(D)	Diningroom.
Eigner	(G)	Owner.
Ein und zwanzig	(G)	Twenty-one.
Emil der Lauschbub	(G)	Emil, the young street brat.
Er kommt schon	(G)	He's coming.
ET CUM SPIRITU TUO	(L)	And with your soul.
Feld Gendarmerie	(G)	Military Police.
Flieger Alarm	(G)	Air raid warning.
Flink	(D)	Brave, courageous.
Frau	(G)	Wife, woman.
Gefreiter	(G)	Sergeant.
Gelderland	(D)	Eastern Province of the Netherlands.
GLORIA TIBI DOMINUM	(L)	Glory be the Lord.
Graafschap	(D)	Earldom, eastern 1/3 of Gelderland.
Graag	(D)	Please, with pleasure.
Grave	(D)	City on the Meuse.(Maas.)
Grebbeberg	(D)	Fortified hills, north of the Rhine.
Grens	(D)	Border.
Grense	(G)	Border.
Grüsz Gott	(G)	Praise God.
Guilder	(E)	Dutch "dollar."
Gulden	(D)	Dutch "dollar."

Gut	(G)	Good.
Haarlem	(D)	Capital of Noord Holland.
Hauptmann	(G)	Captain.
Holland	(D)	Netherlands, (Northwest provinces)
Horst Wessel Lied	(G)	NAZI anthem.
Houtlading	(D)	Lumber stockyard.
Ich bin von Bayern	(G)	I'm from Bavaria.
IJSEL	(D)	Northern branch of the Rhine.
Ik heur niks	(D)	I don't hear anything.
Ist alles bezahlt?	(G)	Has everything been paid?
Ja, das ist ein schönes leben	(G)	Yes, that is a good life.
Ja, sicher	(G)	Yes, sure.
Ja. (Ya)	(D)	Yes.
Jabo's	(G)	Jacht-Bomber. Fighter Bombers.
Jawohl	(G)	Yes.
Jood	(D)	Jew.
Joost van den.Vondel	(D)	Holland's "Shakespeare".
Kaffee	(G)	Coffee.
Kamer	(D)	Room.
Kann der Hans 'raus kommen?	(G)	Can Hans come out?
Kapelaan	(D)	Assistant Pastor.
Kerkhof	(D)	Cemetery.
Kilometer	(Metric)	I mile = 1.6 kilometers.
Kinderstoel	(D)	High chair.
Klompen	(D)	Wooden shoes.
Kolenboer	(D)	Coal dealer.
Können wir helfen?	(G)	Can we Help?
Krankenlager	(G)	Hospital.
Krauts	(E)	Germans.
Krieg	(G)	War.
Kwak	(D)	Ida's family name.
Lauschbub	(G)	Street-rat, brat.
Lebensraum	(G)	Room to live. (Hitler's dream.)
Limburg	(D)	Netherland's most southern province.
Liter	(Metric)	± quart.
Lowlands	(E)	Denmark, Holland and Belgium.
Luft Waffe	(G)	German Air Force.
Maas	(D)	Meuse river.

Market-Garden	(E)	Huge American-British-Canadian and Polish exercise designed to capture Holland's bridges. Sept.1944.
Meter	(Metric)	3+ feet.
Mevrouw	(D)	Mrs. Ma'am.
Mijnheer	(D)	Sir. Mister.
Mof	(D)	A Kraut.
Moffen	(D)	Krauts.
Mutti	(G)	Mother.
Natürlich, kleiner Mann	(G)	Of course, little fellow.
Nederlandse taal	(D)	Dutch language.
Nee	(D)	No.
Netherlands	(D)	Dutch. (official language.)
Nijmegen	(D)	Major Dutch City on the Waal river.
Noch mehr Kaffee?	(G)	More coffee?
Obergefreiter	(G)	Sergeant first class.
Oberleutnant	(G)	First Lieutenant.
Oder ich schiese!	(G)	Or I'll shoot!
Ome.,Oom	(D)	Uncle.
Oorlog	(D)	War.
Opa	(D)	Grandfather.
Opstaan	(D)	Get up.
Ostfront	(G)	Eastern Front (Russia)
Oudje	(D)	Old Dutch Gin.
Panzer Zug	(G)	Armored train.
Panzer	(G)	Tank.
Parlez-moi d'amour	(F)	Speak to me of love.
Patates frites	(F)	French fries.
Pieper	(D)	Potato. (Northern slang.)
Plat	(D)	Flat or Eastern Dutch dialect.
Poulier	(D, F)	Wild game butcher.
Reich	(G)	State. Federal.
Reijnders	(D)	Hotel-Cafe-Restaurant in Winterswijk.
Roermond	(D)	City in the south of the Netherlands.
Ruhr-gebiet	(G)	Ruhr-river-area.
SANCTUS-SANCTUS	(L)	Holy-Holy.
Scheveningen	(D)	Resort town on the North Sea.

Schiedam	(D)	Liquor producing city near Rotterdam.
Schlemiel	(Y)	Klutz.
Schmeckts?	(G)	Does it taste alright?
Schule	(G)	School.
Schwartz	(G)	Black.
Schweinhund	(G)	Pig, dog, bastard
Setzen Sie sich	(G)	Sit down. (Please.)
Sie müsen mahl zum Dokter gehn, Herr Dokter	(G)	You should go see a Doctor, Doctor.
Siegerheits Dienst	(G)	(S.D.) Security Service.
Slagerij	(D)	Butchershop.
Slijterij	(D)	Mini-liquor store.
Smakelijk eten	(D)	Hearty appetite.
Smerig ding	(D)	Dirty thing.
Sondermeldung	(G)	Special Newscast.
Splittergraben	(G)	V-shaped trenches.
Steen groeve	(D)	Clay pit.
Tante	(D)	Aunt.
Touw	(D)	Rope.
Varen over de baren	(D)	Sailing over the seas.
Veluwe	(D)	Northern 1/3 of Gelderland.
Verdomme	(D)	Damn.
Verfluchte	(G)	Damned.
Verzeihen Sie mir	(G)	Excuse me.
Voorkamer	(D)	Parlor.
Vroom, vromen	(D)	Pious.
Waal	(D)	Major branch of the Rhine.
Was machen Sie hier?	(G)	What are you doing here?
Wehrmacht, weermacht	(G,D)	Army.
Wie gehst?	(G)	How do you do?
Wieviel Zimmer haben Sie hier?	(G)	How many rooms do you have?
Winterswijk	(D)	Small Dutch town near the German border.
Womit kann ich ihnen dienen?	(G)	How can I be of service?
Worst	(D)	Sausage.
Yeshiva	(Y)	Jewish school.
Zevenaar	(D)	City on the East bank of the Rhine.

Zolder	(D)	Attic.
Zutphen	(D)	Ancient City on the IJSEL.
Zwembad	(D)	Swimming pool.

About the author

In 1937, the Forrer family moved back to Holland after an eight year stint in Belgium. Three of their children were born during that period including "Little Frits" In the small town of Winterswijk, they took over the old family business in which Ida, the mother, had grown up. They immediately renamed the Café-Hotel-Restaurant "GERMANIA" and called it "HOF van HOLLAND." During that time, thousands of Jewish refugees swarmed across the border from Germany, escaping Hitler's tyranny and many would stop in their Café for a meal or a night's rest. Three years later, May 10, 1940, the Germans invaded the lowlands and France and this is where Frits' adventure starts.

Ironically, the German occupation and oppression was NOT their main concern. The regular bombing by the British at night and the Americans during the day was their biggest scare. (for the parents, that is.) To the boys, watching strafing and bombing P-51's and P-47's was such a fascination, that Frits decided; "THAT'S FOR ME!" Consequently, being drafted in the Royal Netherlands Air Force, Frits volunteered for flight school and landed in the United States for training with the U.S.Air Force in August of '52 and earned his wings in October of '53. After gunnery training in Arizona, the Dutch boys returned home to Holland, "COMBAT READY", and Frits spent the remainder of his military career flying the F-84 Thunderjet.

He returned to the United States in 1957 as an immigrant and brought over most of his siblings who married and settled down and raised families, now totaling 48. His son , a U.S. Air Force Lt. Colonel, commands a C-130 Squadron and his daughter runs a landscape business in Bradenton, Florida. After 20 years in the "book" business and 20 years in construction, Frits now lives with his wife Katy in Gulf Breeze, busily working on his next book and still flying.

CPSIA information can be obtained
at www.ICGtesting.com
Printed in the USA
LVOW01s0305210116
471242LV00002B/2/P